WILD GIRLS

a novel by

Erica Abeel

TEXAS REVIEW PRESS
HUNTSVILLE, TEXAS

FIRST EDITION

Requests for permission to acknowledge material from this work should be sent to:
    Permissions
    Texas Review Press
    English Department
    Sam Houston State University
    Huntsville, TX 77341-2146

ACKNOWLEDGEMENTS
Thank you to Maud and Neilson Abeel, Richard Adrian, and Patricia Chute for their encouragement; Stuart Knoop and Jane Wesman for their expertise; the characters of *Wild Girls*, who made great company for five years; and Otis and Jasper who bring joy. I'd also like to thank Greg Michalson for his generosity in reading earlier drafts of *Wild Girls*, and, above all, Paul Ruffin for believing in this novel.

Cover Design: Nancy Parsons, Graphic Design Group

Library of Congress Cataloging-in-Publication Data
Names: Abeel, Erica, author.
Title: Wild girls / Erica Abeel.
Description: Huntsville, Texas : Texas Review Press, [2016] | "Three college friends from the 50's blaze their own path in love and work, braving the stifling conventions of the age, and anticipating the social thaw that would arrive ten years later. These 'wild girls' pay heavy penalties for living against the grain, but, over the years, rebound and re-set their course, drawing strength from their friendship. The novel follows them from an elite northeastern college, to Paris with Allen Ginsberg, to New York's avant-garde scene in the early sixties, to a mansion in Newport, to the slopes of Zermatt, to Long Island's Gold Coast, as it celebrates the nimbleness and vitality of women who defied an entire culture to forge their own journey."--Provided by publisher.
Identifiers: LCCN 2016015976| ISBN 9781680031034 (pbk. : alk. paper) | ISBN 9781680031041 (e-book)
Subjects: LCSH: Women--United States--Social life and customs--Fiction. | Female friendship--Fiction. | United States--Social life and customs--1945-1970--Fiction. | United States--Social life and customs--1971---Fiction.
Classification: LCC PS3551.B333 W55 2016 | DDC 813/.54--dc23 LC record available at https://lccn.loc.gov/2016015976

To Otis and Jasper

PROLOGUE

It's six A.M. in a Paris just coming awake and she's about to climb to the room of Allen Ginsberg. She pushes open the door of the Beat Hotel, its squawk denting the morning stillness. No sign of the concierge. Too early maybe? In the ancient, dank stairwell she's assailed by odors—from sinks on the landings doubling as pissoirs, "Turkish traps" on little rises off the steps, last night's cooking cut with sweet ghosts of grass—all of it finished with a grandaddy note that might be wafting up from cisterns beneath Paris, maybe from the goddamn Romans. Breathing through her mouth, she cranes up at a nautilus of stairs spiraling to a skylight. Hard to imagine the melting arias of *La Bohème* here.

Room 27, she knocks. *Come in.* Her hand turns the knob, located oddly in the center of the door, and there's Allen Ginsberg, his avid eyes, plushy lips furled around the edges. He's sitting on the bed drying his foot, crossed at the knee.

"What can I do for you?"

"I'm Brett Eigerman, a friend of Gregory Corso and—"

"Wrong room, he's in—Jesus, what time is it? Maybe you better come back later." He finishes toweling his foot.

She takes two steps in. "Actually, I came to see you."

He looks unsure what to do with the news. "So many screwballs come busting in here, you've no idea. Wanting to do interviews about . . . Beats, Beatniks—*what* Beat Generation? When all I want is to hum to myself and rock and write a bible."

"I'd do *anything* for you."

He scratches the sparse curls at his brow. "Well . . . you could wash my socks." Nodding toward a sink. Next to it a double burner and shelves stowing hard-working pots.

She's envisioned something more like . . . a meeting of hearts and minds. She'd play right-hand woman, Boswell to the Beats! She's planned this encounter since college. A witty retort needed, but fatigue from her all-nighter is turning everything *hyperreal* and her eyes smart. For all their hell raising maybe the Beats have clung to convention on some level and expect chicks to keep house for them.

"Wait"—he brightens—"Do you speak French?"

"*Mais oui.*" Emboldened, she moves into the room and perches on the edge of the only chair. Behind Allen, tacked to the wall, the famous portrait of Rimbaud haloed by fair hair.

"Y'know, there *is* something you could do. We're about to visit Celine and could use a translator."

Brett bobs her head. "As it happens I'm reading *Journey to the End of Night.*" Celine's novel has enriched her vocabulary of obscene WWI slang, not what you need to explain to the concierge why the sink you just used as a bidet came away from the wall—but maybe just the thing for a visit to the great writer.

"Gotta see Celine before I go back to the States."

What? Go back to the States? But she's only just arrived!

And now Ginsberg seems to think the audience is over. He moves to a tall mirrored wardrobe next to a window giving on Rue Git-le-Coeur and rummages in a drawer. He lights a joint and motions her over. When she last smoked dope a classmate all in black had a bad trip and needed to be talked down from the sill of a gaping window. She takes a toke, a bigshot, the joint thrillingly wet from Allen's lips. Instantly, she's wheezing like a rusty saw.

"Shit, that hash a bit green," comes his voice.

"I think I better lie down." Shedding her pink anorak, she stumbles toward the bed and pitches onto it like the booty of a forklift. She's down for the count yet conscious, as if recently dead. At some point Allen stretches out beside her. They could be two good children going beddy-bye. He watches her through smudged glasses. "The hash . . . and no sleep," she mutters.

"Mmm," he says, "Gregory's angel."

"*Not* Gregory's."

"The morning has brought a gift of many colors." They lie eye to eye matching breaths *"Belly to belly / the body trembles with happiness"* riding the wave of a boundless present . . .

She must have goddamn dozed off. Allen no longer beside her. "Oh, you know, one of Gregory's chicks," she hears.

"*Another? Gre*-goor-ry! They call up there day and night. *Gre*-goo-ry!" The metallic voice sounds cranked out from something not human. Propped on an elbow, Brett sees, over by the window, the face of a prissy undertaker. William Burroughs, another denizen of the Hotel . . .

"Uh, *what is* your name?" Allen says.

She'd gone back to her pages about Allen and the rest of the story after the memorial for Bodie Curtiz. (A "celebration" of Bodie's life, the program read; she would have preferred to howl at the outrage of Bodie, golden boy of their youth, snuffed.) The story started life as a magazine piece, one of those "My Generation" numbers she'd written in college. It resurfaced as a "Paris Diary" she'd kept in her graph-lined notebook during the time in 1958 with Allen at the Beat Hotel. Then she stuck her pages in a drawer.

After the memorial for Bodie she'd driven with Julia and Audrey to Lilac Close, Audrey's place on Long Island. By Exit 17 she wanted to bail—a visit to their old haunt was bound to invite rude comparisons between those early dreams and the way they'd played out. She almost welcomed the distraction when Audrey, knocking back her second Lillet, hauled out an old grievance.

"Y'know, Brett, I'm into my seventh—or is it eighth— novel and I am pleased to say that unlike you, I have *never* stolen the lives of my friends."

That would be in her lone, loudly ignored, quickly re-maindered, out-of-print novel. Bad idea to drink before six.

"Oh, c'mon, Audrey, we all know writers are ghouls." Julia's honk startles even her Brahmin brethren. "Seems to me I've spotted someone Brett-like peeping out of *your* pages." Brett shoots her a grateful nod. "Anyway, there's no telling whose DNA creeps into a novel. Of course no one could ever capture"—flashing her ravishing Topsy smile—"*me.*"

Audrey's usual sense of fun has gone missing. "In fact, I think the reason you came to Bodie's funeral, Brett, is to write about us—only this time, *all* of us."

Silence, but for the antique grandfather clock in the hall muscling up for a strike.

She thought she'd come for a hit of nostalgia. Or to scout out an old boyfriend—memorials as the new mixer? Or just kinda see folks, she doesn't get out much. But, well . . . *yes.* She'd pick up the story like a time-capsule rescued from the gutter, its degraded images, interrupted music, scratchy voices from a gone world. Start with the Class of '58 and map the from There to Here, capture the confounding sweep of years. *True Confessions* from the Missing Generation, fifteen cents a copy! They'd declared war, the friends, on everything around them; blown past the rules, especially when it came to men *we'll just make it up as we go along.* They'd been so alone out there. Professor Obrecht likened them to acrobats jumping through a ring of fire. *But who, my dear, will catch you on the other end?*

PART I

SCHOOL FOR GIRLS

SENTIMENTAL EDUCATION 101

"But I was in search of love in those days, and I went full of curiosity and the faint, unrecognized apprehension that here, at last, I should find that low door in the wall, which . . . opened on an enclosed and enchanted garden."
—Evelyn Waugh

1954, Freshman

"'Miss Eigerman leaps as though air is her home element.'"

Brett squirmed; unless onstage, she disliked the spotlight, but no stopping Audrey Curtiz, pronounced Cur-teez, reading aloud from the goddamn *New York Times*. The paper's dance critic—well, a third stringer—had covered the group concert at the 92nd Street Y and singled out "Harmonica Jam," Brett's dance to a blues piece for harmonica and washboard. She'd wrested it from herself over solitary weekends in Davenport Theater, the place black except for the bright dance studio in its belly, silent except for her breath and bare feet beating the sprung floor. The rest of the college was off rah-rah-ing the Princeton Tigers or the Yale whoozits, and Davenport felt lonely as hell, but Martha Graham had said, you have a presence that can't be taught, and the piece was going well, the moves pure sass, just rollin' on out and dancing *her*.

"'The piece is antic, elegant, keenly focused,'" Audrey read on. She glanced up through her veiled smile; she had a way of looking through you as she spoke, as if grabbed by a competing insight. "Oh Brett, why aren't you *loving* this?"

"Enough!" Brett said, laughing. She sprang up and wheeled across the lawn in a chain of *tours jetés*. Ginger hair caught in a messy chignon, uniform of leotard and black tights, French striped sailor shirt knotted at the waist. She stopped short of the daffodils hugging a magnolia past its prime, its candelabra of blossoms blowsy and shedding as if it just didn't care.

The other two looked on from the knoll. On fine evenings she and the friends scrambled up to this outcropping of rock above Gilbert Dining Hall, balancing dinner on smelly brown plastic trays. Farther up the hill toward Westerly, Rinko Park, the college "Oriental," perched with a notebook in the fork of an apple tree. Old Rinko was likely working on her opera about the end of the world.

Brett plucked a daffodil. Taking a running start, she drove her front leg forward like a javelin and leaped—just hung out in the air—daffodil in her outstretched hand.

"I want a picture of that," Julia said, "so when we're old and sick and ugly, we'll have something to remind us." Julia Vosburgh was the beauty of their trio, a Pre-Raphaelite Circe with jutting jaw and snakey auburn hair.

Brett, still breathy, leaned back on the heel of her hands. "I know this sounds corny but—I hope we'll never do that 'just girlfriends' number—you know, treat each other like fill-ins for *real life* and disappear when a guy enters the picture." She sometimes wondered what her two fancy friends saw in her and figured it was just a matter of time before they got snatched away by something, someone, some boy.

"Let's drink to that." Audrey reached behind her for a toweled bottle.

Brett nodded in warning toward Gilbert. A couple of co-eds in plaid Bermudas, penny loafers, and detestable *knee socks* came drifting up the path and languidly waved. Lyndy Darling and Cricket Bigelow. Girls with careful hair and careful bodies, parked at this prestigious if offbeat college before the true degree of a June wedding. Members of Foxleigh's deb contingent, who wore oatmeal Fair Isle cardigans with a grosgrain ribbon binding down the center, Breck Girl pageboys, and gold "asshole pins," and who'd arrived already tethered to preppies from Andover, Exeter, and, most exotic, Portsmouth Priory.

Brett sometimes thought of Lyndy's crowd and her own trio as two distinct species peaceably co-habiting the same savannah. She and the friends were warriors pitted against everything the Lyndy's wanted; everything the world *insisted* you want: marriage three weeks after graduation to a fellow who worked at General Motors, end of story. Her little band would not fall into line so fast, oh no; they'd flex their talent in some gleaming, if amorphous future almost certainly involving the arts.

While Lyndy Darling—just last week in the Dudley common room she'd brandished, to squeals of delight, an antique sapphire ring with diamonds on her left finger. "You mean you're going to leave before you get your degree?" Julia, in the lockjaw that could strip the veneer off Aunt Weezie's mahogany secretary.

"But I can finish up any time," Lyndy replied. "As Mother says, 'You won't get another offer like this again. . . .'"

Julia lifted from the towel the bottle of rotgut Almaden they'd smuggled on campus. "Uh oh, don't look now," Audrey murmured.

A small head in a pixie haircut rose and dipped beneath the knoll. May Leach, a disconcerting mix of cloying and slutty, had glommed onto them, mesmerized by Julia's Brahmin allure. They tolerated May because it was kind of fascinating to flip put-downs at someone who *didn't notice*.

"Hi there, come celebrate Brett." Audrey handed over the *Times* and poured May a cup of Almaden in a plastic toothbrush glass.

May scanned the review, pursing her lips, crimson with Revlon's Cherries-in-the-Snow. She stretched her long neck around. "Well, *I* just landed a job in summer stock at the Dennis Playhouse on the Cape." She turned calf-eyes on

Julia, lobbying for approval. "Dennis, you know, is the *crème* of summer-stock."

Dismayed looks all round. No one, of course was all that altruistic, but May made self-seeking so transparent.

"Well, bra-*vo*," Julia said in a voice notably lacking in warmth. Lost, of course, on May.

It made Brett uneasy, the way you could knock May without getting a rise out of her. This girl they carelessly dismissed might just as carelessly turn around and snap someone's neck.

Later that evening a group from Dudley gathered in the dorm's common room for a bull session on the meaning of life. Brett, still in leotard and tights, usually skipped this exercise and headed for the dance studio. The night, though, was fragrant with apple blossom and wisteria, the mild air like fingers trailed lightly over her arms.

In Dudley's common room girls in satiny quilted bathrobes lounged on the sofa or sat cross-legged on the floor in a bouquet of smoke, menstruations, and Elizabeth Arden Blue Grass talc. Lyndy Darling came slapping downstairs in pink bunny slippers, pageboy clasped at the side with a tortoise shell barrette. She settled on the floor beside Brett. "To think you've been reviewed in the *Times*!" Handing Brett the program from the Y concert: "would you autograph this for me?"

From the sofa Aura Folkenflik was expounding on man's relationship to the mystery of being in Martin Buber's *I and Thou*, bible of thunder-thighed psych students. "It's a relationship that stresses the mutual, holistic existence of two beings—"

The sense of this eluded Brett and Brett liked things to make sense. Someone produced, to a chorus of groans, a box of Sara Lee brownies, and discussion shifted to the nature of despair in Kierkegaard's *The Sickness Unto Death*.

"Phone for Aura Folkenflik!" a voice yelled down from the head of the stairs. Aura ground out her Kent in an ashtray overflowing with butts and disappeared upstairs. She was dating a small fellow with a low hairline, editor of the *Columbia Law Review*, whose "prospects" made him the envy of

Aura's friends. Brett couldn't fathom the appeal of prospects if a boy had the sex appeal of a lawn gnome.

A pale face flared like an apparition at the common room's entrance. Nina Winston, dressed in her signature black. She considered them all for a long moment from somewhere north of planet earth.

"Where you coming from?" May asked. The question's twin meanings hung in the air. For all answer Nina floated up the stairs. "I mean, where does Nina get off acting like"— May stretched her neck—"Ophelia-among-the-water-lilies? Her mother is Hildy Winston Lon-geray and they live on Park Avenue. Winston *nee* Weinstein."

They were all poseurs, of course, but Nina was in a class by herself. Brett sometimes suspected that Nina's melancholy, which she trailed around campus like an ebony train, was no wardrobe item you could simply pack away. "Nina was amazing as Emily Webb in 'Our Town,'" Brett said. "When she says—you know, after she's died—'Do human beings ever realize life while they live it?' God, it still gives me goosebumps."

May looked unimpressed, her standard reaction to praise directed at others.

Waving a brownie in one hand, Lyndy Darling was flogging the idea that Albert Camus believed the only serious philosophical question was suicide—but Brett no longer listened. She'd become fixated on the ongoing ritual. A voice from the head of the stairs periodically bellowed down someone's name and *Telephone!* The anointed would struggle up, mounting a show of annoyance at getting pulled from deep thinking—and fooling no one—and flap-slap upstairs to a black phone affixed to the wall. The calls, Brett guessed, were from Dartmouth, Yale, or—most mythical—*Princeton.* If the girl summoned was out, a message would be scrawled with a pencil hanging by a dirty shredding string from a spiral notebook by the phone—messages Brett, to her shame, had read more than once. Abruptly, like in a nightmare, Brett had the panicky sense she'd arrived at the wrong party. That black phone and notebook—invitations to the dance, shaper of destinies—were the true nerve center of the campus.

Lyndy Darling, phone! called the unseen oracle.

Brett watched Lyndy scramble up, philosophy and suicide placed on hold. The dance program from the Y lay creased from where she'd sat on it. Brett suddenly felt like the court dwarf. No one ever yelled down, *Brett Eigerman, phone!* She'd arrived at Foxleigh with her scholarship and her talent but lacking any ties to the world of preppy boys now summonsing forth the girls they'd known from sailing in Dark Harbor, Maine, or Watch Hill and family spreads called Century House and who knew what all? Brett pictured these boys. They'd have last names for first names and English high color and sing "Jerusalem" in cold early morning chapel with a hard-on. Her highschool classmates had gone on to WyoTech Automotive. She couldn't even hope for a call from a boy from her father's City College. Ahead loomed the prospect of yet another solo weekend, Davenport dark except for the dance studio blazing in its belly, the college deserted except for a few pariahs in harlequin glasses in off-campus houses . . . Her box of light suddenly felt like a prison. Of her own making! She wanted to board one of those trains streaming out from Penn Station or Grand Central to the green quads and gargoyles and dreaming spires.

She eyed the dance program lying creased on the floor. She'd pledged to give up the whole rest of life for a career that would last fifteen, at most twenty years. She'd end up teaching girls in training bras—at a storefront School of the Danse in Rego Park . . . between Nino's Haircutting and "We Buy Gold." Brett looked around at the schoolmates she'd scornfully written off because *she* was an *artist*. Even the dimmest girls in this room had found the true path. It was she the numbskull. Kierkegaard, the meaning of life, her fierce ambition—they were nothing but blind alleys. How had she managed to miss out on the true business of college? She was horrified she'd gotten it so wrong. She rose and scooped up the program she'd autographed for Lyndy and winged it in the trash.

Foxleigh College tried to temper the hothouse culture it fostered with a progressive style of education. There was nothing so musty and passé as a *major*. You could spend three years playing the harp and the fourth studying Madame Blavatsky and other spirit mediums. Brett could have cared less. Sophomore year—after her "epiphany," as she called it, in Dudley's common room—she planned to major, and maybe also minor, in Romance.

She knew she was no match for the campus beauties and trust funds swanning around Foxleigh. "Ethereal," people called her. She could work with that. Ethereal was good because a boy could want to do dirty things with you and not feel dirty. And she was a campus star, she packed Davenport at dance concerts, her stories in the Lit magazine were considered *deep*, if eerily similar to Dostoevsky.

In the meantime, she'd found her people. After ghosting friendless through highschool, she hoovered up the attention of Julia and Audrey like the roots of a parched philodendron. At Gilbert, over dome-shaped salmon croquettes or "shit on a shingle," she struck her Intellectual Pose, grody sneaker crossed at the knee over black tights, arm hooked over the chair, smoke from her Viceroy mingling with shafts of sunlight slanting through tall ogival windows. "What Camus means by the Absurd," Brett said, "is not that *life* is absurd, but that we ask it to *mean* something." The friends leaned in, nodding, Audrey Curtiz smiling her private smile. "No one ever gets that right," Julia Vosburgh said, hand shaking from a Dexie-fueled all-nighter writing a paper on Durrell's *Justine*.

She'd acquired her "elective family" after Julia's gorgeous head appeared backstage one night in the dressing room mirror. Their eyes met in the mirror. "You must *always* dance," Julia said. Brett was charmed by the way she said "ohl-wiz," the whisper of graying bra strap, the way her eyebrows aspired to meet in the middle. She'd admired Julia from afar, especially after her show in Davenport Gallery, photos of wraith-like girls among the headstones of a cemetery. "Why don't you come to the Caf when you're through here," Julia said. "I'd like you to meet someone."

Audrey Curtiz, pronounced Cur-teez, looked like a Madonna with a high IQ, and limped. Her half-brother Bodie came from the legendary Hollywood family. "Sorry I missed the show," Audrey said to Brett, "I've been, uh, 'plumping the pillows' of a term paper." "She's been rewriting Cricket BigelowFs hopeless work," Julia translated. Brett liked Audrey immediately, the mischief in her. She feared she might disappoint them both.

Sometimes the lunch group collected Rinko Park, the Korean-Filipino girl recruited by Admissions to meet the Oriental quota. Rinko, a poet-musician, came on all lady-like, pearl earrings, black hair smoothed in a decorous bun, but Brett sensed in her some renegade spirit that would loft her far from Foxleigh's manicured groves. They'd all pitched their tent outside the nicey-nice culture. They'd sooner die than fold into a life, come June, of greeting hubby at the split level door—back foot kicked up—and mixing formula and burping babies. Living happily ever after before you'd even *lived*—a prefab life. Brett considered them subversives Joseph McCarthy had somehow overlooked, a mini Westchester Underground. Among them, only Audrey was still casting around; she'd do something creative, of course, maybe work in publishing, an ideal blend of commerce and literature.

At their round table in Gilbert they hooted with laughter (catching frowns from the debutantes at the next table) over the latest exploits of May Leach, whom they'd dubbed the Whore of Mensa for wearing a diaphragm on blind dates. In her lab book for Topics in Cell Biology May drew orgasms with colored pencils. Over tepid coffee Julia paged through a copy of *Love Without Fear*, the sex bible by Eustace Chesser. "Here's a chapter called 'First Intercourse.' 'The new husband is advised to keep the lights off becauseF—get this—'the sight of his arousal can cause fear and distaste.'" Julia's shriek of laughter swiveled heads at Lyndy's table. Brett had unearthed a manual called *The Good Wife's Guide*. "'Have dinner ready and take 15 minutes to rest so you'll be refreshed when your husband arrives. Touch up your make-up, put a ribbon in your hair.'" Groans. Next, they speculated loudly on which heiress with a hyphenated name the Welsh poetry professor would bag next. And whether a certain senior was actually having an affair with a matronly professor noted for her history of the Wobblies. They took care not to mention the campus romance of one of their own.

*   *   *

On an iron-cold Friday Brett cadged a ride with May and others to Cambridge for a concert by Harvard's Student Orchestra. May was no friend of the heart, like the others; they were fellow foot soldiers in missions to the Ivies. Foxleigh did a booming business with the Ivies—excepting Columbia, with its pear-shaped grinds who commuted from home in the Bronx. Preppies normally only screwed townies, never the nice girls they'd marry—yet at Foxleigh they found, amazingly, a Whitman's Sampler of Nice Girls Who Put Out. Boys converged there for the fall mixer from Cambridge, New Haven, and Hanover, goggle-eyed in anticipation, barely able to believe their luck, all but ejaculating in their chinos at the college's wrought iron gates.

Brett had struck out at the fall mixer; she'd arrived dressed as the can-can dancer from Toulouse-Lautrec, startling the boys in Burberry's and white bucks who'd only ever seen such a figure on posters in the dorm. That fiasco faded, as she and May strolled the cobblestone streets below Adams House, the dorm elected by Harvard's artier types. At the scent of wood smoke she pictured grapplings before a snapping fire, fingers reverently unfastening a stocking from its garter. Her eye caught on a tweedy, long-waisted boy striding by like a young lord, eyes fixed on the middle distance. Occasionally a head swiveled at the sight of her, the float of pink hair and lavender stockings flashing from the circle coat bought with her mother at S. Klein. Brett felt like an interloper peering through the windows at a burnished, unattainable world. They had something here called "final clubs," May told her, bastions of privilege that bolted its doors with a resounding thunk against the likes of her.

The concert was at "Mem" Hall, a High Victorian Gothic pile, which housed Sanders Theater. Its pews lent the place a vaguely religious air, like a pagan temple to worship the statues of Mayflower types flanking the stage. The Harvard-Radcliffe Orchestra launched into Handel's opera *Rinaldo*, a love story with hugger-mugger galore set during the Crusades. Immediately, the string section committed a couple of bloopers. Brett jerked in her chair. Every sour note a fingernail drawn across slate. She might feel like a serf around the lords of Mt Auburn Street—and the 'Cliffies who felt entitled to look like dishrags—but she flinched if even a tympani was flat. She couldn't listen to these student orchestra clowns. No escape, she and May were seated mid-pew. When the soprano launched into the sublime aria, "Let me weep / my cruel fate," her voice wobbled off key, all but taking the aria down with her.

Brett heard only a choir of angels. She'd sighted the oboe player. His name was John Howland, Brett learned in the dim, beery crush at Cronin's, on Dunster Street. "The quintessential Harvard hangout," May twittered. "If you want to be cool order a dimie—draft beer for a dime. Brett, restrain yourself. You can't *stare*."

He was the Ur version of her type: eyes the green of arctic ice, abrupt nose, high blush, long waist, crooked teeth—orthodontia was so Queens. This was as far as you could get from Rego Park, and the toiling men with noses and dark hair sprouting above undershirts, sons of Odessa thirsting for self-betterment, and Uncle Ralph with his radar for spotting the agenda of the military industrial complex in every story in the *Daily Mirror* where he was copy chief. What did John Howland see? Perhaps something so fresh and new it needed to be taken. They melted together.

He invited her to lunch next day at fancy Hofbrauhaus, with its faux Heidelberg facade on Mass Ave. John was not a big talker, but never mind, she'd talk for them both, she'd always lived in books and knew the men's lines, which she actually preferred.

"So, you're on the ski team!" Skiing was the sport of Ivy preppies and Hemingway; her family had played volley ball in socialist summer camps.

"I was captain of the freshman team." His voice a thin, monotone as if piped through a trumpet's mute. Modesty, no doubt. She pictured herself swooping over diamantine Alpine slopes with John Howland to the strains of a Viennese waltz, like in a short she'd once seen at a movie palace in Flushing, Queens like the Alhambra. Not that she'd ever skied.

"Too much fancy equipment now," he went on. "I'll stick with my old wooden skis and boots with no bindings."

"No bindings? Doesn't that mean the boots won't release? Suppose you fall."

He shrugged. "Guess you break your leg. Too many people on the slopes now, especially at Mount Snow. It's gotten a bit . . . Coney Island."

Brett scented tricky terrain ahead, best not explored. She had this lousy habit, though: where even fools feared to tread, she trod. "What's 'Coney Island' about it?"

"Oh, you know, cheapjack."

She cocked her head.

"The New York crowd, Bronx secretaries, people who talk funny," John said.

She let that wash over her, disliking herself, but not too much. By now, with the scotch working its magic, they might be saying any goddamn thing, their eyes spoke the only language that mattered.

The waiter set down plates of bratwurst. He had white wooly hair and a deference straight from the plantation . . . wouldn't sit well with her father and Uncle Ralph, fans of Paul Robeson, but that train had long left the station. The plates lay untouched on the laquered wood table. Desire and food didn't mix, they needed too badly to come close. Desire, Brett noted, was like a hand that reached behind your diaphragm and squeezed. *"I want you"* Dick Diver had said to Nicole. John signaled for the check. The waiter cut a glance at their pristine plates *little Harvard twits* . . . They hurried through the wind-whipped dusk to John's room in Adam's House, where just yesterday she'd peered longingly in. Its halls smelled of polish, sour socks, and semen. John poured them more scotch and put Bach's *Sleepers Awake* on the record player and then there was nowhere to go but each other. They lay entwined on the floor, drugged. John, his musk of puppy and sun-warmed hay, she couldn't get enough. Doing "everything but" got them crazy . . . ebbing, then ramping up, and up, almost combusting—yet not quite— "All the way" might kill her. She heard a record plop down on the turn table: Vivaldi's *The Seasons*. It was nearly five, she'd miss her ride to Foxleigh, but the driving, pulsing strings of Vivaldi's "Winter" got them going again.

In the dark back seat of the car Brett's face stretched in a feral smile. Her life had begun.

At Foxleigh Brett now concentrated on Mail Room Studies. Along with the switchboard, that bank of metal boxes adjoining Gilbert was the second nerve center of the college. Six mornings a week her fingers went scrabbling into the mailbox like a frantic ferret, in search of John's blue stationary. When she saw only daylight through the box, it was an icicle to the heart; she leaned her forehead against the cold metal. But John, what luck, was a letter-writer. He quoted poems at her—"The Hound of Heaven" by Francis Thompson, about the pursuit of a sinner by a loving God. Perfect! Her father was an atheist who took offense when someone said "God bless you." "I fled Him, down the nights and down the days," John wrote.

"I fled Him, down the arches of the years," Brett flung back. "Down the labyrinthine ways / Of my own mind . . ."

And John: "Across the margent of the world I fled / And troubled the gold gateways of the stars."

He drove down to Foxleigh for the dance department's concert, and after, they wandered the campus walks, now sugared with frost. It was disconcerting how much of himself John withheld. As in most of himself. He seemed paralyzed by his own Nordic beauty, like that drug which, injected in its victim, mimics death. John might bomb Stowe's black diamond trails with the Harvard ski team, but his inner rhythm was *molto andante*; his responses arrived behind the beat like a long distance connection. Brett walked beside him pitching monologues into his silence, a dog barking around a fortress. She managed to piece together aspects of him from the scantiest hints, like a biologist inferring the nature of a species from fossil imprints or scat.

Over the following weeks the blue letters unaccountably slackened off, as if their almost-romance had run down its batteries, leaving her to hyperventilate and examine the multiple ways she must have fallen short (had he thought her fast)? She'd never guessed that a problem in a relationship could be not knowing whether you had one.

Then, suddenly, a swatch of blue in the mailbox and an invite to go skiing in Mad River, Vermont. Which must have passed the cheapjack test. She lolled on her Indian bedspread in her monk-like room, envisioning a fire-lit bedroom under the eaves at Ye Olde Yankee Peddlar. John wrote that they'd sleep in his 'n her dorms in the Ski Barn. Doubtless, this was a mark of respect. Brett hated the killjoy who'd invented respect.

For now there was the closeness of John's skier's thighs, as he worked the pedals of the Plymouth on I-91 North. She tried to "draw him out," but he was frugal with words, John. Some day soon—soon!—he'd reveal the enigma of himself. Until that day, the monologue. "My father loved *The Sun Also Rises* but he must have forgotten that old Lady Brett was a lush have you been told you look like this actor John Kerr I saw him in a play called *Tea and Sympathy* on Broadway it's set in a prep school and the other boys start this rumor that John Kerr's a homosexual 'cause he likes classical music and poetry"—*Oops*—"and Deborah Kerr pronounced Car the headmaster's wife goes to bed with John Kerr no relation in the last scene to set him straight and all and just before the curtain she unbuttons her blouse and says 'Years from now when you talk about this—and you *will*—be kind,' which kind of bugs the hell out of me, because why would he be kind? he should think he was the luckiest guy alive, in fact, they were both lucky. What d'you think?"

"I had a teacher once," John said, "George Dewey Pause, who touched boys." He peered through the windshield at the snow now outpacing the wipers. John Howland, Brett thought, had likely been the prettiest boy in the class.

Next morning she crashes down the mountain in a monster snowplow, a position she considers unworthy of her, while John shouts things. Not exactly a ski bunny here, she's sweating like a maniac in her bulky winter parka, as she flings her poles about—"no, plant the pole," John calls. Here in this crevasse a quick check confirms the bones are still intact. Her skis rise high above her, forming an X against the slate sky like something marked for demolition. John brakes just short of her in a *scrape* so graceful and nonchalant, maybe a WASP birthright, it's like her dismissal writ in snow. He leans on his pole, blue cap pulled low, cheeks stung pink, an Aryan god of the slopes. "You don't give up," John says, with grim approval.

She would nudge things forward by sending him poems with a carnal flavor. No more Jesus talk! She wondered why, when it was guys who were famously horny, she needed to nudge anything forward. Then she stopped wondering. A French poem called "The Seven Doors of Love" might move this show along—though she could count only three doors, maybe five. Or maybe Rilke's Phallic Poems!

" . . . now you'll become aware / Of a tower in that wonderful rare / Space in you . . . / And I, blissful one, am allowed entry / Ah, how in there I am so tight / Coax me to come forth to the summit." Uh, a bit brazen?

She chose the middle course of Marvell's "To His Coy Mistress," a veiled argument to get on with it and fuck already: "But at my back," she wrote, "I always hear / Time's winged chariot hurrying near . . . Let us roll all our strength, and all / Our sweetness up into one ball . . ."

John appeared deaf to Time's chariot at his back. They're pretzled on a hooked rug before the hearth in his mother's townhouse in Murray Hill, and he's gotten down to her Merry Widow, a stand-alone boned affair that could have tap-danced and recited the Gettysburg Address. "Where are you in all this?" he muttered. He never found out.

Brett's reconnaissance, aided by May Leach, revealed that the herky-jerky rhythm of their courtship might be due to a lank-haired 'Cliffie with the aquiline nose of her father who was in divinity. Brett pried loose from John the intel that they were still "somewhat connected." It occurred to her that a girl with a father in divinity didn't fuck.

*   *   *

With her sort-of-almost-romance again in limbo, Brett welcomed the distraction of an unexpected honor. A friend of Professor Obrecht was editing an issue on higher education at the *Saturday Review* and looking for students to write on "My Generation." Obrecht put forward Brett Eigerman, a girl who could at least string together sentences to develop an argument—at least *spell*, for godssake—unlike the belles and trust funds in this place that had never, Obrecht thought sourly, surmounted its origins as a finishing school. The son of a renowned Swiss linguist, Obrecht had published one seminal monograph on Flaubert, then prematurely slammed up against the end of what he had to say. Partly out of boredom with his beaten-down, big-boned wife, he'd become infatuated with one of his donnees.

In her essay for the *Saturday Review* Brett pulled out something about the banked ambition smoldering in girls who'd been written off as the Silent Generation. The piece triggered an avalanche of Letters to the Editor. Who was this misguided, "perverted" co-ed who disdained family life and kaffeeklatches and the calling of helpmeet and homemaker? It was sacrilege, un-American, and betrayed an early warping of the spirit, etc. etc.

So she had the power to piss people off. What a gas! She was in good company; she'd read that Kenneth Tynan, the brilliant new theater critic, kept pinned to his desk the slogan, "Arouse tempers, goad and lacerate, raise whirlwinds." Brett thought, I'll be a writer. Perhaps writing could bring the adulation she craved—though what could match the rapture of dancing? After the little whirlwind she'd raised with "My Generation" her star at Foxleigh blazed brighter. Its glow failed to advance the Quest.

Brett had impressed Obrecht though. This awkward, tightly wound girl danced like an angel, and wrote with cheeky authority, her words smartly striking the page like the clack of a typewriter. Yet you feared for her, like a creature lying in the road without a protective shell. Brett arrived in his office one afternoon in the ivy-clad upper reaches of Gilbert to discuss her outline for a contract on Strindberg's *Miss Julie*. She sat on the cracked leather sofa in the dim, book-lined office, enjoying the vanilla aroma of his pipe tobacco. With his alert eyes, sweet mouth, and seal brown hair combed sideways, Obrecht was a reassuring presence. He suggested she explore the play's stylistic innovations more, then struck a match to his pipe.

"How are things going otherwise—I mean, in your non-academic life?"

"Well, things aren't exactly . . . *going*." Or going awry.

Obrecht shifted to the casement window and clasped his leather-patched elbows and sucked at his pipe. "I worry about you, you're such wild girls," he said in his light German accent. He shook his head in mock consternation, or maybe not so mock. Brett assumed he was referring to her little clique, in which she knew he had more than a passing interest.

"Do you know the term *salto mortale?*" he went on. "An acrobat takes a daring leap through a circle of fire, expecting he—or *she*—will be caught by a partner on the other end. You assume, you girls, there will be someone there to catch you. But these young men don't value what's freely offered, it goes against everything they've been taught and asks them to respond in a way they have no capacity for. So they panic and thrash about and inflict a world of harm." Obrecht handed over her outline. "You have many gifts, Brett. I hope you'll find a way to let them flower."

Brett headed up to Dudley along the narrow walk that wound behind the dorms. Dear old Obrecht was a bit of a hypocrite—who would catch *his* wild girl? He meant well, of course, but he spoke for the hateful *niceness* she wanted no part of. If she'd correctly understood Obrecht, she'd gotten it wrong—again. The game was to parlay romance into a marriage proposal. The game was not, as *she* envisioned it, to pursue the varieties of passion and . . . Experience! Forget the Solitaire diamond forever. She wanted to swing over the heights and get drunk on altitude and hurtle through flaming srings. So you landed on your ass—wasn't it worse to miss your life? Why leave adventure to the men? Freedom was wasted on them anyway, they were like the Good House-wives, different anatomy. The workadaddies in grey fedoras; the Thomas Dewey types smiling out from whisky ads "For People of Inherent Good Taste"—they were about as exciting as Tiptop bread. They reminded her of that terrifying last line in *Babbitt*: "I have never done a thing that I wanted to do in all my life." Misfits were more her bag. As Julia said, "we'll just have to make it up as we go along."

Brett was making it up more than most. Over lunch in Gilbert she might laugh the loudest at May Leach's ex-ploits, but her laughter papered over a lack of female savvy possessed by girls since the days of Betty Boop. She'd arrived at Foxleigh illiterate in boys. Her self-effacing mother had never taught her feminine guile and the venerable techniques of man-snagging. After her father's mug shot—in the line-up of six—adorned the front page of the *New York Times*, her mother took to knitting garments for no known human part and stopped speaking.

Brett would have been deaf to maternal wisdom. The demure withholdingness required of girls struck her as sim-ply a waste of time—and she was in a hurry. It puzzled her, those delicate, gauzy tales of a young girl's sexual awakening. *Awakening*? When had she needed awakening? By eight she was in love in a fully adult manner with a ten-year-old White Russian émigré with sloe eyes and a round head. She lacked only a precise understanding of certain details.

East Rockaway High was a blur of metal lockers and boys named Chuck and girls in transparent pink nylon blous-es, who feared a stain on the back of their skirt more than the Atom Bomb. Brett stood alone in dusty playing fields, the hockey team's last pick, a humiliation that keeps on giving. In high school she was as absent as you could possibly be and still register as present, like the whited-out head in a class photo. Dancing, she sprung alive, she was Moira Shearer in *The Red Shoes*. When the teacher's eye settled on the new Japanese girl in class, Brett leaped higher—she could jump like the boys—her arms windmilled light, she *had* to be best. "Brett, dear, there's room for more than one star," her teacher said. No, there wasn't.

She found her people in movies and books. Discovered a kindred spirit in Holden Caulfield, keeping by her bed the dog-eared copy of *The Catcher in the Rye* with the red carousel horse on the cover, and like Holden said "goddamn" a lot, and spotted a phony behind every bush, and wondered where the Central Park ducks went in winter. She found love with Heathcliffe and James Dean. Vronsky in *Anna Karenina*, Birkin in *Women in Love* ("She traced with her hands the line of his loins and thighs . . . and a living fire ran through her. . . .") Montgomery Clift's Sergeant Robert E. Lee Prewitt whose girlfriend called him Bobby. Burt Lancaster, walking in out of the Hawaiian rain on Deborah Kerr, who called him "Major" and sprawled with him in the surf in her Catalina with wide cinch belt. *One Summer of Happiness*, a Swedish film that eluded the censors, sent her home with a fever. It was that scene among the bulrushes, where the hero kisses the neck of a bare-breasted girl. The girl the radiant Ulla Jacobsson who would later marry an Austrian doctor and die in Vienna of bone cancer at fifty-three.

After her "epiphany" in Dudley, Brett was desperate to launch love, knew that "desperate" *repelled* love, which made her more desperate. In her fantasies about boys she would become her favorite characters, or their beloveds, sometimes confusing the roles; she could play either part or both at once, like a one-girl band. She'd come on like Anna K.—or Liza, Dostoyevsky's prostitute-with-heart-of-gold who embraced men's knees. She liked the drama of embracing men's knees.

She was technically a virgin, but thanks to the rigors of her dance training, maybe not all that much.

It was an article of faith around campus that to bring a girl into the circle of family marked a station toward Serious. When a blue letter arrived inviting her for lunch at Mother's, Brett understood she had no margin for error. Fiona Howland ran an art gallery on 57th Street, and the walls of her restored farmhouse in Kent, Connecticut, were hung with paintings by Richard Diebenkorn and Franz Kline.

"Where are your people from?" Fiona said, regarding her with all the warmth of an obelisk.

She couldn't very well say Odessa, then the Grand Concourse in the Bronx, where her grandma leaned out the kitchen window and yelled down to her in the lot when the broiled chicken she'd first used to make soup was ready.

"East Rockaway, Long Island." Garbling words like a needle skipping on a 78 record. And realizing too late your "people" never *came* from the suburbs, they *moved* there to move up. "It's one of the Five Towns," Brett added. It was nothing of the sort, but Fiona had likely never have heard of anything so déclassé and, well, Jewish, as the Five Towns.

"And your father, what did he do?"

"He taught college." Until . . . she saw the *Times* on the table's yellow checked oilcloth with cherries, her mother turned away, hand shielding her eyes. . . . She fought down a wave of nausea from Fiona's lunch of near-raw egg on spinach.

On her way back from the john she stumbled on a grouping of rocks in the living room. They turned out to be an "installation."

"I see," said Fiona Howland, "that you are unaccustomed to living with art."

Let the floorboards part and swallow her. John, she noticed, looked amused. Was he actually smothering a smile?

"Come with me," he said, "I want to show you something."

Once outside Brett thought she might hear from John that Mother wasn't the most cordial soul on the planet but a good egg all the same—but John only grasped her mittened hand tight, and they crunched through the snowy woods down to an ice-bound pond. She'd been granted a reprieve! John pointed at a giant dome of sticks near the pond's edge.

"Look at this lodge the beavers have built. It's as big as a two-car garage."

"A lodge," Brett said.

"Yah, beavers are terrific engineers and construct their lodges using vegetation and sticks, with mud as plaster and insulation. The lodge shuts out light and opens on an underwater realm. All the hard work keeps beavers very fit, did you know that?"

"No, I didn't." Nor had she known how deeply she cared

about beavers and their lodges. All their ingenuity and hard work and fitness—it was so lovely, it made her want to cry.

"We'll come back here in the spring when the woods near the stream are full of jack-in-the-pulpit, dogtooth violets . . ."

She didn't hear the rest, she heard only *future*. This talkiness from John, it was tremendous, like a sea of pack ice breaking up.

He drew her against him, face glowy in the granular snowlight, eyes frankly desirous, lost to himself. "I want us to be together," he said. "I've never been so attracted to a girl."

She ripped open the letter like a kid a Christmas present. "Dear Brett, Could you come to Cambridge next weekend? I'm singing Saturday night in a chamber opera—" She paraded her smile over the salted campus walks. The weekend clearly meant *overnight*, no his'n her Ski Barns. After the tortuous stop/starts they'd finally roll all their sweetness into one ball and climb the golden gateways of the stars. She'd long ago forgiven the Harvard-Radcliffe orchestra its assaults on music.

Pre-departure, in her little room in Titsworth, she packed her white "Viva Zapata" cotton nightgown from the Panamanian shop, and April Violets cologne from Elizabeth Arden in her patent leather hatbox lined in plaid. Suddenly her hand froze: what about love? Well, John wasn't overly expressive in that area, but they'd been heading for this weekend since the night they met. It seemed answer enough. She scoured her every crevice, and made herself dainty with Mum. You needed to be dainty for love, even if bodies weren't always super dainty. She'd been terrorized by those ads—tucked away in the backs of magazines, the subject was so shameful—for douching with Lysol and Zonite. "There's a womanly odor worse than body odor or bad breath," warned one ad. She gave herself an extra scrub. With pink Camay deodorant soap which, if the ads were to be believed, kept bacteria away. And if her stomach growled?

She confided these worries to Julia, who gave a hoot of laughter. "I once had this Alsatian boyfriend. They eat a lot of cabbage-y *choucroute* there. We farted together all the time! Why should I feel uncomfortable to please someone else?"

You wouldn't eat *choucroute* with John, a Nordic esthete, not very animalish. He seemed almost too poetic to know about Trojans.

In her journal she noted the date, February 16, 1956.

The sky dropped a record snowfall on Boston that night. The Harvard orchestra hit its usual clinkers and drowned out John's oddly anemic tenor but never mind, afterward, they walked, arms about each other's waist, through the emptied streets. Car wheels grinding on ice in the distance, great cottony flakes drifting slow and silent across the lights from street lamps—a scene straight out of Dostoyevsky. A muttering wall-eyed landlady greeted them—perfect!—on the stairs of a boarding house with lace curtains. A large bed, humped in the middle and covered with a white chenille spread, owned the room. It was under-heated and lit for a wartime blackout. Their mouths—they can't wait to shed their parkas. Overcome, Brett slides down John, her arms grasping the corduroy backs of his skier's thighs. The move disorients John, who's mainly read puritanical American literature. He must have somehow collected her off the carpet . . . They're past the point of no return . . . She falls back on the lumpy chenille spread, taking him with her, pulls him to her with a force beyond herself, heaving about, at last, struggling to unzip, unbutton, drawing into her everything that's John. They're down to her crinoline . . . the feel of skin on skin, it's too much, almost. She feels it, him, the head nudging her, she all but swoons—

Suddenly she's kissed by air. A shift of weight on the mattress. He must be . . . well . . . it's taking some time. Her eyes open. John's sitting on the edge of the bed gazing down on her, cock rising straight from its thatch of fawn hair saying Yes, eyes of a parson saying No. The mattress springs release. It's a struggle to get all himself into his pants. He hangs there in his parka in the dim room, as if unsure what to do next. She stares up at him, legs akimbo, one black stocking scrolled down her thigh, white eyelet crinoline tucked around her chin like a grandee's ruff.

"I never want to see you again," John says.

Her sexual confidence lay twisted on the ground with its throat cut. She wanted to bathe beneath a sheet like in nunneries. She would *be* a nun, dancing was halfway there. She slept with her hand between her legs, cupping herself like a broken bird.

"It's a mind fuck that's worse than rape," May said. "How on earth did you pull that off?" she added, as if Brett had invented the wheel. She commended Brett to Tenley Baker, a Sapphic cowgirl from Arizona with a high forehead and honey-colored pony tail. Tenley was Foxleigh's lesbian-in-residence and half the campus was in love with her.

"You've got to be cold," Julia said. "A Snow Queen. Any guy screws around with me—God almighty, just let him try."

"Maybe you should thank him," Audrey said cryptically. "Come up to New Haven with me, my brother Bodie's putting on this amazing play." Audrey's half-brother, Bodie Curtiz, was one of those legends that periodically flashes like a meteor through the Ivy firmament. For all response Brett sent up a few bubbles like a torpid frog mucked in for winter.

The world beyond heartbreak hotel was open for business. The snow receded from Foxleigh's walks, leaving runnels of sparkly water at their edges. Across America boys slow-danced to "In the Still of the Night" . . . shooby shooby doo . . . pressing bursting groins against dirndl skirts. The Everly Brothers sang, "Whenever I want you / all I have to do is dree-ee-ee-ee—eam . . ." and the Platters, "Oh yeh-es I'm the Great Pretender / adrift in a world of my own / *ooh*ooh-*ooh*ooh."

Over lunch in Gilbert Brett's group, wreathed in smoke, talked excitedly about Allen Ginsberg and the Beats. Ginsberg had read a hell-raising poem called "Howl" in an art gallery in San Francisco—read with a rapturous intensity that electrified his listeners. It was literally a howl against the conformism sucking the air out of America and driving the best into madness. The Beats were soul-mates. Here in Foxleigh's leafy groves they'd felt alone with their discontents, no one to look to but each other—and now, suddenly—it was like discovering humans on Mars!

There was also a brash new novelist rattling literary convention like a rogue tectonic plate. Julia had gone out with him. "I don't care if he banged out *On the Road* in three weeks on a single roll of paper," she drawled, "Jack Kerouac's a lousy rotten drunk." Kerouac wasn't much concerned with paragraphs and punctuation. His hero Dean Moriarty, con man and madman, stole cars and barreled back and forth cross country, fueled by dope and booze, balling waitresses— "sweetening snatches"—as he went.

Brett thought a girl had best avoid any snatch sweetening by Dean Moriarty. But after graduation she must find a way to connect with these Beats. She especially dug Bardic Seer Allen Ginsberg, with his self-appointed mission of saving America from itself. From Julia she learned that Ginsberg had fled to Tangiers to escape the uproar surrounding the trial of "Howl" for obscenity, and help his buddy William Burroughs assemble a novel so far out and repellent no publisher would touch it. There was talk the Beats might settle in Paris. Brett thought, After graduation I'll live in Paris and meet Allen Ginsberg.

SENTIMENTAL EDUCATION 102

"I started out with nothing in the world but a kind of passion, a driving desire. I don't know where it came from . . . or why I have been so stubborn about it that nothing could deflect me."
—Katherine Anne Porter

Summer of '56 the mercury shot off the charts. Happily, the ground floor sublet in Greenwich Village formed one of those Manhattan biospheres immune to fluctuations of the natural world. Sun never breached the apartment at 320 Jane Street—only reflected light glancing off the sliding glass door in the living room, which gave on a cement courtyard. The place was mainly living room, furnished with beanbag chairs you needed to grind-house your way up from, and a red swing shaped like a satellite dish suspended from the ceiling.

Audrey lived there virtually alone. Last minute Brett had accepted a scholarship to Connecticut College's summer dance program. Julia was "sharing" the apartment on Jane Street only to silence Mother, who'd settled for the summer in Marion, the family place below Cape Cod on Buzzard's Bay. To Celia Vosburgh's dismay Julia had "shacked up" with her photographer boyfriend Elliott Haimowitz in his studio near Gramercy Park.

"Do make an effort, Mother, to broaden your horizons.

Elliott just won a Guggenheim—a huge honor—to document teenage gangs in Spanish Harlem."

More Jews? Well, Guggenheim was the better sort, in theory. "But Dearie, why spend the summer poking around filthy tenements with rats?" With a person named Haimowitz whose people hadn't the consideration to change their name? Children were put on this earth to break your heart.

Julia had always felt outclassed by her friends. They might praise her "little pictures," but whatever talent she owned lacked the engine that drove others to work "crazy hours" on what consumed them. There came that dizzying waking moment each morning when she had to reacquaint herself with a sense of purpose. To get herself going she needed to hitch a ride on someone else's drive—part of the appeal of Elliott. Of course, she'd always attracted men—sometimes absently, like clothes collect lint; she need only marry a brilliant man. But how could that justify your brief span on earth? The man who'd reject her—now *there* was someone of interest, she'd at least respect him for seeing into her emptiness! Oh, it was all too confusing. . . .

Before the advent of Elliott she'd confided in her don, Professor Obrecht, because of his wisdom in all matters.

"My little pictures are nothing more than picturesque. It's a special kind of hell, I want terribly to be an artist, but I don't have what it takes to deliver—not compared to my friends." Oh damn, now Obrecht would trot out the boilerplate about pursuing photography as a hobby that would embellish married life.

Obrecht stood, back to the mullioned window, and re-lit his pipe. He considered her obliquely with his sweet eyes. "You know, every creative person wrestles with doubts about their talent and the worth of their art. And needs to work through a certain self-loathing," he added, thinking he could write the book on that one. "Why don't you forget about competing with your friends and just cultivate your own garden? A la Voltaire's Candide."

Julia wanted to embrace him in gratitude. Obrecht had surprised her. "I'm afraid my only real talent is to make men fall in love with me," she said in her plummy drawl.

"The burdens of beauty should be your worst problem," he laughed. Feeling a stirring in his groin, of course he'd long desired her. He feared the mess that could come of her growing too needy. He suddenly suspected it might be the other way around.

They took to meeting in his office after five, when Obrecht would critique Julia's new series of self-portraits enlisting the "landscape" of her own body. She'd started by photographing friends in an attic room in the house in Marion, its walls mottled from sea-damp. When one day her model failed to show, Julia stepped into the breach—at least she herself was always available. By using a slow exposure speed, she turned her image into a blur, while keeping the decaying walls behind her crisp and clear, creating a haunting, off-kilter mood. She shot a series of herself semi-emerging from ripped wall-paper; then re-shot it naked with only a breast visible, a vaporous apparition. She stepped back to study the prints she'd hung with clothespins on a line. Sprouted goosebumps: she'd somehow managed to summon forth figures from the spirit world.

Brett was amazed by what Julia had stumbled into, and not a little jealous—but she marshaled her best self. "This is ground-breaking stuff. About as far as you can get from—well, 'Which Twin has the Toni?'"

Obrecht puffed on his pipe and studied the prints Julia laid out on the sofa. "I do believe you've hit on a new kind of self-portrait that counters the conventional images of women. You could call these—psychological portraits of the body." His eye stuck on a disquieting image of a semi-naked Julia hanging from a doorway. "This one is almost sacrificial."

It was womb-like and comforting in the sepia light of his office, scented with warm vanilla tobacco, and at some point a shift occurred, a quiet between them like the vexed silence before a tornado. The evening "it" finally happened, a girl was practicing piano in the music studio directly above Obrecht's office; an insistent, hypnotic piece, a question followed by a response, the piano building and relaxing, slowing and quickening, intently chasing a resolution. Julia was kneeling beside her photos spread on the sofa. Obrecht looked on from above, the nape of her neck, the escaped curls. The music quickened, pursued a fresh avenue—like lovers shifting position, Julia thought blurrily. When she turned her face up to him they were so inflamed there was only forward.

"It" happened, Julia joked to her friends, on account of that piece by Francois Couperin. "Like sex made audible."

In her class on "The Heroic Imagination" Obrecht in his scholar mode would be lecturing about the *arriviste* in 19th century literature, girls hanging on his every word and scribbling furiously, and Julia would look at his fine broad brow and the boyish dimple formed in his cheek when he compressed his lips in thought and she would picture him, her sex slave, kneeling between her legs. He was enthralled by the future she contained, she by the forbiddenness. She never wondered where any of this was going. Why must it "go"? She liked meaningless sex—regarded by most girls as suicide lite—liked the purity of it. Why must sex "mean"?

She'd finished with love when she was seventeen, she confided in Brett one evening over coffee in the "caf." After the surfboard stuck through the window of his Austin Healy struck a road barrier and snapped his neck. The road to Marion Boatyard, summer before Princeton.

"Willem was your *brother?*" Brett said, shocked and impressed.

Julia's chin nudged the air. "Oh, half-brother, for godssake."

Brett was intrigued not only by the whiff of incest, but the "halfs" and "steps" spun off by WASPs. Where she came from, a couple could hate each other's guts, but that was hardly reason to start another family.

"Anyway, what does *that* matter?" Julia said in her belligerent style. "We were twin souls, Willem was more me than I am myself."

Hadn't Heathcliffe said that? Brett thought.

"Love happens where it happens," Julia added.

After Willem, it was like some pilot light of the heart switched off. Julia preferred it that way. When she was nine, father was snatched away in a rumpus down the cellar stairs like an avalanche of suitcases. She was banned from his death, solely an adult matter—*hemorrhagic stroke* they whispered—and packed off with her brother to Aunt Weezie's in Marion. Father was the kindness in the house, she his "artistic" daughter. They'd blow down Todd Hill on his bike past the mountain laurel in the fresh June mornings, she ensnailed between his legs on the seat he'd built on the crossbar. Sail the Herreshoff 12 to Naushon, him at the tiller, Newport hanging off his lip, pointing them homeward into molten sunsets from the first day on earth. She howled up in her room till something inside snapped.

Celia spewed a cataract of hatred on *her*, the nearest object to hand—plainly, her daughter was to blame for God's habit of stomping out His finest like a blind camel. Celia knocked her photos—"must they be so unpleasant?" Her dates: "That boy you're seeing"—ice cubes clunking—"is a pansy. What do pansies *do*?" She guessed about Willem, she screamed "perverted whore."

The two for two of father, then Willem left Julia leery of attachment. So this was the deal? Well, fuck that, she would not get caught again. She enjoyed Obrecht the way men enjoyed women—in the moment. She even loved him—in the moment. She possessed a man's heart. It seemed a cleaner, more harm-proof way to get through. Naturally, at some point she'd move on. She might even marry—but only a fellow artist whose discipline and drive would spur on her own work. While Obrecht, an ancient *fifty*, would stay in place and likely get seduced by another student—too sordid, Julia pushed it from her mind.

*   *   *

1 can of Campbell's Cream of Mushroom Soup
½ cup milk
1 cup Birds Eye Sweet Garden Peas
2 cans tuna, drained
2 cups medium egg noodles, cooked and drained
2 tablespoons dry bread crumbs
1 tablespoon butter, melted

Bake for 20 minutes or until the tuna mixture is hot and bubbling. Sprinkle with the bread crumb mixture. Bake for 5 minutes or until the bread crumb mixture is golden brown.

Tuna casserole served Audrey as dinner until the thing acquired a furry green topping. After that it was Swanson's TV Dinners, a foil tray with large compartment for Salisbury steak, three smaller ones for peas, rice, and cling peaches, a bargain at 98 cents. She could hardly wait in the morning to turn the key in the lock of 320 Jane Street and escape to her job at *Mademoiselle* as a floater in the publicity department. When Donna, secretary to the Fiction Editor, was promoted to Assistant Features Editor, Audrey got reassigned to Editorial to log in manuscripts—a bit of forward momentum Audrey found more gratifying than she would have imagined. Three times a week she left the Conde Nast building at 350 Madison Avenue at five, and headed through the homeward-bound crush to her speed-writing class at a Katie Gibbs-style business school on 42nd Street, where steel-grey rooms resounded with the clackety-clack of an army of typewriters.

Audrey had instantly taken to the rhythms of office life. She liked being part of the purposeful hive streaming to work in the morning—though most women were transients, of course, marking time before a husband spirited them away to the suburbs. She liked the steadying tedium of nine to five; the office cart with coffee and danish announcing itself with a bell at three. She liked lunch with the girls at Hamburger Heaven, with its sprigs of parsley at the cash register to zap onion-breath—especially their war-stories about snagging a husband. How cool, too, that alongside "Craze for Checks," *Mademoiselle* published stories by Truman Capote and poems by Sylvia Plath. Plath, of course—patron saint of Nina Winston and Foxleigh's other career melancholics—had once worked at *Mademoiselle* as a hotshot Guest Editor.

Even the lowliest job, Audrey found, put lead in your keel. At age nine she contracted *the* disease that terrorized the land like the Plague. It was that public pool in Flatbush, her mother Lurline kept lamenting. Audrey still woke from the same nightmare, gown in a sweaty twist: she lay trapped in an iron lung, surrounded by rows of identical iron cylinders with human heads, the machines set up in a herring-bone pattern, the souls inside dreaming of train rides and flight. That in actuality she'd escaped this horror made its existence no less horrible. They'd thrown everything she'd touched into a backyard bonfire: clothes, bed, dresser—had to yank her back when she lunged after her "Anne of Green Gables" books.

A year later, her mother was killed by a truck hopping a light. Lurline Shoup had been a hiccup in Imre Curtiz's amorous career (at ten Audrey somehow knew this) yet he scooped up his throwaway daughter, and sent her to school in Beverly Hills with her half-brother, Bodie. The resident wife treated her like the poor relative in a Russian play, eyeing with horror the hinged knee brace on her bum leg. Worse were Imre's operatic rages, all the scarier for being unpredictable. It was Bodie who "caught" her, a stray shuttlecock. *"How cool it is to have a sib, I want to know everything about you."* He forbade his crowd to mock her gimpy gait. Confided his dream for a production of "Our Town" ("the dead must be *present* on stage, mingling with the living"). He introduced her one night to *gasp* Prince Philip at the party at Merle Oberon's.

Though she kept it from the friends, Audrey kind of hankered after the tranquil domestic life they disdained, a world remote from the Curtiz menagerie, with its tumult and contrail of wicked step-mothers. She couldn't imagine herself as little wifey, yet saw no reason you couldn't combine marriage and work—in fact, a future without some abiding task made the floor billow beneath her feet. What work, though? Brett, with her array of talents would do something major, she needed only to winnow down. Julia had hit on a new type of self-portrait—though perhaps her beauty was the surest career of all. As for herself, she could lay claim only to a tender shoot of something she sensed silently greening in darkness.

One day Donna announced, to a chorus of squeals from the typing pool, that she was engaged and would be quitting her job as Assistant Features Editor to plan the wedding. Audrey was struck by how Donna had sloughed off her big promotion like so much dead skin.

During the search for Donna's replacement, Audrey, thanks to her new speedwriting skills, sometimes found herself taking letters from Ella Motley, the Features Editor. Miss Motley had oversized glasses with red frames and a collapsed cleavage and stratospheric standards for writing even a photo caption. Audrey never approached her without dry mouth and sweaty palms. One day toward noon she brought a letter to Miss Motley for her signature. Motley instantly circled with her blue pencil two spelling mistakes. Audrey bit her lip.

"A Sarah Lawrence or Foxleigh girl, no doubt," said Miss Motley without looking up and scanning the letter for further lapses. "You arty types can't spell. And what use is that? Next time you type a letter, dear, check the dictionary."

After the burn of disgrace had subsided, Audrey was visited by an insight. The Donna's were just gusting through, but Motley was a lifer. Like those career women in movies played by Rosalind Russell, tough-talking dames who went on spinsterish vacations in Florence and crept between their cold sheets alone, the wages of ambition.

Audrey suspected that Douglas Widmer would come down on the side of the feisty Rosalinds. When over spring break, on the Red Eye from L.A., this clean-cut dreamboat had buckled himself into the aisle seat next to hers, Audrey couldn't believe her luck. It distracted her from her panic at being encased in an iron lung—this one with propellers and wings.

She read and re-read a sentence from her novel: *"With the coming of Dean Moriarty began the part of my life you could call my life on the road."* She must have read the same sentence five times—while noting beside her the varsity athlete-type, his blue Oxford shirt. *"Then news came that Dean was out of reform school and was coming to New York for the first time."* His chinos with an ironed crease. *"—to him sex was the one and only holy and important thing in life   ."* His scent of Royall Spyce—

A sickening downdraft, and the pilot's voice came on about seat belts. The plane wagged sideways and flopped around, lost to forward momentum. She distilled down to a nugget of pure terror. She heard herself breathing like a dying moose. A warm hand landed on hers on the armrest, where it stayed. The hand felt exactly right.

"It's not dangerous, you know," he said. "Probably hit some thermals, they're bubbles of warm air or rising air currents. Jet wings can flex up to 90 degrees. The plane will be fine, and we will be, too."

She nodded, as the iron capsule went nuts over the bounding skies. His hand rested on hers till the seatbelt sign was turned off.

Douglas Widmer was returning from a pâtént litigation conference in L.A. and they talked, conjoined in the enforced intimacy of seat mates, till the light of dawn pinked the domino-like megaliths spread beneath them.

Back on campus Audrey was useless. Her run-in with polio had taught her to keep her traitorous body at arm's length. Now, it had taken over, this body. She sat in a corner of McCorkle Library doubled up and shivering, hating love. She ordered herself to forget this Douglas Widmer, his clean-shaven cheek and protuberant grape-green eyes and uninflected voice. His bullish neck portended a future fat man, she decided. Two weeks later she was slumped on the common room sofa, listening to Aura Folkenflik expound on Wittgenstein and battling the urge for a third Sara Lee brownie, when someone yelled down she had a phone call.

They met for a drink near NYU, where he was in first year law school, during a rare break in his killer schedule. Douglas seemed instantly to find in her what he required, undeterred by her thin hair and gimpy leg; by-passing the tortuous soul-plumbing of the friends' romances. He loved the "mischief" in her eyes, he said, her skin "color of paper-whites."

"So here's what I love about *you*," Audrey said. They'd stopped for capuccinos at the Figaro, corner of Bleecker and MacDougal. "You remind me of the captain of an expedition to the Arctic I once read about. The ice pack closes in, the food runs out, everything around them goes to hell—they're all doomed. Yet this captain maintains discipline and keeps the men focused on their daily tasks till the very end."

"You call that romantic?"

"Oh, but it *is*. You make the world feel possible."

He shook his head in wonderment. "You never say the expected, you always surprise me" (quirk was a Foxleigh specialty, she thought). "And you have great tits" (she didn't).

Despite the pressure and exhaustion of first year law he stayed unflappable, a word created for Douglas. His flatline voice stroked her like a hand on a cat's pelt. Douglas was about as far from Imre Curtiz's blood-and-dagger operatics as you could get. And the wildness of her friends, which by turns made Audrey envious and anxious. May yakked about something called Ben Wa balls you inserted way inside; Julia had launched her amorous career at fifteen with a caretaker, and claimed she would never love anyone but a brother who'd died young. She and Douglas shared the belief in a middle road between conformity and a path of your own devising. In fact, they agreed on most everything: they hated the 'burbs; liked *Creature from the Black Lagoon* and other cheesy sci-fi movies; The Beach Boys and Frank Sinatra (which her pals dismissed along with all things "pop"). As for s-e-x, Douglas shared a place on East 13th Street with three other law students, which left them little privacy. She and Douglas necked up a storm—but while she always applied the brakes at crucial junctures, he himself never pushed. In truth, despite all the blue balls jokes, he seemed too depleted by Torts and Civil Procedure to pursue anything beyond heavy petting on his twin bed.

It was too good, *too* simple. She was suspicious. Why *didn't* he push? He didn't love her unloveable body, was why. He'd been seduced by her connection to a starry Hollywood family. One evening on a bench in summery Washington Square, the bongo drummers warming up by the fountain, some evil imp possessed her.

"When I was twelve there was a dance in the gym where the kids played a game. The girls each tossed a shoe into the middle of the gym, and a boy who liked you would pick it up and bring it back to you and ask you to dance. My clunky orthopedic shoe lay there, the only one that didn't get picked up. I was sitting in the bleachers with one bare foot and couldn't walk down to get it. A boy finally handed it to me, but he didn't ask me to dance. What I'm saying is I don't want you—you *or* your pity."

His face caved in on itself. "Why are you doing this? I wish I'd been in that darn stupid gym. I would have thought you were gorgeous, I would have kissed your bare foot, the way I'd like to right now, and danced with you all night." His hot baby-I-mean-it eyes knocked her back against the bench.

He bought her a necklace from Tiffany's, a gold chain strung with tiny pearls. She took it off only to shower. That they would marry once Douglas joined a law firm was pretty much understood. It bothered her a smidgeon that Douglas seemed to have no provenance beyond La Crosse, Wisconsin. You wouldn't like my people, was all he said. There had been a fiancee in his past, but he volunteered only that it hadn't worked out. Also the pills. A friend who worked at nearby Beth Israel kept him supplied with amyl nitrate, Demerol and other exotic items that had exceeded their sell-by date. One night in Douglas's room a "quay" something had flattened her in a frightening torpor—something she'd never mentioned to the friends, who would only have prodded her to score them some goodies.

"I dreamed I was a siren in my Maidenform bra."
—Charm magazine

The ferry—really an oversized fishing dory—nosed across Great South Bay. They were pointed toward Lonelyville on Fire Island, a long, narrow barrier of beach and dune along the Atlantic, sandbox to prosperous New Yorkers. Ahead, a bank of charcoal clouds had massed in the peach dusk so it seemed they were chasing darkness. The past week an August heat wave had trapped the city under a giant bell jar, and when a fellow law student offered his family's cottage on Fire Island for a weekend escape, Douglas jumped. Lone-lyville, Douglas had explained, was an apt name, just a clus-ter of houses among the dunes at a point where Fire Island narrowed like an hour glass, far from the rowdy, populous villages. "From the front deck you can practically leap into the Atlantic. Lean back and you'll fall into the Great South Bay."

Audrey eyed a dove-grey Weimeraner reined in be-side its master, one of its legs a-tremble. There remained, of course, the matter of the night. In Doug's room on East 13th they never removed key garments, it was like spooning in an Amish community. Back in the city Audrey hadn't wanted oafishly to spell things out. Didn't they always want the same thing? And it was he who suggested the weekend getaway. Still, she feared that when she blithely agreed she might have flunked some test. Audrey fingered like worry beads the tiny pearls strung along the gold chain from Tiffany's.

The captain cut the speed and the boat headed with a chortling engine sound toward a dock. Audrey glanced at Doug's untroubled profile, his slightly bulgy grape-green eyes, cheeks bronzed by the light. He looked happy and re-laxed and turned to smile at her.

The place was central casting beach house: knotty pine, clam shell ashtrays, fish nets on the wall. Before night-fall they climbed down wooden stairs—he helped her over a broken section—and walked along the ocean. Audrey drew back with a gasp: on the shoreline lay a flat round face, hu-manoid and white, eyes and mouth in a pleading grimace. *Eyeing* them, Audrey could swear, the creature twitched its tail. "A skate," Doug said. "Somehow it got washed to shore." "Look, it's actually pleading for help," Audrey said. "We'll give it a hand," Doug said. He found a stick and gently as-sisted the creature back to the waves, where it disappeared. Audrey couldn't shake the image of the skate's face. To think there existed around them this world of mute suffering!

Once settled on the ocean-front deck, listening to the surf and sipping Doug's "Island Punch," Audrey forgot the skate. "Go easy on that old debbil rum, stuff sneaks up on you," Doug said.

She spread an impasto of mayo, sour cream and chives on the bluefish—a recipe from summers with Imre in Nantucket. She loved cooking for Doug, the wifeliness of it. Old debbil rum must have queered her timing because next thing, flames were leaping from the oven, the crust had caught fire, Doug had to beat down the flames with a dish towel. Audrey noted the pack of muscle shifting between his shoulder and upper back and felt herself go soft and yielding, like a chalice curving to receive him. The charred section made the perfect crust, they agreed, and they took their plates and goblets of Almaden out to the front deck, and ate under a drizzle of stars, watching the waves, their foamy curl silvered by the moon. On a far dune a single window glowed orange.

Among the fishnets hung a large photo of two dainty seahorses wearing tiaras and gripping the same strand of sea grass with their tails. "That's called their 'pre-dawn dance,'" Doug said. He drew her down with him onto the sofa. "It's the male that gets pregnant. After that the female swims over to be with him and they change color and finally promenade, holding each other's tails."

"That's adorable!"

Doug knocked back something with a swig of Pepsi. "Brought one for you." He shook a pink pill from a vial.

"Oh, I dunno, your ole debbil punch is pretty lethal."

He snapped the pill in half with his fingernails the way she'd seen someone kill a tick. "Trust me, this adds something."

She looked full at him. "I want to be super-aware. . . ." No need to finish, he always understood.

"This baby heightens awareness. . . ."

Next, she was on a child's bed, a quilt full of laughing clowns. *It's all good, nothing will happen that we don't want to happen.* She kept kicking her way to the surface, trying to break through, but something kept pressing her back down. That pill . . . No, a weight crushing her chest, her ribs. At her center flared a bright core of fear. She woke in earnest and realized the weight was *him, Douglas.* Collapsed on top of her—asleep? Rolling off her now: "Let's get some of this off." He reached under her skirt and started tugging down her underpants. *Wait*, this wasn't Doug, no kiss, no prelude— but he was boosting up her hips with one hand, muttering "You're not helping much." No, wait. She pressed her knees together wanting at least to turn off the light. Then he was traveling up her till his cock, angry and reddish, was prospecting about her mouth. She twisted her head away. He rummaged for something on the night table. *"Where's the damned*—?" Roughly flipped her over. He hitched her up so she was on her knees, head against the bed board and covered by her skirt, and suddenly she felt something ram into her. She managed to get free *from Doug*? pitching hands first onto the floor, she tried to stand and he tackled her from behind, she crawled toward the door, but he maneuvered so she was wedged between two dressers, head against the wall, when she struggled something metal bit into her neck. She heard her own screaming as he hitched her up around . . . *I'm going to die here. . . .*

She must have passed out. She lay face down on the quilt as if flung there on the tide. She could see a clown's red nose on the quilt and, when she turned her head, a light bulb's glare. Her neck was slimed with blood, her fingers found a giant egg on her skull, there was an odor of carnage.

Saving you for your wedding night you'll thank me for it, he'd said.

I must get out of here. She felt defiled, her clothes, she pulled on her Lanz night gown—she was still wearing her bra and shoes. She tip-toed, though no sign of him. Shivering, she hobbled down the wooden steps, collecting splinters from the broken handrail, and far down the night beach under the pitiless stars that seemed to have drifted higher into space. She labored up the dune toward the bay and walked in what she guessed was the direction of the ferry slip. Then she realized the absurdity of getting a boat at this hour. She was wearing a night gown, she'd left her pocket book behind. She crept under some pilings and lay curled in a ball on a nest of eel grass, trembling, palms pressed together between her knees, until the sun laid golden spokes on the sand.

The morning sky, cloudless, vaulted over an ocean brilliantined by the sun like a glossy pelt. She slipped into the house through a side door in the kitchen. *She must find her bag.* There, under the night table. Shielding her throat, she pulled on her dress over her night gown. On the floor something lustrous caught the light: a flock of tiny pearls.

He sat on the deck facing the ocean, bare foot propped on the railing. He wore a tee shirt and plaid boxer shorts and held a mug of coffee.

"Where were you?" His voice curious and friendly. She saw the pack of muscle in his shoulder and long big toe, prehensile, grasping the deck's railing. He glanced around at her. "You leaving? On a beautiful day like this?" He shrugged. "Suit yourself," he said pleasantly.

*   *   *

Later that August Audrey handed Miss Motley a letter with only one spelling mistake. Miss Motley's eyes were magnified by the red-frame glasses that seemed more weapon than visual aid. "What do you want to do after college? And don't say work in publishing."

This was, in fact, what Audrey, along with most every English major in New York, envisaged. Now she could envisage little beyond hauling herself like a dead limb to the next moment.

"Do you know how many of you English majors come to New York and want to work in publishing?" Motley sneered. "Expecting they'll do something—*creative?*"

For a moment it all hung in the balance. One more word from Motley and she . . . whatever remained of her— would fade like a mountaineer into a white-out. From some underground well she raised an iron fist of defiance. It felt the effort of her life. "Creative?" Audrey heard herself say. "Oh, I don't know. I thought at the very least I'd be publisher of the house."

Motley considered her anew. This girl was barely holding it together. It was then she noticed something appalling on her neck under the pancake.

"Tell you what," Motley said, more brusquely than intended. "One of the Guest Editors is out sick, why don't you take over her assignment?" She returned savagely to business.

The subject was deadly: advice for working girls and young mothers who have no time to cook. No matter, it seemed to Audrey a hand-hold on a sheer rock wall over the abyss. She dispensed with supper, brewed some Chock Full 'o Nuts coffee, and broke out a new pack of Camels. Earlier in the summer—in that remote, pre-Fire Island world—she'd felt abandoned by the friends; now their absence was a relief. She was tired of fending off Brett's probing about Lonelyville, and Julia's rants about going to the police, "getting the man disbarred," etc. She loved them for their concern, but could take no solace. There was none to take. She promised herself never to speak about Lonelyville.

By night's end she'd concocted an amusing bagatelle titled "You Don't Have to Eat off the Floor." Hell, she could make the subject of brushing your teeth *twice* in the morning the key to a happy life.

The silence coming from Motley's office tolled the week through like a funerary knell. Plainly, it was garbage, what she'd written. Walking to the elevator one lunch hour, she was overtaken by Motley whizzing by with her coterie of editors, headed no doubt for a fashion show. Motley paused and peered at Audrey over her red frames: "Oh, *you*: you can't spell, but you sure can write. I want your voice in this magazine. Come see me after lunch."

An important ritual at *Mademoiselle* was the makeover. For Audrey the term meant more than the new doe eyes and chalky lips. She slipped on, like a muumuu, a new snappish, no-nonsense self. She couldn't forgive her own idiocy; why tolerate it in others?

Toward the end of August Motley assigned her to interview Hamilton Fiske, an author of literary spy novels whose latest had been optioned by, as it happened, Imre Curtiz. Fiske lived in Islesford, across the highway from Bodie's place, Lilac Close. Fiske had a sock puppet face and wispy hair that was shockingly dyed, but his energy and brilliance beat out at her. Audrey was barely into her third question when Fiske, who'd been sucking up the Smirnoff, suggested they mosey upstairs to his bedroom.

The only thing that could shock her would be a first time for real. "But I don't even know your middle name," she said. Demure smile. A virgin might be more than he'd bargained for.

"That's funny. I like sarcastic girls." A moment. "Look, I'm going through an ugly divorce, and I thought we could both enjoy a little . . . interlude."

A breeze messengered over the busky scent of marigolds, which Julia claimed smelled like men's crotches. "Tell me, off the record." Audrey leaned in toward him. "With an ugly divorce going on, how do you manage to write?"

"Well, Brenda comes out to the studio and yells and screams at me—and then yells some more. And the moment she's gone I go right back to work. You have to be an animal if you're a novelist."

You have to be an animal. She wondered if she could train herself to be an animal, like an espaliered pear tree.

"Y'know, all you little career girls trying to make it in New York—someone oughta write a book about you," Fiske said, amused.

Years later, in a foreword to her first and most famous book, she'd cite that as her aha! moment, when she closed in on the novel she didn't realize she was writing.

On the train back to New York she smiled out the grimy window, as Long Island's grim little ranch houses flashed by, the above-ground pools, orange corrugated rooflets dreaming of Seville but getting only porkpie hats, their porch railings wreathed in plastic flowers. All summer she'd

been amassing stories the secretaries at *Mademoiselle* recounted over lunch hour—invariably tales about parsing male language, as though it were Quiripi dialect, to decode a beau's
"intentions" and maneuver him into popping the question.
Novelists considered these women and their small bothers
beneath consideration—which was why she wanted to consider them. All her characters, she decided, would work at a
fashion mag with literary aspirations, a thinly disguised *Mlle*.
She interviewed friends of co-workers, their second cousins,
Foxleigh classmates—maybe fifty women in all—anyone
who would sit for a date nut and raisin bread with cream
cheese at Chock Full o' Nuts. Lunch hour she walked up and
down Madison Avenue, deploying her characters and designing destinies, like a kid playing with tin soldiers on a battle-
field. A girl having an affair with a married man. A small
town girl who hopes to marry a preppy playboy with social
ambitions. A girl who loves wholly, innocently in that way of
first love—and . . . Well, Audrey hadn't yet decided on the
ending. One thing Audrey knew: the girl had been ruined.

Junior Year

On a moist October night Bowden Curtiz and his
friend walked into Gilbert, straight and tall and clear-eyed
as two young gods, and Brett forgot she'd retired from romance. They wound their way, magnetizing anything in Gilbert that moved, to the table where Brett sat with Julia and
Audrey, Marlboros angled in the air over tepid coffee. May
Leach, like a coyote smelling bacon, ambled over.

Even before they sat Brett decided she must "get" one
of them. Oh, really? *She*, the great flunk-out in love?

What had they talked about? Replaying it months later,
Brett couldn't say. Words were upstaged by Bodie's scotch-
colored eyes and stretch smile, his creaky laugh; Rufus Porter's green gaze and Roman cap of curls. Rufus looked about
to drown in the vision that was Julia, her frowzled head like
a blown dahlia. Brett was about to drown in disappointment; she ought to sign on with the goddamn Stoics, like

that Greek who lived in a barrel with only his clothes and a stick to walk with.

"I've always wanted to make a movie of *Zuleika Dobson*," Bodie said.

Nods in unison. Bodie's father, of course, was one of those Magyar Hollywood moguls like King Vidor.

Then, silence. It struck Brett that no one had a clue what this Zuleika Dobson might be. "'Death cancels all engagements,'" Brett said, to show that she knew perfectly well.

Bodie glowed at her. "Marvelous line!"

Brett became the molten center of Gilbert. "It's from Max Beerbohm's novel"—ugh, too pedantic, and now the accursed flush went licking up her chest and neck. "Zuleika is a *femme fatale* who drives all the Oxford men mad with love—"

"And can only love a man who won't love her back," Bodie said.

"The smitten suitors"—Brett's burning under Rufus's eyes—"all commit suicide. It's Zuleika's first casualty who gets the famous line about death."

Now Bodie was talking about this far out new play, *The Maids* by Jean Genet, that he was planning to stage for the Yale Drama Club. May all but fell across the table and insisted they drive to New Haven for the opening. Brett saw Bodie absorbing May, Audrey Hepburn gamine, her white skin and scarlet lips.

And Rufus Manning Porter? He talked about his seminar with Yale luminary Robert Penn Warren who'd written *All the King's Men*—"He wants his agent to look at Rufus's novel," Bodie put in—and maybe he talked about racing sports cars at Le Mans. It mattered only that after Zuleika, Rufus Porter's green eyes had quit Julia, to settle, miraculously, on her. Merry, but not smiling. I'll take *you*.

She looked back, aiming for something she'd seen on the Swedish girl in the bulrushes in *One Summer of Happiness*. Trying not to try too hard. They turned dreamy and amused, Rufus Porter's eyes. A jade hand-knit turtleneck hugged his narrow frame, a riposte to the usual pink button-downs. Ivy *and* arty. His features had an ideal straightness, brows and nose like a T-square, like the first man to set foot on the New World.

"Where'd you go to school?" they both said in the same moment. *Oh God.* Somehow they'd gotten outside, she and Rufus, into the October night. The air insinuating and moist, yellow leaves carpeting the dark asphalt of Mead Way.

"Lawrenceville. Founded 1801," he added, self-mocking. "You? Wait, let me guess: not Miss Porter's. Not Rosemary Hall. You're too—Bohemian."

Code, of course, for "fast." She decided to go for broke. He'd probably run for the hills, but attempting to sanitize herself, like at Fiona Howland's, hadn't worked for her either. "Actually, my 'school' was the New Dance Group, a lefty place where the faculty made dances to protest the oppression of sharecroppers. My father got booted from teaching at Queens College for being a 'dangerous radical.' One morning, there he was, front page of the *New York Times*, in a line-up of six mug shots of 'pinkos.'" She kicked at the yellow leaves.

"What a terrible ordeal for your family."

"The neighbors treated us like we had the bubonic plague," Brett rushed on, uncertain she'd heard right. "When our 'dear friends' the Gronfeins saw me, they formed a cordon sanitaire around their kids. Mrs. Crap, the nosey parker next door—"

"Wait, her name was really Mrs. Crap?" Rufus laughed.

"Honest. I could feel her evil stare on me from her second storey window whenever I left for school with my lunchbox."

"I shouldn't be laughing, the whole thing must have been traumatic."

"My father refused to name names." Skip the ten months in prison.

"He stood up to those bastards!"

Brett peered at him, his face in shadow against the lamplight, wanting to hold on to the moment. A dog barked; in the distance an answering bark. Silence lay over them like a lead bib.

"There's something I'd like to tell you." He was engaged, pinned . . . "I'm thinking of joining the Merchant
Marine. Writers don't need college—they need the real
world, adventure. The rotting wharves and cities and ports."

Oy. Dropping out—she heard her father—was prelude
to selling apples in the street and crashing in a Hooverville.
In the Merchant Marine, with his looks, Rufus might get
raped by the cook. "Uh, wouldn't you do better to wait till
after graduation?"

"You can't imagine how stuffy Yale is," Rufus said in
his nasal drawl. "Like the Elizabethan Club. The height of
bliss for my fellow 'Lizzies'"—(so he was a member)—"is to
take tea and nibble on finger sandwiches in musty old rooms
with creaking floorboards. And thumb through archives of
Punch magazine "—(sounded heavenly)—"or play croquet in
the back garden, while congratulating themselves on making
the club, when men in every way superior are shut out."

She was awed that he'd made the club, but that wasn't
his point. Or maybe it was. The easy dance of their words—
so *this* was how it was supposed to be. She wanted to fall
into him like a drowning sailor reaching shore. Abruptly, he
seized her hand. She stopped breathing. They walked hand in
hand past a row of Tudor houses used as off-campus dorms,
empty tonight except for a few grinds who would make good
bait for a serial killer, something about their harlequin glasses. Her palm, horribly, grew sweaty.

"You're the only person I've told." He turned toward her.

She realized he wanted her approval. It sounded like
the worst goddamn idea, but she must do this dumb girl
thing, about as sensible as foot-binding, and tell him what he
wanted to hear. "Maybe you ought to run with it."

His exhale told her she'd spoken right. "You look like
. . . *une brave fille.* A girl with freckles and braids who's just
finished her homework," he translated. As she was trying to
compute whether this was a compliment, his face zoomed in
and his mouth pressed hers. The kiss deepened and grew wet
and wild, they were rocking and grabbing at each other's rain
coats like thieves trying to force an entry. She felt him against
her, a sprung hardness.

As if on cue, a light came on from the vestibule of the stone gatehouse.

Three months later over January intersession Bodie Curtiz invited Brett—"there'll be just a few of us"—to Mother's townhouse on 62nd Street. Mother, who'd been a silent film star, was Imre Curtiz's earliest known wife. Someone had done up the back conservatory with Areca palms in blue and white planters, sisal rugs, teak and rattan up the Wazoo, like some high-end Bombay outpost from Britain's imperial heyday. May sat snugged into Bodie's shoulder on a sofa with black rattan arms and zebra stripes. Bodie was still mad about May then, taking her to opening nights and backers' readings, offering up roles in future productions. The other guests were Bodie's buddies from Drama School and his producing partner, Leland Phillips, two years out of Yale. Leland's large head sat angled atop his neck like a pelican's and he affected a stammer.

Brett was thrilled to be included among Bodie's happy few—or as thrilled as she could be, considering. Loudly absent was Rufus Porter. Brett had learned from Audrey, who had it from Bodie, that the family had freaked over Rufus's plan to split *senior year,* and Rufus had a "sort of breakdown." It was three months since the October night they'd walked Mead Way, a span the length of the Cretaceous period. Each day proclaimed her the least loveworthy person on the planet. . . .

And now oh why? this Archie type across the room was eyeing her like he'd just sighted Veronica. Aggressively homely, with a flaring honker that wagged left in a long potato face, and too-short pants . . . Sweet eyes . . . Pablo someone, and no more Mexican than she. He looked way too impressed with making this cool scene.

It *was* cool. Come June, Bodie's classmates would marry Smithies with "that Ipana smile," and head for corporate jobs at Bendix and Hartford Fire Insurance. They would call the counter man at White Castle by his first name, and talk about how many miles they got to a gallon in their goddamn cars, as Holden Caulfield had put it. Bodie wanted to yank the theater from its doldrums and produce avant-garde plays Off Broadway. He was planning a whole season of "Sam" Beckett. Next, he'd mount *Antigone*—the revisionist French version by Jean Anouilh. "Gotta press on m'man!"—his response to any obstacle. When Bodie was "on," everything became possible and their futures rose up shimmering before them.

"Now the money's in place, we'll kick off the season with Beckett's *Endgame*," Bodie said. "First New York production." He leaned back, expansive, stretching his arms along the back of the zebra sofa.

"Not so fast," said Leland, crossing a saddle shoe over his knee. "There's going to be no New York *Endgame* without Beckett's permission."

Bodie eyed Leland in his distracted manner, as if tuned to a private frequency. Same trait, Brett thought, as his half-sister Audrey. "Who's talking about doing it without permission?"

"Uh, have you forgotten we can't *reach* Becket? We've tried his publisher. I've tried the great man himself—phone, telegram, *pneumatique*, carrier pigeon—"

"Gotta press on, m'man. We'll fly to Paris and put it to Sam Beckett face to face. Over *choucroute* and a liter of beer at Brasserie Lipp . . . Why didn't we do that from the start?" Bodie looked down his arm. "And May will come with us. Who could say no to May here?"

"I know a thing or two about poker—" Pablo broke in.

Slowly they turned toward him.

"—but what kind of a game is endgame?"

They absorbed this. A joke, no?

"It's actually the final stage of a chess game," Bodie said, as if he'd just realized.

"*Endgame* capital E is this *amazing* new play by Samuel Beckett," put in May, shooting a conspiratorial glance at the others. "You know, the author of *Waiting for Godot*?" she prompted.

If Pablo knew, he didn't let on.

"So *Endgame* is about this blind paralyzed guy and his attendant," May rattled on, "and his parents, Nagg and Nell, who have no legs and live in ash cans. But really, it's about the end of the human race. It's hilarious."

"Yah, as Beckett liked to say, 'nothing is funnier than unhappiness,'" Bodie said.

Pablo made a quick eye check around the room.

"'Ever tried? Ever failed? No matter. Try again. Fail again. Fail better.' *Voila* Beckett!" Leland said, jubilant.

"But that's absurd!" Pablo squawked.

"Precisely!"

Pablo's face froze in a queasy half-smile, like a kid not in on the joke.

Brett wanted no part of this. She might be a snot like the others, but at least she planned one day to regret it. Cutting Leland a sharp look: "Look, they're talking about the *Theater* of the Absurd. Samuel Beckett's an avant garde writer whose work captures . . . the perplexity of the human project."

Pablo wagged his head. "The perplexity of the human . . . whoaa!" He beamed lopsidedly at Brett, disclosing a grey tooth.

"Pablo's a man to watch," Bodie said in a grave tone that instantly redirected the current in the room like a V of geese switching course. You wait, he'll end up king of the air waves."

"You in accounts or the creative end?" Leland said.

"For now I'm in sales in radio advertising," Pablo said out the side of his mouth like a race track tout. "But I got this master plan"—a hand chop. "Gonna buy my first AM station in Camden, New Jersey—and then, see, AM's not where it's at. Thing is to get in on *FM*. Buy up stations on the cheap ahead of the pack. But I need a coupla partners to carry me before I hit the FM market."

"How'd you get the name Pablo?" May had emerged from Bodie's armpit and Brett could practically hear her like a slot machine recalibrating his worth.

"Oh, it's a nickname from when we used to play stick ball. I reminded the gang of this Dominican soccer player . . . My name's actually Paul."

"*Stick* ball," said Leland. "Is that like baseball?"

"Kinda—only you play it with a broom handle and spaldeen. It's a pick-up game we used to play in the neighborhood. You use manhole covers for bases and cars and buildings for foul lines."

Her father and uncles had played handball against their

Bronx stoops, Brett reflected—when they weren't studying *Das Kapital*. Pablo, though, seemed more of a capitalist.

"Spalding," Leland said, wonderingly. "What, exactly, is that?"

"Spal*deen*," Pablo corrected.

"To think I've played tennis, cricket, lacrosse without ever encountering a spalding."

"Oh for heaven sake, a spal-*deen* is just a pink rubber ball," Brett said, glaring at Leland. "You know, a round thing that bounces?"

Bodie had been studying Pablo from his own private bubble. "About this 'master plan' of yours. After you've bought your first AM station and you're ready to take the plunge into FM? And you need a business partner? Come talk to me, fella."

March brought a blizzard of phone calls for Brett ("says his name is Pablo, friend of Bodie Curtiz?") A blizzard for real, the big one of '57, left drifts of fifteen feet. The whited-out campus was dotted with crimson caps; voices and laughter hung in a frozen capsule, eerily close. The plowed black-top, her breath in the cold air, followed by the radiator warmth of classrooms and smell of drying socks, acted on Brett like Spanish Fly. She developed crotch rot. Half of Foxleigh had crotch rot, presumably from too little sex, or else too much sex, which also produced cystitis. The campus was a freestanding state of Estrus, in perpetual heat, vaginas atop a box of firecrackers, everything was sex, Kierkegaard was sex, Being and Nothingness was sex, the Revocation of the Edict of Nantes was sex and also the Yale-Darmouth game. May Leach drew orgasms in her lab book with colored pencils, several of which adorned her basement dorm room in Gilbert.

In her seminar, Studies in Victorian Literature, Brett realized she'd been so obsessed with Rufus Porter as a conduit to love, she'd forgotten he was a *person*, with a full complement of human traits. No sphinx of the North, like John Howland. Her audible groan collected glances in the classroom with casement windows in McCracken. Somewhere to her right Professor Lundine was talking about repressive Victorian society. "Consider the sublimation of sexuality in Thomas Hardy. In the famous episode in *Far from the Madding Crowd*, where Sergeant Troy dazzles the viriginal Bathsheba with his phallic swordplay, he's pretty much pantomiming sex. Troy pretends to stab her again and again." Dried white spit collected in the corners of his lips, as it did when he warmed to his subject. "And all this happens," said Lundine, wolfish eyes alight, "in a place Hardy calls 'the hollow amid the ferns.'" A pause to let that sink in.

May Leach whipped out a sheath of pencils and colored furiously.

Brett pictured herself, an ostrich struggling to fly, and crashing along the ground.

Summer of '57

"Citrus Greening causes fruit to turn bitter, lopsided, and unusable, and drop from the trees while still unripe."
—Plant Inspection Service.

The summer sublet on Barrow Street lay below street level, so the window offered a marching strip of feet, but at forty-nine dollars a month the place was a steal, and the block reeked of Village history. Audrey was again the primary tenant. Julia and her boyfriend Elliott Haimowitz—now the youngest member of Magnum Photos—were off shooting the civil rights ferment in Alabama.

Brett spent most nights with Rufus Porter, periodically winking by Barrow to pick up her mail. Rufus had rented for the summer a 2nd floor walk-up on West Street, a mean stretch parallel to the Hudson several blocks south. The single room housed a maroon velvet couch hoarding a thousand smokes and a mattress on the floor; the bathroom pipes sang all night. *La nostalgie de la boue*, Bodie dubbed Rufus's taste in real estate. It was, indeed, a form of slumming. Bodie had once let drop that Rufus was a great grandson of JP Morgan. Rufus shrugged that off, claiming much of the dough had been dissipâtéd by dissolute forebears. Brett loved that beneath the patrician manners Rufus was unsnobbish, even humble. Goodness was not a quality she'd ever connected with passion. She came to associate the squalor of West Street with desire and the divining rod of Rufus's morning cock. The *madeleine* that would always bring back the summer on West Street, its animal happiness that made all seem right with the universe, would be the New York bouquet of grime and a flophouse worth of broken dreams.

One evening on a mail run to Barrow, Brett found a message on the pad beside the phone. "Call Jordan Frankel—an editor at Doubleday," Audrey had underlined. Brett paced excitedly, disappointed to find the apartment empty. Audrey, who'd been promised a job at *Mademoiselle* after graduation, often worked late or went with her boss, Miss Motley, to glamorous "screenings."

"I happened to read your piece on the Silent Generation and, well, it's stuck with me all this time," came Frankel's voice on the phone. "I thought we might have lunch." He suggested the Italian Pavilion on West 55th Street.

Brett leaned against the wall, engulfed by the rank smell of the Ladies sauced with kitchen leavings, her lips compressed in a smile. She tried to conjure up this restaurant Audrey had called a watering hole for publishing types. Here at Stouffer's she wore a white mini-visor and the clinking pile of tips in her pocket sagged like a heavy udder. She'd turned down what, in another life, she'd have killed for: a chance to study in L.A. with the teacher of Allegra Kent and other supernovas of the dance world. But Rufus had taken a summer job in New York as a reporter at *Life*, end of story. At least her father approved. In a sybilline utterance from his St. Helena north of L.A. he said the Stouffer's salary could go toward becoming a school teacher, the only secure job during the Depression.

For her snazzy lunch Brett got dolled up in her ochre and black print shirt dress and carnelian drop earrings. Jordan Frankel was thirtyish, with hound-dog eyes under tented eyebrows, faun-like ears. He had the sort of wounded-boy air that could prove hazardous to a girl's mental health. Brett felt less intimidated.

"Your 'My Generation' piece really captured the, uh, 'other side' of the 50's as a cauldron waiting to boil over," Frankel said. "I get the sense you're bringing news. Your writing has a particular energy and cheeky voice." He considered her, index finger rubbing his lip. "I thought you might turn this material into a book."

A book! Her ambition hungered for employment; she'd been an artist, after all, since age four. Rufus would be impressed (the thought weaseled in) that she, too, was doing a book. She mentally wrote acknowledgements: *To Professor Obrecht, who set me on the path. To Rufus, whom I love.* Frankel was probably talking non-fiction, yet already she could picture this book as a novel. It would be about a small battalion of renegades at war with their entire generation and its suffocating conformity.

"Of course I'll need a detailed proposal by the end of the month, say, to run by my colleagues."

She'd somehow snatch time to write between the gig at Stouffer's and the hours she spent jollying Rufus out of his deepening depression over his job at *Life*. He claimed the canned prose polluting the Luce empire was a novelist's ruin.

"Where'd you get all those freckles?" Frankel said abruptly. His eyebrows shot up in their *circonflexe*. Then he looked alarmed, like a toddler who's touched a hot stove and quickly snatches his hand back.

A bat squeak of something between them; Brett broke eye contact first.

When taken, you inevitably attracted other men, she thought. She emerged on 55th, stun-gunned by the heat. She smiled at everyone in the street, which in New York signifies "tourist" or "bonkers." Yes, she was, amazingly, *taken*. At random moments—brushing her teeth or on the john, where she did some of her best thinking—she'd marvel at Brett-and-Rufus couple, like a miracle bestowed at Lourdes. She couldn't work out how she'd bridged the ravening past with now. Lives contained jump cuts that didn't connect up.

The momentous call from New Haven had come four

months back on a raw March afternoon with no hint of spring. Two portentous knocks on her dorm door, maybe three. Her ear against the receiver. *Come up to New Haven for the weekend.* She leaned her shoulder against the wall, breath caught in her throat, heart hammering, knees unpinned. "Yes," she said.

"I promise I won't lay a hand on you."

"Yes." Replacing the receiver, she slid to the floor. Oh God, please *do.*

The first time was studded with terrors. John Howland had convinced her there would *be* none. She'd stepped onto the platform at New Haven five months back in a cloud of Elizabeth Arden's April Violets, one of a cargo of dates the train had ejected in New Haven for an event called Homecoming. For Brett the word carried private overtones. At Bespoke, a Yalie hangout, she dove into a long booth, Rufus opposite, with Bodie and his friends from the Drama School. Rufus had said something about a hotel. Yale was governed by obscenely named "parietals" which limited female visits. Unlike Foxleigh, where of a Sunday morning, the astronomy professor's son—and campus sex mascot—could be heard belting out "Some Enchanted Evening" in Dudley's second-floor shower. At this hotel—was it called the *Terminus?*—they'd spend the night together. She had actually agreed to this—she felt the pink splotches colonize her neck—she was about to get naked with a semi-stranger in a hotel by the slag heaps. After a single date. Not *even*, the meeting in Gilbert didn't count. . . . And then, he'd *disappeared.* . . . Brett absently forked into her mouth a morsel of the Catch of the Day. To her horror it turned out to be riddled with fine bones, the fish a species designed to exact vengeance on its predators. Brett sat in silence, jaws cradling her packet. To swallow meant certain death; to spit it out, social death—and now an actress was asking Brett about her classmate, this Nina Winston, was she as spectacular as everyone said?—but speech was beyond Brett, she could only nod, eyes bugging, aware of curious looks, Rufus's quizzical green gaze across the table, as she went on nodding, hostage to her spiky chaw. Mercifully, Rufus turned to signal the waiter, and Brett swiftly went *spitooey* into her napkin, which she folded and slipped between black-stockinged knees. Cursing her family, soup-slurpers all, who'd never taught her table arts.

That they'd trampled every convention bound them close. They were also slightly amazed by themselves. Love was a nervous business, Brett discovered over the spring. She hadn't expected this . . . lack of joy. As if she'd journeyed from budding to jaundiced, like a fruit that packs it in without ripening and drops, bitter and unusable, to the ground. After each weekend together in the borrowed walkup on 10th Street, she was on standby, a tight anxious knot awaiting the verdict on some third party, The Relationship: has It measured up? Has she? Are they still a go? She half expected Rufus to wake one morning and say, What's this? It was Julia I wanted.

She could now verify that May's multicolor whorls offered a remarkable visual facsimile.

That summer of '57 it seemed the parties at Bodie's place on Lilac Close would never end. People wanted to rub up against the Bodie magic, the exuberance and creaky laugh. Writers came, one of them the novelist who'd decked a critic for panning his book. Polo players came, and lockjawed preppies, and Jason Schley, who'd just invented teaching machines. Foxleigh's Rinko Park came, trailing an entourage of skanky downtown musicians, her ladylike chignon now an angry dark pyramid. Friends of friends came, and absolute strangers, crashers happy to relieve Bodie of his Tanqueray. Earlier in the summer you could never identify a hostess at Lilac Close; guests took bets on which girl might join Bodie in the Master at the head of the stairs.

But by August the tenor of the parties had abruptly changed. There was now a hostess—if a reluctant one; the revels poured rudderless through the night, borne on their own momentum. Bodie had fallen in love. He'd been thwacked by a thunderbolt, as the French would have it. He lost his sense of humor, combed Islesford for the white asparagus she liked, all but lay at her feet.

It had happened at an audition for his production of Anouilh's *Antigone*. She walked onto the stage in the darkened Provincetown Theater and lead with Antigone's refusal to compromise and save her own life. "*I spit on your happiness! I spit on your idea of life—that life that must go on, come what may. . . . You with your promise of a humdrum happiness—provided a person doesn't ask much of life. I want everything of life, I do; and I want it now! I want it total, complete: otherwise I reject it!*"

Nina Winston's voice belled out in a throaty contralto with catches in it, bewitching, heart-grabbing. Such a big voice in the body of an adolescent boy. Bodie stood, sat, paced; passed from tears to exhilaration—he'd found his Antigone! Deaf to Leland's quibbles, buzzing his ear like a gnat—oh, there were others still to audition? Bodie looked at him, unseeing.

Bodie's inquiries revealed that at Foxleigh Nina Winston had been known abruptly to cancel a performance. She might be an uncanny fit for the part but she'd need a leave of absence from college, and could they really afford a diva? Bodie picked up other rumors: Nina never slept; Nina heard voices; she'd flushed down the toilet the Miltown prescribed by the campus shrink. . . . No, this wouldn't do, he said, luxuriating in the novelty of good sense. Leland Phillips bobbed his large head in agreement.

The following week family business called Bodie back to L.A. for a few days. Just as well, he needed to regroup after the voodoo hex that girl had clapped on him. The interlude in L.A. firmed up his resolve to resume auditions for *Antigone*. No, he could not, must not cast that girl in his play, Bodie thought for the umpteenth time as the plane touched down at Idlewild in monsoon-like weather, and then walked immediately to a phone booth to offer Nina Winston the role and his life.

*   *   *

Past midnight, and no one at Lilac Close had thought to call it an evening. As Brett headed for the john upstairs Leland dealt her a chilly look. She feared he blamed the Foxleigh Circes for Nina Winston's position center stage in Bodie's universe. Nina had displaced not only May, but also, perhaps, Leland. Bodie had put boyish things behind him— Brett smiled at her own phrase. She wondered if Leland and some of his theater cabal were what Holden Caulfield would call flits.

At the door of the guest bedroom she started. Nina was backing toward the casement windows, eyes like a fugitive on the lam. "Whoo! you scared me," Brett said. She emerged from the john to see Nina sitting on the window seat wringing a hand towel.

"We're all getting poisoned, can't you smell the fumes from the vents?"

Brett gave a sniff, *willing* the room not to spin. "Well, maybe a bit of mold."

"It's coming from there"—Nina pointed at a metal vent in the floor. "Don't you hear? Hissing."

Brett sat heavily on the bed. "Julia, d'you hear hissing?"

She'd appeared at the door in a sailor blouse and striped pedal pushers, hair an auburn tumble over her shoulders. "All I hear's the surf kicking up."

Nina hiked her skirts and clambered, ass aloft like a feral cat, onto the window seat, and leaned deep out the casement window. From below rose a babble of voices. The sound of barfing. *He'll sleep it off. . . .*

"Get down from there, for godssake," Julia said, "I'm sure we can sort out this fume business."

Nina complied and frantically wiped her hands with the towel. "Too late, look, it's making my hands bleed!" *What the fuck.* "The blood's all over, it's all over for me." She rushed into the bathroom. Brett was unhappy to hear the lock's metallic click.

"Julia, whatta we do? I mean, shouldn't we *say* something?"

Her chin jabbed the air. "Nina's ohl-wiz playing some part. One day it's Masha in *Three Sisters*—'I'm in mourning for my life.' Another it's 'Golden lads and girls all must . . . come to dust,'" Julia mimicked, mangling the quote. "She carts around gloomy lines like the rest of us Tampax."

The hooch had separated Brett from her ability to reason. Foxleigh girls, it was true, came on all madcap, leaping like spider monkeys from one non sequitur to the next. Lucien Carr, Allen Ginsberg's buddy, once stuck his head in the oven and called it a work of art. "But suppose"—Brett chased after some comet's tail just out of reach—"suppose it's not? Bullshit?"

Nina emerged from the john and sat on the window-seat. "Y'know, sometimes I just don't see the point."

"Point of what, dear?" Julia said sharply.

"Y'know, washing your hair, eating and shitting—anything! Sometimes I want to, y'know, do everything and have done with it once and for all." Her fractured gaze of a cat raised the flesh along Brett's arms.

Brett said, "Listen, Nina, you gotta talk to someone about this stuff. You don't need to be so afraid."

"Dr. Newsome just wants to lock me up in McCorkle snorkel, pickle the porkel—"

"Lock you up *where*?"

Nina eye-balled them. "D'you realize? It's already thirty days and seven hours past the summer solstice, the longest day of the year. . . . 'I always watch for the longest day of the year and then miss it.' Don't you?'" Her gravelly contralto was hypnotic. "'I've been everywhere and seen everything and done everything. . . . Sophisticated–God, I'm sophisticated!'"

Brett got it, a beat late: why, of course! That was Daisy Buchanan in *Gatsby*, who could play the part better than Nina? Maybe she was nothing but a great Mobius strip of parts.

"I have an idea!" Nina said. "Why don't we drive to the ocean, like we always do. We'll climb up the bluffs and watch the moonlight on the water. I love to stand on the bluffs and watch the moonlight on the water. Don't you?"

"Tonight will soon be long ago"—Nat King Cole

The trees looked tired, their green yesterday's news. Summer was winding down, hinting at endings. After her shift at Stouffer's, Brett splashed herself with lemony Jean Nate cologne and traveled the steambath city to West Street, to find Rufus in a funk of envy and self-loathing. A classmate from Yale had, at twenty-three, just sold his first novel.

"I was just on my way out," he said, evading her eyes.

"What's up?"

"Gonna toss this"—he brandished a sheath of papers— "in the Hudson."

"You'll do no such thing," she said, maneuvering him back to the sofa, its innards dangling like an obscene tongue. "Think Hemingway: 'Sometimes there's nothing for it but to write the whole goddamn thing.'"

"Hemingway lived and wrote in Paris. He was out in the *world*. Lawrenceville, Yale, *Time Inc.* hardly counts as the world."

And what did she count as, Brett wondered. "Why don't you read me your latest chapter?" Thankfully, she liked the novel, a kinky Gothic triangle about a brother and sister from a patrician family, both in love with the same woman.

She circled a section with a red pencil: "Maybe nix this passage? Too *Time*-ese. And here"—she bracketed several graphs—"don't hate me, but better to 'show, not tell.'"

Meanwhile, her book proposal for Jordan Frankel remained a stack of three-by-fives in a shoe box tucked under her bed among the dust bunnies on Barrow Street.

Word went round that in rehearsals for *Antigone* Nina was spectacular. Rufus, too, had caught the theater bug and was taking improv classes at the Neighborhood Playhouse with theater guru "Sandy" Meisner. His mantra for actors, "live truthfully under imaginary circumstances," spurred Rufus to "more fully inhabit his characters." The stage-struck beauties around Meisner made Brett uneasy. One in particular, with a fall of straight peach-colored hair and the porny name of Ornella. Ornella was a principessa from a titled family that still had its money.

"Oh, actresses," Rufus said dismissively. "Ornella can do both narcissist and little-girl-lost in a single breath. I'd call her a 'failed narcissist.'" He laughed at his term. "C'mon, where's your sense of humor, I love your humor. She's just a taker, Ornella."

What man was ever deterred by takers? Brett also felt queasy when she thought about Nina Winston. The past spring at Foxleigh in Modern Theater they'd been studying, coincidentally, Anouilh's *Antigone*—by the time Nina auditioned for Bodie's production she'd already inhaled the part. In class Nina had defended, of course, Antigone's lust for martyrdom, and the rest of the girls came down on her— with a vehemence that prompted the prof to call them off. The gangup on Nina continued later than evening in Dudley, a pack of girls manless in the state of Estrus. Julia especially vicious, going all righteous about *authentic* loss—*hers*— "Nina, when have you ever really truly grieved for anyone?" she honked. May, always quick to second Julia, called Nina a "tragedy whore." Had it gone too far?

Then, just last week, the business with the "bloody" towel . . .

Brett collared Bodie one morning in the kitchen at Lilac Close as he was heading out to tennis in his whites, towel slung over his shoulder, goldenness incarnate. She cravenly wanted Bodie's love, and a surefire way to piss him off was to suggest that Nina was in any way imperfect. There are times, though, if you don't speak you hate yourself forever.

"Listen, Bodie, you have to listen to me. I know it's cool to be 'sick' and all, but dammit, sometimes Nina sounds"— *don't say psychotic*—"like she's flipped out. She's convinced we're getting poisoned by fumes from the ducts in the house."

Bodie eyed her levelly. "I've had the ducts inspected and in fact, they *are* emitting microscopic contaminants. I'm getting them replaced."

"I see. But the other night she was talking gibberish, saying stuff like 'it's all over for me' and she doesn't see the *point* and wants to have done with everything once and for all—shit like that."

Bodie's eyes glowed past her. "Doncha see? Nina was riffing on those lines in *Antigone*! Lately, we've been rehearsing

till midnight." He scooped up his car keys. "Forgive me, darlin,' but maybe you're all a bit envious. Nina is a major talent—*major*—maybe a young Julie Harris."

He went on about "the psychic risk in being an artist,"
eluding her like a fish color-coding to its grotto.

After the first timid forays, the daring and thrill of *doing it*, they were lovers in earnest. They traveled each other
like zealous tourists. One night she ended up spread-eagled
atop him so they both faced upward like some two-head-
ed bark. May claimed to have multiple orgasms rolling in
one after another. The thing was, right after she came, Brett
needed not to be touched for a time and suspected that might
be true of other women. . . . This morning a smell of burnt
tar rose off the Hudson. Sleepy Sunday wake-up sex. After,
he stayed semi-hard. She inhaled his sweat in the crook of his
shoulder and . . . something about the way he pressed down
and ground around uncorked from nowhere a second wave
hurling her up over the peak, Rufus's smile tossing above her.

They lay back laughing. Brett felt reborn through every
cell, forgetting to conceal how when she lay back her boobs
lay down, too. His cock rode at anchor against his thigh,
pubic hair matted. Something stirred through her belly and
groin. . . . *Again?* Below on West Street a drunk was imper-
sonating Nat King Cole.

Rufus propped himself on an elbow and fired up a
Kent. "A friend at work just told me about an opening at
the Associated Press to cover the Vatican, and I been thinking . . . well, in September maybe I'd move to Rome." The
bathroom pipes loosed a flurry of indignant bangs. "Oh God,
don't look like that, it's just an idea."

She lay there. They'd just been the same body.

"Brett, why don't you come to Rome with me?"

You couldn't do this lying down. She pulled on his tee
shirt and moved to the maroon sofa, updrawn knees pulling
his tee shirt into a tent. *This is our last dance together,* the guy
sang, *tonight soon will be long ago.* . . . "You know I can't just
leave college before graduation."

He ground the hell out of his Kent in the saucer. "I know." He bunched their two pillows and sat against the wall. "Look, we haven't wanted to talk about this stuff. But shouldn't we?"

"You picked a peculiar time."

"When is *not* a peculiar time?" he said, miserably.

She didn't deign to answer. They'd both agreed sort of, while not spelling it out exactly, that it was too soon to lock in together for the duration, they each wanted Experience and the world waiting out there.

"So . . . what *were* you thinking?" he said.

"I wasn't. Why must I think? I was thinking you'd finish at Yale. Like you said."

"I gave my family a lot of bull to get them off my back, and now this Vatican post just opened up, it's a rare opportunity . . ." *There will be other songs to sing, but there will never be another you . . .* "Another *minute*"—Rufus glared at the windows—"I'm gonna pour pitch on that sonuvabitch."

She buried her nose between her updrawn knees, catching a bouquet of them, their marine juices. Yes, she'd wanted the world waiting out there, the dreams of Paris and running with poets. But at some moment when she wasn't looking, this person here began eclipsing the waiting world. They'd become the world, each to the other. Didn't he feel the same way?

Rufus pulled the sheet over his groin, as though it was the guilty party. "I love you very much." She didn't like "very much," its top notes of "not enough." "But if we stayed together now we'd start seeing each other as a prison—Brett, you've said it yourself! We'd grow to hate each other."

Would we? Never had his insights felt so unwelcome. Yet he was only agreeing with her. Some nerve, agreeing with her! That they were not enemies in this made it impossible.

"You have to live your life too," he was saying. "I don't want you to betray what you owe yourself."

Fucking hell!

"And maybe we'll be together again, who knows? With a world of experience to share. When we've become . . . who we're meant to be."

"No," she said, "your 'experiences' would be against

me. They'd take you away from me. And mine would take me away from you. I would want you to disappear."

He looked wounded—the *chutzpah*! It would have been, well, classy if he'd *proposed*, and then she could have heroically said no, like that martyr St. Agnes carrying around her own goddamn head. Or decided *not* to be heroic. And what were you supposed to do with the love? Oh, why couldn't she speak to him like she was speaking to herself?

"Y'know, Rome and all the rest," he said —"the future feels like an anticlimax. I'll always be looking for you." He shut his eyes and exhaled. "It's too fucking hard. We met too soon, it's the fault of no one. Come back here, I miss you."

CODA

In early September a storm descended on Manhattan like the apocalypse. Lightning bared stunned facades, thunder jack-hammered overhead, to wander off grumbling into the night. By dawn the city gleamed; heads cleared; suddenly it was fall.

Jordan Frankel regretfully "passed" on Brett's proposal; it somehow lacked the cheeky voice of her "My Generation" essay, he wrote. Rufus left for Rome to become the Associated Press correspondent for the Vatican. Brett heard from some well-meaning soul that Rufus was engaged to an Italian actress, a principessa. Brett went on a sex bender. In the spirit of scientific inquiry she was studying, as she put it to herself, sexual signatures; no two styles of fucking were identical. At Harvard there was Fenton H. on the floor of Kirkland House; a madman with a rubbery sneer who lived off campus and claimed the Czech premier as kin; a Polish *wunderkind* with an un-spellable name who composed twelve-tone music. In New York, she made it with theater director Leo G. and his cascading bellies on grey sheets, a recording of whales booming from the stereo, and after that a realtor who, when she got aroused, said *what what*. A Catholic journalist who hosted parties upstairs on Cornelia Street, Bach's solo cello on the record player, and who got so kerschnickered she wasn't sure the transaction qualified as sex. At the wedding of Lyndy Darling and Tip DeGroff in Katonah she tumbled into the orbit of a snooty Yalie, color of Vaseline, even his eyebrows. He must have thought: Foxleigh girl, puts out, yowzer. Brett keeps no memory of the trip to the Albert Hotel in the Village, or his name, just a smell of Lysol, and the harsh perp light in the bathtub where she squats under the faucet, going at herself with a washcloth because he's forgotten to use a rubber or refused and forgotten to pull out or thought, what the hell, who was this slut anyway.

On October 9 Bowden Curtiz's production of Jean Anouilh's *Antigone* starring Nina Winston opened to a packed Provincetown Playhouse. How reed-like and brave Nina looked onstage against the massive boulders that would become her tomb, defying Creon to do his worst. "I am disgusted with your . . . promise of a humdrum happiness. . . ." Nina's husky contralto rolled out into the theater's dark, raising gooseflesh. "I want everything of life, I do; and I want it total, complete: otherwise I reject it! . . . I want to be sure of everything this very day; sure that everything will be as beautiful as when I was a little girl. If not, I want to die!"

Applause, foot-stamping, bravo's. The cast, producers, friends piled into the Lion's Den off Sheridan Square to wait for the reviews. Toward midnight Leland and the stage manager were to run up the block to the newsstand on the square to scoop up the early editions of the papers. People milled about the two-level space avoiding eye contact, perhaps superstitious about premature celebration.

In the Ladies Brett discovered Nina dressed in her regulation black, staring into the mirror. Nina put her finger to her lips. "Don't tell them I'm here."

"Nina, you were sensational, the reviews are going to be great."

"But can I live up to . . . myself? There's always the *next time*."

"That's the performer's curse. But you get up for it, you know? And you make the magic happen—*again*. Besides, you've got plenty of margin for error!"

Nina's chestnut eyes flashed her gratitude.

Emerging from the Ladies, Brett scanned the crowd for Foxleigh friends. There was May Leach with her pixie bangs and long neck, twittering about with a new beau in horn-rims. Audrey Curtiz wore a beige blouson sheath with a bow knotted like a Boy Scout's at the neck. In her Creative Writing class she was midway through a novel about working girls in New York.

A small commotion by the door. Brett spotted the pyramid of black hair and little smile. Old Rinko had sort of forgotten about college to marry an avant garde composer who created tone poems out of mike'd ambient noise. She'd become a fixture in New York's downtown avant garde, whose taste for nudity and assorted provocations gave Manhattan's D.A. conniption fits. She began handing around small vials.

May Leach seized Brett's arm. "Do you believe it? Rinko is distributing 'Parisian air!'"

Bodie hovered about Nina as if to arrange the New York air around her. Watching Nina, Brett wondered why she'd worried. Gone was the intransigent martyr from the play hiding in the Ladies. Cradling a bouquet of yellow roses, Nina looked starry and radiant, accepting adulation as her due.

A caboose-like head appeared in the doorway. The tension in the room hissed like a string of dynamite. Leland came striding toward Bodie and Nina, arms full of papers, but even before he spoke you could see from his eyes that the news was good. The crowd fell silent as Bodie spread the *New York Times* on a table and read the lead aloud. A chorus of cheers. Champagne corks popped. Nina Winston, said the *Trib*, was "a revelation."

Brett stitched through the crush to join Julia and Audrey at the bar. Elliott Haimowitz clicked away at the three friends serving up their best smile. Brett was sideswiped by an odd thought: of their trio only Julia remained undamaged.

Wednesday before Thanksgiving, Audrey flew to L.A. to meet Imre's latest wife. Brett drove with Julia to her uncle's "cottage" in Newport, Rhode Island, its stone terraces lashed with sea-spray, for a spirits-drenched weekend. On an exceptionally mild Thanksgiving day Bodie Curtiz and Nina Winston hopped a cab to her mother Hildy's apartment, its beige *so serene*, on the eighteenth floor of 530 Park Avenue. Some time after the arrival of the Honey Glazed Turkey and Cranberry Surprise, in the presence of Bodie, Hildy and other family, Nina walked to the living room window and tipped over the sill from the eighteenth floor to the courtyard below.

PART II

EX-PATS

"Our journey is entirely imaginary. That is its strength . . . It's a novel, just a fictitious narrative. Littré says so, and he's never wrong."
—Louis-Ferdinand Céline

DISPATCH FROM THE FRONT

"PARIS DIARY, Jardin du Luxembourg, September 20, 1958," Brett wrote in the notebook with blue graph paper. "Chestnut trees lining the *allées*. The rasp of dry leaves scuttling over oxagonal paving. It's the start of the *Rentrée* and students swarm the Boulevard St.-Michel. . . . "

Could she stay? In her bag lay a ticket for the Queen Elizabeth, due to sail from Cherbourg in four days. Why go back to New York? Well, to find a job and a mate was why. Like all the other college grads who'd wrapped their summer-bumming around-Europe and sailed back to the States to be grownups. *Fini* mad love with tawny-haired Herman Jaeger from the youth hostel on Cap d'Ail. His motor scooter put-putting along the Neckar, her cheek applique'd to his back.

She thought of Audrey, Assistant Features Editor at *Mademoiselle* with an actual expense account, living on Fifth Avenue—practically in Harlem, but still. She thought of Lyndy Darling DeGroff. She especially thought of Lyndy at 3 A.M. when she snapped on the light to fake out the fleas in the Hotel Esmeralda, or after breaking the sink she'd used as a bidet. In her last letter Julia had mentioned that Lyndy and her husband Tip DeGroff, a manager at Fiduciary Trust, lived in a brownstone duplex on St. Luke's Place in the Village. She pictured English Calyxware, Tip sallying forth in the morning showered and shark-bright, she smelled the lemon oil on wideboard floors. . . . Yet like a horse fighting the bit, something in her balked. Here it was, her promise to herself since college, an invitation to the grand smorgasbord of the world. She could always downshift later into the safe lane.

She watched students and nannies with toddlers filing out of the Luxembourg through the towering wrought-iron gate onto the Place du Pantheon. Could she do this? A giant dimmer was shutting down the day and she was hungry. "The stubborn dine alone," she'd read in a poem. That was her, all right, she thought, over cassoulet in the Relais du Parc. Haughtily ignoring curious glances, eyes focused, unreading, on a copy of Flaubert's *Sentimental Education*. You could tune out the terrors of solitude when living in the music, but sometimes the music grew faint, like a parade vanishing over the hill, and then whatever you had left in the way of a self would leap its cladding to become smelt on the sidewalk. She reached around to scratch flea bites behind her shoulder blade, a memento from the Esmeralda. Who the hell else was doing this? Could *she*?

Some impetus needed to get her over the hump . . . Hemingway had lived here with Hadley. She rolled out his words like an incantation: "Nobody ever lives their life all the way up except bullfighters." Scott and Zelda . . . Richard Wright, at the Stella on Rue Monsieur le Prince . . . Maurice Girodias—alive, that one—and a smattering of ex-pats who wrote dirty books for his Olympia Press, or hawked the *Herald Tribune* on the Champs Elysees. Gotta press on, Bodie would say, you always regret what you don't do. Hell, she could make money as an au pair, tutor students in English. She'd also have the refund from her ticket on the Queen Elizabeth.

She signaled the waiter for *l'addition*. She wouldn't be entirely alone. Just the other day she'd run into Gregory Corso at the corner of St. André des Arts and the Bou v l' Mich.' She was standing outside a *charcuterie* scarfing a *tartine* schmeared with *rillettes*, a fatty pork pâté that unleashes a gluttony not fit for public viewing. She'd already met Gregory Corso, after a fashion, sophomore year at the San Remo in the Village, and flipped over his poem "The Mad Yak." "*I am watching them churn the last milk they'll ever get from me. . . .*" And there he was on St. Andre des Arts, scrawny as a feral cat, gassing with May Leach, a baby blue angora beret pulled Apache-style over her dark pixie bangs. She had a way of showing up, May, and homing in on the action. And the action, suddenly, was the Beats.

PARIS DIARY, La Rhumerie, October 7. "She stayed out all night," she wrote, "because the Foyer des Etudiants Etrangers, where she'd wangled a room, bolted its great blue door at midnight." (She'd chosen to go with third person. "She" felt freer than "I," more amenable to the shameful and disgusting. To make herself a character in her own story would also help keep panic at bay.)

She stayed out all night because day lacked the hours. She hungered for Paris's every cobblestone, gargoyle, pinball machine, bookstall; its odors of water on ancient stone, fresh-baked baguette, *pissoirs*, bus exhaust, *steack-frites*, garlic, Gauloises. She wandered the *Grands Boulevards* glistening with rain, just as Pisarro or someone had painted them. She journeyed to *quartiers* far off the tourist circuit, where Deux Chevaux, cars like little Quonset huts, hogged the narrow sidewalks, and yellow light from a café belled out into the wet dark. A couple of hookers in black fishnet stockings gave her the stink-eye: had she come to poach on their turf? She must look quite the Ugly American in her shapeless pink parka, its hood trimmed in mangy rabbit fur. Elbow propped on a zinc bar, she re-fueled with a *kir* and *sandwich saucisson* and vamped at her image in the flocked mirror.

She silently saluted Rufus Porter for shouldering the nasty work of snipping the cord. It would have been nicer, of course, if he hadn't snipped the cord in order to become engaged to the principessa, but she supposed life didn't work that way.

Afternoons, with October's advancing chill, she wrote indoors over a double crème at La Rhumerie, café of Anglo ex-pats. The industry that sparked off her attracted glances. A powerful sense of vocation lay upon her. She was prospecting for a theme for the Diary. She'd flubbed her shot with "My Generation" and Jordan Frankel—"but not this time I won't," she said aloud (more glances). One day she'd fire her book out into the world and hope for an answering ping! She'd caught a contact high off the Beats, who lived in a grungy, nameless hotel on Rue Git-le-Coeur in the 5th Arrondissement, a hotel ranked thirteen in a rating system of thirteen. Almost too perfect that their street meant "Here Lies the Heart."

It had started some time in '57, the madness surrounding the Beats—since her arrival in Paris, gone global. Overnight, it seemed, Allen Ginsberg and Jack Kerouac were making all the Beats a sensation. Henry Luce lashed out at them with particular vitriol. The stories Luce published in *Time* and *Life* reviling the Beats as filthy juvenile delinquents and a threat to the American Way of Life—articles Brett devoured in the American Library—only fanned the public's fascination. Even that madman Gregory Corso was getting published in *Mademoiselle*. Audrey had just paid five bucks for one of his poems. They said fuck-you, the Beats, to buttoned-down, nine-to-five, suburbs, appliances, DUZ, Happy Rockefeller, Moloch. Moloch! They were mad to live, talk, on a tear, hairy and wild, writing mad wild poetry, pulling it out of themselves drunk, drugged, putting body and soul on the line, pilgrims in search of huasca from the Amazon to push back the frontiers of consciousness. . . .

Scribbling in the Rhumerie Brett's thoughts swamped her racing pen, she was fired up by Kerouac, "first thought, best thought." Her head thrummed with poetry, she walked the Rue Jacob with Allen Ginsberg's "angelheaded hipsters burning for the ancient heavenly connection to the starry dynamo . . . " His "mystical visions and cosmic vibrations." Gregory's "joyprints of pure air!" She wanted to catch this ride.

Mainly she dug Allen Ginsberg. Unlike wacko Gregory and junkie William Burroughs and alkie Jack Kerouac, pussy-whipped by his goddamn *mother*—Ginsberg was recognizable. The Jewish intellectual as visionary. Though of course he'd also done time in the bug house, holy madness being part of the rebel's credentials.

"PARIS DIARY: First Meeting with Allen Ginsberg, Draft #2," Brett wrote. "Mornings New York leaps awake, snaps to, clicks its heels. Paris in the pinkish grey of sunrise cocked one bleary eye and sidled out as if yielding to an indecent demand." She stood in the raw chill in front of 9 Rue Git-le-Coeur, the Beat Hotel off the Rue St. Andre des Arts and Quai des Grands Augustins. Any kid with his *Europe on 5 Dollars a Day* could direct you to it. A peculiarly Parisian early-morning bouquet of brine, bus exhaust, bakery, cafe noir, open-air pissoir. Once again she'd been shut out of the Foyer des Etudiants and journeyed to the end of the night, or someplace just short of it, like a character from Céline's novel. She was running on fatigue that feeds off itself. She could swear the hotel inclined backwards from its upper floors, like a *flâneur* eyeing her through a pince-nez. At street level, a small cafe with white lace curtains and a couple of spindly aspidistra plants . . . The name J-B Rachou scripted in white across the window, signs for BYRRH, Ricard, *Téléphone* . . . Madame Rachou, nowhere in sight, guarded her domain like Cerberus, with faultless antennae for anyone smuggling in a hot plate or hi-fi that would stress her excitable electrical system—this Brett had learned from May, who was tight with Gregory Corso. May had imparted a trove of data on the Beats before sailing on the QE2 for the States.

She juddered awake to the sound of a voice piped in from *The Twilight Zone*. Last she remembered, she and Allen lay belly to belly in the trough of the mattress. . . . Propped on an elbow, she saw the freeze-dried features of William Burroughs, prissy little mouth rouged like a mime's—another denizen of the Hotel. He was famous for having shot his wife in the head in a game of William Tell. In his three-piece suit and tie he resembled a patrician undertaker. Hard to imagine him negotiating the Turkish traps in the hall with last week's *Figaro* for toilet paper.

Allen had just finished pissing in the sink. He noticed her sitting upright on the bed. "Uhh, *what* is your name?"

Allen introduced her to Burroughs, whose gaze slid shut like a cashier's window. She'd heard that Burroughs was in love with Allen. Like everyone else.

"Brett speaks French," Allen said. "I thought she could translate when we go to Meudon to see Céline."

Burroughs lifted a whey-colored nostril. Brett figured her main offense was that she wasn't an Arab boy. Just one more American chick knocking around Paris with her copy of *Europe on 5 Dollars a Day* and deeply irrelevant to the mission of forging a new consciousness.

Burroughs launched into a harangue, lips barely moving, like a ventriloquist's. "The principal instrument of control that prevents expansion of consciousness is the word lines controlling thought . . ." *Huh?* He made as much sense as *Naked Lunch*, his freaky novel that no one would publish. Allen, riveted, nodded and raised his index finger. Burroughs's talking jag sounded chemically fueled. They said he regularly traveled to London to kick his morphine or benzedrine or smack or opium or peyote or yage or lysergic acid or paregoric or mescaline or ayahuasca or majoun habit.

Meanwhile, she was straining to locate the source of ghostly strains of music—a voice crooning "Only You," as if beamed down from Sputnik. It had no identifiable source—kind of like Burroughs' voice, which sounded piped in from some Stygian realm. She realized the music was emanating from the plughole in the sink. Apparently from another room in the hotel.

"I'm starting work on a big poem," Allen announced—"'Kaddish,' a great formal elegy for my mother." Brett leaned forward, hands on thighs. "*Farewell / with a long black shoe / farewell* . . . I started it in the Select the other day, tears were running down my face. I write best when I weep," he added in his reedy baritone. Lately, though, he had no time to work on his poetry, he was swamped by correspondence.

"Just got a letter from this businessman who read about me in *Life* and congratulated me on leaving the rat race . . . A poet wrote on toilet paper, this guy Leroi Jones, and asks me if I'm for real. I wrote back on toilet paper, 'I'm tired of being Allen Ginsberg!'"

"The notoriety is just starting," Burroughs said. "You can work better here in our little micro-climate than back in the States, and constant bombardment by the media."

"He's absolutely right," Brett put in, voice rusty. They both looked at her on the bed, surprised by her presence.

Allen moved to the window. "Miss Peter too much," he said.

That was his beloved, Peter Orlovsky, back in the States. She was up against a lot. Burroughs loved Allen. Allen loved Peter—and imagined Gregory Corso had some claim on her. Oh, and Allen was queer—though deep affinity could overcome that detail.

Now Allen was talking about a girlfriend of Peter's named Misty. Hold on—so Peter was straight? This was damn confusing. "I've been balling Misty, too," Allen went on. "I really dig her, she's this great chick with a profound Asian wisdom. She's Dutch and wants to move to the U.S., you know. What the hell, I'll marry her if she wants to become an American citizen."

Balling Misty—so Allen dug girls! Perhaps he just dug sex in whatever package it came. Earlier, on his mattress, she'd not mistaken the current between them. Maybe she had just to find a window of availability in his erotic calendar. If he was leaving for the States she needed to move fast.

She sat bolt upright. Burroughs might dismiss her as a junior-year-abroader, but he'd gotten her wrong. She'd found her story. In a stroke of pretty timing she'd parachuted, like a correspondent covering a revolution, right into the front lines. She'd carry back an eye-witness report—as it unfolded—about the creative ferment of the Beats in their Parisian micro-climate. Already, she'd lined up a visit with Allen and Burroughs to the great Louis-Ferdinand Céline, with his pack of hellhounds.

She must have walked back to the Foyer des Etudiants along the Boul'Mich, but when she thought back she had no memory of it. The green hash, or whatever it was, had punched black holes in this momentous meeting.

She remembered only that as she descended the stairs of the Beat Hotel, she heard from on high a noise that sounded awfully like retching. She looked up. There at the top of the stairwell, a small monkey face hung over the railing "Angel!" He leaned farther over the railing, Brett ducking just in time, as Gregory Corso barfed down the stairwell.

GUESS WHAT?

"I've sold my novel to Simon & Schuster. And they're paying me a fifteen thousand dollar advance!" Underline, exclamation point.

Envy fileted Brett deep under the ribs, an ugly cousin, she noted, to fear. It sometimes required the discipline of a Prussian officer to cultivate your own garden, a la Voltaire— Professor Obrecht's one-stop remedy for envy disease. She was always craning her neck and coveting the rutabagas in her neighbor's garden. She refolded Audrey's letter and ordered a second *kir*. Getting on toward five, now, and the Rhumerie rang with the sound of Americans and Brits competing for the worst French in Paris.

Brett had forgotten Audrey was writing a novel—about career girls in New York working at a women's magazine. After her own aborted project with Jordan Frankel, she'd kind of broomed the knowledge under the bed. *Fifteen thousand bucks.* She herself was pocketing 100 francs an hour baby sitting for three rascals and ironing cloth diapers, or were they sanitary nakins, ever mindful of a whip *maman* kept atop the piano to discourage masturbation. Brett decided on the high road. She loved Audrey, she must rejoice for her. It almost worked.

*   *   *

"I'd stayed home from the office Friday with a rotten cold," Audrey had written. *"I'm curled up in my pouffy chair in my bathrobe with a box of Kleenex, looking like hell and feeling sorry for myself, when the phone rings . . ."*

The voice on the other end belonged to a literary agent Audrey had recently acquired from a writer she'd edited at *Mlle.* Lucy W. spoke in a Seven Sisters drawl, and stood up in slowly unfolding segments, and at Smith would have worn Bermudas and a gold asshole pin—hardly the hustler type Audrey pictured as an agent. But here was Lucy asking in her mild way if she'd agree to an advance of ten thousand dollars for her novel. The figure cleared Audrey's sinuses like a hit of Chinese mustard. In dark moments she'd feared her pages would never find a home. She heard some imp in herself tell Lucy "No" to ten thousand, but she might agree to twenty.

After they hung up Audrey paced her tiny apartment and looked down at the bleating cars stalled on 101st Street, irritation seeming to rise off their roofs like steam. The truth was, she would have been surprised *not* to sell the novel; the doubt she'd trundled out was an old trick to buffer disappointment. Since the summer on Jane Street the perception had snuck up on her that success was her natural habitat. When women succeeded they always did a little buck and wing about "luck." Not her. With her tapestry of stories about working girls in the big city she'd tapped into something, well, if not grandly literary, new and racy—girls who weren't virgins, affairs with married men—and she'd work it so that readers would overlook that under the glamour and excitement and glitz lay heartbreak.

She passed a difficult weekend waiting to hear back from her agent.

The signed contract and deadline revved Audrey like a triple shot of espresso. Her girls and their career setbacks and search for love kept her company over Salisbury steak TV dinners, they peopled her dreams. An insight into a character would strike while she was brushing her teeth. A plot point would halt her on Madison and 62nd, so the noontime crowd parted in a double wake around her. Anything—a gossip item in Louella Parsons; a detail from *Exodus*, the new bestseller by Leon Uris; a girl's upturned nose and carmine lips before the windows of Peck & Peck—fed into the world that she was conjuring up, as if feeling her way, hands outstretched, into a dark room. Her characters became more vivid to her than actual people. Occasionally Julia would fix her up with one of her pre-Elliott discards and the guy would take her to Larre's on 56th Street, or splurge on the romantically lit Cave Henri IV. But by the time they ordered the crème brulee, Audrey saw a fatal politeness slide down her date's face like a venetian blind.

Then: an October evening Imre Curtiz, on a fly-by to New York, invited Audrey to a book party. "You remember Asher and Sonia Lind, we skied with them in Sun Valley. Asher argues cases before the Supreme Court, and in his downtime the man tosses off novels." Of Sun Valley Audrey mainly recalled the infernal din of stomping boots in the lodge where she sat with her game leg reading *Bonjour Tristesse*.

She wore a new A-line dress in pink silk shantung, the overblouse anchored by a bow, that she'd bought at Best & Co. for $17.84. Scanning the elderly crowd, she wondered why she'd bothered. She chatted briefly with Floyd someone, a young associate from Lind's firm. The bull neck dislodged troubling images.

A crush surrounded the guest of honor. Asher Lind was small and full of bravado like a braggart schoolboy and wore a bow tie. She couldn't say why this touched her. Audrey drifted toward him, catching the word "Matterhorn." "Every year we ski from Switzerland down to the Italian side, where it's called Cervinia. On the Swiss side of the mountain they serve fondue, on the Italian side you can drink Gavi di Gavi." He had a curiously bent-back thumb and spoke with metronomic precision, an exuberance like Bodie's.

"That high country snow around the Matterhorn can get a bit tricky, with the avalanches," Imre said.

"For novices, maybe," Lind returned. "Last year we

came across an ice cave. We took our skis off and slid down the frozen water on our backs carrying skis in one hand and poles in the other. Extraordinary sensation!"

Audrey must have audibly gasped, because Lind glanced her way.

"Why are you *lurking* there, honey?" Imre drew her in by the elbow. "Asher, you remember my lovely daughter, Audrey."

"I do indeed."

"A fellow writer," Imre added, "about to publish her first novel."

"You don't say." Lind's laughing eyes were all over her face. She had never felt so beheld. And mocked? "Well, we must compare notes," Lind said.

He posed for a photo with a woman whose blonde hair was sculpted into a crown worthy of Queen Nefertiti. His wife Sonia, Audrey guessed. She wore the resigned and determined look of women tethered to husbands who require major management. Asher Lind turned his head just then to look at *her*, like a figure in a painting gazing out of the frame. Someone pushed a book at him. Asher, reaching for it, held her eyes a second longer. Audrey nodded stupidly at whatever Imre was saying.

Ducking away from Floyd, the pesky associate, Audrey headed for the Ladies. She smiled at herself in the mirror, one eye more inward-gazing than the other, thin hair back-combed within an inch of its life. He had annexed her in some fashion, this Asher Lind. A married man, who had to be close in age to Imre. She heard Julia honk, Oh Audrey, you *wouldn't*.

When, after two weeks, she corraled the courage to phone his office to ask him advice about a libel matter concerning her novel, *All You Ever Wanted*, her heart thudded too loudly for her to hear much of what was said. She knew only that he sounded as if he'd been about to pick up the phone himself. They must discuss the matter over dinner, it was agreed.

For the great evening she chose a Chantilly lace dress with a square neckline, cocoa brown over taupe, with a satin bow in back that snapped over the zipper. El Parador on East 34th was like a low-lit garden in Seville, lacking only the plashing fountain. Asher had handled a matter for the owner, who welcomed them and took charge of their order. An ease enfolded Audrey. Asher talked about an upcoming trial to argue for the socially redeeming value of *Lady Chatterley's Lover*. She watched his rueful, crooked mouth, savored his clipped diction with its Boston vowels. He questioned her closely about her novel. Sketched a cunning way she might "open up" a scene.

"Did you really remember me from Sun Valley?"

"Of course I remembered. I always had my eye on you."

"What, when I was a teenager?"

"Always. Imre Curtiz's daughter."

It was naughty and nonsense but she relaxed into enchantment, eyes locking over a raised goblet glinting pale yellow, pauses, the touch of fingertips. He grasped her hand— then let it go, *Imre Curtiz's daughter, after all.* Where was the harm? They felt perfect together. Was there a better reason that nothing could come of it?

Back at the apartment she fell on her bed in her Chantilly lace, pumps hitting the beige pile carpet with a muted thunk, glad for the solitude. Her fortress had been breached, already it was more than she could manage. It occurred to her that she'd come away with expert advice on the matter of libel.

On the eighth day he hadn't called she looked up one of Asher Lind's novels at the library: a caper about oil prospectors set in the Congo, kind of ersatz Evelyn Waugh, pretty feeble stuff, she decided. Mainly she focused on the jacket photo of Asher: impish eyes, pipe clamped sideways between his teeth. And a sentence in the novel where the hero's lover marvels at his hairless balls. Asher Lind was her father's associate and a dimestore playboy, just as well he'd disappeared. Since Lonelyville, Fire Island she'd been living in the country of benumbment, where the living was easy.

When he phoned two weeks later from Aspen—could he take her to dinner at Marietta on East 52nd, he'd handled a matter for the owner—she responded coolly, pissed at the long interval since El Parador; still more, by her willingness to overlook it. God knew why she'd abruptly reappeared on this man's radar. He said he'd been taken up with a health crisis involving his older daughter.

She soaked in rose bath salts. He loved opera, she knew, but she couldn't find her one classical LP of Maria Callas singing Operatic Highlights, so she put on trusty Erroll Garner, a staple in Foxleigh's dorms. He blew into the apartment like a blast from the Rockies . . . Navy sweater, cashmere, suspenders, sun and altitude held hostage in his face. No question of Marietta's on 52nd. She loved him already, his rueful mouth, his smell. "Oh God, I must stink, I wore this sweater on the plane"—but she wanted the stink, all of it, his skin too silky to be young.

She pulled away and righted her clothes. "We're perfect together—but nothing can come of this. The world doesn't allow two people as suited as us to get together. It's what half your damn operas are about." She spoke as if addressing some third party.

"But we can be together."

"You're married. And won't ever not be."

He looked puzzled. "That doesn't have to affect . . . this."

She sat rigid. Her character, Holly, a girl based on a co-worker, had come unstrung from an affair with a married man. "I bet you've had dozens of mistresses."

"Oh . . . not *dozens.*"

Spoken like a lawyer. "You're not going to change anything about your life, you couldn't even if you wanted to."

"We'll find a way, you'll see."

She thought of Holly and her lover who claims to love her, and *does* in his sorry-assed way, yet clings to his dreary marriage, the ease of it. She'd written, "Not everyone is made for happiness." But suppose Holly's lover actually wrenched himself free? You very occasionally heard about such things.

"Listen," Asher said, "I have a big case pending, but after that . . . the truth is, I've been wanting to rethink my life."

Shadowing her thoughts . . . she couldn't allow herself to go down this road. Already she knew this man—she'd *written* him, for godssake!—his horror of disruption and comfort with his groove: three kids, the house in Aspen, Opera Guild, the goodies of his life. Besides, she had no wish to bust up a marriage. There was something wrong, though, with a world that kept them apart. She huddled on her end of the sofa, frowning, arms clasped around her middle.

He reached and pulled her over him, a kid with a marvelous toy.

HERE LIES THE HEART

*"Have nice warm room, large, with two burner gas
stove . . . 9 Rue Git Le Coeur, one block away from
Place St. Michel, out window I can see Seine . . .
Haven't started making it with female angels yet,
just got here, but soon have nice scenes I bet."*
—Allen Ginsberg (Paris, France)
to Jack Kerouac (Orlando, Florida)

*"We were living on borrowed time as well as bor-
rowed money and very little of it."*
—Harold Norse

PARIS DIARY, Tabac St. Michel, October 25. "The
French and Algerians are at war in the city's streets," Brett
wrote from her new base, the St. Michel, a Beat outpost hard
by Git-le-Coeur. From what she could surmise reading the
Figaro with two dictionaries the Algerians wanted the French
the hell out of their country, while the French preferred to
stick around and despoil this last chunk of its empire, though
Charles de Gaulle put it more nicely. Each day brought new
attempts by the Algerians to bomb (*plastiquer*) the Parisian
cops (*les flics*), who cowered with machine guns behind riot
shields like giant mantis wings. They looked like frightened
boys.

Brett was less concerned with blood in the streets than blood from scratching flea bites. The fleas had claimed her as desirable real estate at the Cinematheque, Avenue de Messine, during Eisenstein's *Ivan the Terrible* Part One. She also needed a new room; the Foyer was run like a convent. At the Beat Hotel the *chiottes* in the stairwell on their nasty little rises would inspire her gut to call a General Strike. Lately Cyclops, a weaver with a black eye patch, had been cooking heavily with garlic, and all the tenants were up in arms about the giant garlicky turds he left on the footrests. Surely Puccini's Mimi and Rodolfo had sung their sublime arias amidst less stink, Brett thought, as she climbed to Room 27, breathing through her mouth. Not that Madame Rachou would have granted her so much as a "cell room," with a barred window giving on the stairs and twenty-five watt bulb dimmed by fly shit. This intel she'd acquired from Misty Suharto, Allen's sometime girlfriend, over a *pastis* in Madame Rachou's little street-level café.

"Hard to know who'll score a room at the Hotel." Like most Dutch, Misty spoke idiomatic English. "To make the cut you have to carry a canvas under your arm, or write porn for Olympia Press, or simply be incurably weird—like Cyclops, who hasn't spoken to anyone in two years. As Bill Burroughs says, 'Madame Rachou has her orders.' She digs artists and considers the Hotel an incubator of creativity. You might just get lucky at the Stella."

Brett gazed up at the scrubbed cream façade, gleaming in the city's silvery afternoon light, like a pilgrim sighting Mecca. Hotel Stella, 41 Rue Monsieur le Prince, was ex-pat heaven, famed throughout the Left Bank for the absence of fleas. The Alsatian concierge, who claimed to have fought in the Resistance, kept even its holes-in-the-floor immaculate. Richard Wright had lived here, followed by Anatole Broyard, passing for white and fooling no one, plus the odd American logging a junior year in Paris for her memory book.

"I don't rent to people with long hair," the concierge said. "Not since a *Japonaise* clogged the drains."

Through the *Petites Annonces* Brett found a room in the apartment of a war widow in the Rue Notre Dame des

Champs. The widow must have thought it was still the war and they were rationing heat. Brett's blanket might have seen duty in the Marne; she piled on top every garment she'd brought, including the circle coat from S. Klein. In the morning, stiff and cotton-brained, she tottered off, scratching, to her job looking after three masturbators in the bourgeois Seizieme.

These hassles faded beside her mission of capturing the Beat moment in Paris. This had kind of merged with the mission of capturing Allen Ginsberg. She hadn't worked out how, exactly, this might translate day-to-day. Perhaps she'd become Allen's lover/biographer/assistant. "I want to be a part of Allen's ecstatic project," Brett wrote Julia. "My model is the creative partnership of Sartre and Simone de Beauvoir. But he's scraping together the francs to sail home and the clock is running."

Misty introduced Brett to Chez Ali in Rue St. Andre des Arts, where 250 francs could buy you a mountain of couscous topped with meat whose provenance didn't bear thinking about. She was a game girl, old Misty, with an equal opportunity approach to love. First she'd been the girlfriend of Gregory Corso—who had "offered" her in a letter to Kerouac back in the States as an incentive to come to Paris. Getting traded like sexual wampum appeared to roll right off her.

Next Misty became the girlfriend of Peter Orlovsky. This had flowered into a threesome with Peter and Allen. "It's the way Allen gets to have sex with Peter," Misty explained, blowing the bangs up off her almond eyes.

Brett jerked forward, imperiling her *rouge de maison*. "You're telling me Allen has to bring in a girl to make it with this great love of his?"

"The thing is, Allen is queer and in love with Peter—but Peter digs girls." The smoke from Misty's Gitane mingled with the fug of cooking smells and hashish emerging from behind the kitchen's beaded curtain. "Actually, Allen's all over the map sexually. He once said, 'homosexuality is like mental cancer.' Then he goes, 'I sometimes wonder if I hate women!'"

Misty laughed her little mirthless laugh. "Now he sleeps with Peter, girls, boys. After Peter went back to the States I slept with Allen—kind of for old times' sake, y'know? I came, he didn't." She spooned more couscous onto her plate. "Allen's a great soul. He's offered to marry me so I can become a U.S. Citizen."

"Uh, making it with all of them, don't you feel kind of . . . *used*?"

"Maybe I use *them*. Y'know, some day I'll be at a PTA meeting, or the church bake sale, and I'll be smiling away because no one will bloody know that I fucked Allen Ginsberg and Gregory Corso in the same day."

Brett made a note to question Misty about the choreography of a threesome. Like who put what where? Did someone give the signal to switch, like in musical chairs? At some future point she might need to know.

Misty signaled for the check. "I just heard this old girlfriend of Allen's—obsessed with him for years—jumped out a window. Now she's in the bughouse. Bellevue, I think."

"Question," Brett wrote in the Diary: "Do the Beats drive women insane? Or are the women crazy to begin with?"

"November 20, 1958: tomorrow Céline!"

Tout droit mademoiselle, messieurs.

The locals waved them on past shabby villas with flaking stucco. Louis-Ferdinand Céline—reviled WWII collaborator and genius novelist—was a recluse, but Allen had managed to chivvy out his address. Allen made a practice, Brett had learned, of paying court to all his heroes and had been turned down by Ezra Pound.

"What d'you all dig about Céline's writing?" Brett ventured, locking her step to Allen's. William Burroughs, in a three-piece suit and fedora, moved ahead and pointedly ignored her.

"Céline's prose has the frenetic style of wised-up street talk," Allen said. She loved his school-master's baritone, its furry vibrato. "Kerouac's writing has the same rush of fast excited talking. Jack's been trying like Proust and Céline to include all the little private thoughts you normally wouldn't mention."

To speak of Kerouac and Proust in the same breath seemed a bit much. Apparently Allen considered all his writer friends geniuses.

"I flipped over Céline's humor," Brett said. "The section set in French West Africa in *Journey to the End of the Night*—"

"You've read Céline?"

Pretty insulting that he'd forgotten. She let it pass. "As a matter of fact, I've read Céline in the original French," Brett said, her tone not modest. "I paid this French student to translate the slang—a good Catholic boy, so sometimes he was too embarrassed. But it was worth the hassle. Especially since the English translation is"—a beat—"*expurgated.*"

Allen swiveled to look full at her as if she'd just backed, beeping, into his zone. "Listen, you've gotta tell me more about that," he said, eyes drilling her.

Ferocious barking, they'd arrived. A dilapidated two-story villa fenced in with barbed wire. Amidst a tangle of vines, the sign for Céline's wife's dance classes: *Lucette Almanzor, Danses Classiques et de Caractere.*

Céline appeared, shouting behind him at the dogs, maybe mastiffs, as he motioned for them to come in. He seemed glad to see them. They sat at a rusting iron table in a courtyard behind the villa and his wife brought them coffee. Céline was wrapped in ratty scarves and three moth-eaten sweaters like a *clochard*. He had a superb head with beautiful grey eyes and arched brows and thick silvered hair combed back, very much the foxy Breton peasant. The dogs, in a pen behind the villa, snarled deep in their throats. A cat, Bébert, rubbed against Céline's grotty pants.

"Do the dogs ever kill anyone?" Allen asked.

"No, I just keep them for the noise," Brett managed to translate. She feared she'd oversold her skills as a translator. Reading Céline she'd mainly acquired a vast vocabulary of obsolete words for "shithouse."

"His name is Toto," Céline replied to Allen's inquiry about the parrot beadily observing them from its roost near by.

He gave Céline a copy of "Howl," poems by Corso, Burroughs's *Junky*. Céline glanced at the books without interest and laid them sort of definitively aside, muttering something about *la presse*.

Brett realized their host had no idea who they were and thought them reporters.

"What do you think of Beckett, Genet, Sartre?" Allen asked.

Céline waved his thin blue-veined hand in dismissal, fingernails rimed in brown mold. "Every year there is a new fish in the literary pond. It is nothing." Clearly he thought of himself as the greatest French writer and no one was paying attention to him.

Was he on good terms with the neighbors?

"Of course not. I take my dogs to the village because of the Jews."

Brett fudged that last part in her translation. Allen had caught it, though. He shot her his gaze-of-the-twelve-tribes-of-Israel.

"The postmaster destroys my letters," Céline went on, "The druggist won't fill my prescriptions. . . . " Brett was losing him now, *merde, alors*, he was tumbling over the words, herky-jerky the way he wrote. . . .

She would bluff, dammit. *Improvise!* Kerouac would approve. "There is very little levity in humanity," she translated. Christ only knew what Céline had actually said.

Burroughs looked at her, suspicious.

"People are not like Ariel, they're more and more like Caliban," she went on. Either she, or Céline, or both were talking le boolsheet. Burroughs chilled her with his eyes of a homicidal cleric. The dogs meanwhile had set to howling, they might all be inside a novel by Céline.

Who was saying something now about the Danes, what shits they were, the Danes . . . Brett knew he'd been imprisoned in Denmark for collaborating, but the rest was speeding by her. . . . Finally a sentence came clear, she grabbed onto it like a sinking sailor a buoy:

"You don't know a country until you know its prisons!" Brett said, triumphant.

Allen raised a papal index finger and Burroughs leaned toward his host, delighted, and the two merrily got down to comparing notes on prison stays.

Meudon gave Brett a passport to Allen's soirees at the Beat Hotel. He held forth by the kitchen galley, his messianic style a force field sweeping friends, screwballs, and the occasional French writer up to Room 27. Brett, too timid to claim the one chair, sat on the bed under the portrait of Rimbaud, black-stockinged legs stuck out, getting contact high on a stratus cloud of hash. She was a camera, snapping it all for the Paris Diary. The round work table, stack of books, manuscripts, red Royal portable typewriter. The sink and double burner, beneath it a little "pantry" with colander, ladle, cheese grater, frying pans, a gourmet cook's mini sauce pan, a box labeled *Riz*. Allen, the Talmudic stoop and thinning forelocks, his eyes of a Jewish saint. Green corduroy shirt and trio of pens stuck in the pocket like an accountant. Tweety-bird lips furled around the edges. His smile, goofy and snaggled-toothed. How could she nab him alone again?

A rogue asteroid crashed the room. Gregory sighted her and dove for the bed. "Wanna ball with me, baby?" She darted out of reach swifter than a sailfish, and stood against the far wall, eyes beamed on Allen's portrait of Rimbaud, his floaty hair. No one here hassled Gregory about his courting style. Hell, he was a downhome Rimbaud, his bad boy antics something to cultivate.

"The old forms of poetic metrics are too confining," Allen was saying, deep into an Allen-esque talkathon. "A poem should be transported along the line of the poet's breath like a saxophonist 'blowing'"—raised index finger to cement his point. Then he was on to his latest effort to persuade Girodias to publish Burroughs's *Naked Lunch*. Girodias wasn't having it; a purveyor of erotica, he failed to see how vaginas with teeth and talking assholes might be erotic. For Allen, getting his friends published was a sacred mission. "The book's a work of genius about the lust for control over the minds and hearts of other people . . . a vision of what Hell might be like . . . an enormous breakthrough into truthful expression!"

A pause to *faire pipi* in the kitchen sink.

Axel Laffont startled, as French visitors to Room 27 invariably did. Axel, a chronicler of the avant-garde, was a potential impediment. He was skinny and handsome in that beaky Gallic way, and had an eye for *les filles*—which in Room 27 meant her. Allen, she feared, had an eye for Axel. The snarled traffic of desire ran, Axel wants Brett, who wants Allen, who wants Axel.

Early morning, she decided, might again be her window of opportunity.

She found Allen sitting on the bed, grouchy as hell— she might have been the meter reader Madame sent up to inspect the electrical. "Don't you ever sleep?" Allen said.

"It's too exciting to sleep. Listen, maybe I should come back another time."

He fired up a Gauloise and waved it at her in the spirit of, well, here you are and, well . . . fucking *hell*. He exhaled. "I was robbed."

"My God, are you okay? Who did it?" She perched on the sole chair. The room smelled of ham bone and dope.

It came out that he'd picked up an Arab kid at Caveau La Huchette—Brett knew the place, a den favored by highschool dropouts with wispy beards . . . And then toward dawn, a knife drawn . . .

"Jesus, you're lucky you weren't hurt." No point reporting it to the police, of course, thereby calling attention to an expired *carte de séjour*, or, more likely, none at all—or, worst, the circumstances of the theft.

Allen shrugged. "I offered him my wash 'n wear shirts but he just wanted money."

Brett realized he *had*, in fact, been hurt—wounded by what had likely been a sex-free evening, forget the knife. It made her indignant that Allen had to put up with that kind of shit. She wondered if it happened often.

Down in the Hotel's little café, Madame, blue-rinsed and aproned, bustled about behind the zinc counter, while Mirtaud, the Hotel's calico cat, draped herself across the radiator like a ratty pelt. Two sips of Madame's *café* lofted Brett to mach speed. The hour felt electric with possibility.

"I'm scared that all the people who make my belly flutter would probably reject me if I looked at them crying," Allen said.

How could a visionary-prophet be so insecure? "Maybe they wouldn't all," she said. Suddenly remembering Misty's intel that Allen had been in love with Neal Cassady and offered to supervise his intellectual education in exchange for sex.

"My mother was a schizophrenic. It screwed me up and conditioned me. On this acid trip, once, I realized that all women and my mother are one—for me, anyway—and that I'd cut myself off from women because I was afraid I'd discover my mother in them, or have the same problems with them that I had with her."

Was he giving her fair warning?

"Francoise, this French chick, was really hung up on me but I didn't take it seriously." His eyes slid away. *Stay with me*, she telegraphed. "As a kid I was starved for physical contact and affection. I must have been a sexpest to the whole family."

"I was a sexpest—to my first quote unquote boyfriend."

"You?" He exhaled to one side. "I would have sex-pestered *you*. What happened?"

"Nothing. That was the trouble. I was very young and it fucked me up for years."

"If you were very young then, what are you now?" He rubbed his forehead, fading on her again like a dying light bulb. "'Little Kissing Bug' my father used to call me. I once told Jack, 'I'm alien to your natural grace. I'm not a child of nature, I'm ugly and imperfect.'"

"But who wants perfect? That means I would have to be perfect." She blushed at her presumption.

He zoomed back in, eyes broody behind the smudged glasses. His hand lay close on the table. "Angel, I really dig you. With you it doesn't feel forced. Your hair—it's such wild, crazy hair, like a higher you reaching up, attuned to cosmic vibrations. A sun-flower 'seeking after that sweet golden clime.'"

The rasp of the outside door, then a commotion of air and Gregory stood beside them, shirt hanging out of his fly. Giving off odors of day-old mackerel. Mirtaud leaped from the radiator to take shelter behind the bar.

"Gotta read you my new poem," Gregory said, treadling the floor. "'Budger of history brake of time,'" he declaimed, waving about a sheet of construction paper. "It's called 'Bomb.'"

Damn! Brett thought, Allen nodding excitedly.

"You . . . Bomb . . . Toy of Universe . . . Grandest of all snatched-sky . . ."

"Yes, yes, go on!" Allen said.

"How would you define the Beat Generation?" Axel Laffont asked one night.

"There is no 'Beat Generation,'" Allen said irritably, more nasal than usual from the catarrh the Beats all passed around like re-purposed gifts. "It's all a hex, a term invented by journalists and academics to further their careers and make money by writing articles. Most of our preoccupations are technical. Nobody really knows what we're doing and an endless stream of bullshit flows through *Time* and *Commentary* written by ignorant sellouts who have no artistic insight." Axel looked disappointed.

Actually, Brett had more than once wondered how, exactly, a few writer friends—Allen, Gregory, Burroughs, Kerouac—comprised a "generation." They seemed more a group of loyal buddies than a literary movement. In fact, they seemed like each other's wives. Allen came on like a den mother, hawking their manuscripts, tending to meals. At times his routine resembled that of a good French bourgeoise. Around five he'd shop in the nearby market in the Rue de Buci, with its bounteous outdoor stalls of produce in season, its pale leeks and emerald-black sea urchins briny and gleaming in pubic nests. Then, back to the hotel to start dinner—for whoever rolled in; his hospitality was exemplary. From room 27 a top note of simmering lentils and Bayonne ham bone—or his ultra-filling spaghetti and potato soup—joined the massed fug of dope and doody in the stairwell.

It killed Brett how Allen nourished and nurtured, the way he'd doubtless been forced to with his mad mother, who'd ended up with a spike through her brain. Allen turned living cheap into an art—of necessity. Even with his growing fame, advancing like the growing clamor of a mighty army, he still needed francs to pay Madame Rachou or the *laiterie* that had advanced him four days credit. Allen got money from Burroughs; sometimes Jacques Stern, a Rothschild crippled by polio who threw temper tantrums, high on coke, from his wheelchair. Harry Vietor, another rich American, arrived one night with heroin and his cast-off suits from Saville Row—and launched into the story they'd all heard more than once about how he'd blown James Dean.

Brett was fascinated by Allen's indifference to material goods and all the *stuff* America wanted you to want—and only a misfit wouldn't. Allen's indifference was no pose. The spirit and creating poetry—bringing forth the "dark river within" and unleashing his own wild naked mind—that alone mattered. Back home people coveted split level ranches and RCA TV's. Allen harvested "epiphanous moments." He improvised minute to minute. Happiness was discovering the great Apollinaire! He visited his tomb at Pere Lachaise, where he left a copy of "Howl" for Apollinaire to read in heaven. His poem made Brett cry:

> *Peter Orlovsky and I walked softly through Pere Lachase*
> *we both knew we would die*
> *and so held temporary hands tenderly in a citylike minia-*
> *ture of eternity*

He rhapsodized over Gregory's mad mouthfuls of language. "He makes poems like God makes brooks," he told Brett. "Gregory's probably the greatest poet in America, and he's starving in Europe." Brett found it hard to square "the greatest poet in America" with the Gregory she knew who depended on the kindness of monied girls, left a trail of barf, and wore pants embellished with come.

Pawing the sheets for warmth in the widow's house on Notre-Dame-des-Champs, Brett felt a foreboding in her belly. She heard Obrecht in his office at Foxleigh but who will catch you on the other end? She thought of Nina Winston on the wrong side of the ground, poor mad Nina who had somehow been failed by them all. She thought of the girls who'd found safe harbor, Lyndy Darling DeGroff in the duplex on St. Luke's Place, sorting through burp cloths and onesies, and opening the door of her new Kelvinator to show how crisp the lettuce stays. Aura Folkenflik Ogus, snugged with her lawyer husband in Teaneck, New Jersey. Julia and Elliott in his studio in the Flatiron District, poring over negatives together with a loupe. Audrey, in her perch above Fifth Avenue and 102nd, must be lonely—the wages of love with a married man—but she had a glam job and a book contract.

She tried not to picture Rufus Manning Porter, who'd aborted the search for Experience to marry the principessa. They lived in the former hunting lodge of a Cardinal, she'd learned from one of those souls put on earth to impart such news.

Conjuring all this Brett had a bad moment. But an evening in Allen's room, and she was pulled back into the music and Allen's faith that the sacred mission of poetry and art, the holy life of the spirit was the central business of the universe. Of course one passport to holiness was smack; or whatever elixirs the hotel's inmates concocted in their rooms, some in the spirit of hunters out to ensnare exotic quarry from the frontiers of consciousness. Brett stayed clear of drugs, partly because the Hotel offered a cautionary parade of junksickness. Gregory was beset by infernal shakes and sweats and itches, the works, then puked his guts out. Burroughs, with his whey-colored skin, yo-yo'ed between habits and apomorphine cures with a Dr. Dent in London, who sounded like one of his own unsavory characters.

"Years later," Brett would write—now on an IBM PC—"when she longed to be someplace else, she'd think of

Paris '58 and Room 27 at 9 Git-le-Coeur, the beating heart of the universe, where something new was getting born, and she had a piece of it. Even with the flea bites, starter consumption, and battle to keep warm she knew, This is where I want to be. In the same moment she was living it she was filling time to the brim, all her windows open, everything she'd want to explore blowing in."

DESIGN FOR LIVING

"The door you didn't try / where could it have led?"
—Stephen Sondheim, *Follies*

It was a life of pleasures snatched on the fly: slivers of weeknights; phone calls—just to rub voices; furtive clutchings. Literally—en route to an event with Sonia, Asher would ask the cab to wait below, zoom up in the elevator and grab Audrey in the hall; she developed a crick in her neck. It reminded Audrey of a crack about Bodie as the only man alive who could double park in front of a whorehouse. Once—no waiting cab this time—Asher made it into the apartment, and to her dismay raced out to *Sunrise at Campobello* with their juices on his fingers. Clearly, this couldn't last. Audrey lived with her bags packed—not checking out though. He had delivered her back to the opening chapter she'd been robbed of one July between the Atlantic Ocean and Great South Bay. Asher was surprised, and moved. You were saving yourself for me, he joked. She wept. He feared he'd offended her, sounded caddish instead of reverential, which he was. He kissed her from forehead to knees. What depth of sadness lay in her he couldn't fathom.

For her part, Audrey spent hours parsing Asher's refrain, "I want to change my life." Was it a ploy or sincere? A

ploy that Asher had *convinced* himself was sincere? A state-
ment in good faith that stood zero chance of altering the
status quo? Men, she suspected, used language as a kind
of test drive to see how things might play out, but with no
commitment to making them actually happen. That's why
there were no female Einsteins, Audrey thought irritably;
women wasted their best years trying to decode male language. She knocked off an article for *Mademoiselle* called
"Manspeak."

Occasionally on tap was the luxury of an evening
out for dinner. Asher was a master breaker of dates so this
became an iffy proposition. Some excuses felt less flimsy
than others: his daughter Esther, who was hydrocephalic,
had suffered some health crisis; you'd never lie about that.
(Asher's secretary, Audrey soon learned, protected his secret
life and vigorously defended his more outrageous cancel-
lations.) They sometimes ate at Del Pezzo on 34th street,
an ornate brownstone frequented by singers from the Met-
ropolitan Opera. Naturally, Asher had handled "a matter"
for the owner, who greeted them with a bow and news
about the new shipment of truffles and a discreet smile for
this woman not Mrs. Lind—Asher traveled a special route
lined with discreet smiles. Another stolen luxury was the
odd night at the Opera, where Asher belonged to a club
that provided private boxes. At the point in *The Marriage
of Figaro* when Susanna sings, "Come and fly to the desire of who adores you," she melted against him, reaching
for his hand. Asher shrank back; she'd forgotten they were
sandwiched between his firm's partners and their lacquered
wives, who hosed her with hostility. During intermission
they ran into Floyd, the bull-necked lawyer who'd pursued
her at Asher's book party. He cut Asher an admiring look:
why you old dog.

"This married lawyer of yours," Julia said, "it's so wrong,
he's got all the power. I mean, Elliott and I are a team. And why
should you get the wife's leftovers? Don't you deserve better?"

Exactly what her character Holly might say. Audrey made
a mental note to change it to "the wife's *leavings*." "And he's
taking 'my best years!'" she said, fingers raised in mock-horror.

"Y'know, there's some truth to those clichés. Asher's getting a free ride—it's all to his advantage."

"That's a tacky way to think."

Of course she'd endlessly played the same tape to herself.

Like all lovers, they liked to revisit their origin story, pinpoint the earliest glimmer of attraction.

"It happened at your book party," Audrey said. "Even though you were pretty silly, boasting about skiing the Matterhorn blind drunk."

"I was hoping to impress you."

"You didn't even see me."

"I could feel you listening, Imre Curtiz's daughter. Actually, it was no idle boast, after a glass or two, I once outskied an avalanche. . . ." He launched into tales of backcountry exploits in Crested Butte, Colorado where avalanches were rife. "The slope opened a gash that ripped across the mountain like a zipper, and I had to dive into a shallow crevice for protection."

"Where's the fun in that?"

"It's fun if you know what you're doing. I once took a three-day course on learning how to analyze snowpacks. Avalanches are made up of water and the trick is to make like a swimmer and stay on top of the snow—do the crawl or dog paddle, just swim, swim, swim!"

As in all such arrangements they could never spend the night together. One evening Asher phoned to say Sonia would be in Colorado—ski season was starting. "There's an inn I like called Cliffside, upstate New York near Garrison, overlooks the Hudson." A moment. "I was thinking we could spend the weekend there. I'm arguing a case in Albany and I could meet you there Saturday. We'll catch the last of leaf season, the foliage along the Hudson should be spectacular."

After they hung up, Audrey's euphoria over this "progress" suddenly went flat in her mouth. Why should her schedule depend on Sonia's athletic pursuits? She heard Julia talking about the "wife's leftovers." Firing up a Camel, Audrey then worried that she and Asher were built only for brief passionate encounters. In truth, she'd never spent even an afternoon with a man who wasn't a psychopath.

As the limo Asher had sent curved along the Taconic Parkway, she couldn't shake her crankiness. "If it doesn't work out, Asher can always slide back into his marriage," Julia had said. "While you could wake up to find you've missed your life." By the time the limo crackled into the gravel driveway to Cliffside, Audrey was in a fury at both Asher and herself.

The room was perfect: antique Ogee mirrors, fireplace banked with logs, lashings of pillows at the head of the four-poster bed, a patchwork quilt angled across it. She came downstairs to a glassed-in terrace. A smell of chrysanthemums cut with wood smoke, lovely country inn smells. Over at a corner table a couple leaned their faces together. Audrey ordered a glass of Gavi di Gavi. With each sip the irritation burned off. Far below rolled the mighty Hudson, calming, hypnotic. Asher's exuberant style, walks under burnished trees, the talk that never ran out . . . At the thought of Asher's car speeding closer, she wasn't sure she could get through dinner first. An eerie voice from the future bowled back at her: *Take this, now. Don't wait to be happy.*

She signaled the waiter for another; already he was hurrying over, anticipating her request. "A call for you Mrs. Lind," the waiter said.

He'd been delayed, she thought, heart too high in her chest, but the moment she heard his voice she knew. *His daughter Esther . . . an attack . . . waiting for an ambulance . . . Sonia flying in from Denver . . .*

"Audrey, please, say something. Talk to me . . . Audrey?"

She had no words, no right to anger, a child was sick. Their little getaway, all those pillows, it felt dirty.

"You would have canceled in any event."

"Audrey, that's ridiculous, I'm as disappointed as you— *more!* Nothing could have stopped me coming except— Listen, I'll send another car to get you. Or stay a bit"—his voice trying for levity—"and enjoy the fall foliage—"

She hung up.

She was lucky, there was still a late train to New York from Poughkeepsie. The puzzled innkeeper hoped Audrey had not been too disappointed by the foliage. Because of the summer drought, she said, the colors had been dull this year and in any event they'd had no leaves since mid-October.

She told the secretary she shared with the College Editor that if Mr. Lind called, she was to say Miss Curtiz was in a meeting. Each unanswered call bulked up her muscle, as if she'd been lofting eight-pound weights. She swelled with malevolent satisfaction like a serpent gorging on mice. The pink orchid plant he sent to her apartment she handed off to the doorman, after dropping the inscribed card in the trash can by the mailboxes. Nights after work she put her shoulder to the novel, shuttering out all distraction *to be a novelist, you have to be an animal.* She reveled in her power to leave herself behind like some war-torn land.

Several weeks of this, until one night in her apartment she absently answered the phone.

He was there at the Algonquin to greet her. In his bow tie and tweedy jacket he resembled a middle-aged college kid and looked smaller, as if humbled, he'd shrunk. She beat back a rush of love and counted to five.

"Audrey, I know you to be fair-minded," Asher started in his metronomic tenor, double-jointed thumb on display—"so please, you must forgive me for something that was utterly beyond my control. A child was in trouble, I did what was only right—believe me, I was devastated." . . . blahbedy blah . . . "The last thing in the world I wanted was to hurt you."

At this she almost flew out of control. Men, in her limited experience, always expressed contrition for "hurting" women, presuming they had the power to *hurt*, when mostly they had the power to deeply *annoy*. He went on about the rotten timing of that weekend, and she sipped her Lillet, steadied by its tangy nectar and the ambient hum. She nodded in sympathy, glowed with understanding.

The relief in Asher's eyes revealed he hadn't expected it would be this easy. "On some level you were right," he said— her empathy flushing him into the open. Audrey scarcely dared breathe, as he semi-confessed to mixed feelings about the weekend. "With Esther's illness I pretty much need to be reachable by Sonia and couldn't see how to swing that without, well, something I can't manage yet—not *yet*. But you'll see, after this big case I'm working on, we'll find a way. . . ." More language in that vein. She noted the clever lawyerly hedging and loopholes, wondering if he taught that in Trial Practice at NYU. She kept her gaze warm and complicitous.

Since the Cliffside debacle she'd had plenty of time to reflect. In truth, she'd tired of Asher Lind—tired of *them*, the situation, its predictability. A sense of futility had invaded her. The separation had allowed her to recognize that investing in Asher was like throwing money away, and this offended Audrey's eminently practical nature. And sexual shame. Alongside a child in trouble, their avid pursuit of pleasure was like those grotesques in Hieronymous Bosch sticking penile shapes into holes.

Her turn. She told Asher she loved him and had spent many nights fantasizing about the things they might have done in that room with all the pillows in Cliffside—he reached out, but she slid her hand away. "Trouble is, I need what everyone needs," she added, in the event this might have eluded him. "Someone to come home to at night and talk about work over a martini and snuggle with under the quilt on winter nights. I want to be one of those dumb tourist couples you see everywhere, with peeling sunburn and cameras and dopey shorts, just ordinary Ugly Americans seizing their moment in the sun." She laid this on the table in the tone of a bank teller peeling off bills, watching his ruddy face lose color. His admiration and awe blew out at her. She felt him fall harder in love, putting all this love out there, her refusal burning it off like morning fog.

"Asher, don't call me, it's better for us both, I'm sure you agree." She checked her watch. "Well, I'm off!" A huff of relief, like after a tiresome chore. "Miss Motley has given me a pair of house seats for *Fiorello*." To which she'd invited Floyd Susser, an associate from Asher's firm.

*   *   *

Audrey had wanted at times to kill the Monster of Lone-lyville, for whom no demise would be too cruel; her father Imre; and now Asher Lind, who was taking his sweet time about departing her system like a lingering ear infection. She could also clobber without a qualm Floyd Susser, a world-class bore who could riff pedantically on almost any subject (reducing you to silence for fear of uncorking the next monologue). Floyd also had unusual digestive habits. At the movies he'd race to the john right at the film's climax because it "gave him the urge."

Luckily, Audrey could kill people off in her novel. In a new chapter of *All You Could Want* she had just rid the earth of Holly's married lover Dean in a fatal boating accident. Dean had promised Holly to "rethink his life" after a big promotion came through. Then his wife had "accidentally" become pregnant again—just one of many cards Dean could pull out of the deck for preserving the status quo. So the best solution had been simply to kill the bastard off. Reams of language were wasted protesting otherwise, but in truth, husbands preferred the comforts of the rut to happiness—for the Dean's of the world the rut *was* happiness.

Such matters Audrey chewed over during weekends in her "writing retreat," a little ranch house in Islesford she'd rented below market for the off season. The house was in the townie section near the bay—light-years from the old money glamour of Lilac Close—up a short steep driveway and sequestered like a deer in the scrub oak. Evenings, she'd sit, legs on the coffee table, and dream her characters' destinies over a glass of Lillet. The woods outside, illumined by a spot, copied the amber in her glass. At some point she'd heat a Swanson TV fried chicken dinner—"new and improved!"—with buttered potatoes and mixed vegetables, all on its individual tray divided into three triangles, the biggest for the entree. The package depicted a chipper wifey in a shirt dress with pocket book and bag of groceries, a figure she and the friends had reviled in college, and whom Audrey now found herself envying, sort of. Sunday she woke to chimes from a little white stucco church down the road.

On a Saturday towards midnight Audrey decided Dean's death would be too much of a downer. She needed to feed the dreams and buoy the hopes of "her" readers, the mute, invisible women whose stories had been deemed too trivial to tell—who else cared about their little triumphs and tragedies, anyway?

Design for Living/draft #2 Audrey typed. Dean survives the boating accident with a few broken ribs. Holly decides to embrace the role of permanent Other Woman. To convey the appeal of such an arrangement Audrey had only to draw on her own intoxicating, early days with Asher. Audrey banged out a new scene on her Olivetti: Holly contrives to "run into" Dean at a squash tournament at the Harvard Club, and after, they move on to drinks at the Algonquin Hotel where Holly lays out her design for living.

Nope, her readers wouldn't buy it. She fired up a new Camel and squinted through the smoke at a tremor of ochre leaves. Like her readers, Holly would want kids, you betcha, their footfalls and little voices, she'd want PTA, piano lessons, Rex the dog, February White Sales, a Westinghouse Roaster Oven, and meat-and-potatoes-sex with a husband who walked in the door at night saying *hi honey, I'm home*, smelling of commuter train and the *Times*.

Draft #3. Dean lies in the hospital, stroked out from the accident. His wife, of course, keeps vigil, while the family and hospital staff treat Holly like a vagrant and bar her from visiting him, italicizing the sordidness of her position (Audrey slammed home the carriage of the Olivetti with a fury). An ailing mother calls Holly back to Bumfuck, Nebraska. Enter kind widower with silver sideburns . . .

Yah, she'd go with that version. Audrey shifted to the sofa and put up her bad leg. She smiled to remember the buzz she'd gotten from conjuring Holly's life as the Other Woman; reached for her smokes. Didn't living solo sometimes suit her? Despite everyone yammering she'd die miserably alone? When the work was going well her book people made excellent company. Perhaps she did better at weaving the destinies of her characters than pursuing her own. To weave she needed solitude, savannas of it. She also needed, might as well face it, Asher. Just not all the time.

The problem, of course, were the wretched weekends, when other couples would be enjoying Sunday brunch, prefaced, of course, by morning slow love—something she could only imagine since she and Asher, always pressed for time, made it like birds taking a shit between two storms, and look what had happened at Cliffside? But suppose she packed weeknights with Asher with weekend-ish pleasures; then, come Friday hightailed it out to Islesford? Asher would be getting away with bloody *murder*—but who in the universe was keeping score?

Audrey imagined the commentary such an arrangement would inspire in "Tell me Doctor," a smarmy column in the *Ladies Home Journal*, which had lately addressed the issue, "Where should we stop in petting before marriage?" (She could hear Julia's shriek of laughter.) The Doctor would tell her she was selling herself short because she believed no one could love her unreservedly. The Doctor would be right. With her scraggly hair, gimpy leg, and un-perky breasts, she'd never felt herself an appetizing package like Julia or Brett. Yet Asher reliably found her arousing.

How to engineer a reunion? Audrey suspected that because she'd found the strength to dump him and delivered a lethal hit to his pride Asher was permanently hooked. She would need to test the waters.

Audrey riffled through the waste basket and plucked out her discarded Draft #2 of Holly's scheme for getting back with Dean. She'd typed,

"The squash courts at the Harvard Club were on the fifth floor. Holly ordered a chardonnay from a bar by a window giving on 44th Street and found a seat in a sort of bleachers just out of sight of the players. Dean and his opponent, both in transparent plastic goggles, set to whacking the ball at walls. Between sets Dean leaned his forehead into the squash court wall to catch his breath. . . . "

The chardonnay at the Harvard Club was rotgut, but this was no wine-tasting—she'd gotten herself here, and up to the 5th floor squash courts, and that was all that mattered.

Till this moment she'd followed to the letter the scene she'd written for Holly, even worn the same sleeveless black velvet cocktail dress. Now she'd have to climb out of her pages and work without a net.

From the top row of bleacher-like seats, Audrey watched Asher and his way taller opponent whack a ball in the bright box below, the geometry of the whizzing ball and its happy *thunk*, a flex of the knee to smash a low one, the adroit ballet to avoid colliding. Did they know how devastating to women they were in their white, droopy-drawer shorts? She watched Asher, a wily David flush with victory, towel off and chat with a fellow club member in wire-rim glasses. The man brayed like a lunatic on furlow. He was the publisher of Arden Press, another David, who was battling America's prudery. For years Asher had been working on a case that would argue for the literary merits of Arden's unexpurgated *Lady Chatterley's Lover* and consign the dirty-minded censors once and for all to the dust bin.

Asher glanced up, icing her heart. "Why, Audrey Curtiz!" His hey-old-buddy tone. Oh God, had she completely misread him? Or was he feinting to put off observers? Next she knew, he'd slung an arm around her shoulders, anointing her with sweat, and was marching her off in a playful way she'd always loved to a corner of the room giving on 44ᵗʰ street. Audrey worried that the harsh light might reveal her eyeliner had been clumsily applied with shaking hand.

"Christ, I'm happy to see you," Asher said, looking not the least happy.

Over drinks in the seedy parlors of the Algonguin Hotel, just down 44ᵗʰ street, Audrey laid her terms on the table in a neutral voice like a labor arbitrator. Able lawyer that he was, Asher hedged about ski rituals, sick daughter, Sonia this and that. Audrey eyed him coldly. She hadn't even requested national holidays. Yet over the following weeks when they met for dinner at the off-*piste* restaurants chosen by Asher, she discovered he was prepared to carve out more room for her than she'd ever imagined. There would be trips, there would be birthdays, there would be a life—just not a husband. "I'm going to Brussels to see a client," he announced one evening in December. "Can you manage time off from the shop? I want you to see the Flemish Primitives in Bruges. And the Ghent altarpiece, a marvel." February they went to Grand Case, a little fishing village he'd discovered on the French side of St. Martin's, dancing every night in the harbor-side *boites*. March belonged to Zermatt.

Audrey sometimes pitied Holly.

BOY GANG

*"In the '50s if you were male you could be a rebel,
but if you were female your families had you locked
up . . . Someday someone will write about them."*
—Gregory Corso

Brett eyed the blue airmail letter on the little marbled table at the St-Michel. Pablo Sobotka was coming to Paris on business and hoped she'd show him the Eiffel Tower and "the sights."

Pablo had been a low-level complication in her life since, well, that vexed period roughly a year back after Rufus Porter had decided to cover the Vatican and Ornella. Late that summer, Pablo had shown up at one of Bodie's croquet parties at Lilac Close. Not one for genteel sports, Pablo hung on the sidelines gassing about his latest buys in FM radio, all poutered with his own smarts. Brett watched the women watching Pablo, mentally remodeling this fixer-upper, costing out the sweat equity against major *prospects*.

Later, a Lilac Close ritual, they all drove to the ocean, a straight shot from the house, and scrambled up the high bluffs to watch the moon on the Atlantic. Without precisely meaning to she stayed behind with Pablo. They worked up a fine heat in the lee of the bluffs (though love on sand is a highly overrated exercise). After, Pablo said, you cried, and considered them engaged. She cried because his schoolboy reverence was a turn-on and *post coitum omne animal* hap-py. At the time she'd been a bit ahem indiscriminate. Even racked up a night, long overdue, at the Hotel Earle in the Village with Bodie. Because he was there. Though maybe not so much, sexually speaking.

Pablo—at least his earning potential—had somehow appeared on the radar of her father in the depths of Bellflow-er, California. He'd written her in Paris to "snap him up." There must exist a whole borough of heaven, Brett thought, peopled with fathers urging their daughters toward the one who would catch them and keep them safe. If only the daugh-ters could listen. If only she could sort out her own feelings. Pablo talked like Nathan Detroit; his fixation on her thrived without encouragement—like the roots of banyan trees grab-bing nourishment from the air. Yet the thought of losing this thing she'd never had with someone she didn't want made her afraid. Nights in the widow's meat locker she sometimes burrowed into the idea of Pablo like a down coverlet.

Brett fingered his letter. She couldn't notch the idea of Pablo into her life in Paris. She'd been nowhere near the Eiffel Tower. Room 27 at 9 Git-le-Coeur, Café St.-Michel, Ali Baba, the tiny *epicerie* where Hotel residents shopped at 2 A.M.—those were her "sights." Pablo had signed off with "I can be the man you want me to be." It squeezed her heart, he sounded like John Alden or someone.

They met for English tea in the peppermint-striped bar of the Pavillon Opera where Pablo was staying. He looked on in wonderment as she bantered with the waiter in her faux-fluent French, and ordered *Viennoiseries*—"French for Dan-ish," she translated. Pablo seemed a rough draft of the person he was working toward. The grey tooth had yielded to white porcelain, while his fingers served as pusher for crumbs from the *Viennoiseries.*

"It's all happening for me now"—a brown crumb stuck to the corner of his mouth. "Business is through the roof, gotta new two-bedroom on East 66th. Brett, I wanna share it all with you."

She scumbled together some grateful words. "The thing is, Pablo, I've kind of got a life here now."

He looked caught out at failing to understand. "Gotcha. Listen, I can fly over to see you every month or so."

"I'm working on a book, so that might be, well, a disruption."

"A book—fantastic! But you'll come home eventually, won't you?"

"Being an ex-pat is kind of open ended." Shit, she ought to cut him loose. "Pablo, what do you like so much about me?"

He chuckled, absurd question. "The gals in my office, they all just wanna get hitched. You—you're an ex-patriot, a writer, you wear your hair like—like a Parisian. I mean, you're"—his hands formed two large parentheses—"different from the rest. Lookit—do your thing here. And I'll wait."

Her fork paused mid-journey. "You mean, you'd actually wait?"

"As long as it takes."

With Allen, lately, it felt like three steps backward for every two forward. In an interview with Art Buchwald in the *Tribune*, a postscript noted that he was close to raising the fare to sail home. Meanwhile, with their growing fame, the Beats were invited around Paris to meet other poets and artists, like high school misfits suddenly grown popular. Now Allen had disappeared into his "joint psychoanalysis" with William Burroughs. "A great psychic marriage," Allen called it.

Shut out of this unholy project, Brett logged long hours at the Café Bonaparte, which offered serious heat and the odd glimpse of Jean-Paul Sartre. She came across a sentence she'd written in the Paris Diary on a contact-high in Allen's room. "The gargoyles hunch high above the city spitting night." Ugh. Kerouac swore by "first thought, best thought." But suppose it was "first thought, shittiest thought?" Brett glanced up at the electric blue dusk on the Rue de l'Abbaye and was sucker-punched by loneliness.

A finger of cold air weaseled under her scarf. Gregory

Corso gusted in. The Boastful Fireman, Brett privately called him, for his habit of hosing the environs with semen. She'd been dodging him since he'd taken to declaring, like the Left Bank's Town Crier, that he was "mad for a pink-haired angel."

"Angel!" he sang out, spotting her. "Your gasoline dress!"

Gregory's book was called *Gasoline* so maybe this term for the jewel of her wardrobe, a maroon blouse and skirt from Peck & Pack, was a compliment. This evening she was pleased, for once, to see him. Gregory had a tender, take-charge side like a small, mad mommy.

"Let's go to the Pantheon," he said, jigging in place, his yawp attracting stares. "We'll fake out the guards and spend the night communing with the spirit of Victor Hugo!"

Here was an idea that could come back and bite her in the ass. Suppose Allen found out?

They slunk around the tomb of Victor Hugo in the mortuary light, the air that hadn't circulated since 1885, but the guards threw them out at closing. They roamed the Rue Mouffetard like a pair of truants, she on the slip-stream of Gregory's manic energy. They blissed out over the North Rose in Notre Dame—Gregory claimed its blue was heightened by sniffing horse. In the Mistral bookshop they hunkered down among Brits with dodgy teeth living *la vie Boheme* before going up to Cambridge. Watched, terrified, as George Whitman, the bookstore's owner, gave himself a "haircut" by setting it on fire.

At dusk they escaped the November rains in the Café de l'Odeon. "Usually, when I meet a girl I ask her how much money she has, and then I demand half of it," Gregory said.

Her own poverty had made her an exception. She not-ed how the belled section above Gregory's wide mouth was chimp-like, as if his maker hadn't bothered properly to finish his creation—yet he had an acquired appeal, Gregory, with his alley cat frame and tousled mop, not to mention the fast-est hard-on in the West. It was unclear when or whether he bathed; he might be self-cleaning like a cat, or moving too fast for the dirt to settle.

"Allen and I picked each other up at a dyke bar in the Village. It was beautiful. I was about six months out of prison and Allen just digs my face, see, 'cause he's a homosexual, right? Allen was the first gentle person and dear friend. He's the closest thing to me in life, my guardian understanding angel. He introduced me to Kerouac and Burroughs. Man, he so loves me. I told him, I'd die for you."

Brett loved Allen's love for his buddies—imperishable loyalties that evoked Roland and Oliver from childhood books. Gregory's shenanigans had made him as welcome on two continents as a leper. In Nice he'd managed to insult Picasso, arriving back in Paris with a gun. "I went to the Deux Maggots and aimed the gun at everybody and screamed, 'Why did I starve in Nice? You bastards!'"

Allen just smiled like a doting uncle at what he called "Gregorian" lunacy. Allen harbored boundless empathy with people the world kicked aside like detritus: muttering drunks, loonies who heard voices, the *clochards* on Paris metro gratings with pissy pants and red-rimmed eyes. Nutso Peter, who called himself "crazy as a wildflower" and wrote in "Frist Poem," "mistory fills the air." Maybe they formed a continuum with his sad, mad mother.

These grand friendships had a way of schlurping into sex. There had been some funny business back in the States between Allen and Kerouac. Allen had been mad for Neal Cassady, super cocksman and model for Dean Moriarty of *On the Road*—in fact, got caught on his knees blowing him—by Neal's wife Carolyn. Burroughs was hot for Allen. . . . There was the troika with Peter and Misty. . . . Within this sexual free-for-all, Brett suspected, lay a code to which she lacked the key.

The maitre d' at Brasserie Lipp directed them to a good table—the prime real estate doubtless Bodie's doing. Brett sped through the intros so Gregory (suctioned onto her like a whelk) could sit before anyone spotted the silvery logo on his corduroys. Bodie and his wingman Leland were already sharing smirks. Tip DeGroff, who seemed pretty lit for this early in the day, tried to explain to the waiter how to make a bullshot—"bouillon, juice *de tomate*, and beaucoup vodka." Beside him, his wife Lyndy ballooned beneath a navy maternity number with a red faille bow at the throat.

"We've just come from an art show, Yves Klein's 'empty' exhibition,'" Tip said, making air quotes. "Mind you, it was literally empty—not a stick of anything in this supposed 'art gallery.' They should have named the show 'The Emperor's New Art.'"

"But Dadso, Yves Klein meant for *us* the *visitors* to be the exhibition," Lyndy said.

That Tip was a philistine and boozer struck Brett as a fair trade for the Village duplex and the family compound on Mt. Desert, Maine they called the "camp." Then she remembered Julia's latest letter—"*The day after the honeymoon, Tip was off to the races—the Americas Cup and the rest of the yachting calendar. He clean forgot he had a wife! Worst of all, he's been coming on to* me." To think that in her Parisian squalor she'd often envied Lyndy. Brett noted uneasily that at her side Gregory had turned antsy like a kid needing to pee.

"You can blame it all on Marcel Duchamp," Bodie said, delighted by the idea. "Duchamp was exploring the question, What gets to be called 'art?' His 'Fountain' was a major landmark."

"At least a fountain is a visible object and can be a thing of beauty," Tip said.

"Duchamp's 'Fountain' was a porcelain urinal," Leland said.

"Well, your *Doo*-shomp should have his head handed to him," Tip said.

"Look man, Marcel Duchamp is one of my genius heroes, man," Gregory jumped in, imperiling glassware. "Just met him and Man Ray at a party, man. Ginsberg kissed Duchamp's shoe and asked for a blessing. And I cut off Duchamp's tie."

"Good grief, whatever for?" Tip said.

"To show him we loved him, man."

Tip inclined toward Gregory like an anthropologist who's encountered someone who never attended St. Paul's and Yale. "Tell me, my friend, how do you support yourself writing poetry? Are you affiliated with a university?"

"My university was Clinton State in Dannemora where I got turned on to Shelley. That fucker was beautiful. But after I got out I stole again. I tried work. But I can't make it because I just don't live in this possible world, I don't know what it is. My book *Gasoline* brings in money, Kerouac sends me money, Allen too. So I don't have to worry about anything as anal as rent or food."

A harried silence. Everyone sat as if with an ear cocked for a coming tsunami.

"Oh Brett," Lyndy burst out, blue eyes swimming— "I'd almost forgotten to tell you, we went to the Paris Opera Ballet and I remembered you once went *leaping* across the lawn at Foxleigh holding a daffodil!"

Tip had moved on to vodka martinis. Lyndy talked silkily about her work on the board of the Penal Ministry and the rewards of giving back. "I do think it's important to give back, don't you?"

Gregory twirled his hair with his index finger like strands of spaghetti. "What do you—what does she know about fucking prison, man?" Brett placed a hand on Gregory's thigh, but he brushed it off. "I was sent to the Tombs at age twelve. For five months, no air, no milk and the majority were black and hated the white and abused me terribly. And I was like an angel, man, because they stole my food and beat me up and threw pee in my cell—"

"Why don't we save that for after dessert," Bodie said.

"—and after, I was sent to Bellevue, where I spent three frightening sad months with mad old men. And they peed in other sad old men's mouths. So where was your fucking penal reform then?"

Tip's cheeks bore two raspberry stains.

Gregory stood, knocking over his empty wine glass. "Paris is beautiful when it's Paris and not vacationing Ivy-league."

Bodie patted the air above the table, as if to placate everyone.

Happily, the garcon arrived with the *harengs* and a platter of *huitres*. They talked of Algerians causing havoc in the streets, riot squads with shields on every square, the taped-over trash cans. Was it even safe to take the Metro?

"Gracious, Paris just isn't the same!" Lyndy said.

"Well, the FLN does have a point, all they want is independence for Algeria," said Brett who read the Commie paper *L'Humanite*. "And the French police are using gestapo tactics. They're actually boasting about throwing Arabs in the Seine."

"My word!" Lyndy said. "Oh, Brett dear, the girls are throwing a shower for me next month. Would you consider flying in? Julia, Audrey, Aura—*everyone's* coming!"

Tip, pretty tanked by now, eyed Brett. "You know, I quite enjoyed your Gregory. What was it he said? 'I don't live in this possible world.' Quite *extraordinary*."

"What exactly are you doing here, darlin'? Hasn't the whole ex-pat trip kind of run out of steam?"

Brett flicked an uneasy glance around the Select, Hemingway's old haunt, where she'd met Bodie for a drink before his flight to New York.

"Allen Ginsberg and the Beats are here," she said. Of course Allen's imminent departure threatened to ring down the curtain in Paris and shift the scene to wherever he was going. As for what she was "doing here" as a not-so-innocent abroad, harder to articulate.

"Look, there was this great moment in Paris," Bodie said. "In the twenties with Hemingway and the rest. And then another wavelet of ex-pats, still coasting on the magic of the Lost Generation. But now?"

Bodie signaled their waiter, a sloe-eyed boy with obsidian hair, for another round.

She'd not be the one to say it, but yes, except for the Beats, her timing was a bit off and the third wavelet of expats in Paris were mostly the tag end and dregs who'd arrived late to the party, as they were stacking the chairs and dousing the lights: college grads between lives, no longer students but not yet an account executive or lawyer—or, if you were a girl, a Mrs. and mom; a few losers rehearsing for a lifetime of drift; academics on Fulbrights researching dissertations that no one would read; liberal arts types like her, eking out a few *sous* babysitting and tutoring. No, this wasn't exactly the Paris of fucking Hemingway writing one true sentence, the truest sentence he knew, or checking out Fitzgerald's dick in the *toilettes,* or Gertrude Stein saying, you are a lost generation, that's what you all are!

"You and the Beats are on a whole different trip," Brett said. "Allen's a spiritual seeker in search of a cure—for the sickness in America he calls 'shutdown.'"

"Fair enough. But where do you fit in?"

"I'm writing about the creative ferment of the Beats in Paris."

"Is that so. You'll show me pages?"

"Soon. When did you get so friggin' cautious?"

The handsome waiter dipped by. Bodie's eyes followed his hips, the narrowest in Montparnasse. "Darlin,' it's not *me.* We all know a guy can screw around all he wants, as long as he wants—but a girl?" He gestured in his ungainly way, a whisker behind his words. "You really do worry me, you have no sense of survival."

"Because I don't live according to *McCall's?*" Nervous laugh. She thought of Misty and the other "female angels" the Beats passed around like baseball cards. Allen's ex who'd landed in the bughouse. And what about Neal Cassady's castoffs among the used condoms along US 6?

"I had dinner with Pablo in New York," Bodie said. "The man's been snapping up FM stations"—he shook his head in wonderment. "He might be seeing someone." Brett kept her smile aloft with clothespins. "What's going on in your little head?"

"I'm thinking that I can't afford a shrink, so like most of the world I'll just have to live crazy."

Bodie laughed. "Come home soon, darlin.' I'm telling you because I love you."

"I love you, too." Something big came into her throat. "Oh Bodie, it kills me that you worry about me." She sucked air in through her teeth and for a moment they sat enjoying the old warmth. Since Nina's death a rift had opened; Brett feared that in some way Bodie blamed her crowd.

"The truth is, I've gotten involved with Allen Ginsberg," she blurted.

"Clever, darlin,' isn't he queer?"

"Allen's kind of . . . fluid, along a spectrum. And he digs *me*."

"Here you are chasing after a homosexual"—the word sounded clunky in his mouth—"when a perfectly nice man—" She waved him silent. "So how, exactly, *do* you see the future?" he said.

"It's the present I'm focused on." The sacredness of the moment, she didn't add, fearing his mockery.

Bodie's tawny eyes focused on something past her shoulder. "You don't want to have regrets, you know."

"Oh Bodie, won't we all no matter what?"

SOCKS

On an afternoon sunk in maritime damp, Paris a monotint of gray and grayer, the stars aligned.

She was picking her narrow way along St. Andre des Arts, heading for the Odeon metro and American Express, pondering Julia's letter. *"I'm so proud of you, we all used to yack about living abroad, but you actually went and did it."* The thing was, lately—maybe since talking to Bodie—she'd lost the way forward. Lately she wondered whether tonight she'd again eat horse meat alone, and if you could get crabs from the *bains-douches publics*, and whether Julia would marry El- liott, her Magnum photographer, and who besides Lyndy DeGroff and Aura Folkenflik were making babies.

Suddenly, up ahead—Allen. Goofing with a *clochard.*

"Where you going?" they said in unison. Allen gazed skyward, lower lip stuck out in a grin. A fine drizzle crimped his departing forelocks and misted the horn rims.

"Well, *I'm* going to the Louvre and you, angel, are coming with me." He nudged her around in a do-si-do and Brett forgot American Express and weddings and babies. "Been sniffing horse, best way to see the Uccello," Allen said.

She wove around an oncoming walker, faintly amazed by this excursion. She'd begun to fear that "female angels" were something of an abstraction for Allen. "You're not afraid of getting hooked?"

"I use junk as pious experiments to see what type of visions I get. Wrote Part II of 'Howl' under the influence of peyote. I don't get hooked 'cause I can't live without working."

They started over the Pont St. Michel past knots of artists with sketch pads, and leaned their elbows on the stone balustrade, and looked down at the Seine. She coughed discreetly. She and the Paris Beats might all have low-grade TB.

"'Under the Mirabeau flows the Seine,'" Allen intoned in his baritone quaver, conducting with the index finger of his right hand. "And our amours . . .'"

"'Love vanishes like the water's flow," Brett picked up from Apollinaire's poem, "'Love vanishes / How life is slow / And how Hope lives blow by blow.' The line's much better in French: *'Et comme l'Espérance est violente.'* How *powerful* hope is—and resilient. In English it's distorted by the rhyme."

"Yes, much better!" Allen raised his index finger like John the Baptist.

What shaky knowledge of French she possessed never failed to impress Allen. They watched the river below, its roiling coils of olive grey. It was easy around Allen, normal conversation and behavior didn't apply; how could they with a man who casually peed in the sink in front of company, and at parties said, let's get naked, and used the resident toothbrush?

"You want things too hard," he said abruptly. "You need some of the ancient Asian calm and wisdom. You need to let go and just lay back and let it happen." He cut her a broody look. "Things with Bill are settling into a good groove," he went on, Brett flattered by the confidence—doubtless the effect of the horse.

Thanks to Misty Suharto, the self-appointed *yente* of the Hotel, Brett knew that Burroughs had been mad for Allen, and still felt he had some claim on him—it seemed the Beats were big into unrequited love. Burroughs also went in for torturing Allen's cat and typing in his room when Allen wanted to be alone.

Suddenly Allen started in about Peter, how in the beginning it was like a cold celestial fire. . . . "We agreed that he could own me, my mind and everything I knew, and my body, and I could own him, and all he knew, and his body and we'd give each other ourselves. We vowed that neither of us would go into heaven unless we could get the other one in."

Brett's hopes listed like the *Titanic*. Yet this celestial fire bit didn't exactly square with Misty's intelligence that Peter was straight and didn't really dig sex with Allen. *"Peter just has sex with Allen as a kind of favor—and provided there's a woman involved. I once heard Allen trying to convince Peter to meet him in Milan, and Allen says, you wouldn't have to make it with me if that's what's making you shy."*

Since Peter had left for New York, Allen went on, he'd had sex with Bill—mainly to avoid offending him.

Brett stumbled on the curb as they swung parallel to the Seine along the Quai des Tuilleries. Ghoulish Bill and sex didn't belong in the same sentence—though all this sexual consideration would have done Emily Post proud. Brett failed to understand the fetish everyone made of Burroughs, including Madame Rachou, who thought him quite the gentleman, with his grey trilby and tie and three-piece suit, but might well have feared for her cat Mirtaud. Satanic Bill, Brett had heard Burroughs called.

"Bill and I have now moved beyond the physical," Allen said. "We're talking about a new model for relationships."

"Oh? What kind of model?"

"A kind of open sexuality. The idea would be to find a way to spread the connection between us and extend 'Love Bliss' to many other people. Bring other people into the relationship without sacrificing intimacy."

"But how do you handle, well, jealousy and possessiveness? Aren't they kind of hard-wired into us?"

"Oh, we'll eventually figure out a way to get beyond that," Allen said.

The great bronze door to the holy of holies had swung open. The drizzle was now a mere suspension, as if getting breathed back to heaven.

At the Louvre they swam past guards who observed the crowd with bored, watchful eyes; wove around clots of sluggish tourists wearing tan Hush Puppies and draped with camera gear, all looking for the *Mona Lisa*. Allen knew exactly where to find Uccello's *Battle of San Romano*. They stopped before a battle scene against a black ground, more dreamy than warlike. At the center a soldier on a rearing black horse gives the signal for attack, though the battle looks more like a strange ballet for automata and carousel horses. Together Brett and Allen looked at the painting, something she always found disconcerting. Like, were you supposed to say something? She pictured Professor Rubin at Foxleigh, spritzing neosynephrine while silhouetted against a slide of *St. Peter Healing a Cripple.*

"I know you're in love with me," Allen said, eyes soldered to the canvas.

Brett focused on the gleam of a helmeted eye, heart doing a loop-de-loop.

"The adoring way you smile at me. Like a mother. Not *my* mother, thank God! Christ, the chicks who go for me always look like my mother. And smell like her, their hair—the smell of death. Don't idealize me, I don't deserve it."

"You don't have to deserve, it's for free." A moment. "Anyway, I just dig you as you are."

"You hardly know me."

"I do though, I . . . *recognized* you, like I've always known you." Oh, why couldn't she say something more original?

"Francoise, a French girl I met here, was really hung up on me. I probably hurt her a great deal because I didn't realize the consequences or see that it was real. It's a big neurotic problem of mine, not recognizing genuine affection. I thought, anybody gets fixated on me must be a misjudgment of some sort."

"Since when has judgment got to do with it?" Think of him and Peter. Peter was an Adonis but in his poems he wrote "shues" and "mistory" and "knowtice," and called himself crazy as a daisy and demanded piss be sold on the market to help people get to know each other and came from a family of mental patients. So . . . *judgment*? Why wouldn't Allen look at her? Here beside him she might be as recessed away as Mona Lisa in her plexiglass cage.

"She came to my room and climbed all over me—" He shuddered. He was still on goddamn Francoise, who maybe had death in her hair. "I was so closed off. I didn't see it, as I might now."

"How might you see it—now?" Brett was afraid to breathe.

"Well . . . as a chance for an open situation. I'm troubled that men"—a loud group of Germans pushed through, muffling his words—"and I'm afraid of oblivion."

"So you'd like a child."

"You know, it might be good to have one's self-importance broken up by 'a Zen master in the house all the time'— that's how Gary Snyder describes his kid."

"Allen, why don't you stay in Paris?"

"Gotten too hung up here with my identity as 'Allen Ginsberg.' I gotta go be nobody again."

"Back in the States you'll not be nobody, for sure!"

"But life here has been frantic and second-rate, everybody in my room all the time. I'm over-anxious to please, I can't write when I'm *expected* to cap 'Howl.' I need to stare at the ceiling and empty my head of junk."

"You could post at-home hours—"

He turned toward her, finally. "But then how would I have met *you*?" He smiled, lip catching charmingly on a tooth. The crowd was giving the Uccello a pass and they occupied a private zone. "I mean, look, there's cops with machine guns on every block, it's a big drag and the soul of Paris seems dead."

"Yeah, but everything's opening up to you here."

"I need to make practical plans with Peter for next year. Or next decade. . . . "

The words stung, only for a moment. Love Bliss would sweep her into the circle.

Allen's hot eyes unpinned her at the knees. "Where do you come from anyway?"

"Queens, actually."

"You're like a girl in a fairytale . . . in danger out in the dark woods. You have a wild fine mind, finer than any girl I've met, really. Such a lovely, classy face . . . " He pulled her to him and his glasses struck the bridge of her nose and the pens in his pocket her boobs. His smell of Gauloise and ham bone and something pungent and dark. She smiled against his lips and felt his answering smile and they took each other's mouths and tongues, straining to come closer, climbing, trying to scale each other, his hands boosting her ass, there goes the neighborhood—

"*Alain, te voila! Ah, je m'excuse.*"

They jerked apart. Allen's glasses were cockeyed. He pushed them to the bridge of his nose with his index finger.

Axel Laffont raised an eyebrow in amused surprise and licked her over with his eyes, a male pastime on Paris streets. The Dutch painter from the hotel appeared, and a couple of freelance photographers who worked the cafes.

They'd arranged to meet here. In front of the goddamn Uccello.

Then: as a regular in Room 27 at 9 Git-le-Coeur, Brett found herself invited to Harry Vietor's bash at La Perouse. Her fleet step carried her along the Quai des Grands Augustins toward the legendary restaurant, known for private dining rooms with *chaises longues* to accommodate palate-cleansing of the horizontal sort. A *bateau mouche*, lights ablaze and eerily empty, cruised the Seine. Reports of Algerians gunning down people in cafes and the metro had culled the herd of tourists.

Straight ahead Laperouse gleamed jewel-like in the violet dark like an unmoored pleasure dome. Inside it was Belle Epoque up the Wazoo: rosy glow from scrolled candelabra set in red velvet walls, murals of naughty pastoral frolics, mirrors veined in crackles. Waiters grandly swung silver trays bearing *foie gras* and little enameled boxes of cocaine. Fortified with a *coupe* of champagne, Brett stitched through the crowd in search of Allen.

A fracas, as Gregory blew in sporting his black velvet "courting cape." Brett spun in the opposite direction. The previous week, against her better judgment, she'd climbed to his garret, room 42 at the top of the Hotel, to hear him read the completed "Bomb." Two stanzas in, he jumped her—so much for "better judgment," clearly a fictive region of the psyche. She was saved by a rival hammering on the door and hollering *Gre-goo-ry*! (She later reflected that since Gregory's resting state was a hard-on, sex would be less a distinct act than simply Gregory to a higher power.)

There was Allen—her heart drum-rolled—three pens in the pocket of the wash 'n wear threads he wore to parties. He was talking to a man with a creased, hound dog face and low-set ears—some movie director. Truly, no one could talk as animatedly as Allen, she could feel the vibrations in her heels. She took the measure of his hunger for making the scene—travel everywhere! meet everyone! . . . Jean Genet! Ismelda! the Shah!—and it was only just beginning. How did that square with Allen's need to go be nobody again?

She hung back, stroked by the Gallic melancholy of Charles Trenet. "*Que reste-t-il de nos amours?*" What's left of our loves? "*Que reste-t-il de ces beaux jours . . . de ma jeunesse?*" And those beautiful days of my youth?

"Why you look so serious?" said Axel Laffont. During the nights in Allen's room, she'd not been oblivious to Axel's beaky charm.

"I feel nostalgic for my youth."

"How do you support *l'Hotel?*" Axel said. "The filth, the smell, *c'est infect.*"

Support . . . "Oh, you mean how can I stand it? Guess we all dig a chance to live history as it's being made."

"Yes, they make great poetry. Beel Burrough—I think that he desire to make the world mad." Axel touched a finger to her carnelian drop earring. His musk mingled with the feral suffering of what had become his black leather jacket. "It's the same color as apricot jam. I like very much apricot jam . . . Why don't we leave here. I live not far, Rue de Seine. *On est un peu bousculé ici.*"

"*Que veut dire bousculé?*" Brett said distractedly, scanning the restaurant for Allen.

Axel eyed her slyly. "Al-lenn prefers the men. But perhaps for you he make an exception."

She smiled inscrutably. *Hard for Allen to be the aggressor*, Misty had said, *he needs a lot of foreplay . . . After that, pas de problème. . . .*

"It's a pity that he leave."

Panic clawed her. "Allen's leaving?"

"*Il a touché à l'argent.* He get the money for the boat."

And then Allen was beside her, just like that. He grasped her arm. *You knew*, his eyes said, his hand moving up and down her arm. They stayed like that, Allen's hand moving on her arm, with no idea what to do next.

A joint was produced and they found a private dining room that looked to Brett like a satin-lined coffin. Allen and Axel were soon laughing at the least remark. She'd only made a show of inhaling. She could barely swallow. *Allen had the money for the fare home.* He went on about the movie director—John Huston it turned out—and Bill's plan to show Huston a screenplay about a junkie—and again Brett was struck by Allen's appetite for the world's players. Across from them, his eyes panned from her to Axel and back. Brett's brain lit up like a pinball machine. Not your ideal scenario but . . . With his French sophistication, Axel would be game. She tried to envisage the blueprint for a threesome, everyone "goofing happily," as Misty had once put it. She had no wish to goof happily with Axel.

They perched on the bed in Allen's room like three crows on a telephone wire. The sweet smell of hash shook hands with the ghost of spaghetti-potato soup. Axel startled, head whipping around—someone balling here in the room?—then realized the sounds were emerging from the Delphic oracle in the sink. Axel relaxed back on his elbows, hip against Brett, and toed her foot. She turned a melting gaze on Allen. "Let's get naked," Allen said. Brett felt Axel stiffen along her flank.

"*Ah, ça non.*" He shot to his feet, thin lips a single line like Dick Tracy's. "*C'est pas mon truc, ça,*" he muttered.

Brett and Allen looked up at him from the bed like chastened children. Axel had never taken off his black leather jacket. She felt wounded for Allen. He'd put up with a lot of this kind of crap. They remained sitting side by side. Without the troika was she enough? Outside an ambulance, its wail of an air raid or impending apocalypse, reminded Brett of Madeleine getting rushed to the hospital with appendicitis. The great silence of the Paris night closed in again.

Brett looked at Allen's profile that his mother had loved, his out-thrust bottom lip, the large whorl of his ear. She wanted to make him know in very particular ways how deeply attractive he was. A leftover sob broke in her throat—and then, skin on skin like a mercy.

There were parts she couldn't remember, Brett wrote in the PARIS DIARY several weeks later, but what she couldn't remember, she would leave blank, rather than make it up. . . .

A small Pisa of saucers rose before them on the round zinc-edged table, marking each café they'd ordered. Allen was still jawing about Gregory. Predictably, he'd come busting in that morning around ten. She barely listened. Their night of love had left her glowing, crotch well-used, her every part re-jiggered and camped squarely in the living world. *"The weight of the world is love"* . . . Since dawn in the trough of the mattress—Allen beside her, nose addressing heaven—she'd been drafting the next chapter of her life. Pack it in here and follow Allen home on the QE2. Meet up with him at some pad on the Lower East Side, of a size to expand the circle of intimacy. Never mind that love with Allen had been unlike anything in her resume. The prelude so drawn out she'd felt almost like a one-woman team of paramedics on a coronary victim, she might briefly have dozed off. After, he clutched her like a pole-vaulter who's aced it.

"—and now he's in his golden period." Damn, was Allen still gassing about Gregory? "'Coit Tower's worthy of Dylan Thomas and 'Fern Hill!' I couldn't stand to throw him off course."

"But Gregory's got nothing to do with you and me," Brett said. "I don't dig him that way, and he's always got some chick—"

"Uh, unh, this is different, I've never seen Gregory so hung up on someone."

"I've done nothing to encourage it."

"Are you sure?"

She cursed Gregory's run-off mouth. "He's not a serious man, he's more like a lunatic child—"

"Dammit, that's how people always put Gregory down!"

His tone evicted Brett from her euphoria. She felt nauseated from Harry Vietor's bubbly, no sleep, the morning's caffeine offensive—and now the awareness that Allen's nonsense about Gregory was no nonsense.

"That childish egotism is just a facade," Allen said. "I'll never understand why nobody gives him the respect and money he deserves." He fired up a Gitane. "I don't feel enough of that erotic romance around the belly to stick with one chick the rest of my life"—(so it *wasn't* Gregory)— "I don't even want to sleep with just one man! Maybe if a chick had the same detachment as me and wouldn't suffer continually from my lack of erotic interest. But angel, that's not you. By a long shot. You'll get married and be happy you didn't do something crazy."

"*Crazy*? What's crazy is Peter doesn't even dig you, he likes women." Her voice attracted stares; from two tables over Cyclops turned his eye their way. "Why do you want to be with someone who cringes at the thought of sex with you? Services you. And as long as there's a chick in the bed. Go fucking love him. Neal Cassady, too! So they can live off your brain and your fame and then ball girls. And you'll live down on your knees. . . ."

Allen eyed her as if mildly surprised by her company. He dragged on his weed, exhaled to one side. Her mini-explosion had glanced off him like buckshot off the Yamato. She lit one of his Gitanes with a shaky hand and waved it around. He would split now, stick her with the check. Hell, he'd already left.

She suddenly saw that Allen would remain with Peter in whatever fashion; clearly there were mysteries of the soul to which she was not privy. She saw that Allen would stick by all the buddies, all of them geniuses of course, no matter how mediocre or demented or criminal. His loyalty was admirable. Touching! As for Love Bliss, she'd run up against the boy gang. Peter and the boy gang! Life's grand adventures, love included—*especially* love—were with the boys. Allen would go home and save America from itself and try on his new celebrity and composit his legend and sleep with any straight man who'd stand still for it. He would pull the boys of his youth close—Peter, who found him disgusting. Gregory, Burroughs. Neal Cassady waving his cock from "Howl." And as for those sad waitresses Cassady had balled along the highways of America—the "snatches" he had "sweetened"— let them fall to the ground in gratitude.

Allen dug her wild fine mind *finer than any girl I've met* and for one night he loved her, the body never lies, and he dug Misty's Asian calm, enough to marry her so she could get a green card—*my name is Allen Ginsberg and I sleep with whoever I want*! But they were footnotes, Brett Eigerman and the rest of the chicks. Gregory and Cassady screwed them, Burroughs shot them in the head. And Allen? In his roll call of all that was holy women hadn't made the cut. Only by an act of concentration worthy of Rodin's Thinker could Allen remember women existed at all.

"I suppose I shouldn't take this personally," she said, "but I fucking *do*."

Allen's eyes burned at her. "Don't you think if I could just take a pill and love women I would? Then I would love you and we could get married. And you could do my laundry and feed me and take care of me."

What? Was this the prophet of the universal spirit, savior of America, confidante of William Blake and chaser of cosmic awe? He sounded like *Woman's Day.* "And I'd put a ribbon in my hair," she said, shook by a giggle.

He cocked his head at her.

"Y'know"—she fluttered her fingers—"pink satin, or maybe red. And have a martini ready and take off your shoes. And wash your socks." A hiccup of laughter. "I just remembered. That first morning in your room, do you remember? you said I could wash your socks."

"What's so funny?" A man the color of cinnamon stood over them wearing a parka with toggles. Behind him two cats lugged camera gear. Ryding Carter, culture reporter for the *Herald Tribune,* had arrived to interview Allen before he sailed for New York.

Brett reached around for her pink anorak.

Allen grasped her elbow. "Angel, don't go."

"Who's your lovely friend?"

Allen introduced them.

"You are lovely."

"Well, why wouldn't I be? I'm twenty-one."

Ryding Carter thought that the height of wit and suggested they order lunch. A gaggle of Ginsberg watchers had picked up his spoor and collected off to one side. A kid with a beard like pale pubic hair came over and asked Allen to autograph his copy of "Howl."

Brett fell on her *croque monsieur*. Never had grilled cheese and ham tasted so fine.

Carter took out pen and pad and Allen told him he planned to meet up with Peter Orlovsky once he returned to the States and figure out from there what next and get drunk with some Buddhists. "I want to get out of the 'literature business' so I can write again." Carter seemed more interested in *her*.

"And you, my dear?"

"*Moi?* I'm writing about the ex-pat scene in Paris—actually, us. All of us."

"Maybe I can be of some help. Why don't you stop by the paper?" Carter handed her his card.

The photographers had finished setting up. Brett shifted out of the way, but Allen pulled her close. A flash bulb popped. Allen whispered something in her ear that might have been I love you. Love came easy for the boy gang when you had one foot on the QE2. She would cast off, too—with them, their story, hers to keep and let crystallize till it was ready to be told. Another flash bulb. She marveled at the sahara of human perversity, and smiled for the camera, for posterity, and for the photo of Allen Ginsberg—"girl unidentified"—that would grace many volumes to come.

SILKY

"I've always felt rich people have more scope for behaving badly, or for behaving amusingly badly . . ."
—Allen Hollinghurst

New York, Spring 1960

There was only so much ghetto you could take.

She'd had two years with Elliott Haimowitz, for her a good run. Elliott was the youngest photographer in Magnum, sexy in that way patented by Jewish men, and a one-man crusade to document urban blight across America, which pumped her own flaccid ambition. As a bonus, the name Haimowitz gave Mother hives.

Julia had tired, though, of garbage alleys on East 100th Street, the sad dwarf, foul-smelling hovels in Alabama. That photo of a dying man on his pallet caught by Elliott's camera in the very act of staring eternity in the face—some images were better left unrecorded. To think they'd spent an entire night with those greasy hoods under the Coney Island boardwalk! Not that she couldn't rough it—she'd sailed in the Gulf of Maine, for heaven's sake, with the *Titania's* head always out and everyone pooping over the deck and no shower for a week. But the Gulf of Maine was *clean* roughing it, and with Elliott it was yellow strips of flypaper and mice boldly streaking through the kitchen and toilets like the black hole of Calcutta. She'd caught herself feeling almost rivalrous with squalor. Elliott seemed more enamored of gangs and heroin addicts than of her. Though he never looked at another woman except through a lens and she had only to say the word and they would "make it official." Now he'd disappeared in Mississippi to record the fight against desegregation, while she sat alone in New York. No no, there had to be a more expansive life.

Julia had reached a crossroads shortly after her opening the previous month at the Sperling Gallery on 57th Street— a vanity gallery where artists *paid* to show, if the truth be told. Elliott, off on a "freedom ride," was conspicuously absent. Julia stood among the guests in a kelly green princess-seamed dress surrounded by photos of herself—quasi-naked in more than a few, with a hint of gauze-veiled boobs and pubic smudge—literally coming out of the woodwork like an X-rated wraith. "There's a danger and mystery to your work," a dealer had said. "Unfortunately there's no market for art photography." Mother had said only, "must it be so unpleasant?"

The chatter around her crescendoed; no one much looked at "the work," as Julia called it, except for sidelong glances at the nudity. To judge by the absence of red dots, no one was buying either. Why, they regarded the opening as a party with wall treatment! Bodie Curtiz swept in wearing a Chesterfield coat with black velvet collar. "Christ, hey," Tip DeGroff intoned. Bodie went glad-handing around, his rusty-hinge laugh riding above the chatter. He lobbed her a "good stuff, darlin'—and that's a knockout dress!" He was sorry he had to dash, a preview of *Camelot*. Thanks and fuck you, Bodie.

Lyndy DeGroff was nattering away with two biddies about Cricket Bigelow's elopement with—the horror!—a Dominican band leader. Julia saw her brother Hendrik standing alone, eyes bright like a startled wildebeest in the Serengeti, unnerved by the urban jungle, a poster boy for depleted gene pools. The elevator spit out . . . why, dear Professor Obrecht. He stepped forward with a cane. Julia flung her arms around him, what it must have cost him.

As the crowd was thinning, Julia's gaze alighted on a single red dot. Someone had bought a photo! One of her favorites: a girl suspended from a door frame, ecstatic or crucified, the moment both haunting and erotic. When Julia questioned the gallery manager, he said the buyer had wished to remain anonymous.

"I'm an artist. You're a dilettante. A Sunday shutter-bug."

She flung her G&T in his face and clomped down the four flights of stairs and paraded her fury and impotence through the urine streets of Alphabet City till the hour turned unsafe.

That Elliott had a point made her madder. She had an artist's soul; talent, even. Yet at the prospect of sweet-talking snotty dealers and hustling her work in an indifferent market—Julia felt something in her go fatally slack. Dillettantism afflicted her women friends like the black spot disease that hit Mother's phlox mid-August. The women surrounding the Beats, Brett had told her, had ended in the bug house, or taken a powder. Julia longed to be an art boor, grabbing what she needed from life—i.e. an exciting man—and kicking aside anything, man included, that interfered with the work. Audrey was managing something in that vein. Brett, the surprise disappointment, was working for a publisher of pulp fiction in a pocket Siberia south of Macy's. Nights she worked on her memoir about the Beats in Paris. Julia wasn't holding her breath. It was disloyal, but she'd laughed when Elliott called Brett "a schlemiel of love."

Elliott was so married to photography he seemed barely to notice she'd broken up with him.

Julia bunked down temporarily in a guest bedroom in Lyndy DeGroff's brownstone on St. Luke's Place in the

Village. Julia felt she inhabited a different universe from her oldest friend—and second cousin; everyone in the etiolated Vosburgh circle was somehow related. But how dear of Lyndy to put her up, especially with her toddler Miles scaling anything on legs, and a new baby expected. Lyndy embodied their shared girlhood—getting the curse, Miss Porter's, dances at The Club in Marion, cruising on Buzzard's Bay to Cuttyhunk and Naushon. When Lyndy asked her to be godmother to Miles, she accepted out of politeness. To her surprise, she went gaga over Miles DeGroff, his round eyes and dirty knees. The child was still in training pants, yet already she had visions of taking him to the "Nutcracker" at Christmas, and Central Park Zoo to watch the seals get fed, and Rumpelmayrs on Central Park South for black-and-white ice cream sodas. Years later she'd remember saying, I loved you from the day I set eyes on you and I loved the world better because you were in it.

Julia took a job at the Greenleaf Gallery on 57th Street funded by a collector friend of Imre Curtiz. Greenleaf showcased the groundbreaking new artists called post-Abstract Expressionist, among them Color Field painters, and "Pop artists" like Andy Warhol, Roy Lichtenstein, Tom Wesselman. (The gallery's most ravishing piece, people joked, was Julia.) She inventoried paintings, kept records of sales, decorated openings with her presence. The job required only a fraction of her brain, but it offered a temporary roost, a pause to regroup. With the city now turning caressing and warm, Julia looked restlessly around, impatient to assume her life like a young royal his crown. She checked out the news in her bathroom mirror, her straight brows, boxy jaw, clay-colored nipples. Was it too ghastly to . . . adore yourself? She simply saw herself refracted through the male desire she aroused. Why should she go to waste?

Too soon for her date with a real estate broker in the East 60's, so Julia wandered Central Park. An early blast of heat, a rehearsal for July's inferno, had turned New Yorkers limp. Young mothers sluggishly pushed carriages in a rolling carnival of diaper bags, soggy pretzels, and whiny toddlers. If this was what women aspired to it seemed to Julia they'd been sold a bill of goods. At least they were launched, these mothers. She'd stalled out in her prime.

She sat on a bench, and tacked her hair into a messy French roll, moist tendrils at her nape. There loomed the unattractive prospect of summer with her family in Marion, an enclave of large frame houses on Buzzard's Bay where no "Hebe" or "colored person" ventured. Her brother Hendrik had made a profession of tracing the Vosburgh/Lansing genealogy, and logged many hours in Marion downing G&T's with Cousin Weezie, with her charcoal mustache. Julia's current boyfriend was cut from a similar cloth. Meredith "Digger" Osborn, yachtsman and associate at Debevoise Plimpton, was so conservative he believed America had been usurped from the Brits. "You *like* this stuff," he marveled— "stuff" being their late-night sessions on the DeGroff's sofa that left her primed to combust. In summers past, photography had insulated her from Marion's ambient futility; now, with the work lying fallow, the place would not be bearable.

Julia gazed up into the trees' awning of green, fearing she might be tainted by a family history of depression. A languid breeze parted the leaves to reveal a swatch of blue—she grew mesmerized by the blue, the bluest of blues, a blue from Tiepolo, the blue of heaven— And then, as easily as a page being turned, she saw the way forward.

She walked on, oblivious to the heat, past a field where uniformed kids were playing softball. She would make her *life* her art. She would need a cohort, a co-conspirator—in fact, a husband. They'd pull around them a salon of artists and great minds. Spend spring on the Riviera like Sara and Gerald Murphy, the perfect model! She might even, like Sara on the beach in Antibes, wear her pearls down her back. One catch: the Vosburgh cash was running low. She was hopeless about money, but knew that Hendrik had squandered a pile on a fountain in the pond in Marion which had wrecked the plumbing.

It was still early for her appointment; she decided to swing by Jason Schley's weekly soirée on Fifth Avenue and 62nd. Brett had been "dating" him, if that was the word; Jason didn't overthink dates, he just phoned at 10 P.M. and said hop a cab over. Julia thought his sexual etiquette could use a major overhaul, but at least he'd had the vision to invent Teaching Machines and sell the thing to Xerox. And his crowd was bound to be less predictable than the regulars at the Yacht Club, stiffs in rep ties and belts with whales, all working in advertising or finance or for Mr. Luce, and apprenticing to die of cirrhosis.

Julia perched on a lime velvet window seat with a flute of champagne. Her eyes landed on the host. Jason lasered her a look of hope that she quashed like a bug. She spotted a Brazilian journalist, or was he a CIA agent? . . . shifty-eyed and the bronze of a basted turkey . . . a fellow named Slocum, the publisher of hot new Arden Press, with an alarming bray of a laugh . . . The suppressed yawn watered her eyes. Failing all else, she could pack it in with Meredith Osborn. She'd wear the antique French lace veil that belonged to her ancestor, Armand de Seychelles, who was guillotined during the French Revolution. They'd live in the East 70's, and attend St. Thomas on Madison Avenue, and eat over-cooked lamb on Easter Sunday, and name their babies Meredith Jr. and Osborn, and decorate the tree Christmas Eve. It would be enviable.

Loud laughter in the hall, and a *whoosh* of energy blew in. Beige raw silk blazer and yellow tie—did the man think he was Jay Gatsby? Leland Phillips, skull cocked on his neck like a pelican's, padded in his wake. Guests swam into Bodie's orbit as if pulled by some law of physics. Julia absorbed the spectacle of Bodie Curtiz, the stretch smile in his square-jawed face, the way he vanished behind his whiskey-colored eyes into his private movie.

From her perch on the window seat Julia went perfectly still. Something silky parachuted over her and she exhaled. Why, of course! How had she never thought of it? Bodie Curtiz, creator of worlds. He was putting Off Broadway on the map, making it up as he went. . . . He had panache! Like his father and the other movie moguls who'd given America its dream of itself. Meredith Osborn would want a wedding on the Entrepid with a four-gun salute and sailors in dress white and on their wedding night he would shallowly poke at her and she would come anyway; like Brett she was probably over-sexed and could barely touch herself or pee without getting turned on.

"Bodie Curtiz is only *half* Jewish, Muthuh," she would say. "But the Nazis wouldn't have given a damn, so I guess that makes him *100%*!"

Julia suddenly loved being alive. Of course Bodie was likely too *driven* to be a sensualist. But she'd gorged on sensual, maybe it was time to raise the curtain on a new act.

They said Bodie had never gotten over Nina. Oh, *They* talked all sorts of nonsense. She was strafed by a worse idea: if *she* had never dreamed of connecting till now, neither had he. In fact, had Bodie Curtiz ever sought her out?

Julia smoothed the skirt of her gingham dress and swam through a wave of new arrivals toward Bodie's entourage. Among them stood a woman with tragic, kohl-rimmed eyes who came on like *The Dying Swan* of zip code 10021. She was a producer for the David Susskind show.

"Ed Albee's play is about isolation and alienation in a commercial world," Bodie was saying. "Ending's a real shocker."

Julia maneuvered so she stood directly in Bodie's line of vision.

"Where you opening?" said the producer.

"Provincetown Theater if we can get it."

"Other producers won't touch *Zoo Story* on account of the obscenity and violence," the woman said in a smoke-cured voice.

"That's because other producers are frozen in the past and scared of their own shadow. We've got Asher Lind on board in case the Manhattan D.A. gets hot 'n bothered. This Edward Albee's going to be huge. The new 'absurdist' playwrights are going to revitalize theater. . . ."

Julia had stopped listening. Further details had ceased to matter. She had stuck her face directly before Bodie, flashed him her most ravishing smile, what she named the "flame-thrower"—and he'd shown all the interest that Lyndy displayed when greeting the guy from Di-Dee Diapers. This Julia had not envisioned.

ARDEN PRESS

The partitions in primary colors suggested a kindergarten. Brett had, in fact, arrived at the nerve-center of avant-garde publishing in New York on University Place in Greenwich Village. Arden published *Waiting for Godot*, the Beats, Eastern mystico hoo-ha. And soon, the unexpurgated *Lady Chatterley's Lover* by D.H. Lawrence. Bayard Slocum, Arden's publisher, was leading the charge against the morals squad over at the Post Office, righteous letches who got to decide what was obscene or "socially redeeming."

She'd reported here for her first day of work at nine sharp in her Career Girls best—Navy, nylons, udder-like garters—only to find Arden Press deserted. The very air asleep. She sat galloping her fingers on what she hoped was her desk in a windowless back office. You didn't land Publicity Assistant at Arden Press without industrial strength connections. After her inglorious return last summer from Paris, she'd languished at a publisher of sci-fi pulp on paper of a quality found in Parisian *toilettes*. Then Audrey prodded Asher Lind, revered around Arden as a crusader for free speech, to drop the name Brett Eigerman in the ear of Bayard Slocum. . . . Somehow they'd neglected to tell her not to report to work till, what, ten? She sat as the minutes sluiced away, pondering how she would orchestrate her move from the girl ghetto of Publicity to Editorial, and take authors of deathless prose to lunch.

A click of high heels in the hall. In the next partition a secretary had arrived. The girl unwrapped her biale and cream cheese and voluptuously dialed a number. "So how's the bursitis today, Aunt Harriet?" After that, a brief session of hunt-and-peck on her typewriter, which seemed to exhaust her. Another phone call. "Oooh, don't tell me, is he a look-no-further?"

Finally Brett's boss blew in wearing little white gloves. At last it begins! Iris Demerrit shot Brett a distracted but not unfriendly look. She was blue-eyed, with a box nose, spray of pale freckles, and brisk, masculine manner that called up one of the Hardy boys in drag. Iris made a dive for her pealing phone and settled in at her desk, giving Brett her back. "Oh, the living room faces north? That won't do. . . . Yes, I *know* painters like north light, but he's not a painter."

To wrangle the morning into shape Brett decided to reintroduce herself to her boss. She sidled up to Iris's desk, which sat a knight's move to the left of hers against the wall. Timing had never been Brett's strong suit; Iris, ear to the phone, frantically presented the palm of her hand to hold her off. Iris must be preparing to launch a publicity blitz for a new title. She must learn all aspects of the biz, Brett thought, before making her segue to Editorial.

"Good morning, I'm calling about your Junior-one with 'w d b f.' Does that mean a *real* wood-burning fireplace?" Iris's palm was still signaling Brett to hang back. "How big, exactly, is a Junior-one? Criminy, *300* square feet?" Next, a call about a prewar with marble bath. Then a sunny brownstone floor-thru overlooking communal gardens . . .

Over the next half hour Brett got a crash course in New York real-estate-ese, from brand nu appls, to drmn bldg, clsts galore, grt location, prwr hdwd flrs—and above all, *pristine*. Plus a sampler of Iris's preferred expletives: "Criminy," "Jiminy Creepers," and "Shoot." Toward noon Iris swiveled around in her chair, apparently recalling the presence of the new hire. She set Brett to work filing reviews of Arden books in the beige file cabinets, then strode off for lunch like a cow poke heading for the chuck-wagon.

At 1 P.M. a bear-like figure in shades shambled through. Arden's Production Designer, Brett learned. Cat never showed up before noon, sometimes not at all. Bayard Slocum had boozed with him one night at the Cedar Bar, an art world hangout on University Place, and hired him, though the guy's only experience had been the Navy and designing covers for a publisher of Christian westerns. Brett was unacquainted with the genre of Christian westerns, but felt at home around Bayard Slocum's capricious style. Honoring one's every impulse was a form of entitlement she'd seen in Bodie and other WASPy types in college, who found introspection morbid, indecisive . . . in a word, *Jewish*—and equated recklessness with *high spirits*—especially since Father, or somebody, would pick up the tab for whatever dumb-ass scrape.

By three Iris still hadn't returned from lunch. Brett refiled reviews so she'd appear indispensable and not get fired on day one.

In the following weeks Brett graduated to updating reviewer lists and addressograph plates; answering phone inquiries about pub dates; mimeographing press releases; sticking into review copies enclosures that no one read. She also discovered that Bayard Slocum, the great proponent of free speech, withheld the right from his employees. When crossed, his bellows of a gored ox would rock the back offices. "Bayard means well," said his secretary Oralee, who functioned like a wife explaining a savage mate to the world; "it's just that he explodes first and thinks about the consequences when the smoke has settled." Besides, he was deeply frustrated by Henry Miller's refusal to grant him permission to publish *Tropic of Cancer*, Bayard's dream since adolescence. More alarming than Bayard's rage was his joy; from the front office his laughter of a spotted hyena on speed ricocheted around the halls, raising the hair on Brett's nape. None of it boded well for a segue to Editorial. Meanwhile, Brett's studious observation of her immediate boss disclosed more about Manhattan real estate than the craft of publicity.

One Monday the galley of a new title arrived on Iris's desk: *The 120 Days of Sodom* by the Marquis de Sade. The cover art soon followed: a clutch of 18th century ladies, bosoms overflowing corset-front gowns. Behind her left shoulder Brett could sense a firestorm of creativity.

"Get me Bloomingdale's on the phone," Iris quacked like a warm-up man in the Borscht Belt. Eureka! The campaign had come to her! A window display at Bloomies! *120 Days* would ride the wave of the current fashion craze for retro, corset-style dresses. Mannequins in lace-up bodices would stand in Bloomie's windows before giant blow-ups of the 18th century originals on the cover of Arden's book. It would be a trifecta of promotion, history, style! Bloomies appeared intrigued. Iris doubled her original order for the covers, which would surely be in demand at other department store displays around the country. They were going national!

A Bloomies executive with a dim memory of Western Lit 102 smelled something unkosher about the title. Or dipped into the book, a pageant of sadism, depravity, and coprophagia to outdo the *Merck Manual of Sexual Disorders*. The Bloomies deal went belly up; the covers arrived back at Arden like a shipment of strontium 90. Brett felt a solidarity with Iris; Arden's female employees were rather like fleas along for the ride on the haunches of a wooly mammoth. She winced to think of Iris slinking back, disgraced, to the office the next day. But Iris arrived later in the week in patent leather peep-toe pumps, buoyant as a skylark. She'd located the perfect apartment!

If the nature of book publicity remained a mystery, Iris Demerrit offered lessons of a different order. Chipper and confident was the ticket up. No matter that Iris's true business at Arden was to find an apartment for her boyfriend, Edward "Neddy" Shyer—while reporting to a warm, well-lit place, air conditioned in summer, and taking people to lunch on an expense account. Iris reasoned that if she could roust Neddy from his shabby-genteel furnished studio—a way of consecrating his bachelordom—and get him into an *unfurnished* one-bedroom in a grt lc, F/S bld—*pristine*—he'd come round and marry her. It wasn't as if Neddy couldn't afford to move—he'd made partner at his white shoe firm, belonged to the NYAC, and was listed in Who's Who—prime requirements in a mate, Iris had confided in Brett. To judge by the angst emanating from her desk, he was also a master breaker of dates, often departing impromptu for business in

Paris, where the French, to his misfortune, would pronounce the name Shyer as "*Chier*," as in "to shit."

Discovering her boss's deep agenda unsettled Brett. Was she making the same mistake as in college, where she'd been blindered by ambition? At Foxleigh, she'd belatedly understood that the true business of college was the search for a mate—then neglected to marry the first man she'd slept with like everyone else. As a result, she sometimes feared, she'd volunteered for permanent dislocation. Iris might indeed be showing her the way. Unfortunately, the only candidate on the horizon remained Pablo, whose devotion had definitely crossed over into the pathological.

Brett undertook her duties in slow motion, spreading them like jam over a jumbo slice of bread. Even so, for alarmingly long stretches no one at Arden Press appeared to require her services. Brett wondered why they were paying her sixty-five dollars a week.

At least there was life outside the office. Hard to say how the affairs began, only that they reliably did. Jason Schley, who collected the lettered and the *louche* at his soirees, taught her about Wilhelm Reich-style orgasms. You were supposed to bellow and howl to break up "body armoring" so you wouldn't get cancer. Mid-party she made it with him on a mat on his bathroom floor. Did she love Jason? Well, you'd love Jason like you'd love a Komodo dragon. Call her a discriminating nympho; there were worse things. Brett wondered could you just slide into the marriage deck farther down the line? Or did you reach a Lily Bart moment in her house of mirth—ho-ho-ho—when it became too late?

JUNGLE GARDENIA

From her earliest years Julia had only to dodge male attention. Now her history of conquests had hit a glitch. She was tempted simply to phone Bodie and say . . . well, what, dammit? That she couldn't will the phone on the night table to ring made her groan out loud.

She persuaded Audrey to throw a dinner party. "Bodie's a tricky number, be careful what you wish for," Audrey said cryptically. She'd redecorated the apartment on Fifth and 101st Street within an inch of its life (a bit *Bloomingdale's*, thought Julia, accustomed to heirlooms passed down from generations). A giant doll house she'd bought on a trip with Asher resided incongruously in a corner of the living room.

Audrey seated them together. Julia's hand jumped badly when she raised her glass of chardonnay; she feared she reeked of Tuvache's Jungle Gardenia. She turned toward Bodie, armed with questions. How had he discovered Edward Albee? And *Zoo Story*? How would he face down D.A. Frank Hogan? Oh, and Mother knew the Reed Albees of Larchmont!

Bodie presented a woven silk shoulder and fell into animated conversation with a fellow on his right. A geeky astrophysicist with no-color frame glasses named Winty. Julia caught fragments about an asteroid on schedule to nick planet earth. . . . A coming apocalpyse . . . Bodie's appetite for astronomy appeared all-consuming. Why, it violated common courtesy!

Julia was tempted to lean across Bodie and colonize Winty for herself, but their boorish tone of "us men" talking science left no opening. To her left, meanwhile, a jumpy editor named Jordan Frankel talked excitedly about a book he would soon publish called *The Leopard*. With her entire being focused on the science seminar on her right, Julia could barely frame cogent responses. Across the table, Audrey sympathetically rolled her eyes at Julia and leveled a cold glare on Bodie. Julia poked at the poulet Marengo Audrey had cooked from Julia Child and half hoped the asteroid heading their way would do its nasty business. She took her own apocalypse home early, pleading migraine.

Was Bodie playing some sort of game? She paged back to some gossip about Leland Phillips—Bodie's *shlepper*, as he was known—but decided he was just that.

She might as well be grown up about it: she'd kind of selected Bodie like a dowser locating a gemstone; any "attraction" had been one-sided, her private fantasy. Amazing, the power of auto-suggestion: she'd had herself wedding Bowden Curtiz at a *mairie* in Paris; attending backers' auditions for new plays; shaping the city's cultural life—and retreating afterwards to bedclothes scented with cedar. Julia sensed that with all his swagger, in the matter of women Bodie was an innocent.

She permitted Mother to call Meredith Osborn her fiance. She listened with an abstracted smile to talk of a big wedding in Boston's St. Alban's Church, bastion of high Episcopalianism. Meredith said she resembled certain figures in its stained glass windows by Edward Burne-Jones.

Julia focused on Meredith's best quality: remoteness. It fit with her current vision of marriage as something resembling Celia's 18th century *ecritoire* from which you could pull, like a secret compartment, a separate life.

One day in the gallery's files Julia came across the name Bowden Curtiz. He'd recently purchased a painting called

Girl with Ball by the pop artist Roy Lichtenstein. The beginnings of a migraine sent her to a daybed in the gallery's little
office. She wondered how she'd get through the Lichtenstein
opening the following week.

She ought to have bought the lavender "mod" Mary
Quant dress in a larger size. She knocked back a second wine.
When she sighted Bodie—alone, she noted at warp speed—
she felt her poor heart might seize up. She fled to the far side
of the gallery and focused on the painting before her, *Girl
with Ball*, as it happened—Bodie's. A smiling girl in a bath-
ing suit held aloft a beach ball. She'd been lifted from some
ad and reworked in the style of a comic strip using Benday
dots. As Julia looked, the girl's rounded mouth and smile
seemed to curdle into a grimace, then a silent scream—meld-
ing with her own as she felt a side seam of her Mary Quant
dress split open.

"Brilliant, isn't it? I love the way Roy mocks the moral
seriousness of art."

Julia recognized at her elbow an important collector, small, dapper, chesty as a capon. He guided her—Julia
clamping a hand across her ribs over the gaping seam—toward another comic book-style painting that read, "Look,
Mickey, I've hooked a big one."

The collector said, "D'you know how Roy got started
with this style? His son pointed at a Mickey Mouse comic
book and said 'I bet you can't paint as good.'" He wobbled
with silent mirth at his remark and Julia heard her own
laughter, metallic above the chatter.

They moved on to *Turkey*, the giant bird sitting there,
legs obscenely folded back, oven-ready.

"To the untutored eye, it looks an exact reproduction,
doesn't it?" The collector, a Continental type who reeked of
cologne, had taken Julia's elbow. "But in fact, Lichtenstein
has worked a sly transformation. See, the forms behind the
turkey"—he gestured at the painting with second and third
finger—"are taken from the great French still lifes of the
late 19th century. The genius of Lichtenstein is to create an

original artwork *pretending* to be a copy. Say, could I take you to dinner?"

Julia leaned into him and promised she hardly knew what.

"I thought you were engaged."

Julia turned to find Bodie standing beside her. His face was blotchy above the pink linen jacket.

She thrust up her chin. "What's it to you?"

The collector made a quick appraisal and melted into the crowd. Bodie glowered at her, un-Bodie-like. Seized her wrist, squeezing hard.

She started to cry. "Don't tell me you're concerned about male honor."

"Maybe I am," he said uncertainly. He appeared as un-strung as she.

"And suppose I *am* engaged?"

"Let's get out of here."

"What are you talking about? I'm working."

"Darlin,' maybe just this one evening—"

Bodie steered them to a wall against the gallery's office. "We have a lot to say to each another." His eyes appeared strained as if he'd stared into the sun.

"Uh, tell me please, when did . . . *this* happen?" She opened her hands to frame some invisible entity. She was furious to think that he'd not been fooled by her sad maneuvers. "What kind of perverted game are you playing?" She'd meant to say "perverse."

"*When* did it?" They were talking a shorthand understood only by them. "I dunno, after your opening I couldn't stop thinking about the way you looked in that green dress, I hardly paid attention to *Camelot*. It's not a game."

"My opening at the Sperling was months ago, and you hung around for all of three minutes, it was damn patronizing." She winced to remember him at Audrey's dinner.

"I wanted to be very cautious. I needed to be sure."

There was some sort of logic here, not a promising one, yet it seemed late to worry.

"I kept thinking of Zuleika Dobson and . . . her conquests," Bodie said.

"The cock teaser at Oxford? What a sophomoric idea."

"Maybe so, darlin,' but you are a bit of a femme fatale, you know. The truth is—I was afraid of you. Listen, why don't we go to Le Pavillon? It's right near here, across from the St. Regis."

She said nothing. She owed it to her tattered dignity.

"We've lost a lot of time as it is."

"Listen, I'm not interested in bullshit numbers and people who run hot and cold," she lashed out. "Or dates. I loathe *dates*." She looked to one side. On the wall a comic-strip girl with bright red hair cradled a phone. The bubble read, "Ohhh . . . Alright. . . . "

"Well, hu-llo!" Bodie laughed. Julia twisted her neck and looked down at her white skin in the gaping dress.

He laid his hand against her ribs like a ritual act of possession.

She battled feebly with what his warm hand had ignited. "I'll come with you if—"

The noise in the gallery made it hard to hear. He stuck his head forward. "If?"

She shook her head no.

"Julia Vosburgh, are you proposing to me?"

The following Sunday morning while he was in the shower, Julia shrugged on Bodie's white terry-cloth robe, poured herself a mug of Colombian, and wandered through the loft to inspect his art: a female nude by Willem de Kooning; a pastel of a barn by Wolf Kahn; works on paper by Roy Lichtenstein. Off in a privileged corner, flood-lit by a skylight, a photo by Julia Vosburgh.

CAREER MOVE

"As for a woman, what kind of man sells his soul for a gash? A fucking veritable GASH—a great slit between the legs looking more like murder than anything else. . . . Every time I look at a woman now I almost get sick thinking about it."
—Jack Kerouac

She moved through Arden like some independent contractor directing her own little show, with only the dimmest notion of what the bosses in their front offices were up to. She had as much connection to Arden and its agenda as the station agent at the Sheridan Square subway stop. Iris had all but forgotten her since Neddy Shyer had detected a flaw in the pristine one-bedroom in Gramercy Park, and it was back to the Classifieds.

Brett sometimes encountered Owen Argento, a multi-hyphenate—writer-junkie-criminal—and sort of Arden's house mascot. He roamed the halls in a paisley western shirt and Bolo tie, his crag of a schnoz plying the air like a phallus. Argento wrote "literary" porn—a critic had touted its "capacity to corrupt minors"—and claimed his only interests were "sodomy, lesbianism, and smut." He occasionally hit Brett up for lunch money. He was said to be working on a novel about a club kid junkie who accidentally asphyxiates his socialite girlfriend. Brett learned that after getting his young wife hooked,

Argento had sent her out whoring on the Lower East Side for cash to score smack. It got Brett crazy, the notion of this wife, she thought of the lost women paddling in the wake of the Beats.

Sometimes Brett poked her head into a dim interior room where a woman of a larval pallor laid out *Greenwillow*, Arden's revue, on what looked like a pool table. It published provocative voices from around the globe—the Beats, Jean Genet, and, yes, Owen Argento. Why, here was Gregory Corso, an excerpt from his journal.

"Brett finally digs me, but I no dig her any more."

Whoaa, if she'd finally dug him, it was news to her. He went on, *"Found a rich young many-languaged girl at the Sorbonne who wants to see me every day."*

And here was "Footnote to 'Howl'":

The world is holy! The soul is holy! The skin is holy!
The nose is holy! The tongue and cock and hand and asshole holy! . . .
Holy Peter holy Allen holy Solomon holy Lucien holy Kerouac holy Huncke holy Burroughs holy Cassady holy the unknown buggered and suffering beggars holy the hideous human angels! . . .
Holy the cocks of the grandfathers of Kansas!

And women? The cocks of the grandfathers of Kansas had made the cut, but where were holy the women?

"You're in the red hot center and you're giving up already?" Audrey had no use for failure, doctors, or psychoanalysis. "D'you realize Arden was just written up in *Time*?"

Brett realized. The piece, "Free Speech Crusader or Filth Racketeer?" called Arden a "whip-lashing live cable of zeitgeist!" It was galling to be at the heart of the zeitgeist yet out of the geist.

For Audrey the advice game was a one-way street. Brett had more than once tried to raise the subject of Asher Lind, whom she viewed as an opportunistic vine strangling Audrey's young life. Whenever she tiptoed toward the subject, she got Audrey's sudden smile and, "Now, don't *you* start."

*   *   *

Goaded by Audrey, Brett stepped, unannounced, with her superb carriage, into Bayard Slocum's office.

"I think I could make a better contribution to Arden Press as a reader in Editorial." Slocum's eyes in his death's head skull took her in uncertainly; possibly he was blitzed on the martinis from lunch. "I could begin"—addressing the bridge of his yellow tortoise shell glasses—"by reporting on submissions by French authors—you see, I lived in Paris and I'm fluent in French—and also work with authors to polish delivered manuscripts." *And pursue authors of my own* died in her throat.

A dangerous silence, like the moment just after a baby bonks his head. Slocum's face constricted in hilarity.

"Oh, you'd *polish* Sam Beckett? Take a blue pencil to *Molloy*, then maybe *Malone Dies*?" The hyena laugh. A sickening downdraft of silence. "Who are you and why are you here?" Before she could enlighten him: "Women come around here, wanting things, wanting to be . . . wanting to revise Beckett, dear God!. . . . Women should stay home. I can smell them when they hang about me, I can smell their periods."

Brett felt vacuumed into some petrified zone beyond horror. Did this mean she herself wasn't . . . *dainty*? She backed out of Slocum's office as if departing the West Wall and fled to the Ladies. Slocum had shared additional insights on her profound unsuitability for work in Editorial—but she could think only of those ads in the back of the *Ladies Home Journal* warning women to douche. Failure to maintain feminine hygiene caused a husband's withdrawal of marital sex, the ads amply hinted. One photo showed a wife rattling the locked door of the conjugal bedroom, banned by her failure to be "fresh" and "clean" by douching with Lysol—"three times stronger than powerful carbolic acid!"

Waitaminute—if you could be *too* fastidious that was her. Brett performed a test—the limberness conferred by dancing had many uses. Things A-okay. "You don't have the usual swampy female smell," Allen Ginsberg had said. A high point of his appreciation—and an aspect of the beloved that

Shakespeare had missed celebrating in the Sonnets. Too bad she couldn't share Allen's testimonial with Slocum.

Jubilation reigned throughout Arden. Over a game of ping pong in Paris Henry Miller had finally granted Bayard Slocum permission to publish *Tropic of Cancer.*

Henry Miller had never registered on Brett's radar; she decided to check out the book Slocum had worshipped since adolescence. She opened at random to a page:

"You can forgive a young cunt anything. A young cunt doesn't have to have brains. They're better without brains. But an old cunt, even if she's brilliant, even if she's the most charming woman in the world, nothing makes any difference. A young cunt is an investment; an old cunt is a dead loss. All they can do for you is buy you things."

Maybe censorship wasn't such a bad idea after all, Brett reflected, at least on a selective basis. The notion of being written off down the line as a "dead loss" added as much good to the world as elephantiasis. "Brilliant" and "charming?" Who the hell did Miller think—? With his pig eyes and skin like ground veal—and doubtless the working parts the color of turkey gizzards and no longer working—Miller might himself be a deader loss than—

Calm down, Brett ordered herself; she was getting too agitated for an office setting, grinding her teeth and courting dental work, not advisable at a salary of sixty-five dollars a week. And the scumbag in *Tropic* was simply a character, the author's *persona*, yeah, that was it, and Miller was striking a blow for freedom of expression. Brett turned toward Iris, who was winding up a call to a friend's wedding registry at Tiffany's. Maybe Iris, who sometimes read the books she publicized, could enlighten her.

"Could you tell me why Slocum and Arden are so gung ho on this?" Brett showed Iris the offending passages.

Iris had lately been in a tetchy mood—the apartment ploy had failed to advance her romance; and she'd never much liked her assistant, who daily witnessed her humiliating, Sisyphean efforts to roll her affair up to the altar. Her blue eyes flashed with righteous rage. "Hush, d'you realize you're questioning the whole, uh, raisin detray of Arden?" She thrust a sheath of papers at Brett and nodded toward the beige file cabinet.

In the following days Iris was distracted from her stressful romance by occupational therapy: the need to mount a major campaign for *The Tropic of Cancer*. The brain waves from Iris's desk pulsed across the office to Brett's corner like the transmitter from RKO Radio Pictures. Something dazzling was slouching toward University Place. . . .

"I got it!" Iris exclaimed one morning. Arden would throw a huge launch party at the just-opened Peppermint Lounge, the hottest club in New York. They'd stage live tableaux of scenes from *Tropic*. Decorate the joint to look like a Parisian night club. Parisian hookers standing around! Nude women taking baths in champagne! "Jeepers!" Iris said in her crackly Olive Oyl voice, overcome by the audacity of her vision, "it's gonna be like Busby Berkeley!"

Unfortunately, the upcoming publication of *Tropic* triggered a new round of obscenity trials across the nation; the cost of arguing for freedom of expression were dragging Arden into the red. Someone must have pointed this out to Slocum, notoriously lackadaisical when it came to anything so dreary as business. The following week a dark, otter-sleek fellow—an efficiency expert, it was whispered—made the rounds of the office, clipboard in hand. Iris took a sabbatical from the realtors and focused on calls to model agencies for Parisian hooker types; Brett filed and re-filed the same contracts, and after eight go-rounds, lower lip drooping, typed a contract free of whiteout. She'd been nursing a bold new plan to hopscotch to Editorial.

Brett had often pressed Oralee—who functioned as both office manager and Slocum's psychiatric manager—to give her a shot at writing reader's reports of manuscripts submitted for consideration. It was an opportune moment: the righteous censors kept Slocum and his editors in court defending *Tropic*; stacks of unread manuscripts gathered dust on Arden's shelves. Oralee suggested Brett start with submissions from the "slush pile"; surely no harm in that, as those sorry outpourings from wannabe "authors" were rarely publishable.

Skipping her usual two hour lunch in Washington Square Park, Brett checked out the manuscripts Oralee had left for her appraisal. The first was *A Life of Jesus* with illustrations in color pencil. Several more of this caliber, and then to her surprise she turned up *Baobob* by her old classmate Rinko Park. Since dropping out of Foxleigh Rinko had become a fixture of the downtown art scene, creating works difficult to classify. Which—duuhh—was kind of their point. *Baobob* was difficult to identify as a book: it turned out to be largely blank pages plus an occasional drawing attended by a tiny, mind fuck of a haiku.

In the same stack on Oralee's desk—or rather, off to one side, if one were to be boringly technical—lay a manuscript—clearly a Xerox copy—titled *Fiend's Journal* by Owen Argento. Brett summonsed an image of its dissolute author, Arden's combination mascot and welfare case. With all his hustling, pimping, cop-dodging, and schnorring, he'd actually managed, God bless 'im, to submit a manuscript for consideration.

An air conditioned silence hummed in the empty front offices. Oralee was at lunch. Iris had left in a dither for Best & Co. on Fifth Avenue to buy a summer frock for Neddy's law firm's annual summer party, a lavish affair at a castle in Westchester. Though *Fiend's Journal* had not, strictly speaking—or even un-strictly—been assigned her, it found its way to Brett's desk.

Her lamp at 320 West 90th burned late into the rainy night as she polished her report on *Fiend's Journal*. In a rigorously crafted argument Brett had concluded that aside from its formal innovations *Fiend* was a failed book, less a novel than an act of auto-destruction and apology for despicable behavior, particularly toward women. Arden Press, she concluded, should pass.

The phone. Jason Schley, after a very long interval. Usually it was just, Hop a cab over. Tonight it was an invitation to Paris for the coming weekend. They'd stay at the Georges V, hit Fouguet's, the Rodin museum. She'd be back in the office Tuesday morning.

The Georges V! She'd hardly recognize Paris without flea bites or broken sinks. She'd visit her old haunts, Git-le-Coeur and the Beat Hotel—was Burroughs still there? St. Andre des Arts . . . the couscous joints . . . the horse chestnuts would be in bloom. . . .

"Lemme get this straight. We'd leave two days from now, correct?"

"Uh, my plans just came together. . . ."

"I see. Y'know, I would love to go to Paris, Jason, but I need a great deal more than the Georges V or anything you could offer. Like an engraved invitation and two months' notice. And a petition to City Hall for the right even to call me. Why don't you go fuck yourself."

Shrieks of hyena laughter ricocheted through the halls. Slocum was back and things must be ticking along nicely on the Henry Miller front. But that pesky efficiency expert was again making a pass through the office; to produce an effect of working she marshalled the skill of Alfred Lunt and Lynn Fontanne. The expert grilled her on the precise nature of her tasks at Arden. As she babbled about the challenge of updating reviewers' lists, he sidled up close. His sebaceous glands could have lubed the new Buick Invicta, and now, incredibly, he was proposing they meet for a drink after work at the Cedar Bar down the block.

Back at her desk, Brett's hands went clammy at the thought of submitting her report on Argento's novel. Slocum could segue in a heartbeat from joy to fury. And her report hadn't exactly been, er, assigned—yet her literary acumen would so impress him such details would fall away.

Iris's phone. Neddy Shyer sounded delighted to hear her voice.

"Could you please give Miss Demerrit a message? Tell

her I have to be out of town next week on a case and won't be able to make the office party event. Thank you, dear." A moment. "You'll be sure and give Miss Demerrit the message, now, won't you, dear?"

Oh brother. No wonder Neddy had been thrilled to get her. And called during lunch hour when Iris was certain to be out. Brett envisioned the conniption fit his message would unleash, something resembling Tinguely's auto-destruction machine with all its parts flying apart, which had recently scandalized visitors to MOMA. Brett dutifully recorded Neddy's message, not without a little sadistic frisson, on her pink message pad. Then, she skedaddled into Slocum's deserted office and placed her reader's report on his desk

She was hijacked by Oralee before she could step off the elevator.

"Oh, my God, what have you done? He's livid!"

Brett moved into the hall, blinking stupidly at Oralee. Bayard Slocum came barreling toward them. He stopped short, skidding like Road Runner.

"Is this the one?" Slocum said to Oralee, his glare all but incinerating Brett. "Are you the cretin who wrote that d-d-drivel?" Slocum was flushed an infarction rose. "Whatever did you think you were doing? In fact, who *are* you, anyway, and what are you doing here?" Turning to Oralee: "Tell me, does this . . . person . . . *work* here?"

"I gave you stuff from the slush pile," Oralee hissed. "What possessed you to write about *Fiend's Journal*? What were you thinking?" Oralee placed her fingertips to her forehead. "Don't you *know*?"

"Know what?

"For godssake, Slocum thinks of Argento as a literary colossus. *Fiend's Journal* is Arden's big fall/winter book!"

*   *   *

Brett had no memory of returning to her desk. She sat chewing over thoughts of her nullity, when suddenly Iris rounded on her, hosing her with a stream of invective from which Brett, shrinking back, extracted the nugget that she, Brett, moronic screw-loose screw-up that she was, had never delivered the message from Mr. Shyer, had instead left it sitting on her desk WHERE IT WAS USELESS! useless as Brett herself, because did Brett imagine she, Iris, would look for her messages on BRETT'S DESK? From the fusillade of insults Brett gleaned that Iris had learned about Neddy's sudden change of plans about the office party only by accident from Iris's girlfriend. For a moment she felt indignation for Iris and furious at her shithead boyfriend.

The Thursday before the July 4th weekend Brett Eigerman was "laid off." Iris had been promoted to V.P. of something. After cleaning out her desk, Brett turned to her boss.

"Hey, I got a nifty idea for a launch party for *Fiend's Journal*. Why not hire a bunch of skows decked out with lights to parade around Manhattan's waterways? Wait"—presenting a palm—"even better, how about renting a ferry, maybe one from the Circle Line. It would be kinda like a ship of fools. On board you have taste-makers and guests mingling with apache dancers, fake cops, and pimps. Oh, and junkies, of course, who'd be pretend shooting up below decks or in corners."

Brett carried away, like a little goody bag, the glint of admiration in Iris's eyes.

BEGIN IN GLADNESS

"Every time a friend succeeds, I die a little."
—Gore Vidal

Depending on where you stood on the great wheel, June 1962 was a month of celebrations. *All You Could Want* sneaked onto the best seller list. Julia Vosburgh and Bodie Curtiz threw a book party for Audrey—now Audrey Marsh—in Bodie's art-filled loft on Greene Street. The last of the sun lay lashings of red gold over the dropped living-room, a smell of wet plaster wafted in from the street. Bodie was on the horn in a back bedroom, sweet-talking a player on the city's zoning board. His passion to move and shake had found a new arena: the conversion of Soho's warehouses into lofts for "aspirational" buyers.

Julia was full of her beauty this evening, her eyebrows striving to meet, breasts shifting like sleepy puppies beneath a muslin camisole plucked from the attic in Marion. After a brief waltz with slenderness and fashion, Julia was yielding to her natural heft. Not for Julia, a neat body punished by girdles and cinched waists, boobs ready-to-launch missiles in circle-stitched satin. If there was one thing Julia wasn't it was neat. Fleshiness became her, rhymed with her pre-Raphaelite allure. It all looked good to Bodie, who thought Julia's largeness, indifference to makeup, and hints of silvered hair betokened class.

Julia waved everyone over to the spread on a raised dining section: her famous rumaki, deviled eggs, steak tartare. Mateus Rose d'Anjou.

"*Chéri*," she crooned. She stooped to crush her little godson Miles DeGroff to her decolletage. He was a beautiful child, pale and withdrawn, with a malevolent look. He'd been the first baby in Julia's circle, she loved him madly, down to the grime on his knees; even when he barfed in the lobby of *Babes in Toyland*, kneeling to tip his head delicately forward like a fountain sprite. "Julia has a magic way with Miles," sighed Lyndy, whom Miles generally ignored.

"That child could be Tadzio in *Death in Venice*, all he needs is the sailor suit," said Brett (privately convinced he'd grow up to be an arsonist).

"Oh, don't even *think* that." Julia nuzzled Miles's hair. "A homosexual was in love with Tadzio."

A fuss by the door, and Rinko Park, their old Foxleigh classmate, made her entrance. Something suggestive and accusatory about that pyramid of black hair; it spoke of pubic swatches and internment camps.

"I hope you'll come to my show next week at the RG Gallery on Madison Avenue," Rinko said. "John Cage is coming and everything, and maybe Marcel and Teeny Duchamp."

Julia's gracious smile curdled. She regularly had to battle the envy that lay dormant in her system like herpes, triggered by any woman who'd stayed the course, and this evening was proving a rough patch. Audrey, who'd taken Marriage and the Family in college and kept a dollhouse in her living room, had produced a bestseller. Now Rinko Park, who'd composed operas in Foxleigh's apple tree—and surely been the most ludicrous of them all—would have a show in a bonafide art gallery. Not a vanity space you had to pay for, like her. With *Teeny Duchamp* coming! Julia mumbled something and headed for the john to deal with the wreckage of herself.

*   *   *

The heat—they had to be kidding. The manholes could double as skillets. Brett ducked into the Parthenon at Broadway and 107th which, like every self-respecting Greek diner, sported a crystal chandelier fit for Versailles. The glacial air conditioning quickly sealed the layer of sweat like a second skin.

"I'm separated from my second husband and good friends with my first," Rinko said straight out over iced coffee, as if she and Brett had kept up since college. "He's in Seoul."

It sounded complicated, Brett thought, quasi-hypnotized by Rinko's little singsong. Despite the heat Rinko was draped in black *schmattes*.

She'd been living in a loft on Broome Street, Rinko went on, where she'd been paying $50.50 a month. "It's also a studio where I show my friends' art and all that kind of thing. La Monte Young just gave a concert there—he's a composer—and Charlotte Moorman, a cellist. The D.A. is always after her and everything because she performs topless." A little smile bracketed by double dimples. "But now I'm being forced out of my loft."

Apparently, the clutter generated by the artistic ferment in the space had metastasized and literally shoved Rinko out onto the street. Brett pictured getting ejected from her own apartment on West 90th Street by a glacier of dreck. She was sweet, though, old Rinko, with her shallow head, like a moon or theatrical mask; the amusing way she peppered her singsong with American argot, "that kind of thing" and "you know?" Also, since getting "laid off" from Arden, Brett was behind on her rent and Dr. Raul Connor, her landlord and owner of the brownstone, was eager to find a pretext for eviction. She constantly badgered him to fix the leak in the living room ceiling. And he suspected she was on to the nature of his practice. He billed himself as a chiropractor, but to judge by the Puerto Rican women who came weaving up, green around the gills, from his basement quarters, he had a side gig in abortion. Rinko homeless, Brett jobless—the match was made.

*   *   *

Instantly they found their groove. Rinko set up in the back bedroom. Brett remained in the sunny, if leaky, front room giving on 90th Street. Olive green walls, a sofa of foam rubber on a plywood frame, the bed snugged into an alcove. A narrow hall made a dog's leg turn to a misshapen kitchen and the bathroom, the whole back end reminding Brett of her deviated septum. With Manhattan's dearth of rent-controlled apartments in safe neighborhoods, the place was a find. Brett lugged a teak strappy chair from Goodwill up four flights of stairs, envisioning salon-type evenings with her new roommate and avant garde friends.

Brett's cooking skills barely extended beyond frying a Minute Steak: smother with Adolf's Instant Meat Tenderizer, drape in wax paper, pound with hammer. Rinko, to Brett's delight, cooked Korean savories like "Bibimbap"—rice topped with spinach, mushrooms, bean sprouts, and spiked with red pepper paste. They carried their plates to the living room and ate sitting cross-legged on the floor before the leaky bay window and gabbed like old-style girlfriends late into the night. Rinko's father was a prominent businessman, distantly related to Ferdinand Marcos of the Phillipines. Junior year she'd quit Foxleigh for lower Manhattan's cold water canyons, acquiring two husbands along the way. Her family was not amused.

"La Monte Young and I once lived for two weeks on nothing but foie gras. Someone sent it as a Christmas present to his manager. We walked around the city feeling big and important, as if we owned the place." Rinko's mouth curved in its little lunar smile, framed by the dimples.

To cobble together cash, Rinko had worked as a translator of Korean for Campbell's Soup. "Now I'd never touch it 'cause I know what goes into it and everything. The worst is Pepper Pot soup, the tripe." She was also a musician. At Foxleigh she'd been working on an opera about the end of the world.

"You play an instrument?" Brett's chopsticks closed on a 'shroom.

"My voice is my instrument. I use the screams of women in childbirth in my music. I'm attracted to what it can express in terms of human suffering."

In the light of the goose neck lamp the hillocks of Rinko's cheekbones and, yes, inscrutable smile anchored by the double dimples gave her a delicate beauty. Other times she looked flat-faced and sallow, tented behind the fierce black hair like Wumei the warrior queen. She was low-slung in the seat, bandy-legged, droopy up top. This scarcely deterred the American male, apparently unable to look at an Oriental female without sex secrets of the East dancing in his head. Suitors quickly smoked her out at the new address. Pablo Sobotka, ever bobbing in Brett's wake, might have been the one man in the Tri-State area immune to Rinko's siren call. She returned the compliment by pronouncing Pablo "crass."

Rinko kept the suitors in line, to Brett's amusement, rather like the recreation director of a cruise ship. Harvey Lawyer hadn't made the cut as a lover, but was recruited to protect her from Manhattan's District Attorney, who was on a crusade to keep the world safe from the pubic hair on display in avant-garde theater. One evening two dozen yellow roses arrived on 90th Street from a famous Brazilian architect. "I hate you," Rinko told him over the hall phone and hung up. How he'd offended was unclear; perhaps he was the wrong color or simply old.

They ate lunch in a wedge of sunlight at the foot of Brett's Indian bedspread, and Rinko shared her love secrets.

"I never eat scallions for several days before a date," she said in her little singsong.

Often a bridesmaid, never a bride, went the Listerine ad to combat hal. There was also Clorets gum.

"And"—the little half-smile—"I have this secret muscle way up inside," Rinko said.

"Like, what does it do?"

"You know, clenches and unclenches."

The secrets of the Orient. Brett assayed an inner clench or two.

Rinko's hypnotic singsong, their cozy dinners, and late-night bull sessions laced with laughter soothed Brett, still jangling from the pasting at Arden. She'd made light of it, and could have seen it coming, but everyone knew that "laid off" was simply fancy for "fired." Brett sometimes feared she might be programmed to fail on every front, like someone with a reverse Midas touch who turned everything to shit. In Rinko she'd found an ally. They were, each in her fashion, dissenters from the straight world outside their door, the army of permed wives putting hubby through dental school, or Gal Friday's waiting for him to "pop the question." Rinko created a "work on paper," a lock of Brett's copper hair pasted across her own black, which she intended to include in her book *Baobob*.

This opus was wandering the byways of publishing like a jilted bride. Brett couldn't bring herself to reveal that she'd encountered *Baobob*—mostly blank pages with freaky "instructions" ("stare at the moon till it becomes square")—in Arden's slush pile. She tapped her sole connection from her publishing career, and arranged for Rinko to hand deliver the thing to Oralee at Arden Press, who would place it on the desk of the Managing Editor. What better home for Rinko's book than with publishing's enfant terrible? *Baobob* arrived back at 90th Street in record speed with a terse note: "Arden is in the business of publishing literature, and whatever this artifact might be, it does not qualify as such."

Brett donned her best consolatory face. "Forget Arden, it's basically a loony bin run by the craziest inmate. On to the next."

Rinko looked at her, impassive. "I've added you to my list of inspirations for the book," she said. Then she padded past to run a bath, leaving Brett with her sympathy like shirttails hanging out.

It kind of blew Brett's mind, how Rinko simply shook off rejection like a wet Retriever. Rinko couldn't muster the attention for such a thing as rejection, she was moving too fast and in many directions. Rejection was simply the lag time of a slow-witted world lumbering along behind the curve.

Fall 1962

Labor Day jolted New York back into gear. Brett continued the unemployment line shuffle in design-challenged spaces that informed people precisely where they stood on the food chain. Paris sheltered its dreamers, the idled could aerate their imagination over a *pastis* at the Select; in New York you were either on the bus or a bum. And a worm had entered the cocoon of 90th Street. If you didn't serve Rinko's art, Brett was learning, you inspired as much interest as the strappy chair she'd hauled up from Goodwill. She began to harbor irreverent thoughts about Rinko's art.

She huffed up five flights of a loft to view Rinko's latest work, *Hump Me*, a hillock-y stretch of canvas on the floor that instructed the viewer to do just that—and galumphed back down. A record downpour in October inspired *Rain Piece*. Rinko invited her cohorts to 90th Street for her "concert" of drips, as water traversed the window frame of Brett's bed/living room, to go *splick* in a bucket. A second pail was produced for a collateral leak, setting up a counterpoint.

Nam June Paik cozied up to Brett on the sofa. "Rinko, she take art off wall and pedestal and make art accessible for every man." Paik (pronounced "Pike") was a "video artist" who worked with old TV sets, and played Boswell to Rinko's Samuel Johnson. He spoke a strange gumbo of Asian-English, hiked his pants high with both belt and suspenders, and wore a perennial smile of a lewd Buddha.

The next week another of Rinko's people, La Monte Young of the greasy ponytail, played a seven-hour concert— the repetition of a single note—in a derelict warehouse, as the audience clanked up and down in a freight elevator.

Audrey, whom Brett had dragooned into checking out the scene, lasted fifteen minutes.

"This 'art' is about the sanctification of boredom," Audrey said in her chirpy, good-humored style.

"But if you want to be hip, you can't admit you're bored."

Brett suspected she was hopelessly tethered to logic and form and other Old World artifacts, milk-fed as she'd been on 19th century novels by Flaubert and Stendhal. *Square*, Rinko had intimated more than once.

Rinko padded into the apartment one night with a groin injury from a piece that instructed viewers to pelt her with jelly beans. She stretched out with an ice-pack on the foam rubber sofa. "Why you working temp jobs and all that kind of thing when you could be, I dunno, making dances, like you used to?" Rinko said.

"Well, to pay the rent, for one thing." And the phone bill, which she awaited with dread after Rinko's midnight calls to Seoul. "So I can work on my memoir about the Beats in Paris."

"Memoir? That's like first this happened, then that. It's in the old mold, you know?"

"Yeah, life is one damn thing after another, as someone said. I don't think we'll get away from that any time soon."

"Oh, I want to mix up all the boundaries. My art asks for viewers to complete it, like a call to action and everything." Rinko sat up and swung her feet to the floor. "Maybe some day you'll write about me." The little smile.

Brett smiled back. Maybe some day I will.

While Rinko was working the leading edge, a new president had arrived. The fifties were finally giving up the ghost. Usually deaf to pop culture, even Brett caught the strains of "Blowin' in the Wind." Across the pond there was something called The Beatles. Change was blowin' for women, too. Jackie Kennedy was the wife who'd landed the ultimate prize, of course, and got to schmooze in French with Andre Malraux in the White House—while Marge treated the family to Pillsbury's Hungry Jack in a split-level home with picture window. But women were also taking their cues from *Sex and the Single Girl* and Doris Lessing's *The Golden Notebook*. May roomed with a girl going to law school, one of two in her class. Aura Folkenflik had made Reporter at *Newsweek*. She'd bellied up to her desk in her ninth month, and gone into labor in the cab to Mt. Sinai, doing her Lamaze panting, feet braced against the partition, to the terror of the turbaned cabbie stalled in traffic.

Brett pounded a Minute Steak in her crooked kitchen and pondered an irony she might have enjoyed had it concerned someone else. The world was catching up to the pocket rebellion her crowd had launched, no permission asked—while she herself had lost traction.

The home life wasn't helping. Rinko's pieces were turning hazardous. Brett lay on the sofa circling want ads for Glamor Jobs, when she smelled smoke. She found Rinko cross-legged on her bedroom floor, lighting matches and watching them burn out.

"It's called *Flame Piece*," Rinko said. "It makes people think about, you know, our mortality and everything. George Maciunas invited me to perform it next week at his gallery."

Brett was in no hurry to encounter Maciunas, the ringleader of something called Fluxus. Supposedly, he took literally the dictionary meaning of the term as "bodily release, a flowing or fluid discharge from the bowels or other part."

A rapping on the door. The sulfurous smell of *Flame Piece* had set aquiver the nostrils of Dr. Connor, who'd been changing a light bulb in the hall.

"You got problem with electrical?" He sniffed the air, mustache twitching, like a grey fox scenting prey.

Brett thought *Flame Piece* rather haunting, but how to explain it to old Connor? He was a virtuoso of ethnic slurs and called Rinko the *Chinita*. When Brett explained Rinko was of mixed heritage, he varied it with *Boonga*. (After they'd asked him to unclog the bathtub drain, Rinko became *La Puta*.)

"I was ironing and the blouse got singed," Brett said, signaling with her hand for Rinko to stay back.

Waking to the season's first frost Brett smelled schism in the air.

She couldn't have said when the apartment fell to the downtown avant garde, whether it was gradual or a sudden coup, but it was now officially Occupied, the Upper West Side's very own Sudetenland. Every second evening artists stomped up the stairs to present—what? performance art?

or—or—"Happenings," yeah, that was it, the new "theater" by Allen Kaprow, the latest thing! Brett was too busy searching for a nook in her pad free of artistic activity to care. She retreated with her notebook to a nest of towels in the bathtub. A thumping on the door, someone urgently needed the sink! To dye a jock strap purple for a performance piece.

Video guy Nam June Paik arrived the next day with his cellist-muse Charlotte Moorman, bearing a live chicken under his parka for a work whose nature eluded Brett. Within minutes Connor's knuckles met the door; he must have heard the goddamn chicken squawking in Paik's coat during its journey up the stairs. Connor didn't look happy. Perhaps he harbored festering memories of discrimination, the flunkies of imperialists barring him from carrying livestock on planes from his native land.

"We make 'Happenings!'" Paik said excitedly. "You watch? No performance ever the same twice. No more wall between art and audience. We break down fourth wall!"

Connor's eyes narrowed. "Not here you don't, no construction." Turning to Brett, he indicated Paik: "Tell General Tso here no construction."

The phone. Paik, who happened to be standing next to it, picked up. It turned out to be Brett's father.

"Who is that strange-sounding man and why is he answering the phone in your apartment? It's not *correct*, think of the impression it gives. I thought you were sharing the apartment with a nice girl from college."

The artistic Occupation of 90th Street marched in tandem with an uptick in traffic to the back bedroom. La Monte Young, not the tastiest item on the menu, hadn't made the cut. Nor had Nam June Paik, smiling, devoted, and horny. "I want to get in Rinko's pants," Paik confided to Brett, "but she like white guys." The whiter, the better. Brett woke one morning to find the resident lover was Warren Finnerty, star of *The Connection*, the Living Theater's notorious new musical about junkies hanging around waiting for a fix while a live jazz combo played onstage. En route to the bath Brett sighted Warren standing like a ghost in the back bedroom, a fair match for the sheet doing duty as a toga. White trash junkie sexy. Brett couldn't delete from her mind the giant boil plaguing his character in *The Connection*. She put paper down on the toilet seat.

The following week Brett collided in the hall with—here was a new one—her own date from the night before! She knew she ought to get pissed; instead, she was tickled by crazy laughter. Like, how did Rinko bring it off? Last night she'd brought back Laird someone for a glass of vino. . . . Rinko blows in, sashays around, a second bottle is produced . . . and then, Brett's lost the transition . . . whoosh! the guy got vacuumed like a dust bunny into the back bedroom.

Brett escaped to the Public Library on 42nd Street and Fifth, its cavernous reading room. She looked up from her notebook across the rows of tables with green lamps at the scholarly and the homeless, and wondered how she'd become a squatter in her own apartment. She struggled to work up a head of anger at Rinko. Her normal responses had slipped their sprocket; she was only dismayed by herself. She knew what she *didn't* want—what she did, not so much. She was like a clay figurine with only rudimentary features pinched in. Rinko Park might have sprung fully formed from Minerva's head. Even from 42nd Street Brett could sense the thrum of Rinko somewhere in the city, her droll bossiness, her religion of her own importance, as unshakable as Joan of Arc's. Rinko was impervious to the snickering at her art, converted the snickering, too, into art, a win-win gambit. So where did that leave *her*? She was an extra, a spear-carrier standing by to serve Rinko Park's vision, her rendezvous with greatness. No, not greatness. Rinko was too subversive and sly and slant-wise for anything so grandiose, so uncool as greatness. Which wouldn't keep her, Brett sensed with a little shiver, from latching onto something, or someone, that would catapult her from the fringe to make the world her stage.

A sudden vision of the apartment in flames. Brett collected her things and hurried down 42nd Street toward the Seventh Avenue subway. To the west loomed New York's monoliths, windows glittering and laser-sharp against a cold orange dusk—Allen Ginsberg's Moloch! She was captive to a runaway car hurtling down hairpin curves and narrowly losing it.

*   *   *

With Paik's *Opera Sexualis* a new corner was turned. The pipes had burst in his loft and Paik arrived with Charlotte Moorman at Uptown Avant-Garde to run through a section of the work. Charlotte sat in Brett's front room furiously bowing a piece by Alban Berg that sounded like cats in heat. Except for a bikini fitted out with Christmas lights, she was naked.

A rapping at the door. The artistic activity here must be putting a dent in Connor's practice, Brett pictured the hapless patient below, abandoned in the stirrups. Before Brett could stop him, Paik emerged to greet the doctor with his toothsome smile.

"Ho ho, you don't like Alban Berg and twelve-tone masters?" he said—or something of the sort.

"*Como? Me estas volviendo loco.*"

It was the friggin' UN up here.

"I warn you many times about the racket," Connor said to Brett, pulling at his little dictator's mustache. He craned his neck to get a view of the living room action.

"Racket!" Paik said, smiling ear to ear. "'Racket' is music, too, if you know how to hear. I make sex part of musical performance. You a doctor, you appreciate. Sex a part of art and literature—why not music? The highlight of my piece—"

Brett shouldered Paik aside. Connor had no need to know about the highlight of Paik's "Young Penis Chorus," which consisted of ten men sticking their dicks through a paper curtain in time to the music.

"We'll be sure to keep the volume down," Brett said.

Connor's eyes betrayed a glint of amusement at what must appear to him the frivolities of people unhampered by the need to perform basement abortions. Then he glowered, pulling at his mustache: "I want the *Chinita* out."

Brett wanted La Monte Young out. One evening she arrived home from the 42nd Street Library with fever chills, to find La Monte stroked out on her bed, greasy pony tail fanned across the pillow. He crashed there, Rinko said, because . . . Brett was too feverish to retain her explanation; she remembered only that Rinko seemed puzzled she needed one.

Fortunately, George Maciunas, CEO of Fluxus, never

ventured north of 14th Street, as if the air uptown was composed of methane ice crystals like Uranus. One of his artworks was a series of little boxes called *Excreta Fluxorum*, inspired by an Italian artist's collection of ninety cans titled *Merda d'Artista*. Maciunas's boxes housed a carefully curated assortment of animal poop, Brett learned from Rinko—from a tiny mouse turd nested in a pill capsule to a dried cow pie—all classified in Latin. There was reportedly a container for a Cro-Magnon specimen, plus the doody of *Unicornis fantasticus*. One evening Brett sniffed suspiciously at an envelope on the little hall table next to the phone. Labeled in Rinko's hand, "Tortoise shit for G.M."

Swell—so long as Maciunas's oeuvre resided south of 14th Street. Later that month his building fell to a developer—Bodie Curtiz, as it happened, who was scarfing up great chunks of downtown. *Excreta Fluxorum* was in need of a new home. Rinko stepped up to the plate—possibly, Brett suspected, because Maciunas would also be welcome in the back bedroom.

Rage pressed up through her ribcage and throat. Calm down, Brett told herself. She didn't listen. "Waitaminute, d'you mean to say he's gonna bring boxes of shit in here?" she spluttered. "No way."

She and Rinko stood facing off in the hall. Brett suspected she looked scary. She'd been smoking too much, sleeping little, and couldn't throw off a bronchial cough. Her periods were lasting so long they shook hands with each other mid-month. A doctor had recently confirmed that she was suffering the after-effects of her visit to a section of Paris overlooked by tourists.

"It's only till George finds a new place," Rinko said. "You know, *Merda d'Artista* sold for its weight in gold to a major collector and everything." For a moment, the hacking, haggard presence confronting her in the hall seemed to register on Rinko. "Something John Cage taught me," she said, in a conciliatory tone. "It's alright to be wacky."

They stood so close Brett could feel Rinko's breath on her face yet they might have been standing on separate planets. *I've gotta get out.* And she saw, suddenly, that she could change course.

WEDDINGS

Newport, Rhode Island, September 1963

It was all wrong. She was trapped at this slung-together travesty of a wedding, and nothing for it, Cee Vosburgh resolved, but to hold her nose and get through it. That Julia had chosen this odd date, the Sunday after Labor Day, was the least of it. After "shacking up" in that warehouse in the slums, she'd rushed into this thing without warning, barely three weeks ago. Cee fought back tears of indignation an onlooker might mistake for a mother's happiness. Why, Julia herself had learned of her own marriage plans from a friend's phone call! Bodie had been just too occupied with his real estate deals to inform the bride himself. No proper invitations, of course, much less engraved ones from Dempsey & Carroll, no Wedding Registry at Tiffany's. The minister a Unitarian, meaning a communist or Jew. All of it dictated, of course by Bodie. Julia, who had never listened to anyone, least of all her mother, just slavishly went along with whatever this man wanted, with no regard for how things are done. The man's supposed charm was just a little too flashy for her own taste—and a "something" she couldn't puzzle out. Of course, married to a half-Jew, Julia would be dropped from the Social Register. And to think, she could have married that peu-fectly lovely Meredith Osborn!

Last night over a nightcap in the library, Julia drops another bomb—maybe the reason for the rush. At least she doesn't quite "show" yet, she's always been statuesque, so unlike the willowy Lansings. This not a first; sophomore year there was that quick trip to Havana . . . Oh, where had she gone wrong to have such a daughter? Thank heavens the child had stopped taking those dreadful photos.

A flapping like wet sheets getting shook. Cee looked up at several mourning doves knocking about a belfry shedding curls of paint. A shaft of sunlight pierced through a section of stained glass window that had lost its stain. Lord, this place was a wreck. Even with bright sun, the little stone chapel—up the road from Gentian Court, her brother's place—harbored a mortuary chill. A quavery contralto started up that gave her the willies; mercy, was that a man's voice? Julia had said she wanted a piece called "Come Ye Sons of Art"—sung by a eunuch, apparently. . . . Cee glanced at her brother Theo, his trembling hands edging toward the color of her Damson plum preserves. Theo the proper person to give the bride away—but of course Julia had vetoed anything so "retrograde," she'd walk down the aisle on her own, thank you very much.

Cee craned her neck around at the sparse gathering dotting the chapel's pews. Behind, sat three maiden aunts, neighbors in Marion. Weezie, the mustachioed one, held on her lap Fletcher, a soiled white terrier with crusty eyes. Bodie's father, Imre Curtiz—or Curteez, might as well get used to it—and his half-naked wife, who looked roughly Julia's age. Cee nodded a purse-lipped greeting at a clutch of Julia's old classmates from Foxleigh. Lyndy De Groff pregnant again, poor dear, you'd think she and Tip were R.C.'s. Julia's tarty friend May wearing a hat like Carmen Miranda. There was Bodie's stepsister Audrey, her tea-length blue frock with scalloped neck perfect for an afternoon wedding; now there was a girl with a sense of occasion. The mystery being why Audrey hadn't yet attended a wedding of her own. They said Audrey had written a shocking best selling novel; enough to scare off any beau. That blond fellow to Audrey's right probably one of Bodie's theater people and much too pretty for a man.

Julia's dear friend Brett looked positively ill, her skin the color of the plaster in the chapel. Tommy Grierson hanging all over her. Tommy called himself an explorer, and if he didn't watch his step he'd get eaten by cannibals, like Nelson Rockefeller's son Michael. Imagine, a boy from such a nice family getting boiled alive by savages with plates in their ears. Cee shook her head at Brett-and-Tommy, spooning as if they were at a drive-in. It made no sense, young people today. Marriage was no picnic and a whole lot easier if you closed ranks with your own people.

Bodie emerged from an anteroom. His white suit and pink shirt about right for the commodore of the Yacht Club, did he think this was a regatta? He looked expectantly toward the entrance. The eunuch's voice floated eerily through the chapel and all heads turned as Julia came swanning down the aisle in her own bizarre costume. She'd had the gall to wear the antique French lace veil that had been in the family since Armand de Seychelles. Her white satin and lace dress was marked with water stains, something from the attic in Marion. Apparently she'd confused a wedding with Halloween. Julia sailed, smiling, toward her intended—the child did have beautiful teeth, like all the Lansing-Vosburghs. Her girth made the hem of the dress wildly uneven, dear Lord, she might have just rolled out of bed with the groom. He moved to join her. At the sight of his red sneakers, Celia Vosburgh thought she had just about seen it all.

The reception was held on a slate terrace bracketed by the cottage's two wings. Gentians, punched up to a Day-Glo violet by the sea light, bloomed in cracks between the slate. Beyond the house a stone wall clad in pale green lichen ran along a headland; the sea below bellowed at the rock face, occasionally geysering gobbets of foam above the wall. Clouds bowling swiftly overhead released a platinum spear of sun.

Brett lofted her second goblet of champagne. What a gas, this Gentian Court, one of those Newport mansions called "cottages." Gothic gloom, ruined choirs, the hosts looking low on red blood and stalking about on stiff legs and inclining from the waist, Good to see 'ya. Brett spotted a blond actor type—a dead ringer for Oscar Wilde's lover Bosie—and briefly wondered who he was. Tommy's godfather, Archie, was taking liquid nourishment with another crusty old commodore, their noses host to a lacery of red veins like crackles on Ming porcelain.

"That new catamaran is something to behold," Archie said. "Both its hulls rise out of the water and the boat just shoots over the surface, free of the water's drag."

"Ayuh, bloody flying machine," his friend said. "She'll do 50 miles an hour, an Indy 500 without brakes."

The notion of this boat flying over the water and planing on air . . . free of the water's drag—it gave Brett a rush. Suppose you could live that way?

May Leach directed her saccharine smile at Brett from under a hat laden with posies and rolled toward her in segmented sections like a caterpillar. Had she actually crashed the wedding? Anything to lay her adoration on the altar of Julia.

"Y'know, your friend Tommy Grierson's got that old school charm." May considered Brett from beneath her brim. "He was just explaining to me how a cocksman steers a boat. He's actually rowed in the Henley Royal Regatta."

"I think the term is pronounced *kok-sin*."

"Anyhoo, he's quite the adventurer. He's traveled to Papua, New Guinea and hung out with the Hasmats, this ancient tribe of head hunters. Brett, you could have an exciting life with him."

"I think it's 'Asmats.'" You'd quicker curl up with a head hunter before you'd trust May's concern for your well-being.

And where in the scheme of things to fit this Tommy Grierson, her "older man," now introducing her round to the Vosburgh side, graceful and easy, his hand at her elbow? They'd met when he enrolled in the French class she taught in the adult extension of Columbia to waive her tuition fees.

The past winter, the face-off with Rinko about housing cans of artist's *caca* had delivered the kick in the ass she needed to plot a new course. She'd always lived in books and she saw she could earn her keep from that, she would get a Ph.D. in literature, a salary, the title of Professor—a new life!—if she got cracking, she could make the spring term at Columbia University. She took asylum there like a political refugee fleeing an occupied land; in the stupendous quiet of a carrel high in Widener Library she could exhale. The academic world opened its arms to dreamy types like her, unfit for the nine-to-five of life; offered a refuge to muscular brains who could solve Fermat's last theorem, but could scarcely get off an elevator or tell you the time of day. She returned to 90th Street only to sleep.

Pablo had located Brett in her little carrel in Widener and looked around like Amundsen surveying the wastes of Antarctica. "Whoo! Where is everyone? I couldn't spend more than ten minutes here." He jiggled his leg. "But I sure admire you for doing it. Just think, some day I'll have to call you 'doc.'"

That was before Tommy blew into her French class. She'd fallen for him partly because he got excited about the subjunctive. "Sheer genius, this separate tense—or rather, mood—that expresses desire versus reality!" Tommy had a weathered, lupine face, stuck-out ears, indignant hair like the crest of a ruffed grouse. He'd traveled the planet's remotest corners, where tribes had "never departed the stone age," and was now looking to "put down roots." His family history gave Brett pause: boozers, suicides; during her manic phase his mother had once bought out half of Bonwit Teller. In 1963 self-destructiveness, as elegantly practiced by the upper class, played better on the green quads of Princeton than the asphalt grid of New York. The tide was turning in America toward the go-getters, raw energy, it was leaving the aristos behind to sip their G&T's and putter about their waterfront property. As if all along America had never really been about anything but money.

Yet here was this nice man wanting to marry her. Beginning a sentence, "Once we start making babies . . ." Shrugging off the gyn problems that had plagued her since Paris, problems the male brain couldn't process. Tommy drove them to his godfather Archie's compound in Pound Ridge, where his extended family played touch football and croquet with an ebullience verging on hysteria, and married each other in its chapel. He walked her around the green estate heavy with summer, full of their future. Brett was flattered, grateful. Struck by how the love of men felt almost entirely fueled by fantasy.

"Come with me, I've something to show you."

Tommy motioned with his head toward a solarium with several busted panes extending from a wing of Gentian Court. Then Brett spotted Pablo, his hair daringly long to his neck. A twinge of guilt. She'd forgotten, but of course Pablo would be here, Bodie was enamored of him. Pablo squeezed out a smile as he took in her and Tommy. It made the day go dull. Brett waved with two fingers.

Leaving the door of the solarium ajar, Tommy pulled her behind it so they were hidden from the guests. Then he tipped her back in a Fred Astaire move for a tongue-y kiss. . . . Brett laughed at the childishness of the maneuver.

Tommy said, "Maybe it's time for you and me to get going, too." She was twenty-six, almost an old maid, she could be sprung from Rinko and the madness of 90th Street. "We could elope," Tommy said, "just run down to City Hall. Why bother with the rest?"

An after-image of Pablo's awful smile hung in the air.

Well, she'd brought off the wedding with aplomb. In matters requiring aplomb, breeding helped, thought Julia, amazed to be keeping company with such words. Yet without her lifelong training and inborn skill in massaging appearances—plus the focus of a Flying Wallenda—she could easily have lost her footing.

The previous evening, before the wedding, she'd travelled the drafty halls in search of Bodie, tipsy and skidding on Persian carpets from the sixteenth century (Auntie, a relic from the Victorian age, had stuck them in separate rooms).

She found him propped against the pillows of a four-poster bed, nose in a script. "I've chivvied you out of your lair," Julia said, flinging herself onto him.

"Careful," Bodie said, rescuing the script. "You and Celia put away a few?"

"I was thinking of that Mae West line: 'is that a gun in your pocket or are you just happy to see me?'"

Bodie's hand tightened on her shoulder. "Won't it upset the little bugger?"

"Oh, darling, not this early." She straddled him, hiking up her night gown, and he rolled her off and rose over her, the sheet caught between them Bodie there for her through the sheet—but by the time they yanked away the bedclothes—

"*Goddamn.*"

From the cliffs below Gentian Court the muffled growl of the surf. Julia eyed his somber profile on the pillow edged in lamplight. She should have known better than to tempt fate the night before the wedding. "Darling, we're both nervous about tomorrow. And you worry too much. It's supposed to be just fine till the 7th month or so."

She caught his look of dismay. "7th month? I'd have thought you'd have this . . . melon by then. In any case—"

Don't say, It's not you. Because it is me, that's exactly what it is, Julia thought, the booze steering her down a bad path. She said, "I'm sorry, I wanted you too much." They'd neglected to mention in "Tell Me Doctor" that a side-effect of pregnancy was ravening horniness caused by venous congestion.

"You shouldn't have to be sorry."

Oh God, let's not fight, not tonight.

He looked down at her along his shoulder. "Is there such a thing as 'too much?'"

Was this an actual question? Or, since they both knew the answer, was it an epitaph for Bodie-and-Julia before they were out of the gate? "I shouldn't have started."

"You have every right to start," he said angrily.

Shit. Don't even try to make things right, not tonight and half-crocked. Distract him. "Cee has been rather a good sport, don't you think? When you consider how much she loves ceremony—in fact, that's all she loves."

Bodie reached for his Marlboros. The motion somehow shorted out the bedside lamp. He fired up a weed, dark forelock falling over his forehead. The light stuttered back on. "This joint must date back to Newport's Quakers," he muttered. "When I sat on the chaise in my room it collapsed," Julia said—and then they were laughing, at rickety heirlooms; at Theo and his wife, themselves relics whom Bodie called the Rodney Ushers; laughing at the incongruous mix due to descend the next day on Gentian Court: Imre Curtiz, with his Hollywood swagger and silver quiff and child bride mingling with—could you imagine?—Weezie and Uncle Archie. "What do you make of Brett and Tommy Grierson?" "Doesn't have legs," Bodie said. "Just as well, I've heard Tommy once had a, uh, 'dissociative fugue,' whatever that is," Julia said. "A bit awkward, with Pablo coming." But what could compete with Tenley Baker—they were laughing again—now engaged to Jason Schley? "I mean, Tenley was Foxleigh's lesbian-in-residence," Julia said. "I think women can play at such things, don't you? Men, I'm not so sure."

Bodie killed the cigarette and switched off the light. Julia curved herself against his back; he secured her hand tight against his ribs. Shortly after the high of the early days, Bodie had started to need to get seriously plastered before doing it and then all the sauce would make it a lost cause or it would be love in the fast lane. That her resting state was randiness made things easy for Bodie, she was primed to explode at a touch. She'd once thought of proposing they consult a shrink. She'd instantly thought better. And when she couldn't match his tempo—well, she'd learned, once Bodie's breathing turned regular, to squeak through on her own. A practice at which she's become distressingly adroit. Back in Gilbert Dining Hall the friends had wondered why Jake Barnes and Lady Brett never thought of sixty-nine. Now there was something Bodie liked—as a one-way trip. Perhaps women, with their folds and briny secretions like Cherry Stone clams were yucky. Elliott had not found this the case, she thought, feeling disloyal.

She would not, Julia resolved, regard this evening as a harbinger. She would not. She did not go back on decisions.

She had chosen to make her life with Bodie and any problems could be worked around. Bodie was exciting, bending New York to his vision, taking wild leaps that could land badly but leaping—that was the main thing! He'd recognized in her a kindred soul and partner for the grand adventure. She could not have chosen wrong. What mattered now was only that they'd come this far and would move ahead. Except in the sack, she and Bodie were perfect.

November 1963

Rinko landed a concert date at Carnegie Recital Hall, and on 90th Street it was now show time all the time. It was also show*down* time, Brett thought. She balked, though, at playing philistine. Rinko & friends were about to lay a stick of dynamite under New York's clubby, convention-bound art scene—and she should impede this signal event?

The pre-concert frenzy coincided with her preparation for the Orals. Musicians, artists, and squatters bunked in at 90th Street among half-eaten cartons of pork fried rice and crusts of pizza. Cigarette butts floated in Styrofoam cups. The place was alive with the sound of music, or what Rinko called the "sound of turmoil."

The slog of cramming for the Orals, pick-up meals, no sleep, and, often, no bed of her own, hammered at Brett's already fragile health. She put in fifteen hour sessions in the carrel at Widener Library, force-feeding herself centuries of literature. Once past the hurdle of the Orals, she'd be on her way, liberated from unemployment lines and the maelstrom that was Rinko. Tommy stood ready to spirit her away to the orderly stations of life. At the same time she felt tugged in a separate direction. She'd look up from her books, suddenly haunted by a scene in Central Park. One afternoon in the spring before she met Tommy. *"It wouldn't matter, we'd have each other."* She pictured a tennis ball balancing atop a net. . . . She threw herself back into Voltaire. Love could wait. Or maybe it couldn't. Instinct told her that the world doesn't put itself on hold while a girl finishes her work; that she might return from her labors to find things not as she'd left them.

On a cold November evening that felt like snow, Brett pushed open the wrought-iron door in her lobby to the sound of . . . cocking her ear toward the stairs—murder. Or shrieking pigs getting readied for slaughter with twists to their tails. A glance down the back stairwell toward the Cabinet of Dr. Connor. Nothing. She raced up to the fourth floor.

On the sofa, Nam June Paik. Clutching a microphone, Rinko, in a slight crouch, brows contracted, teeth bared, squinting in rage, anguish, feral abandon going AHEEEIEE-IIIIEEEIIIEE . . . her small body a bellows pumping it out through her pelvis and back and throat . . . a shriek like a Kamikazi pilot . . . then infernal yodeling—melting now into wails, groans of rapture, grunts and little whimpers, laughter—shit, that must feel good, Brett thought through her horror—then a volley of rhythmic shouts that could only be—

A fist pounded the door.

Silence. Connor pulled at his little mustache. Brett began, "It's 'the sound of turmoil,' a new type of music my roommate is rehearsing for a concert at Carnegie Hall, well, the recital hall, you know, a few steps east on 57th—"

"If she don't stop I call the cops and throw you both out on the street. You owe me half the rent."

"Eviction Piece!" Paik cried. "We turn it into Happening and get it on video."

"It's the sound women make in childbirth," Rinko objected after Connor had left.

"Oh, I would have said—" Brett didn't finish.

"He's like all men," Rinko shrugged, "they say what I do with my voice is too animalistic and everything because they're afraid of women, this very powerful energy in us. Without us there would be no human race and all that."

A donation from a mysterious benefactor covered Rinko's half of the rent. But not the long distance calls to her first husband in Seoul. As in Seoul, Korea. Long calls, long distance. The phone was under Brett's name. She tore open the phone bill, braced herself against the wall, and slid to the floor.

Rinko emerged from the bedroom with her dainty step in a duffel coat. She glanced down at the bill lying in Brett's lap. "Oh, you don't have to pay that," she said airily. "You just order a new phone and get a different number and everything, you know?"

You don't have to pay, Brett heard. "I—I can't just get a new phone, I can't do that."

"Why not?" Rinko said, as if impatient with a slow-witted domestic. "I did it several times. On Broome Street."

Brett stood. "And I don't have the money to pay this." She waved the bill. Rinko stared at her like someone not familiar with the language. She's about to give a concert at Carnegie fucking Recital Hall—and this person is pestering her with a *phone bill*?

Brett stared back. All these months, she'd been living in a *ménage à trois*: her, Rinko, and Rinko's ambition. She hadn't been that dumb as to miss the ambition. What she'd failed miserably to grasp was the scope of it, cosmic, stretching beyond her sightlines and blotting out the horizon, a leviathan with webbed wings and coils and horned back, lumbering forward to obliterate all obstacles. Like her.

It was cold in the apartment but Brett felt herself go radioactive with sweat. "Listen, the phone's in my name but that fucking bill is yours, so deal with it however you decide. No way will I 'just order a new phone.' I'm too bourgeois. Rinko, I really admire you, I do. You change people's brains around, you rock the world off its axis—I mean those screams—it's primal, the voice of existential rage. No other woman out there's doing that." She paused, this aria was going the wrong way. "Listen, I know you think I've, well, sold out—but not everyone has the guts to be an artist. I don't have your vision, your drive, your . . . tenacity. Maybe I did once, but then it dissipates, like with most people. I no longer have dreams—I have a game plan. Get my Ph.D and pay my way by living in books." A moment. "Aren't you ever afraid?"

"Of what?"

"That there'll be no one to catch you on the other end?"

"I never think of it. I guess I'm more like a guy than most guys."

"Listen, Rinko, I've got to pass the Orals, it's my shot. But the way it's been here, with the noise and madness"—she put her fingers to her forehead—"I can't think, I can't eat, I can't sleep, I can't get into my own bathroom, or even my own bed."

Rinko's face betrayed no expression. "Maybe you shouldn't look at things that way. John Cage once said, 'There is no such thing as an empty space or an empty time. Try as we may to make a silence, we cannot.'"

It would later conflate in Brett's mind in a nightmare montage: Rinko's concert at Carnegie Recital Hall and her own twisting, Luciferian descent. Rinko shrieking; herself shedding her insides, so the one seemed to feed the other in a vicious loop. The moment Rinko started in with the banshee howls—of a volume to make the dry run on 90th Street sound like "My Way"—Brett knew she had to find a john. In a bar on 56th Street, in the dim, coffin-shaped Ladies—an old-fashioned water closet with a chain—clots sluiced out of her, the size of half dollars, the size of crab apples. Later she lay curled in a fetal position on the living room floor where she wouldn't destroy the mattress. At 3 A.M. she dialed Pablo's number. No one picked up. Go to the ER immediately, a doctor said. She woke, packed with cotton batting like a stuffed turkey, in a large common ward to rival the olden "foule wards" for venereal patients.

Never mind, she's over the moon on Demerol and back in springtime Central Park among the flowering cherry and magnolias. Daffodils blow on the hill in a fanfare of yellow. The faces of New Yorkers, normally set in grim lines of forbearance *what have I done to deserve this* wear smiles. She and Pablo find an empty bench. Affixed to its back is a small metal plaque with a name and dates—1940 -1962—and the inscription "It is what it is."

Pablo slings an arm around the back of the bench. "You just do your thing—and I'll wait."

"Pablo, I'm not sure I can make babies."

He crosses a leg over his knee, enormous shoe nicking her shin. "It wouldn't matter. We'd have each other."

"You don't mean that, everyone wants a family."

"If you can't, we can't. That's all. We'll be our family, you and me."

Words her great-grandfather might have spoken to his bride, both of them happy and poor, on a bench in springtime Gorky Park, Minsk, among poplars two centuries old. Here in the Demerol ward those words blow open doors, one door, then another, then another. He'd follow her through failure, illness, fuck-ups . . . murder! . . . un-altered and off the rack, unexpurgated and unimproved. . . . She has only to walk through the first door.

On a grey November noon Brett emerged from her carrel at Widener and headed toward the Chock Full 'O Nuts on Broadway for coffee and a cream cheese on date nut bread. She instantly sensed something off. Everyone was leaning forward, angled forward, like fleeing shadows. A woman wept in her parked car. There might have been a terrible accident. From across the street a girl shrieked at someone, "Haven't you heard?" Now Columbia's buildings were spitting out people into the leaden noon. Brett went over to the woman in the car. *The most spectacular single American disaster since Pearl Harbor*, went the car radio.

Television organized the day and the mind, knitted people into communities. Walter Cronkite's voice cut the unthinkable down to manageable size. November 24th Brett, stretched between numbness and disbelief like everyone else, watched the funeral with Tommy Grierson and his family in Smithtown. President Kennedy's gun carriage, came the voice of Cronkite, was to be drawn up Pennsylvania Avenue to the great rotunda of the Capital. Jackie's two children would stand with her before the national audience. The children dressed in powder blue coats and red lace up shoes . . .

Caroline in a black headband . . . John squirming, his tiny fist clenched behind his back . . . the widow, swollen eyes fixed on the caisson and six matched horses . . . the million people lining the funeral procession . . . In the silence, the clopping of the horses' hooves could be heard on TV and radio. Images kept repeating in an endless loop: Caroline in the black headband. John John in his little short coat saluting his father's coffin. The tragic widow in the black veil.

The swiftness of the blow intensified the national trauma, Brett read in the *Times*. Impelled Americans to draw close to those they cherished.

In the murky interval between her slog to prepare for the Orals and her sojourn in the Dickens ward, Pablo had done a fade to black. But this was no time to stand on ceremony. National traumas focus the mind. At issue was a life: waking to rain on Sunday morning, a key turning in the lock, the day recounted over drinks, ordering in Chinese, a toddler: don't touch, hot, a tour of old haunts in Paris, White Sales, big birthdays . . . Tommy knew what he wanted. Yet did he, really? She might not recognize the "Brett" Tommy wanted. She conjured up the catamaran skimming so fast over water nothing held it back. But where would she land? The thing was, you needed to land. She was tired, way too soon, but there it was, tired from love, spent from love spent.

The Oak Room of the Plaza, with its massive wainscotted windows on the park, felt guaranteed to shut out all harm.

"I'm not sure how to say this," Pablo began—

An intake of breath. "I'm not sure how to say it either," she said, cutting him off, excited to tell him her news.

Across Central Park South a carriage horse in a plumed purple head dress, the Tyrian purple of royals, stood alongside the curb, offering a lesson in forbearance.

PART III

"The things we have never had remain:
it's the things we have that go . . . "
— William S. Burroughs

WIFE

Memorial Day 1980, Eighteen Years Later

You could hardly count yourself among the Islesford elite without an invite to Audrey Marsh's Memorial Day party at Lilac Close. This evening marked the first of the 1980's and spirits rode up the flagpole. In honor of the new decade Audrey had camped up the party in red, white, and blue: bartenders spun blue slushies, cooks decked in stars 'n stripes flipped burgers and rotated franks, even the popsicles were colored patriotic. As always, Audrey liked to mingle art with money. On the terrace out back, developers with their pulled and lacquered wives and venture capitalists with spreads like airplane hangars yukked it up with writers, painters, and the "big mouth" journalists attached to the wealthy like egrets to cow pies.

Occasionally a woman caught her heel on the terrace's crumbly brick. The grounds of Lilac Close remained defiantly un-manicured. A grey barn graffitied with lime moss sagged earthward; the terrace moseyed into grass erupting in a field of wildflowers. Beyond, a stand of crab apple trees torqued into gnarled poses by winter winds framed a marshland that stretched to the horizon. Lilac Close, with its "original Islesford" old money dishevelment, was a rebuff to the hyper-landscaped homes of the *nouveaux* who assumed Nature was there to be customized like any other purchase.

"Isn't the view *divine*?" Lyndy DeGroff and Julia stood out back, eyes fixed on a tinseling pond dripping over the far horizon. "And Bodie is where? Does he ever stop working?"

Julia's jaw tightened. She smoothed the waist of her signature Marimekko, an ankle-length culotte splashed with bold orange and white orbs. "Ever since Bodie leased this place to Audrey, he never sets foot here," she said by way of an answer. "Why? Because it's a shrine. He spent one summer here with *her*."

For Bodie a house was mainly a chance to pull a real estate coup by 'flipping' it after a couple of years. Just as she was settling in. Julia sometimes felt like an upscale migrant worker. Bodie's perpetual motion so ran against her world in Marion where generations returned to the same jumble of rooms with faded chintz and the permanent smell of roast lamb in the pantry from Sunday Lunch and walls blotched with sea rot like the age spots on Cee's hands. Bodie had currently installed them in a manor-style house wrapped with verandas bordering potato fields on Millstone Drive—a place more *Out of Africa* than Islesford. In an effort to throw down an anchor, Julia had planted a perennial border of pink lilies, yarrow, and phlox along the south veranda. On the rise beyond the barrier marking off the parking area, she'd put in a bed of Montauk daisies, just masses and masses of them.

Julia smiled toward a boy hanging off the bar, one hip out-thrust like the youths beloved of Greek sculptors. Lyndy's first child—whom Tip treated like a foundling laid at his door—and her own naughty godson. Lavender tee shirt under white jacket, Ray-Bans a la *Miami Vice*, bowed lips, the scar/dimple on his left cheek—he looked far too pleased with it all, something only the charmed and very young could carry off.

After it turned out she and Bodie were not going to make babies, Julia had poured her longing for a child of her heart onto Miles. He was her little love—peu-fectly *cunning*, Weezie cooed. She took him to the *Nutcracker* suite (forgetting to pee beforehand, he danced it through in his seat), and Rumpelmayers on Central Park South for black-and-white ice cream sodas. *The Little Prince* became their touchstone book; when the fox asks the Little Prince to tame him—by sitting closer to him every day—Miles would peer up at her to see if she would cry (she always did). When he was older, they went to the Philharmonic's Young Peoples Concerts, chatting backstage with Bodie's friend Lenny Bernstein. Whenever Lyndy checked into McLean's to tweak her medication, Julia would sweep Miles off to Bodie's latest house in Islesford. She planned to take him one day to Paris, the Parc Zoologique. Over the years, they forged a shorthand of looks and code words to signal dismay at the obvious or stupid remark.

Then, as in a dream, Miles was gone, to Andover, to Princeton, gone from her. They'd never gotten to Paris. Now twenty, or was it twenty-one, Miles seemed a bit effete, if she were to be objective, which she was not. Last year he'd caused a flap by carrying on with the wife of Tip's associate at Fiduciary Trust, adding fuel to the shocking dislike Tip DeGroff had always shown his oldest son. Now Miles had taken a "leave" from Princeton and lived in a cottage in the Islesford Dunes where he made driftwood sculptures and built ocean kayaks. Julia worried her policy of deny-the-boy-nothing was partly to blame.

A photographer from the *Islesford Star* corralled the hostess and friends for a picture. Audrey, hair center-parted and pulled into a scraggly nub as in college, looked cheerful as a bullet. She flashed her abrupt smile. Audrey still smoked Camels when everyone else, voting for longevity over fun, was dialing down on bad habits. Really, Audrey shouldn't play Russian roulette with her health, Julia thought. With the current craze for self-examination, Audrey liked to say "my breasts are the only part I never wash."

A man with eyes set wide in his skull like a Hammerhead joined the photo shoot. Julia recognized an investment banker whose "townie" wife had disappeared some years back under shady circumstances. A prime suspect, he'd never stood trial, the whole unpleasantness had been snuffed, and he'd knit back into Islesford circles like shrapnel the body heals around.

Julia touched Lyndy's sleeve. "There's Audrey's beloved,

Hugo," she said, motioning with her chin. A man with the face of a dissolute cherub hung like a turkey vulture over a pale black woman cradling a bichon frise. "He's working all the angles. That lady with the doggy is a producer for Food Channel." Hugo was hustling his new cookbook, Julia explained, and hoped to launch a TV show combining interviews with cooking. It was refreshing here in the guile capital of the world, how Hugo made no secret of milking Audrey's connections.

"Why does Audrey put up with it?" Lyndy said.

Julia thrust out her jaw in a belligerent way she had. "Do I know? I guess to keep Hugo on board." God I sound like a bitch. She frowned. "In some way they're all 'family' to Audrey, you know—Hugo, the producer, the bichon. And let's not forget the key family member: Audrey's, umm—well, I like 'artistic consultant' better than ghostwriter, don't you?" She looked out over the marshland. "And of course there's also—"

"Oh yes, I was about to ask."

"—Asher Lind."

A crisis with a cooler, the striped popsicles were turning to slush. Audrey glanced around in search of Hugo. He'd locked onto a restaurant critic in a dippy-brimmed red hat. Really, as co-host, shouldn't Hugo at least keep an eye out? She got more host action from her handyman Alex.

Audrey threaded her way toward the kitchen. She knew how she and Hugo must appear—especially to the money barons with blooming wives who were more than a little familiar with quid pro quo. To them Audrey-and-Hugo was an item easily decoded: connected, fortyish woman serviced by go-getter stud. She didn't give a damn; she'd lived too long in defiance of the playbook she'd been handed at the gate. She enjoyed advancing Hugo's fortunes. He was her project. She liked how, when he got around to it, they made love. Sex with Hugo was tidy and to the point, so close to not fucking at all she sometimes wondered how they pulled it off. After, she got to sleep alone, an underrated pleasure. She suspected that their . . . alliance, you might call it, also suited Hugo, who kept a tight rein on his priorities.

Alex had mended the cooler. Audrey thanked him profusely. In a fairer world her handyman, with his competence and clear, frank face, would be a CEO. Alex was indispensable in keeping up Lilac Close. Literally. Last month a section of dining room ceiling had sluiced to the floor in a cascade of plaster. "The house just needs maintenance," said Alex, unfazed, and promptly returned with his workmen. He somehow managed never to impose his messy personal life, fodder for the Islesford gossip mill. His wife was a looker who'd been known to cruise the Islesford railroad station where the illegals regularly hired themselves out for per diem work. One day she caught the eye of an arbitrageur who was in and out of detox at Gracie Square Hospital. Alex simply showed up at Lilac Close as usual.

As she was leaving the kitchen to rejoin her guests, Audrey was waylaid by a caramel girl with a mess of rough curls. Rachel Dempsey, an intern at the *Islesford Star*, was the adopted daughter of a diplomat with far-flung postings, who'd acquired a rainbow family—along with the ire of his Park Avenue co-op board for "bringing down the tone of the building."

"I love your work. Could you autograph this for me please?" Rachel handed Audrey a copy of *Class Notes*.

Audrey graciously obliged, her flowery signature buffed by years of practice, the bold "A" releasing a scrawl like a jet's contrail. So many book parties . . . The first at Julia and Bodie's loft in Soho—had Rinko Park been there, little Rinko who was now mega-famous? She herself was no slouch. She jetted around to promote her novels on morning TV shows with identical anchors—a blonde plus cartoon-handsome male; had *her* table at Elaine's, went to the best parties. She liked all this. After bobbing on the margins, there's deep satisfaction in making the cut, a revenge of sorts, though the anger never quite disappears. In New York, city of dreams where only the cleverest or luckiest gain traction, it's everywhere, the anger.

Audrey handed back the signed copy of *Class Notes* to Rachel, noting the molded cleavage. Her own now getting that collapsed, crepe-y look; on the sly she would actually reach down and reposition her boobs. Audrey stared for a moment at this girl with the dew still on her, and abruptly recognized her young self. The difference being that Rachel was one of an army marching under the banner of feminism. While they—she saw Brett leaping over the lawn with that silly daffodil . . . they'd had only their defiance and each other. And now . . . could Rachel know she was ogling an impostor? Hard to pinpoint when the well had run dry. Maybe since she'd learned the word *deficits*. Perhaps it would have happened anyway thanks to the seductions of the city.

She'd always done her best writing mornings when the brain seemed primed to grab onto words and thoughts like a climbing plant's opportunistic tendrils. These days she rose toward ten. Usually tasting like an ash tray. She'd somehow lost her appetite for the slog of writing, the solitariness, the ruthlessness needed to refuse all Incoming. They'd loved to brainstorm about characters and plot points—Asher conspired with her in believing stories necessary. Lately she caught herself thinking *what's it for*? Like poor crazy Nina who'd lost her appetite for living, God help them all. She herself had lost her imagination for the happy endings required by her readers. At the doozies she came up with lately, she'd catch herself laughing out loud. They had not escaped the odd critic trying to earn his keep, but Audrey Marsh had become critic-proof. She'd also become a plagiarist. Of herself. She'd struggle to wrestle something into words; sense it was eerily familiar— then realize she'd said it better four books back.

At least she didn't cannibalize her friends. Like Brett, whom she'd divorced. All those years as Brett's shadow editor and hand-holder, shaping up drafts of her pieces for *Newsday* and the *Village Voice*. Then Brett produces that traitorous novel—who was it said no good deed goes unpunished? One episode cut particularly close. Though Brett had gotten it wrong. Some day she might be tempted to tell Brett how very wrong—but why give it away? their stories, their lives were their capital. Brett had missed the "Audrey" character's main story: among the old friends, it was she, Audrey, "exploited" by the dastardly Asher Lind, who'd found big love. She couldn't say the same for Brett, who'd surprised everyone, herself included, by marrying Tommy Grierson—maybe as retaliation. In fact, Audrey thought, lighting up—delighted to feel the itch of inspiration—why not get down and dirty and weave a pair of revenge-crossed lovers into her own next novel? Rather than getting married to someone Brett had married *against* Pablo. He, in turn, had likely married May to get back at Brett.

Think of all the trouble Pablo and Brett might have saved everyone by marrying each other! Only May had come out ahead—materially, that is; it was no secret that Pablo hated her. They'd started married life, that cluster of idiots, primed to crash and burn. Brett bore much of the blame, of course, with her dithering and bizarre brand of snobbery. Brett was one of those dangerous "innocents" who damaged the lives she touched. The "all-for-love-one" of their group— had she ever really loved?

Baby, come to me . . . Ain't no second chance / you got to hold on to romance . . . The song drifted outside from the radio sitting on the kitchen counter. Audrey killed her cigarette. Patti Austin? *Baby, come to me / this was meant to be / because I can't go back to living without you . . .*

The cheesiest of pop songs, and she and Asher had loved them, their guilty pleasure; danced to them evenings in her little ranch house among the scrub oak on Red Dirt Road, she kicking off her Capezios and still a bit taller . . . *Gotta have your love around me . . . Because I can't go back to livin' without you . . .* His smooth cheek, his odd crooked thumb. The delicious sweaty musk of his Navy cashmere the first night he'd flown in from Aspen. *Gesundheit Sprechstunde.* Strange she should remember the name of that magazine.

Can I help you with anything Miss Marsh?

She startled to see Alex standing by like a polite school boy. He wore tan work boots with white socks folded over at the ankle.

"Thanks, Alex, you've helped so much already. If anyone asks I'll just be a moment."

From the window seat of her bedroom she watched a lone rider at Topping Stables trotting round a ring, round and round, a chestnut mare, a dream rider, posting up and down, up and down . . . Oh, the good times when there was nothing to do but get closer. Even married, there was enough of him to go round, it had never stopped amazing her. It was *she* the real wife. Asher's official spouse hung like a faint blur in upstate New York where she bred Fox terriers, only occasionally checking back into their apartment on East 86th Street for some social or family event. Or a health crisis involving the hydrocephalic daughter. They traveled, she and Asher. St. Martin's in winter, the Creole fishing village of *Grand Case* where they ate the spiny local lobster and danced at a beach bar strung with colored lights called *Le Moon*. Istanbul in spring, where they shuffled with herds of tourists through the Blue Mosque and woke to dusk and slow love to the sound of minarets calling the faithful to prayer. In Paris, right off the plane, they hit a cafe and ordered a *double crème* and *steack tartare*. At the d'Orsay, if it wasn't shut down by a strike, they called on a favorite Monet: a farmhouse in winter nestled like a hind behind a wooden gate topped by a black magpie, lemony sunlit snow edged by moats of bluish shadow, its hiddenness and deep contentment. Happiness is selfish and story-less—and to much of the world an irritant. That included Brett and Julia. They somehow seemed uncertain about where they'd touched down, foreigners in their own lives.

As for Lyndy DeGroff, the woman never tired of warning her about the hazards of love without a contract. "Marriage is a disincentive to abandonment, that's why it was invented." Failing to understand that she *was* married in all the ways that counted. Lyndy hardly a model of marital bliss. Tip was a husband *in absentia*, always taken up with the Fastnet Race and the America's Cup. Raising four rambunctious boys on her own seemed to have driven Lyndy round the bend. Even with just Miles at home—the other three were now in boarding school—Lyndy needed tune-ups at

McLean's to adjust the dose of lithium. She might do better to soak up the good air around Zurich where *Tender is the Night*'s Dick Diver had romanced Nicole. *We must return in summer and hike to Z'mutt . . .*

They'd planned that February to meet in Zurich where Asher had a legal "matter"—never discussable, which charmed Audrey. After Zurich they'd travel to the magical town of Zermatt. Asher had a longtime ritual of skiing the Matterhorn area with his little "posse." They skied the Swiss side of the mountain, then the long run down to Cervinia on the other, Italian side, all in one day. The hotel arranged transportation back to Zermatt. Afterwards, over dinner of fondue or a meat pie called *pastetli*, Audrey would smile like the tolerant mother of unruly boys while Asher and his buddies rattled on about skiing off piste in fresh snowfalls they called a "dump," and she'd savor her image of Asher when they first connected, bowtied and boyish and playing hotshot skier.

To reach Zermatt, which was closed to cars, they took the train to Visp, then boarded the little cog railway that rose almost vertically along terraced farms. It was snowing lightly and the air smelled of woodsmoke and pine and in the distance sleigh bells tinkled. A horse drawn sleigh carried them along the Bahnhofstrasse, Zermatt's main drag, to their hotel. Unlike the flashy new chalets flying a sea of flags, the elegant old Monte Rosa Hotel offered only a discreet brass plate. White walls and red shutters, balconies wreathed in little lights, a pine-paneled lobby smelling of lilies and banked fires. They woke to intoxicating air and a view beyond their windows of pitched roofs heavy with snow. Over to the right towered the cockeyed pyramid of the Matterhorn, its peak girded in clouds.

On the first day—a "pub crawl," as Asher put it—a cable car bore them high to the mountain lake, *Schwarzee*. From the cable stop they walked to a hotel-restaurant beside the lake and ate a leek-and-sausage dish called *Papet Vaudois* and drank cider sitting on the deck on rawhide chairs, faces offered to the sun.

Audrey was snapped from her glaze of contentment by a boisterous greeting at her side. Vanilla blonde, Euro accent, old friend of Asher's. Inger. Audrey's antennae instantly radioed that the old friend had once been mucho friendly. Plans were laid, they would all meet up later that week. Audrey wondered why when two people have had sex it sticks to them like pollen. Prodded about Inger, Asher laughed it off with lawyerly evasion. He left next morning for the slopes before Audrey woke. He would phone after they skied down to Cervinia to let her know they were heading back.

A leisurely breakfast of *birchermuesli* and a small bread called a *burli*. Audrey walked Zermatt, the Matterhorn always in view, ever changing character: at one point it resembled Dr. Seuss's cat in the hat, with its slightly bent stovepipe peak. At the town rink Audrey leaned over the railing to watch the skaters. Something poignant about people in bright colors skating round and round to Viennese music, blame *Love Story*.

An unwelcome image of Asher's friend Inger from *Schwarzee* carving the slopes with Olympian thighs. "Your basic nightmare" a woman in her current novel called a version of Inger. Asher was already stepping out on his wife, was this the pattern he'd repeat with his girlfriend? Audrey surprised herself by thinking that whatever came her way from Asher was everything she could ask. Any more and she'd turn barmy with happiness. *"I fell for you when you were fourteen." "Good thing we didn't get together then." "Yes, but think of the time we missed!"*

She strolled along the Bahnhofstrasse; managed a *"Gruezi!"* to a shopkeeper and bought picture postcards. Around lunchtime she tracked down the place on Lienertstrasse Asher had discovered—"still untouched by the Twee squad"—and ordered the local perch; *rosti*, a Swiss potato pancake; and a sweet *pulla*, a cardamom-and-cinnamon-spiced bun. "We must return in summer and hike to Z'mutt," Asher always said. Z'mutt was a tiny hamlet of twenty houses snugged in a high mountain valley. It offered views of the Matterhorn at its jauntiest and meadows of Alpine wildflowers: blue trumpet gentians, heather, yellow Lillium, and sunset pink *Alpenrosen*, really a rhododendron. Audrey would object she couldn't manage the trek, Asher would say they'd take it slow and steady, she could use a walking stick like the Swiss hikers—but then summer came and went and they failed to return.

By 3:15 the light was dropping and skiers were coming off the slopes; a serious mountain cold rose off the ground warning that daytime had been but a frivolous interim. Turtling into her fur collar, Audrey hurried back with her uneven gait along the Bahnhofstrasse to the Monte Rosa to wait for Asher's call. They had their own ritual of apres-ski. She found sex too madly exciting after Asher came off the slopes, bringing his smell of animal exertion and high altitude, like their first time in her apartment. She would come too soon, before getting over the crest—something like what must happen with teenage boys.

Still a good hour or so before dusk. Audrey set to correcting the galleys of her new novel. Her attention snagged on a glaring error in chronology; when had copy editors stopped doing their job? she thought irritably. The single revision required re-jiggering in other chapters; a novel was a delicate organism. Glancing up, she startled to see lights winking from the houses outside the window. She checked her watch: almost five. The light fell at four. Asher hadn't yet phoned? Absurdly, she looked over at the red phone on the night table to confirm this was so.

Audrey took pride in avoiding hysteria. Reaching for one of the Monte Carlos cigarettes they sold here, she focused on Brett, her anti-model in panic control. Brett kept a Xanax on hand for everything from a stuck elevator to a stuck zipper, she hadn't realized till now how much she disliked this aspect of Brett, and she was worried how one "Audrey Curtiz" might figure in this memoir Brett was supposedly writing. . . . The clock had moved one minute.

Most likely there had been a glitch in Asher's transport back to the hotel.

Wouldn't he have phoned?

The hand holding her cigarette jumped like something not attached to her.

She wondered if Inger had been of the party to Cervinia.

She dialed the hotel desk to see if she'd missed a message. No, *Madame*, no message. Rather than sit and embroider scenarios, Audrey decided to head over to Elsie's, a small wooden chalet popular with the apres-ski crowd. Perhaps by hanging around the room and fretting she was keeping the phone from ringing.

The place was steamy with the breath of young Swedes wearing ski pants with suspenders and sweaters zipped open at the throat. Their high color and laughter and animal health. Audrey forced herself to drink a second Lillet; the longer she stayed at Elsie's the greater the certainty of finding a message from Asher at the hotel. He was reliable to a fault. Professor Obrecht used to say Tolstoy's characters felt so real because they could be inconsistent. Asher was being inconsistent and real, he'd have stopped at some apres-ski joint on the Italian side to take the chill off, and neglected to call. A joint filled with rowdy Italians instead of Swedes named Anders, like the one coming on to her. She'd never known someone so gregarious as Asher. Chatting up a fellow passenger on the crosstown bus, he could turn a load of crabby New Yorkers into a cargo of smiles and good will.

Maybe he'd run into more old friends, like Inger, from years of skiing Zermatt. At the après-ski he'd order *Gluhwein*, a warmed spiced wine—German sangria, really. Or maybe a *Calanda Edelbrau*—skiing worked up a fine thirst. On her right Anders was hoisting something called a *Bombardino*: eggnog, whiskey and brandy, whipped cream on top. Asher took it without the whipped cream. Inger reminded Audrey of the baroness in *The Sound of Music*. After a certain age you rooted for the silken, hurt baroness, not the fresh convent girl Maria.

Sorry didn't call sooner, got delayed . . . Sorry to make you worry . . . Back in an hour . . . We'll go to the Fluhalp, the best venison . . . Anders had a goggle tan like a raccoon. He said, Smile. She was concentrating on whether it was all right to go back to the hotel now. While picking through Swiss francs, losing a few to the floor, she heard a silence fall like the drop of a canvas. Over by the corner TV. The bartender and Swedes had turned their backs to her, riveted. A reporter in ski gear stood with a mike in the floodlit snow, talking about a sudden, unexpected "dump" near the Breuil Cervinia glacier. The transceivers had picked up the signal of one skier buried in the snow, but gotten there too late. "Those who survive the initial impact of an avalanche," he explained to the viewers, "have fifteen minutes before the warmth of their breath melts the snow around their face, which will refreeze into a casing of ice that suffocates them."

The clerk from *Reception* with the discreet voice approached her the moment she walked into the Monte Rosa. She waved him silent, the man's mouth kept moving. An avalanche on the Italian side . . . Monsieur Lind in the little hospital in Zermatt . . . In his pocket they'd found his passport, along with a receipt from the Monte Rosa and the key to his room. Since they'd checked in together, the authorities had notified Audrey Marsh.

The ski patrol had picked him up and taken him to their hut, she was told at the hospital. He'd gone over the edge . . . tumbled over 100 yards . . . cracked his head and was in a coma . . . She heard the word "intracranial." How had she been so stupid? How had she imagined their lives belonged to them? She asked to see him but when she did there was no one to see, just a mummified figure and tubes all over. He was helicoptered to University Hospital in Zurich. By the time she arrived at the vast forbidding complex, they were operating again to stop a second bleed in the brain. Hours later she was told to wait in a room with thumbed magazines and a coke machine outside Intensive Care while they "cleaned him up."

The following morning she asked at the nurses' station to see Asher Lind. The nurses exchanged looks. "Who are you?" "I'm his friend." They conferred in German. Only family were allowed to see a patient in Intensive Care. "I'm his beloved." "Only family," a nurse repeated, her mouth like a mail slot. Frau Lind has arrived, the mail slot said.

They couldn't stop her from sitting in Family Waiting. Audrey sat all day in the *Warterzimmer fur Familienangehorige*. She sat perfectly upright and still on the waiting room sofa staring straight ahead at a fish tank that contained dead fish. Or artificial fish. Hanging now and forever among little castles with turrets. She pitched over on her side on the sofa. It might be nighttime. She became aware of murmuring, a smell of starch. Hands got her vertical. Someone offered her hot coffee in a styrofoam cup. A hospital volunteer in civilian clothes brought her a sandwich and kindly said she must eat.

By 10 P.M. she was the only person left in the waiting room. She had to leave now, the volunteer said. Audrey asked for information about the condition of the patient Asher Lind. The volunteer said only family is privy to that information. Audrey returned to her room in a little hotel near the hospital and unwrapped her sandwich, some kind of wurst, from the hospital volunteer, and watched TV. On the TV a man announced that the Concorde operated by Britain and France had entered service, cutting transatlantic flying time by 3½ hours. A $2.00 bill had been issued in the United States.

Over the next days she sat in Family Waiting, a copy of *Gesundheit Sprechstunde* in her lap. She never got past the cover bannering a *Sprechstunde mit* a smiling *Frau* Dr. Zimmermann. She regularly spotted Sonia Lind walking by in the hall. Over the years she'd somehow erased Sonia, yet here she was, defiantly real and deep-voiced, the blond bob and protuberant mouth like Leslie Caron's. She was Asher-sized.

One day Sonia came into Family Waiting and sat beside her. "You won't want him now."

It was that bad, then. *You were just there for the good times*, Sonia was saying.

Asher's head had been struck by a slab of snow like a giant cinderblock. Audrey heard words: *traumatic brain injury . . . structural damage . . . atrophy . . . encephalopathy . . .* "The doctors said that another man might emerge with major mental impairment," Sonia said. But Asher, with his fierce will, was doing better than anyone had the right to expect. "There would be deficits, of course."

Deficits. Wasn't that something financial? She pictured the lights winking in the dusk outside her window at the Monte Rosa, the moment when the terms changed. She wanted now for time to pass quickly.

He had come out of the coma babbling about her, Audrey. In French—Sonia glanced at her and they almost smiled.

Over the next days they took to sitting together in the Waiting Room. Sonia's harsh lovely alto. They'd married right out of college. Her father, a prominent Washington attorney and counsel to two presidents, had been important to Asher's career. A few years in she learned about his affairs but when their second daughter was born with grave health problems they'd pulled together as a family. After that Asher went back to his serial flings, usually with married Europeans—but none of that disrupted their life. Until—Sonia's inhale pinched her nostrils.

"I used to read your novels and be afraid I'd find him there."

Audrey turned her head away, then back. "I'm sorry I fucked up your life."

Sonia's stony profile.

Well, what did she expect? A warm embrace and *kumbaya*?

"My husband will need massive amounts of care."

My husband.

Sonia had turned now to look at her. She planned to move back to Manhattan from upstate, she went on. There would be intensive rehab, therapy, with both daughters living in California it was essential she be on hand, though the daughters would help, too. "My husband has not been the most conventional, but when push comes to shove, our family pulls together."

There seemed a lot of space and cold as if they were conversing from across a great arctic waste.

"Do you want to see him?"

The evening lights winking on across from the Monte

Rosa, the artificial fish floating forever among their castles, her apartment on 57th Street—these would mark the perimeters of her world.

"Men," Sonia said in her rasp. "Somebody has to be the grownup."

She met him for lunch four months later at Circus on East 61st. She had almost to look away. His features had been disarranged like some unfunny Frankenstein joke; one eye, open at half-mast, had relocated to the wrong address. His sentences didn't make sense. He became irritated by her failure to understand. A random word would set him singing old songs, *I want a girl, just like the girl that married dear old dad.* The word "kick" brought on Cole Porter. *I get no kick from Champagne,* he crooned from across the table. *But I get a kick out of you.* He was all lyrics, Asher.

"You seem to be bouncing back," Audrey said brightly.

"I'd like to bounce with *you.*"

He grabbed on to words hand over hand, the words were what kept him swimming above the avalanche. Wily, brilliant Asher, who'd delighted in demolishing an opponent in the cross. He could still captivate the waitress—though she kept glancing at Audrey, not sure what she was dealing with.

Audrey had once read a magazine article that proclaimed you grow from loss. In fact, you shrank from loss. Since Zermatt she'd lost chunks of herself, like an airplane dropping parts mid-flight while managing to stay aloft. Old joy came back to her in a rush; she reached for Asher's hand across the table. "We *knew* how lucky we were. Every moment we knew. If only other people could be that happy, just for a moment."

"Lucky." His brow drew into a fine concentration. "L.S./M.F.T. Know what that stands for?" She squeezed his hand hard to draw him back. "Lucky Strike Means Fine Tobacco."

At another lunch Asher announced they must plan a hike up the valley to Z'mutt in the spring to see the meadows of *Alpenrosen*. "'The Great Spirit of the Mountain breathed his own peace upon their hurt minds and sore hearts.' Mark Twain." The next day Asher called to say he'd decided to get back with his wife. "My wife Sonia," he added.

He phoned Audrey six times a day. He adored her, wanted to squeeze her thigh, loved her smile and the way they danced . . . *We could have danced all night, we could have danced all night, and I'd have begged for more . . .* Audrey said she loved him too but it was better for them not to talk that way. They made another lunch date. The evening before, Sonia phoned to ask if Audrey would mind seeing Asher back to their apartment afterward. He couldn't always be relied on to find his way home. The doorman had been alerted.

Over the years Audrey came to believe that life contained a happiness quota. She'd gotten her allotment. These days she lived off past happiness, drew from reserves carefully apportioned out like drops of water from a stranded hiker's canteen and found that it sufficed.

I'LL MAKE YOU A STAR

"He diss me!"

Huh? Brett, with her shaky grasp of lingua ghetto, wasn't sure what "dissed" meant, but to judge by the fracas in the back row of the classroom it wasn't good. A zephyr of ripe garbage drifted in. The classroom—part of a warren in the former Pemex Chemical Company that housed O'Dwyer College—lacked windows, and Brett always kept the door open. Unfortunately, the loading bay for the cafeteria leavings yawned just down the hall.

"Look, this is a college," Brett said evenly, "and whatever issue has come up back there, this is not the place to pursue it. Let's move on."

Brett had spent the last several minutes of English Composition 99 vainly trying to explain to her students why they should avoid cliches. Morale lay below sea level: though the word "remedial" was absent from the course title, the *first* level was Comp *101* and the students were not fooled. They'd ridden here on the wave of Open Admissions which, starting in 1970, invited anyone who'd made it through high school to attend the colleges comprising City University. The catch: New York's disastrous public schools were forced to focus more on violence management than education, graduating kids who were barely literate. So here at O'Dwyer College it was Remedial everything. Except for one sour colleague of Brett's who called O'Dwyer a "home for men," none of the profs complained. At least none who'd nabbed a tenure-track position, a pathway going extinct in a university that found it more cost effective to work the hide off part-time adjuncts. Like Brett.

"But Shaquan diss me," the girl loudly reported from the back row.

The offender sat balanced on the base of his spine, arms folded across his chest, legs akimbo, the crotch of his jeans somewhere around his knees.

The request "please see me after class" formed in Brett's mouth, but she hesitated. For one thing, she wasn't sure if the plaintiff's name was Lashawna or Tayshawna. Since inscribing names in her blue roll book, Brett had been struggling to match them to students. She had more success with Latino names. Or Kevin and Mary, attached to pale pimply kids who'd landed here at O'Dwyer dazed and Sister-whipped from Immaculate Heart Central. One name stubbornly defied pronunciation: Q'J'Q'sha—and its owner always accused Brett of failing to call on her but luckily she rarely showed up. Brett's cred was down around her ankles and she was viewed, to judge by the sea of hostile gazes before her, as an emissary from the oppressor's camp, complicit in all the scourges that had landed on black folk since the first slave ships left the *Ile de Gorée*. A woman whose mother had hired their mothers to trek down from Harlem to clean toilets. For all they knew, Brett—with her spiffy bellbottoms and mod tops—had recruited for latrine duty someone's aunt (pronounced "ahnt") from this very class.

The "see me after class" bit also routinely brought jeers, causing further disruption. And Brett needed to tread carefully in the case of Lashawna or Tayshawna. The girl usually clattered in late on stiletto heels, displaying major cleavage, fringed leather, and long nails laquered with acrylic museum-quality art that curled like talons. Reportedly, she turned tricks. O'Dwyer had placed . . . Laquanda—that was her name!—on probation and Brett feared her own complaints might trigger Laquanda's expulsion, a responsibility Brett thought it prudent to avoid. Anyway, "conferences" with students in her office rarely proved productive. Inevitably they

included some inner city version of "the dog ate my homework," stories that involved a knife-wielding boyfriend who'd
"snapped," a brother who'd violated parole, an ahnt taking
a bullet to the head while sitting in a car outside the projects in Bedford-Stuyvesant. Stories marshaled to explain why
the student had slept through class, or spent it in the hall,
or was still unprepared to take the make-up quiz—"Teach"
shouldn't take it personally.

"Hey Miss, Laquanda diss me first," Shaquan said. He
glanced around for confirmation.

"Uh, in college we generally call the instructor Professor." Brett heard the word "bee-atch," followed by snick-
ers. Kevin and Mary from Immaculate Heart, their faces
the color of turned skim milk, stared ahead as if blindered.
Brett's two allies—a boy from Ivory Coast and a stern young
girl from Brownsville Houses, noted for its three-foot rats—
looked unsure where to put their eyes.

Brett said, "Why don't we discuss the whole thing later." She scanned a paper stained with coffee and what she
hoped was ketchup. "Kevin, try to avoid such expressions as
'it's raining cats and dogs' in your writing. That's a typical
cliché. And: 'beat around the bush' and 'go with the flow.'
Also stilted phrases like 'in this day and age.' Sometimes it's
better just to write the way you talk."

"Like muthuhfuckuh?" someone muttered, to appre-
ciative cackles.

"Shut the fuck up," said a Dominican student. Several
others turned on him.

"Excuse me, this is a college classroom," Brett was again
moved to remind the group. Melting pot? In here it was a
shark tank. For reasons Brett little understood, the Domini-
cans were reviled by the other Latinos, while everyone hated
the Asians who were considered robotic goody-goodies, kept
their own counsel, and always pulled A's.

"Yo, I don't see what's wrong with 'go with the flow'"
put in Shaquan. "Like, everyone know it mean you jus' . . .
go—with the flow," he mimed.

"You're right—but that's not the issue," Brett said. "In
writing it's better to avoid language that's been so overworked,

it ceases to evoke. It's dead language." Brett stopped, at a loss to explain. With their shaky English, a cliché, to some of these kids, must appear like a life raft in the Atlantic.

"*Dead* language?" Shaquan slid impossibly lower on his lumbar vertebrae, legs akimbo. "*Dead*? You dissin' Kevin."

Kevin's eyes flicked sideways, yearning for the exit.

"Look, my mandate here is to teach you how to improve your writing. It's called a critique. I'm offering a critique."

"Man, she dissin' *us*," Shaquan said excitedly, his neighbors concurring.

Something about the rudeness of "she" pushed Brett perilously close to the edge. Meanwhile a separate loud discussion dissing her teaching technique was in progress, while others had taken to chanting *Go with the flow, go with the flow.* Hey, waitaminute, I'm on your side, she wanted to say, my Uncle Lou played *Songs of the African Veldt* on his victrola in Rego Park, I believe in Open Admissions, I marched against tuition, I hate the lousy public schools and O'Dwyer's shithole of a physical plant, the folks who rule America *want* brawls like this so no one will notice while they make off with the loot—but I am not the enemy and *none of this is personally my fault*—

Instead of saying this, Brett scooped up her roll book, briefcase, and bag the class watching with sudden disquiet—and walked.

She would have liked to keep walking. She would have liked to head home and churn a piece for the *Village Voice* mocking what she called the "feminine upkeep" expected of women through a final polish. But you couldn't just go AWOL on your class. For the moment, she'd regroup in her basement office, even if the asbestos and mold messed up her sinuses. Her hand hovered over the phone: she ought to contact Security about the class's "unruly" behavior. But they might send one of those students who majored in Security and were doing a brisk business in the resale of pricey textbooks lifted from the profs' offices. Security might report her classroom issues to the Provost, and then when she came up for tenure, someone would cite Professor Grierson's "lack of rapport with the students." On some level she couldn't blame the students. She wanted to be somewhere else and they could smell it. In fact, she wasn't altogether there, though she handed back papers and assigned grades and wrote on the blackboard, "let's eat grandma" versus "let's eat, grandma" to demonstrate that "grammar saves lives"—inspiring ribaldry about eating grandma and comments of "nice ass" and "she hot." "Miz Grierson always act like she be off in her own world," a girl had written on the student evaluations, where Brett fared poorly.

As a grad student, high in her little carrel at Columbia's Widener Library, she'd harbored a more exalted vision of the academic calling. That vision surely existed somewhere—just not at O'Dwyer. She'd emerged with her shiny new Ph.D. exactly as the market for college teaching in New York had cratered, and the new population of students was giving CUNY a nervous breakdown. You didn't *teach* Dickens at O'Dwyer—the place *was* Dickens, spiked with Hubert Selby's *Last Exit to Brooklyn*. Her department chairman—cadaverous and asthmatic from inhaling the asbestos *de maison*—got a break from remediating only with the Shakespeare elective that was listed every third semester. The course was usually canceled for lack of students.

This chairman had noted Brett's mental absenteeism, along with her skill in evading Committee Work, which Brett considered a major time-eater, useful solely for snagging tenure. Her journalism was not much appreciated either: it was "popular," not scholarly, maybe even pornographic. Brett suspected envy might be a factor.

Because she was getting read, reaching the larger public. Since the early 70's everybody wanted to hear from the women. Sitting in the 110th Street playground with Tommy Jr., she'd been electrified by Vivian Gornick proclaiming in the *Village Voice* "the next great moment in history is theirs." She clipped the article, issue of Nov 27, 1969. Women writers were bringing the news, *were* the news, making history—and couldn't have known in those heady days how swiftly, after *making* history, many would *become* history, and "their" moment passed to others. Everyone was reading *The Female Eunuch, Sexual Politics, Against our Will*. With *The Myth of the Vaginal Orgasm* you need read only the title. No one had much use for periods any more, and there were pamphlets on menstrual "extraction." There were memoirs by mad house-wives and man-haters duking it out in the erogenous zone and a screed by Andrea Dworkin proclaiming all hetero-sexual sex is rape. And there was Gloria Steinem. A bitchy friend of Audrey's wondered why someone as pretty as Gloria cared so much about feminism and didn't just marry a media baron.

From the sidelines Brett had been itching to bust into the action. A rainy spring afternoon, Tommy Jr. napping, and she sat doodling on the kitchen butcher block . . . Sud-denly time collapsed backwards and she was twenty-one on the Pont des Arts with Allen Ginsberg as he talked about "widening the circle of intimacy." Today they called it "al-ternative lifestyles." New Jersey, of all places, was a hotbed of "key parties" and "group sex." Brett slid off the kitchen stool. Here was the story that would crack her in.

She picked up the scent of a couple named John and Mimi, high priests of Open Marriage, and they agreed to an interview for her "spec" piece exploring the issue of possessive-ness. "If I sleep with Eva, a woman I've been seeing for twelve years," John said, "I'm not taking anything away from Mimi. The way I see it we all come out ahead." "I like the space," Mimi said, as Brett scribbled in her notebook. "My affairs work out better if the man is already married and has a prima-ry relationship in his life." Mimi recommended twice-daily sessions with a vibrator to unblock creativity, and the couple wished Brett godspeed, and sent her to check out a "group marriage" in Quincy, Mass. The co-weds felt so easy around each other they took dumps with the bathroom door open.

Florets of balled up paper littered the floor around Brett's typewriter. Past midnight, but you could phone Au-drey at any hour.

"I can't write this."

"Stop that!"—Audrey's standard response to defeat. Brett heard a match strike. "Here's an idea," Audrey said through an exhale. "By paragraph three you've got to tell people *why* they're reading this. Give it a shot and if that doesn't work, hop a cab over."

She mailed her article to a name she'd picked off the masthead of *New York* magazine, the glossy an editor named Clay Felker had liberated from the Sunday section of the *Herald Tribune*, and made essential reading for strivers who enjoyed envying the enviable. She'd almost forgotten about the piece when the kitchen phone rang later that week. Little Tommy was bawling, indignant they'd run out of Pop Tarts.

"Where you been hiding?" came a voice. "Why haven't we heard from you before? We're gonna run your piece in the issue hitting the stands in two weeks. Oh sorry, Byron Schlitt here from *New York*. Come talk to me."

Brett scooped Tommy up in her arms and wiped snot from his nose and kissed the baby crease at his wrist, the darlingest in creation. One day she must find a way to tell Audrey she loved her. Audrey made it hard, she was resistant to what she considered "sentimentality" like a mallard's feathers to rain.

"Beyond Monogamy"—bannered on the November 10, 1974 issue of *New York*—unleashed a tsunami of furious letters. Brett crowed; she hadn't lost her power to annoy. One midnight it struck her that the article lacked a crucial insight. Who were these people kidding, with their alternative lifestyles? Only a matter of time before someone's nose got caught in the door. From Quincy to Parsippany they could fuck each other blind, and that wouldn't keep them from soon being dead.

I'll make you a star! The promise hung in the air in *New York*'s caffeinated warren of cubicles on 32nd Street. Brett was one of the "almost-famous," a sardonic observer of high-bourgeois rituals in *New York*; how do I know your name? people asked at parties before bestowing their attention. She sped airborne along the walks of Central Park, past old people on benches and softball pick-up games, stories pinging in. The times offered a ridiculous abundance of material. Why not do a piece on women who leave the boorish husbands they've "grown away from"—then, oops, forget they might need to make a living? The guy remarries a woman free of militancy and stretch marks, makes new babies, forgets the support payments—and *voila* wife #1 becomes a candidate for welfare.

Follow your bliss, Joseph Campbell had said at Foxleigh. But journalism was a crap shoot compared to Academe. Could she rely on her husband? They'd leaped into marriage and woken up in it like two strangers in a motel bed. She married survival, grabbed onto this man like *The Raft of Medusa* who saw nothing wrong that a baby wouldn't fix. Why he married her she wasn't sure and thought it prudent not to ask. Tommy worked in Development at the Parks Conservancy, which appeared to believe that paying a living age was vulgar. She feared he was only dabbling in New York's religion of work, he preferred to hang out at the Explorer's Club and talk about piranha fishing from a dugout canoe. Her husband sometimes seemed an oldstyle adventurer come to roost, incongruously, in an America up to its eyeballs in revolutions; he dreamed of the rainforests of New Guinea while everyone else fumed about "fascist pigs" in Chicago. He deserved a bigger love. They were happy, in a negligent sort of way, and when she became pregnant they felt blessed.

Over the years the Grierson money had been pissed away, but tribal loyalty made Tommy and his "bride"—and now little Tommy—welcome at sprawling waterfront houses in Marion, Mass., passed along for generations. He was good at the good life, Tommy. There were July 4th weekends at Uncle Archie's compound up from Cee Vosburgh's place; cruises with prep school friends on the *Kookaburra*, a fifty foot yawl chartered from Bill Buckley; anchorages in enchanted harbors in Newfoundland where they OD'd on lobster and Dewars so they could barely find their bunks below. The new money in Islesford, Audrey quipped, liked their outdoors clipped and climatized. Tommy's people took theirs straight up, braving forty knot winds on Somes Sound or lightning storms on Aspen's Buckskin Pass.

The members of this extended set were high spirited

and, after Marion's noon whistle, higher than the Piping Plovers knifing the sky above their nesting ground. Occasionally, after his second 'toonie, Archie—a blowhard with a bulbous lavender nose—might let slip a crack about "Hebes," or marvel that his nephew's Harvard roommate answered to the name Perlmutter. Tommy would dismiss Archie's bigotry as senility compounded by "the sauce." On her side, Brett came to regard the relentless *breeziness* as an avoidance of introspection. Perhaps generations of privilege and ease had made certain types of brain work unnecessary to survival, so the anterior prefrontal cortex had gone flabby. The Locust Valley lockjaw itself seemed armor against thought. They were sporting even about death. Tip DeGroff's brother, ravaged by a hideous disease, waxed downright jolly about the prospect of relocating to Brooklyn's historic Green-Wood Cemetery. "It's a National Historic Landmark, with 19th century sculptures and mausoleums!" He'd be in the impeccable company of DeWitt Clinton and Louis Comfort Tiffany.

Brett came to see this New England enclave as a parallel universe. Ensconced in derelict mansions on prime waterfront, flying burgees from the Beverly Yacht Club, sipping bullshots and quoting William Buckley between regattas and rounds of croquet, they seemed doomed to irrelevance. They'd stepped away from the driving wedge, their story had been written and annotated. They were living out of their own archives. Be careful what you wish for, she sometimes thought, amazed by her old fetish for WASP-world. Yet here was little Tommy Jr., with her mother's lovely grey eyes, at six months sitting ramrod straight on the sofa and "reading" books and laughing at words like "niblet"—already a wordsmith? In Tommy Jr. she had wished right.

Too often now the rough patches got smoothed by booze. Or punched up by booze.

"Development is just a fancy term for holding out a tin cup," Tommy said one evening.

"Maybe you could use some of the connections you've made to move to a better job."

"I should, yes, I should start asking round."

"Maybe update your resume."

"I should, yes."

Loud sigh. "I mean, if you spent half the ingenuity looking for a job that you spent working on Tommy's Halloween costume . . ."

"And if you ever stopped scribbling and spent any time on Tommy at all . . ." He chucked back his Maker's Mark. "Is there anything I could do that would please you?"

"That's a cheap shot, you always globalize to avoid looking at a specific issue."

He socked her. She walloped him back and there they were, whaling away at each other. Each unhinged by separate disappointments. They stopped as suddenly as they'd started, frightened of themselves. She stared up at him from his family's Tabriz. She was pregnant again.

With the roof of Africa they hit a new low.

"Think of it, a walk-up to the roof of Africa," Tommy said, ice cubes clinking. He settled his lanky frame in the Queen Anne chair. "Non-technical, but Kilimanjaro's altitude makes it challenging. The outfitter's an old friend. They've agreed to give me a leave at work."

"But the baby's due in August. I thought the plan was to wait till after the baby."

"Oh, I should be back a good month before."

Trying not to tear up. "Oh Tommy, that's cutting it so close."

Oh Tommy, he mimicked.

Let it go, you know he can be childish. She focused on a snapshot on the sideboard of Tommy lying in the grass at Archie's place in Marion, dandling his son high over his chest. He was a dad who diapered and hit the floor to build minarets with Legos and, yes, concocted the best Halloween costumes ever.

"Lookit, I know it's not ideal but I've been training for a year and I'm in peak condition to summit. The timing's perfect."

The timing's perfect—did he hear himself? She felt the baby sharply elbowing its cozy chamber, as if in protest. That her body could do this filled her with gratitude and awe.

"Just think, you'll get some 'quality time' to spend with our son."

She shut her eyes *let it go*. During the stamina training he'd gotten chummy, her husband, with a donor to the Conservancy, a chipper lady jock with a squared-off stance and blond streaks. Brett decided against asking if she was of the party.

"He's walking on the roof of Africa when you're in your eighth month?" Julia honked.

She found it hard to understand Brett's coziness with shabby treatment, how shockingly little she demanded. Julia had a theory. In their youthful hungers they'd flung themselves at men who only knew how to trash "dirty girls." She herself was a cold witch, no male shenanigans could survive the Death Star of her scorn. With Brett, right out of the starting gate something in her had shriveled.

A member of Tommy's expedition got altitude sickness, which delayed the ascent. Then a monster rainfall, unprecedented for that time of year, made descent by the planned route too hazardous, creating further delays. The baby arrived three weeks early. Tommy raised no objection when Brett told him she'd named her Bella. Her grandmother's name, an Old Country name from the shtetl. A name to make the Marion crowd roll their eyes and reach for the Maker's Mark.

Audrey invited Brett to a meeting of the new Women In Media group for a support-and-gab-fest called networking. Audrey had just been elected president. After the awful business with Asher, friends had rallied round. But everyone was so busy now "juggling"—careers, babies, sessions on the trapeze at Kounovsky's on 56th Street, husbands. Harder now to find time for the friends.

Brett, who'd not seen Audrey in a while, was dismayed at her appearance up on the podium. Bulging middle, hem sagging above mottled calves, hair wispy on her high forehead—Audrey was veering toward slovenly. She stood at the mic working through items on the group's agenda, spinning off irreverent asides in her plummy voice, referring to the group as "Friends of Scarlett O'Hara" and occasionally smiling at some private joke. She looked a bit mad—did no one else notice? Sitting on her little *faux* gold chair, Brett's heart sang to think of Audrey hacking out her own path twenty years before women's lib, defiant and full of cheer. Business wrapped, the women pounced—on each other; the room rocked like a party fueled by top grade cocaine. It was new and their moment in sisterhood. No one could have imagined then that twenty years down the road a culture burned out on feminism, so *yesterday*, would wash over them like winter's high tide—movement stars, deserter wives, publishers, best-selling writers, crusaders against patriarchy—dumping them high on the beach like so much flotsam.

"Someone I think you should meet," Audrey said, collaring Brett. "Kristi Hauser just started *Verve*, a new magazine that targets working women. Tells you how to hire—and fire—a secretary, not how to *be* one. *Verve's* the farthest thing from that slavering over how to please your man stuff in *Cosmo*."

Audrey steered Brett toward a dark-haired whippet of a woman doing battle with late-life acne. Kristi Hauser regarded Brett as if totting up her possible uses. Brett thought she might be witnessing the new approved version of femaleness, liberated from the oh-please-love-me-please edition of yesteryear.

"I've had you in my sights," Kristi said. "Ever since those marvelous pieces for Clay. We must have lunch."

It was never a question of "if." It was only a question of "when." And who would make the call.

Maybe not, Brett would think. What possible good could come of it? Even to think about it felt disloyal. Tommy,

more wary of her past than he let on, referred to Pablo—
whom he'd seen at the Curtiz parties—as Cha-cha-cha.

She'd sighted Pablo earlier that winter in Central Park
from across the new "adventure" playground on 81st and
Fifth. She sensed the whip of his head and eyes zooming
in—a nano second before seeing him. Twenty-four degrees
with the wind chill and he wore a lowlife Shriner's hat and
light windbreaker, like the New York weirdos who walk
around coat-less in frigid weather—to prove what? They
eyed each other across the state-of-the art jungle gym, its
rope bridge crawling with kids kitted up in snow suits and
red hats, their cries brittle in the frozen air, and she wondered at the years of living they'd clocked: births, anniver-
saries, the beat of little footfalls, *socket!* don't touch, sunlight
on the parquet, warm tumble of sheets, the smoked salmon
and *Times* and park strolls and Chinese and ennui of New
York Sundays—all of it.

"Are you a good father?" Somehow they both knew the
basics.

"Pretty self-absorbed, but I suppose I am, in my way.
Are you a good mother?"

"Kind of like you."

His eyes that curious light pigskin with dark pupils,
schnoz a trumpet flare wagging to the left, crooked grin.
Charcoal pinstripes, yet still the kid with the high-bounce
spaldeen. They sat catty-cornered in Menchanko on 55th
Street in the populous noon of midtown lunch and it hadn't
mattered who'd made the call, it felt forbidden and rich, a
furlough from the KP duty of conscripted life. Pablo talked
about his FM business and switching KQV to an all-news for-
mat; a real estate project with Bodie out in Islesford. Around
them bristled a thicket of words not spoken.

"We have a lot to say to each other," he said, low in his
throat. "And we've only scratched the surface. If we started
we wouldn't be able to stop."

"Are you happy?"

"May married well in terms of money."

Well, there was an answer. "My children," she said, "I never knew I could love anyone so much."

They'd managed to take the vitals.

"Your articles in *New York*—damn, you're good!" He sounded miffed, as if she'd slipped one by him.

"Were you in love with May?"

"I was in love with you."

With flawless timing, the waiter was upon them to take their order.

"You gotta come to the Young Concert Artists benefit we're doing at Carnegie Hall," Pablo said. "I'll comp you. Actually, I just joined the board. I'm tight with Maestro Lorin Maazel," he went on in a burred voice. "Meeting everyone, Barenboim, Pavarotti . . . I have everything you wanted now."

Someone might have yanked a lamp cord from its socket. Had he really said that? She cocked her head and smiled, one of those, No, *really*? smiles.

"But the 'everything' I want is more talent—and last I checked only God is dispensing that. Also, getting by on four hours sleep so I could have more life." She placed her napkin on the table. "I'm on deadline," she lied.

They kept coming back, drawn by an itch to decrypt the enigma code of their past. They got a buzz off each other's gluttony for work; like him she would die, quite literally, she believed, without work.

"You need a bigtime agent," he said. "This Ber-neece of yours, I dunno."

Brett maneuvered a morsel of eel into her mouth. "She handles lots of women writers—"

"Listen, I was at this party thrown by the Young President's Club, and I met a guy who knows this hotshot agent at ICM, Hollywood connections up the kazoo, I'll set up a meeting—"

"Thanks, but I like Berenice."

He'd invested in Bodie's latest real estate project, a condo designed by Renzo Piano that would replace two SRO's on 98th and Riverside. "We'll 'relocate' the residents, mainly junkies and dealers."

"Y'know, I read about that. As I remember, most of the tenants are not junkies, they're old people, welfare mothers, and folks who've fallen off the grid. I sometimes feel one scrap of shitty luck away from them."

"I would never let anything happen to you," he blurted.

They both looked startled, as if pitched into a time warp.

"Where do they relocate those tenants *to*?" she said, annoyed at his presumption but maybe a beat late. "A homeless shelter that's swarming with roaches and sexual predators?"

"C'mon, look around you, building, construction everywhere. There's no holding back development in this city. Catch the rising tide—and then you're in a position to give back. I just made a, well, substantial gift to Naropa, this Buddhist study place out in Boulder. Started by Allen Ginsberg. Didn't you once know Ginsberg in Paris?"

This sushi was giving her acid reflux. "I believe money for worthy institutions should come from the public sector."

He looked at her in admiration, as if he didn't quite deserve her yet. "I never told you this, I was afraid of how you'd react"—he lined his chopsticks up on the edge of the plate. "Between foster homes I used to sleep on subway trains."

"I was a stupid snot in those days. I haven't forgiven myself, but I'm hoping some day you can."

Each time they met she decided it would be their last. They met out of nostalgia for their youth, their future billowing out like a giant spinnaker catching the wind. They were haunted by the tease of what-might-have-been; the sense that their lives had gone one way, and perhaps not the best way, when they might plausibly have gone another. Or maybe Pablo came to rub her nose in his swanky life—and she to confirm she'd been right all along.

March 10th, 1980 Jean Harris shot Herman Tarnower, the Scarsdale diet doctor, and every woman writer in town wanted a piece of it. Passion, murder, feminism, class—here was the story, Brett thought, that would finally break her out. In the kitchen she heated up the chicken fricassee the new Haitian sitter had cooked Bella and Tommy for supper.

The front page photos from the tabloids lay spread on the table in the dining room, which also housed Bella's bunkbed. There was Mrs. Harris en route to the arraignment, the mink, her blondness and patrician air, the pale blue eyes wide and uncomprehending. Looking out from behind the police car grille, hunted and dazed.

"What's wrong with that lady?" little Tommy asked, always eerily alert to adult matters.

"She made a bad mistake, sweetheart. But maybe she'll find a way to fix it. Eat your lima beans."

This story was hers. Jean Harris could have been *them* at Foxleigh, one of her crowd. *Her.* Jean rises to become headmistress of the Madeira school. Then, fifteen years into their virtual marriage, "Sy" Tarnower steps out with a younger, blonder edition—and the past swings round and cracks Jean in the teeth. She goes bonkers, default position of women down the ages. Drives five hours through rotten weather to Dr. Tarnower's house with a gun in her purse—to kill her*self,* she claims. Already Brett could see the lead.

She replaced the receiver and leaped around the bedroom in a little Hopi dance. She hadn't even lobbied for it. She'd launched a telepathic desire into New York's vast webbing of hungers and desires—and *ping*! Kristi Hauser asks her to cover the Jean Harris trial for *Verve.* Kristi had indeed kept her in her sights. The hot new book in town was the perfect platform.

She paced the bedroom. She'd never felt easy with success. Like Audrey. Or Rinko, to judge from afar how she wore her celebrity. For her, the prospect of success offered a rainbow of opportunities to blow it, a disorder somehow traceable to a snowy night in Cambridge, though she couldn't sort out how. Get too fortunate and the gods might zap you with a disease, just to even the balance and keep things lively in Olympus. Living in nonentitude, moderately unhappy, was more her thing.

The headlines that March briefly took a rest from Jean Harris with news of the city's latest budget crisis. Brett arrived at work to rumblings about "painful cuts" and shutting down entire colleges within CUNY. Like O'Dwyer, with its image of Remediation Central.

Brett's cadaverous Chair, seemingly oblivious to the rough air ahead, informed her over a productive cough that an instructor was moving to Arizona. Maybe also suffering from asbestos lung. "That means we'll have a tenure track position open in English. Of course the competition is fierce," the Chair said, reflexively recoiling from the musk of desperation she gave off. "Y'know, it would increase your chances if for a change *ahem*—you would publish something scholarly."

Tenure track. Brett rocketed uptown on a 2/3 train, her car a captive art gallery for a budding Franz Kline. Tenure was the promised land: good money, promotions, *benefits*— a home-free honey of a package which, unless you exposed yourself in the hall, they couldn't take away. The only hitch, she belonged to journalism.

In the interests of harmony, Brett had given up pressing Tommy on the job front—but she knew he was digging deep into capital. Her promotion to Assistant Professor would secure their rung in the middle class. They might loft bullshots with Bill Buckley on the *Kookaburra*, but come Monday she was squeezing out remaining toothpaste with pliers. They hired French-speaking Haitian sitters, who charged way less than the nannies requiring their own room with bath and TV whom the DeGroffs found through the *Irish Echo*. Redaline, the Griersons' current sitter, cooked up fiery *rotis* of obscure animal parts, while brooding over a fiancé who'd run off with her sister. Her predecessor had simply not shown up one morning. And now special counseling might be needed for Bella. She was a pretty child, her little face haloed with fuzzy yellow hair like a Christmas angel's. A child of few words and shy of eye contact, tippy-toeing around some private fairyworld and concocting games with her "friend" Andy—perhaps, Brett thought uneasily, to escape the friction between her parents.

*   *   *

With the launch of the Jean Harris trial that November Brett forgot about benefits. It was carnival time in media land, the courthouse packed with hundreds of reporters and photographers jockeying for prime space. Shana Alexander was there, her angry smile. Fragile, feisty Diana Trilling, with her greyish-pink up-sweep, tobacco-cured voice, and a disdain for Mrs. Harris that floated off her like the stale perfume that also floated off her. Suburban housewives had driven four hours to attend. You'd think it was 18th century London where people swarmed to witness a public hanging, scrambling to score seats in Mother Procter's Pews—only the pie sellers and gin shops were missing.

Brett loved sitting ringside with the press. Mrs. Harris arrived each morning in Chanel-style suits—the jacket lined in mauve silk—with her hoity-toity manner, her memories of trips with Tarnower to Paris, Kenya, Ceylon. She took notes, studied transcripts, hid her tears behind big shades. The whole gestalt pissed off the jury of Archie Bunkers and key-punch operators controlling her fate. Even though Harris had merely coveted a swishier version of their own lives.

A centerpiece of the trial promised to be the Scarsdale Letter which the young, fresh-faced prosecutor planned to read to the jury. Harris's fate hung on her true intent at the time she pulled the trigger, and the letter, the defense believed, would demonstrate her love for Tarnower.

The reading of the Scarsdale Letter ran up against the very day that Brett's Comp 99 class was to be observed by a superior in rank. The cruel timing all but set Brett writhing on the faded living room Persian—already she'd been canceling classes to attend the trial. High marks for teaching technique were paramount in nabbing a tenure track job. But to miss hearing Mrs. Harris's secret heart exposed was to hamstring her article. Brett fed and bathed the kids and put them to bed. Tommy swung in the door with his bouquet of bourbon—often now the case

"Just had drinks with a Parks deputy commissioner who's moving on. Looks like there might be an opening in capital projects I'd be just right for."

"Tommy, that's tremendous, I am *so* excited."

Tommy operated according to his own clock. Pulling together they could float this boat after all.

The night before the Scarsdale Letter was to be read in court, Brett considered calling in sick at O'Dwyer.

"I wouldn't burn your bridges on the teaching front," Julia said. "I mean, Tommy once had a 'fugue thing-y—'"

"Yup, know all about it, and his aunt Gertrude jumped from a window in a Philadelphia hotel on her wedding night. As a matter of fact, Tommy's in line for a much better job." It was not productive to speculate on the Grierson gene pool, especially when she thought of her children. She also suspected that Julia's take on Tommy was symptomatic of some disappointment with Bodie and their failure to have children. Whatever his flaws, Tommy was a terrific dad, especially compared to the jerks she'd recently written about for *New York* who flaunted their "fathering" creds to prove they were "male feminists."

"C'mon, you can finesse the article." From Audrey, voice garbled voice on the other end of the phone. Brett guessed she was tippling Lillet. "You can cobble together the Scarsdale Letter from the tabloids and other articles. Trust me, no one will notice except you."

In the end, Brett sucked it up and took Comp 99 through its paces with such brio, her inquisitor checked the box "Clearly Superior." That same day, the world went on as it does, whether you're fucking there or not. The Scarsdale Letter was read in court—damning Mrs. Harris by exposing her fury at her young rival, whom she called "your whore," and her pain over being "jeered at as old and pathetic" and treated "like discarded trash"—and the jury convicted her of second-degree murder.

At the coat check of The Four Seasons Brett narrowly collided with Jordan Frankel. She was not entirely pleased to see him. Jordan Frankel had once "passed" on her book proposal—a lifetime ago, way back in college. One never forgets a rejection, especially one that's justified.

"Brett Eigerman, just read your piece in *Verve* on Jean Harris. Good stuff!" He'd acquired a short salt-and-pepper beard and sloppy middle. He glanced at her ring finger.

"Thank you. It's Grierson now, Eigerman for writing." She touched her fingers to her hair. For this important meeting she'd had it stylishly ironed straight by George Michaels, Mad Ave's panjandrum of long tresses. "Actually, I'm having lunch with the editor of *Verve*, Kristi Hauser."

"You don't say." His bushy brows tented his eyes in the sexy hangdog way she remembered. "Smart girl, Kristi, she's writing the next chapter in magazine publishing. Tell me, what prompts women to end their names in 'i'?"

Even a little seedy and sour, Frankel was attractive, especially if a girl was up for doing a bit of rehab. Marriage sharpened your perception of men. You could view them through the clear lens of nothing-at-stake. "How's life at Doubleday?" Brett asked.

"Finito." There came a murky tale about his imprint, internal strife, a publisher "who didn't like my face"—then boiler plate about "pursuing new opportunities" and "irons in the fire." He was here—he shrugged toward the entry—about a Conde Nast startup. "I gotta tell you, I remember our lunch—what, fifteen years ago? Your dress, the color of—spicy brown mustard."

"I would have said ochre," she laughed.

"Whatever color, it was pretty dazzling." He eyed her under his tented brows. They kept looking at each other, and the air went wavy around them. "But you mustn't keep Kristi waiting"—his hand shot up. "We ought to have lunch before too long," he mumbled. New York-ese for one month north of never.

She hung in the lobby for a moment. It was a grain of sand in her eye, those pages abandoned in a drawer, her Paris Diary, or memoir, or . . . whatever. She'd left herself sitting with Allen Ginsberg at a zinc-edged table in the Café St-Michel, arrested in time like one of those eerie plaster-bandaged sculptures by George Segal.

*　　　*　　　*

Brett made a show of appearing at home in the important hum of the tall, copper-hued Pool Room of the Four Seasons. Kristi, evidently a regular, greeted friends, the only moving part in her face the mouth, endowed cartoon-like with a life of its own.

"Oh, a pathetic tale," Kristi said when Brett mentioned bumping into Jordan Frankel. "Topflight editor, one of the best. Then he has an affair with his publicist at Doubleday, gets her pregnant and refuses to leave his wife. The girl insists on having the baby. Frankel denies it's his—though he's been with this girl, apparently, for five years. Messy enough—but when the girl's the daughter of the firm's publisher? Please. Of course they had to unload Frankel." Her mouth smiled. "I dislike messes, don't you?"

Brett followed Kristi's lead and ordered the Maine lobster risotto. The moment the waiter left, Kristi leaned in:

"We'd like you to come on board *Verve* as Contributing Writer. You'd do a monthly feature on enterprising women who are setting new trends and changing the culture. We don't want to be seen as anti-male, so it's important to find the right tone. When men read about successful women they see Western civilization crumbling."

Mmhm, mmhm, Brett nodded excitedly. As Kristi went on about the types of stories that would be right for *Verve,* an impolite question came knocking.

"Well, the truth is we couldn't pay much for a while," Kristi answered. It would be something nominal at first— had she said a penny a word?—but once they turned profitable—and she had every expectation the magazine would take off, it was targeted to a growing niche—the pay would be competitive with, say, *New York.* "I know it's a bit of a gamble," said Kristi, reading Brett. "Starting a magazine is high risk, you've got to psyche yourself up. But consider it an awfully good bet, we're riding a wave and I believe we're going to be *big."* She eyed Brett shrewdly. "Think it over, it would be a full time commitment—more. I'll need to know, say, by the end of the month."

Brett left the restaurant in a state of nervous elation and headed toward Park Avenue. White tulips nodded in the center island and the spring breeze promised new beginnings. She'd agreed to weigh the offer over the next two weeks—but that was just for form's sake, a maneuver counseled ahead of time by Audrey.

Waiting for the light to change, she suddenly thought of Tom Drake. No one ever thought of Tom Drake. He was an actor who'd played the upwardly striving son of coal miners in a movie she'd seen in her youth in Flushing. His dream is to go to med school, but he gets his feet wet in the rain because he forgets his galoshes and then catches pneumonia and fails the exam. It had always spooked Brett to think how one chance event could sabotage your shot.

The light changed and she strode across Park Avenue.

Short of a Tom Drake event, the next moment was hers.

ANCIENT STARLIGHT

"Ah ha ha ha / Stayin' alive / Stayin' alive"
—the Beegees

He'd been on the phone since lunch. Julia pictured a monstrous umbilical cable snaking beneath oceans to snow-bound New York. Get me Henry, Bodie barked at the assistant he'd flown to Cancun. Okay, then get me Zaha . . . Tell her I want it yesterday . . . She's—*what? Out of the country?* You can't be serious.

Julia had recently read in the Science Section of the *New York Times* that the universe was moving farther away. And no matter what galaxy you happened to be in, all the other galaxies were moving away from you. Maybe that explained her expanding loneliness. It wasn't just life with Bodie—it was a cosmic condition. That she couldn't conjure where all these galaxies were moving to brought on a malaise that called for a double Stoli. Her watch said four hours too early.

She lay beneath a thatched umbrella on a chaise that two employees had ceremoniously draped with white towels, folding the head-level one into a pillow. They'd holed up for the week at La Maroma, a five-star resort on the Mayan Riviera that might be keeping half the Yucatan in *huaraches*, in a waterfront suite named Sian Nah—Mayan for "House of Heaven." In the lobby a parrot feathered in psychedelic teal and topaz exhorted you in a humanoid voice to pay your bill.

A new telescope, she'd read in the Science Section of *The New York Times*, detects light from the earliest stars. Although those original stars are long gone, the light from them is still traveling toward us so what the telescope's picking up is ancient starlight.

Julia watched with wry amusement her husband's style of taking a vacation. He was haggling about a lower fee with an architect who hadn't yet understood he was outclassed. Bodie could have a third career selling carpets in Istanbul's Grand Bazaar. For his latest, grandest project Bodie had recruited a roster of hotshot architects to build an original modern house on spec. A gamble, since the current taste in Islesford ran toward Olde English McMansions, with dormers and pilasters and Palladian hoo-hahs spreading across dune and sod like the pox. The developers and nabobs of finance who dominated Long Island's Gold Coast had a jones for anything resembling the restricted golf clubs and Bridesheady country seats their forebears would have approached by the Service entrance. ("Think Yiddish, build British," Bodie liked to joke.) Yet he was convinced that people with the right blend of bucks and *aspiration* would go for his one-of-a-kind modernist houses by the likes of Philip Johnson and Sir Richard Rogers—undeterred by their location on scrub-land near the aiport and a swamp that he'd bought at fire sale prices. Bodie was naming the project—God love 'im—The Houses at Lilac Close after his family's place on the "right" side of the highway.

"The standard new homes in Islesford are . . . banal. Bereft of architectural forethought."

He must be talking to the *Islesford Star*, Julia guessed, recognizing the phrase she'd given Bodie. "Thirty-five houses houses that are esthetically fresh by top designers makes this a world apart from the usual subdivision." A moment. "I think of myself as an artist, not a developer." Julia twinkled at him. Only from Bodie would this not sound pompous.

For a moment she saw herself as a dormer junking up the clean modernist lines of Bodie's "vacation." She reached for her tube of Bain de Soleil and schmeared it over her pale thighs, the scent of the apricot *geleé* conveying her back to the early days with Willem, his hard-on pushing at her Jantzen.

The Julia-and-Bodie of the 60's—had they become ancient starlight? On one thigh she noticed a delicate tracery of purple spider veins. Every time you turned around, another of age's affronts! She'd taken to plucking out white pubic hairs.

"And we'll pass out videotape clips showing the site from the driver's seat of a sports car," Bodie was saying.

Overkill, Julia signaled to her husband, waving her index finger. He sat straddling his chaise, smooth chest bare, white pants tied with a drawstring. At forty-six he was lookin' good, her husband, thanks to the tennis, and maybe a "touch up" he'd mysteriously disappeared for. Still, he appeared taken down in subtle ways like some early-stage Dorian Gray, especially his skin . . . biscuit-colored. Behind the shades his pupils, Julia knew, would be dilated; he'd be too wired to eat much dinner. The rituals of coke—the chop-chop with razor or credit cards and hoovering it up your schnoz—felt alien to Julia. Blow didn't jibe with New England pleasures, like freshly shucked Little Necks washed down with icy Tanqueray.

She grew hypnotized by a fuschia bougainvillea blossom swirled on an invisible current in their dunking pool. Checked her watch: *damn*, three and ½ hours until her first transfusion, hold the ice. Even in a five-star you couldn't risk ice. She pictured the bar, where it would be dark and cool and they'd be playing the Beegees. When had she started trying to move minutes? She remembered getting knocked out for a D & C during the infertility workup, how she semi-enjoyed the whoosh into nothingness.

Those early years with Bodie the fun never stopped. There were trips to Paris to see "Sam" Beckett and lovely times at the Hotel des Ecoles in the Latin Quarter, three pink houses with the air of a country inn, and a garden where in fine weather they took their *bols de café* with *tartines*. There were backers' auditions to raise money for plays. Bodie almost always deferred to her judgment; she figured among the city's "taste-makers." They filled the loft on Greene Street with a Who's Who of people in the arts, media, finance. The money men needed artists to goldplate their greed with a patina of culture; the artists needed patrons. Julia preferred, to think of her evenings as latter-day *salons, a la* Gertrude Stein. People flocked to Greene Street drawn by her and Bodie, their brilliance and connections and largesse. With their double threat alliance they'd invented the power couple before it had a name. Julia's career as a photographer—and what a soul-sapping slog—lay far behind. Her medium was marriage to Bodie Curtiz.

Perhaps the razzle dazzle faded when Bodie shifted from theater to real estate. He'd started with Soho, carving its original cast-iron housing stock into trendy lofts. Then he turned to scavenging through failed savings and loans for cheap properties around Beverly Hills, churning out huge profits. Theater, Julia surmised, had continually rubbed his nose in the ghostly leavings of Nina, a name pronounced only when they were completely sozzled.

Julia realigned her own interests. She traveled with Bodie and a group of architects to Dakar, Senegal, where he was investing in a planned "garden city" that would resemble the town of Portofino, Italy. They explored the water-besotted region of Saint Louis, where the owner of the funky *auberge* was still laundering their sheets when they arrived, and they woke to early love and the sound of cocks crowing. The lakes and mangroves and Baobabs, the appearance of a purple heron, goats roaming free in the streets—Saint Louis ignited Julia's old ambitions. She shot fifty rolls of film.

An evening on Greene Street to show her slides. When the lights came up, she was mortified see half the guests had dozed off.

"I mean, all those goats in the streets—you can only look at so many goats," Audrey said.

"But it's about the work, the way this shot is framed."

"Of course—but other people's trips are a bore except to themselves. Why not go back to those photos you used to do? The freaky ones of you coming out of the woodwork naked?"

"I'm more interested now in capturing the world outside myself."

Then Julia was off with Bodie to St. Petersburg, borne on the wave of his latest enthusiasm: the Russian wooden churches on the nearby island of Kizhi. She mounted a slide-show in the loft of the haunting, fantastical structures shot in every light, including the silver of an oncoming storm. "These onion shaped domes symbolize heaven in the Russian Orthodox tradition, and were constructed with wooden shingles—just imagine—without using a single nail!"

A few heads swiveled to glance up at a buffet with champagne goblets and *petits fours*. Julia's gaze landed on Audrey's boyfriend Hugo. His nostrils frilled as he aborted a monster yawn.

Julia tobogganed into depression. Her photos—which had once provoked—now put people to sleep. She brooded, feet curled beneath her, on the celadon velvet sofa in the loft's cozy inner library. Face it, she was just a dilettante and gussied-up consort mirroring her husband's interests—precisely what she and the friends once vowed at Foxleigh never to become! *Heavy with useless experience*—the line hung there like fleecy sky-writing. From a high shelf she pried loose the book by Adrienne Rich.

> You, once a belle in Shreveport
> Your mind now, moldering like wedding-cake,
> heavy with useless experience . . .
> In the prime of your life.

Julia poured herself a curtain-raiser of dry vermouth. There was plenty of money now from Bodie's real estate deals; better to be moldering and useless while sipping Brut Champagne in first class than getting the bends in coach. "You've got 'uptown problems,' when you think of most people's mean, scrimpy lives," Brett said.

But Bodie's dough seemed to come at a price. Julia had caught the rumors, of course, about her husband's less than kosher dealings. Like her women friends, she considered business something that only men did and even appeared to find interesting. She occasionally glanced at letters to shareholders and annual reports on Bodie's desk, with the graphs and six-month total returns; the column of ratios to average net assets. God bless him for dealing with such things! She also wondered if all business, not just Bodie's, didn't kind of blur the line between legal and less legal. She thought about the Vosburghs; the fuzzy stories she'd picked up about grand-dad, who was such an old dear, and how he'd worked for a firm that acted as a U.S. base for Germans who helped finance the Nazis—stories she hoped were more innuendo than fact. As Balzac had said, "Behind every great fortune lies a great crime." With Bodie she found it prudent to see, hear, know very little. And then . . . the unthinkable.

It was the height of the Season at Islesford, with its big ticket benefits and horse shows and muscular social striving. So different from creaky old Marion and its ramshackle club-house and Laser/Sunfish Regatta and *lack* of striving since where you'd landed at birth was exactly where you needed to be. She and Bodie were throwing a small dinner in their house in Islesford on Millstone Drive. For some time, he'd been super-harried, aborting conversations when she entered a room, conferring with associates late into the night. This evening, even with a tableful of dinner guests, he remained glued to the phone in his study. "Be there in a sec, darlin,'" he repeated, waving Julia away.

He finally came into the dining room, the wide smile laminated on his face, as the *tarte tatin* was being served. Leland Phillips, his sideman—unkindly known as "Bodie's schlepper"—cut him a questioning look. That Julia inter-cepted. Bodie's smile hadn't budged. A cool wet nose nudged her ankle. Julia lifted her Dachshund Min onto her lap, felt her little beating heart between her hands. She breathed in the lovely nutty scent of Min's chestnut coat.

The following week Bodie told Julia he was going to Singapore. Building was booming in Singapore, they were pioneering a neo-tropical style, and he wanted to explore a casino project there. It would be a longish trip, he alerted her. His amber eyes looked opaque as when he was trying to hornswoggle a contractor.

Julia tucked her right fist under her armpit in a way she had. "Tell me what's really going on."

"I *am* telling you."

"You're not fucking going to Singapore."

Five o'clock and the late summer light through trees dappled the burnt sienna wall of Bodie's study. He ran his hand through his hair. She'd never seen him so deflated; she wanted to shelter him from whatever idiocy he'd stumbled into.

"Julia"—turning his face away—"trust me, there are things you don't need to know. I'm just . . . going to be away for a while, let's leave it at that."

"I may not *need* to know but I want to know. I'm your wife, dammit." She walked to the window and looked at her Montauk daisies on the rise out back. Spun around to face him. "Bodie, whatever it is, I don't judge you."

"It" came out, finally, the story of a "tangled deal" some time back involving land in Quogue. He'd been accused of making false statements to federal regulators. His lawyers had unsuccessfully fought the charges—without merit, Bodie insisted—and he was going to be spending twenty-seven days . . . "out of town," he said, not meeting her eyes.

Julia blinked back tears; crouched to caress her three Dachshunds, milling about her ankles. Their seal-like sleekness. How ignoble to pity her*self*, when she ought to be closing ranks with her husband. She rose and straightened her shoulders. "Lovey, since I'm not going to be seeing you for a month, let's go out tonight and have a great dinner. We'll go to Harborside and order champagne and lobster."

Julia fended off inquiries from Mother about Bodie's latest travels. To friends she rattled on brightly about Bodie's neo-tropical casino and Singapore, "a wonder created out of a tear drop," and Singapore's spectacular ascent from third world to first world status, no natural resources except its small population and excellent geographical location—why, it was a socialist economy that worked!

Word got around anyway—Bodie never lacked for enemies—that "Singapore" was in fact the rather less exotic minimum security Federal Correctional Institution in Loretto, Pennsylvania.

JOBEROO

"There is only the trying.
The rest is not our business."
—T.S. Eliot

"You'll never guess what. Bet you dollars to dough-nuts." His eyes unanchored and glassy.

"Tommy, not now, I've got to talk to you."

"I quit the old joberoo."

"You *what?*"

"You heard me, I quit—"

"Wait, I thought you were in line for Deputy Commis-sioner of, uh—"

"You don't even know what I was in line *for*, do you?" He folded onto the flame-stitch Queen Anne chair, legs akimbo. "That job didn't work out, and anyway, it would have been the same old bullshit. Holding out a tin cup, fan-cier title."

"Oh, Tommy I'm so sorry—I'm sure something else will turn up—something better. But the timing's really bad. I had lunch today with Kristi Hauser—at the Four Sea-sons—and she offered me a job to write full time for *Verve.*"

"Great! You're better off at *Verve* than that dumping ground for welfare cheats—"

"Don't start with that . . . listen to me. *Verve* wouldn't

pay much at first, maybe no money to start, and I'd be quitting O'Dwyer and . . . if you're not working, how we gonna manage?"

"Actually, I will be working. Jus' signed on with an outfitter to lead trips to the Asmats in New Guinea."

"Oh Tommy, be serious."

"It's challenging, I know, but our customized trips make it safe to explore the islands that time forgot."

She stared at him in horror. "Are you smashed or something?"

"Oh, there you go," a phrase that always flipped her switch.

"What about *us*, your family?"

He looked confounded by the question. "What *about* it? Contract's only for a month. Though I'm hoping to spin this into other gigs for collectors of Asmat carvings . . ."

"Tommy, have you totally lost it?"

"I've just *found* it—found the life I want."

"You can't just split, you can't."

"I'll never give up my kids," he said stoutly. "Especially since you're so busy busy—"

She started to cry.

"Now you can see . . . Cha cha cha," he sneered. "Face it, you never wanted to be married to me in the first place. You've ohl-wiz had one foot out."

Carry on alone with two children? A seam opened in the floor. "I want to keep our family together. Tell me what I can do." She'd grovel, she'd do anything to keep her family.

His eyes focused wide of her. "There's nothing you can do. It was a mistake from the start, it's ohl-wiz been wrong—"

A presence, then, like an intake of breath. In the entrance to the living room a small figure in jammies with blonde angel hair clutching Andy bear.

Later that week, Brett, who had not been "doing well," received a phone call informing her that Tommy Jr. hadn't shown up for school that morning. Her heart seized up and she went straight to: *Etan Patz.*

It had happened two years ago, 1979, yet parents in New York were still freaked about Etan Patz. Six-year-old Etan Patz had walked one morning two blocks to his bus stop in Soho and gotten swallowed by something monstrous and evil at large in the city.

"Redaline, where is Redaline, Tommy's sitter?"

"Calm down, Mrs. Grierson." The woman from school is saying, "I'm sure there's some explanation. No, we haven't seen the sitter either."

Brett phones the police. Standing there in the kitchen, phone wobbling in her hand, she makes a mother's deal with God. She dresses Bella and slings a raincoat over her nightgown—since Tommy split, she's taken to sleeping in, setting Bella up with coloring books and crayolas in her bedroom. Before she can lock up, the phone again.

"Brett, it's all right, everything's going to be all right. You must be beside yourself, but little Tommy's been with Mother, and now he's here on Greene Street with me and everything's fine. Hop a cab down and I'll explain."

Brett can't flog the cab on fast enough through New York's rush hour, cursing every UPS truck, driver from Jersey, and a minibus for the disabled. "Hey, lady"—the driver eyes her in the rear-view—"you in a hurry, you can take another cab." Through the rain-pocked window the trees with their white spring blossoms inch by.

Brett finds Tommy astride the antique horse Bodie bought from some French carousel. She swoops down and crushes him against her. Bella wants to climb on the horsie but Tommy calls her "silly little girl" and she starts to bawl, and just the normalcy of kids fighting makes Brett want to bawl with happiness. She distracts Bella with the coloring book and crayolas she somehow thought to bring.

"Call it a failed kidnapping," Julia starts, when they're out of earshot in the library. "Tommy intercepted the sitter at the bus stop near the school, and told her he'd arranged with you to spend the day with his son. He's sly, Tommy is. Then Tommy takes him to his godfather Archie's place in Turtle Bay—empty, because Archie's in Kenya. And through the sheerest luck, the guardian angel of children, I'm convinced,

Mother stopped by Archie's place to see to some ceiling leak she was meant to check on. She spots Tommy in the hall with Tommy Jr. and confronts him . . . Cee can be *ferocious*. She managed to get out of him that he planned to whisk little Tommy off to Port Moresby, in Papua New Guinea for Chrissake. He'd actually researched the schools there run by the U.N.! Right there in the hall Cee gave Tommy the what-for and informed him that children not only belong with their mother—any judge would deem him mentally unstable for wanting to take his child to a place with malaria and typhoid without proper vaccinations. And of course his 'ridiculous little caper,' she called it, would *kill* old Archie—imagine if the tabloids got hold of the story! Didn't the family have *enough* skeletons? And just like that—Tommy caved. Maybe he was relieved. So . . . here we all are. Cee has redeemed herself. It's amazing, I never thought I'd say anything remotely positive about my mother."

That evening Redaline phoned Brett to say that her fiancé would be joining her in the States after all, and she no longer wanted to work for Brett and Monsieur Grierson, *une famille pas du tout comme il faut*, and in any event, she wanted her own room and TV.

Brett felt ripe for a breakdown.

She decided she'd give it a pass. Breakdown was the way to go if you could have it at McLean's like Lyndy DeGroff. Not some snakepit like Bellevue or Long Island's Pilgrim State where Allen Ginsberg's mother had been lobotomized. Bottom line, once a mother, you can check your breakdown rights at the door.

She sat with a yellow number two pencil and yellow legal pad at the little antique desk in the living room and ran numbers. Hire an English-speaking nanny with references and you could forget about money for food and rent. It was back to the classifieds in *Haiti Liberte*, and good luck and good night. Another certainty: she'd be a fool to count on Tommy for support checks from the land that time forgot. To care for the children she needed to nail tenure at O'Dwyer, kiss asses, write papers of interest to three people in East Jesus, ramp up the old teacher-student rapport. No more dialing it in between magazine gigs.

Kristi Hauser was relieved when Brett phoned to say she would not be accepting the job at *Verve*. She'd picked up gossip about Brett's deserter husband and a troubled child etc. Kristi had zero tolerance for domestic messes and unstrung ex-wives. Women writers would kill for the job on *Verve*, she needed to staff up, and lack of talent in New York had never been a problem.

Brett became known as a fierce disciplinarian around her new neighborhood, largely Dominican, in Washington Heights. She marched her kids around, barking orders at Tommy Jr. and Bella like the Marine Gunnery Sergeant from *An Officer and a Gentleman*. In the A & P they followed her down the aisle, solemn and pale, arms linked like a miniature couple. Instinctively, they knew to protect the one person who protected them. People mistook Brett for the big sister. The support checks from Tommy slowed to a trickle; she heard that the gig in New Guinea hadn't worked out. Oddly, it pained Brett, the thought of Tommy broke. He had such a flair for the good life.

With no money for sitters, they went everywhere together: adult parties (where the kids read *Tintin* on a mountain of coats in the bedroom). Rambles in the Palisades— "pick up the pace, goils," Tommy would call behind him. The occasional movie—*Saturday Night Fever* had traumatized him for life, Tommy would confess, laughing, over one college break. A restaurant where The Boyfriend allowed them—their eyes saucer-wide—to order a *second shrimp cocktail*. The Boyfriend was a constant, if transient, figure of the Grierson household, and tended not to stay long. He would check out Bella perched on the sofa in her jammies, silent and fuzzy-haired, reading *Five Little Peppers and How They Grew*, which she'd fished from a garbage pail on Dyckman Street—and sing the I-don't-think-so Halleluja chorus. One boyfriend called to say thank you. "Spending time with you and the kids made me realize I want a real family of my own."

Brett thought sometimes of Allen Ginsberg, now liver-lipped and one eye at half-mast, who, after his reading at PEN, didn't recognize her or pretended not to, and she thought of Rinko, now a supernova on the world stage, and she thought of the good times with Tommy, and drinking bullshots on the *Kookaburra*, and her babies getting born, and she could hardly conceive how she'd gotten from there to here.

The coldest night of the year, and they've ducked into the Lion's Den in the Village, following a smoky party with wall to ceiling books. They order the special: roast pork with gooseberries. The children's bright eyes and burnished cheeks. Abruptly it comes to Brett that she can imagine nothing better than the three of them sitting here together, eating roast pork with gooseberries, and she thinks, *this is happiness, I'm so happy.* She's rich in love, love that's effortless and buoyant, far from the roil of romance, striking heart notes from a different register. Setting aside the vast separate galaxy of romance, the world of Tommy and Bella and her feels complete—an insight she takes care, over the years, not to burden them with.

The following October when Brett came up for tenure, CUNY was walloped by yet another financial crisis. "Painful" choices had to be made—painful, that is, to those not making them—and the Board of Higher Ed decided to shut down such "under-performers" as O'Dwyer College. Brett returned to cobbling together a non-living wage as one of the CUNY's famously exploited adjuncts, crisscrossing the boroughs to three different colleges. Changing times have a way of dispatching even the best of ideas to obsolescence. Though *Verve* had once filled a niche to perfection, a feminist publication targeting professional women who spent their own money was now considered, well, beside the point, even faintly embarrassing. Five years after its founding, *Verve*, losing advertising to *Vogue* and *New York*, ceased to publish.

WORKUP

When Bodie eventually netted $8.4 million on the transaction that had landed him in "Singapore" Julia didn't know whether to laugh or scream. She honored her promise not to judge him. Yes, she often felt pushed to the periphery of his life, yet the whole package of Bodie—his energy and flamboyance . . . even shadiness—continued to enchant her. He loved her back, could she doubt it? For her 35th he'd thrown her the party at Tavern on the Green, rounding up childhood friends from Marion. "To my beautiful wife," he began his toast. An ovarian cyst sent her one dark dawn to St. Vincents, and Bodie all but took over a hospital wing. He set up his office in her hospital room; hectored doctors and nurses about his wife's care; ordered a case of Dom Perignon to serve visitors; fussed and buried his nose in her neck; slept in her room on a cot. Bodie Curtiz, it was plain, adored his wife.

But over the years what she privately named the *lacunae* had widened. Especially after the baby business.

She'd miscarried soon after the wedding. They both confessed to feeling relieved; way too soon to have children. But at odd moments, off camera, Julia mourned. It would have been a boy.

Then in her thirties Julia went off the pill. Nuthin' doin.' Julia feared she and Bodie might be too selfish to make children, their bodies knowing something they didn't. She contracted baby lust. She wanted to pad around belly first, steering herself like a bus, hands supporting her back the way she'd seen Brett and Lyndy do in the third trimester. She could see this mini Julia-and-Bodie, his little face fully formed like Renaissance painters portrayed the infant Jesus. Each period was an accusation, a mark of personal failure. Maybe God was punishing her for those trips during college to Havana and Dr. Spencer's in Pennsylvania.

Her gyn doc prescribed an infertility workup. Julia was thirty-seven and the window narrowing.

Cautiously, she broached the topic with Bodie. "Oh Jule, I don't know," he said, pacing the loft's sunken living room. "I mean, you and I take up a lot of space."

"We'll turn my studio into a bedroom."

"Jule, don't be obtuse, I wasn't talking that kind of space. Aren't things wonderful as they are? Why change anything? Darlin,' I don't want to share you."

"There'd be more of me to go around," she laughed. "Just think, we'd have a little 'us.'"

He stood legs crossed at the ankle of his bell bottoms, back to the night window. Behind his squarish face a black pane across the street abruptly bloomed yellow, and from where she sat on the new leather Italian sofa Julia could make out a solitary woman bending to some task.

"What's this 'workup' thing anyway?" Like most men Bodie was ignorant of female physiology and skittish about things medical.

She bumbled around trying to explain ovulation, the basal temperature charts she'd need to keep to detect its arrival. "The workup's a two-way 'thing, y'know. It might not be *my* problem." Ignoring his affronted look. "Remember Aura Folkenflik? Her husband's sperm swam crooked because he'd smoked so much dope, and they had to use a turkey baster." She explained about sperm counts and what Bodie would be expected to do.

"I think not," he said haughtily. "Somehow I don't see myself in the waiting room of a masturbatorium."

"Well, it's not *elegant*, but you focus on the end game."

"Paging through stained porn rags in a cubicle? How

does some Jewish fertility doc whose mother forced him to go to medical school ascertain what would turn me on?"

"Now we're getting anti-Semitic? And it's infertility."

"Look, if it doesn't just . . . happen, maybe it wasn't meant to be."

"Bodie, we're friends in this. Why you coming on like a Neanderthal?" They could explore other routes, Julia went on, having studied the brochures from the doctor's office. Like monitoring cervical mucous to predict ovulation.

"*Mucous?*"

"Oh don't be childish. You take a sample of cervical secretions and stretch it between two fingers to test for the right consistency. During the peak time it's cloudy and slightly stretchy, and the best time to have sex. The sperm can survive for up to seventy-two—"

She broke off—at his expression of horror. No, disgust.

A phrase leaped out from a novel: he loves pussy. To judge by Bodie, the "he" in that novel formed a special male subset. Early on she'd sensed that for Bodie certain intimacies were more duty than pleasure. She would hang on the edge, almost there . . . almost. But sensing his impatience, as if he were sentenced to hard labor, it froze her soul. Julia would think of Elliott, who could play her in maddeningly delicious ways, got turned on by *her* excitement, his power— the whole lovely complicitous dance. It got so that on the rare occasions when Bodie slid south she would bat him away and pull him upwards, he would come too fast, then get angry she wouldn't let him go down on her, she fearing he was too finicky to go mucking around among their fluids . . . Oh, they'd become a disaster area in bed.

"—I mean, if you have to start stretching . . . mucous," Bodie was saying, "if it comes to turning ourselves into hospital labs . . . no, no no."

Julia tucked a fist into her armpit. "It's me, my whole body."

"You just said it could be me as well," he said generously.

"I mean I'm repulsive to you. You should see your face."

"That's insane! I just hate the way everything gets so medicalized and clinical in America. They've taken out the joy." The phone pealed in the study but for once he ignored it. He sat beside her on the sofa and raised the back of her hand to his lips. "I adore you. How do you *get* these ideas?"

The phone started up again and then Bodie was sucked back into work, problem with a contractor in Mendham, New Jersey. He eventually agreed to follow the temperature chart. She imagined he operated like this in business—both signing on and reneging. Desire on demand, as Bodie jokingly called it, did their sex life no favors—and failed to get Julia pregnant. Now in the bedroom on Millstone Drive they slept in a California King so vast they might inhabit different time zones. When she voyaged across the tundra in the dead of night toward Bodie's warm back, he would capture her venturesome hand and tuck it companionably against his chest, murmuring about an early appointment. "With us it's always the husband has the headache," Julia griped to Brett.

Very occasionally there were alcohol-laced encounters—in the pool house on Millstone which contained beach gear and a bathroom. The place had become an unlikely erotic magnet. They'd baptized the move to Millstone with a hot session on the pool house's mildewed striped float, doing it doggy style the way Bodie liked. The smell of sun-dried canvas and fishy tackle evoked for Julia the summer boys of her youth. Lately Julia sometimes sneaked off to the pool house where no one could hear the vibrator—women all had them now—which sounded like Uncle Archie's Boston Whaler. She'd once felt that "companionate love" (as Brett had called it in an article) plus a crammed calendar could mask the lacunae. Might as well cover a tiger trap with straw. What a waste of herself, she was made for love. It was too perverse, a white marriage with so appetizing a mate. And what was *he* doing for sex, this mate?

"Maybe Bodie's just not a very sexual person," Brett said, "he could have low testosterone." She neglected to mention how, one boozy night at the Hotel Earle off Washington Square—a Foxleigh annex—she'd come by this judgment.

To "dock" her randiness—the way breeders clipped dogs' tails—Julia took to climbing the tall bluffs on the beach down the road from Lilac Close, then hiking miles along the ocean. Walking by the "gay" section one afternoon, she spotted a sculpted body that belonged to a landscaper friend of Bodie's. Bulging out of his blue Speedo.

Of course she'd picked up the innuendos about Leland, long enamored of Bodie—who treated him like a water carrier. Julia stopped to watch a sandpiper skitter shoreward, its tiny feet eluding the lip of the wave by a hair. Did Bodie dig men? She'd picked up no sign of it. Nothing effeminate about him. The one thing, there had been that . . . hallucination. A lifetime ago—Gentian Court, 1963—the night before her wedding . . .

In the bedroom at Gentian Court she'd snapped awake, dry-mouthed and jumpy, setting up for a monster hangover at her own wedding. The moon cast a silver pane over the empty sheets on Bodie's side. He wasn't in the loo either. If he was stewing over their little sexual fiasco, she must find him and reassure him. She pulled on his pink cashmere Shetland over her nightgown. The sky bowled back high and black, Jupiter pinned like a diamond brooch below the moon. She stepped around the gentians now folded for the night. Had she heard voices? Instinctively, she melted into the shadow against the solarium. The voices came louder. Julia peered around the wall. Two figures were coming along Upper Cliff Path, silvered by moonlight. Too far to see details, yet these figures with little purchase on the solid world spoke of intimacy. The shorter one, fair-haired, shifted to point at the Orkney Light—and the taller man stood revealed. Julia's eye flew to the red sneakers. She pressed her fingers to her breastbone, inclining like a diva receiving an homage. The pair headed down grassy steps to Lower Cliff Path, their bodies sinking, heads riding above the bayberry till they vanished. The night reclaimed its mighty solitude and Julia swayed in place, uncertain the pair had passed this way. Back in the bedroom Bodie lay snoring on his side.

Ginned up Djinns, Julia thought, as she drove back to Millstone in the falling light. Or did dreams know better? When she was growing up everyone sniggered over "fairies" and "homos." She herself had always felt the sensual pursuits, in whatever package they came, were all good. God's gift to humans. It was different, though, for the guys. Bodie and friends had been terrorized by that shrink Charles Socarides, a bogey man who'd darkened their college years, and made a career of "curing" homosexuals. She suspected the guys had never gotten over it. They might eye The Mineshaft on Washington Street, and Rawhide and the other "leather bars" along the West Side Drive through the windows of their Beemers—but they would drive right on by.

At Millstone Drive Julia fixed herself a double Chivas Regal and sat on the sofa in the emptied day with her feet tucked under her, not bothering with lights. She could hang out at a lesbian bar. But she didn't even like to touch her*self,* much less another woman. She could become a housewife hooker, like Catherine Deneuve in that movie *Belle de Jour.* Maybe she could apply for the white glove prostitution ring of Xaviera Hollander, the Madam who'd written *The Happy Hooker.* Slot sex into her routine, like flossing. Trouble was, with all the feminist hoopla about equal opportunity in the sack, sex as sport failed to interest her. She wasn't into the new freedoms. She'd done the new freedoms fifteen years ago.

ROAD SIGN

"The fifties was the bad decade."
—Gore Vidal

August 1979, Islesford

That day the heat spiked at ninety-eight. At dusk it still weighed on the land like a Biblical scourge. From the fields off Millstone Drive drifted the baneful smell of Temik, the liquid pesticide sprayed on potato crops to kill parasitic nematodes. Temik was Islesford's signature August scent, its late-summer logo. Local environmental groups were fighting to ban the stuff, which seeped into groundwater and caused cancer and birth defects. Apparently it was indestructible.

Julia unstuck herself from her pool-side chaise and headed for the house to help Blanca bring out the frozen daiquiris, olives, and smoked tuna pâté. In her forties she still resembled a Burne-Jones beauty, crimped henna hair now paled by threads of silver. She wore a red-and-white shift by Marimekko, a designer now out of style, except among fashion-averse wives of academics around Harvard Square.

She wrestled with the sliding screen door, jamming as always in its groove. It struck Julia that long after their little dramas on Millstone Drive had played out, the Temik would live on.

Rum and tuna pâté seemed to revive the house guests. Leland Phillips, permanent fixture in Bodie's entourage. Tip DeGroff, on leave from Lyndy, who was getting her medication tweaked at McLean's. Audrey's Hugo, bunking in at Millstone while Audrey was on the coast promoting her new novel (a squirrels' nest had started a fire in the attic of Lilac Close, and Alex was supervising repairs). They formed the sort of handsome group who, glimpsed in a restaurant, make other diners feel they've chosen the right place.

Toward six, there was a general movement to dress and drive to an art opening at the Vera Tang Gallery in Islesford. Julia chose to stay behind with her three Dachshunds, who lay panting, their little bellies working, in the shade of the veranda. Hugo looked too sozzled to join the others. She'd never warmed to this man who'd fattened his career on Audrey's connections.

His Cookalong show was going "like gangbusters" he announced from his chaise. "Next up, while I'm dicing and slicing at my on-set counter, I'm gonna interview celebrities. A-list movie stars and world leaders!"

Julia wondered how long Audrey would remain part of the equation. A lady bug alighted on a red orb of her Marimekko.

"Care for a top-off?" Hugo hoisted the Mount Gay Special Reserve from a glass table. She waved her hand no and he freshened his drink. Behind her shades Julia pretended to doze but Hugo chose to remain oblivious. "Y'know, in the beginning everyone knocked Bodie and the Houses at Lilac Close. The deep pockets don't go for cutting edge design, they want the fuckin' Cotswolds yadda yadda. But now's all"—his words slurred—"falling into place. The man's got vision."

Julia only half-listened. The past weekend she and Bodie had fetched up loaded at the pool house among the kayaks. It had not been a success. A sentence kept recycling in her head like a trapped musical phrase. During a garden tour in Islesford, somewhere by the box woods, she'd caught the tail end of a conversation. A landscape designer saying, *he's our little discovery*. The "he" pointed any number of ways.

It occurred to Julia that Hugo had been warming up to share something she might not enjoy hearing.

"Hell, I shouldn't say this."

Shit. "C'mon, the things you shouldn't say are usually the most worth hearing."

"No, really . . . I shouldn't . . ."

Julia waited. The lady bug lifted its carapace to display translucent fairy wings and resettled from a red to a white orb of her shift.

"So, Tip told me Bodie's been sorta walking in on him."

Julia snapped mega awake. She eyed Hugo, his face of a dissolute cherub. "Heavens. What do you mean?"

"You know, when Tip's changing or about to take a shower. To cop a look."

"He must be misinterpreting. Tip's a bit of a peacock, don't you think?"

Hugo topped off his glass again. "I dunno, the man's going around saying he's not sure what team Bodie is playing for."

Julia was slow to parse the expression, then her mind took several sharp turns.

"Jeez, the husband of your oldest friend, your *house guest* for Chrissake, and he's spreading rumors! Another thing—well, maybe I shouldn't be telling you this." Hugo had swung around to face her, legs akimbo. Pale curls sprouted on his inner thighs.

"Oh, why don't you anyway?" Shifting onto her side and imprisoning her arm. Careful to keep her tone offhand, as if fearing to scare off a cardinal from the bird-feeder. She wanted to be very careful not to scare him off.

"Well, no harm meant, but a person who shall remain nameless spotted Bodie at Studio 54 and, well . . . you do know about the 'VIP basement'"—Julia's heart was banging around like a rat in a garbage pail—"where the busboys give blowjobs—?"

At the car door's slam she bucked in her chair. The guests stepped through the heat like walkers on the moon. *A bitch to find parking . . . All the day trippers . . . That was Islesford in the summer for ya'* . . . "You made the right call," someone said at Julia.

She thought she might be ill. She pictured tiny Icarus in Breugel's painting, plummeting seaward, a city of souls oblivious.

Bodie came round and kneeled by her chaise and kissed her between the breasts. "How's my beautiful wife? Look who I brought back, darlin.'" Julia nodded distracted hellos at Bodie's on-site engineer for The Houses . . . A Polish builder . . . Vera Tang's husband Simon.

Bodie sauntered into the house to organize a new batch of daiquiris.

Julia pulled her Marimekko over her head and walked over slate still hoarding sun to the pool. The water felt not much cooler than the air, its liquid dimension. She submerged in the shallow end and observed her guests behind slitted crocodile eyes. Would Bodie be so brazen right under her nose? She studied the guests like suspects in an Agatha Christie house mystery. "Need a jazzier prospectus for the Houses," Bodie was telling the engineer. You couldn't be an engineer and into men. Leland too old a story. Scratch Tip DeGroff—he'd be happy, if she gave the sign, to run off with *her*. Was he spreading rumors about Bodie to pave the way? No, Tip too New England for such duplicity.

Leland Phillips had collared her once, at the 40th birthday bash Bodie had thrown her at The Water Club. *"You're making it work, aren't you."* How could she have let that pass?

You had to know when two people were making it. It would not get by her, she had the sex IQ of Einstein. Desire had an afterlife like the Temik in the potato fields. There would escape a spritz of lust, a gesture held in check. There would be a polish to the cheeks. A display of *not* looking at each other, as subtle as a clown act.

Julia slowly breast-stroked the length of the pool, then back. Hugo had fallen asleep, head back, mouth agape. Why, when men dozed off, did they look dead? Bodie, barefoot in loose linen pants, appeared immune to the heat, blabbing with the builder now, topping off drinks, the creaky laugh, smile stretching ear to ear. The perfect host! Well, almost.

He was blond, gym-buffed, generically handsome. Cock angled diagonally under his tight white jeans like an occult road sign. Remote and dreaming toward the fields, not quite of the party. A married man, Simon. Which said little. She should know.

Julia sank. Hair fanned about her like the wings of a manta ray. She'd known, in some fashion, in the phantom way you know one day you'll die. There were degrees of knowing, apparently. You could know without naming it, deny it full citizenship, and that way you never had to deal with it. She surfaced, blowing out water.

"Any cooler in there, darlin'?' Bodie called. "Julia's a water animal," he said.

She dove back down. The good news: she was exonerated from disgustingness. It wasn't *her*. She stroked under water to the pool's far end, surfaced with a snort. In fact, her husband adored her—in whatever part of him that didn't involve fucking. That ghostly couple at Gentian Court on her wedding eve—maybe no mirage? Why they'd been all around her, Bodie's—she shied away from words—*pansies*, fairies, fuck it all, cycling through. Leland was likely a discard. *He's our little discovery.* You bet he is. People must be having a good laugh at her expense.

Julia climbed from the pool and headed barefoot over the tepid slate toward the house. *There are things you don't need to know*, Bodie had once said. You bet there are.

"Oh, Jule, did I tell you?" he called. "I made a rez at Harborside for eight." Julia kept moving toward the veranda and slid the screen door half open. As usual it stuck. "Darlin'? Need some help?" With a violent motion, she rammed the door from its track so it hung sideways like a broken wing. "Oh dear, time for a little wife-comforting," Bodie said.

Out on Greene Street she finds herself unable to hail a cab and then can't get *into* the cab or the window down or think where to go in the cab. August, no one in town. "Just drive around," she says. The cabbie fixes her in the rear view mirror: "What you say, lady?" "Just go downtown to Battery Park." She wants to put her fingers in Bodie's eyes, break his teeth. "Or uptown, go uptown. And *then* downtown." She curls into fetal position on the seat. The cabbie thinks, *carajo*, another *loca*.

Simon. Merely a legible name scrawled on a palimpsest over a shadowy swarm.

He stands watching her stuff clothes into a Vuitton bag. Deaf to her insults, all vile. "Be sensible, Jule, we can move beyond this."

"Why don't you go fucking live with Simon?"

"Because I want to live with *you*. Why can't you understand that?" He's exasperated, as if she lacks some radical failure of comprehension. "When did you get so parochial and small- minded?"

"You've stolen my time—years, hours, minutes."

"We're happy. You know we've been happy."

"You, undoubtedly."

"*And* you. That morning in Saint-Louis in Senegal—"

"I want a divorce."

"Oh, I'll never agree to that," he says gravely.

"You'll—*what*? You're not even my husband, not in any way that counts."

"Lots of things count. I love you counts."

"Love me how? What does it *mean* the way you love? Using me as a cover while you cat around? Why don't you drop the charade and live your real life?"

"My real life is you. I adore you. Why must everyone fit a one-size-fits-all?"

"Oh, fuck off."

He was crying. Now what. You don't measure up as a man, she was about to say.

Labor Day at Lilac Close. From the marshland an electric thrum presaged autumn. They sat on the terrace out back, "just us chickens," doing damage to an Entemann's Crumb Coffee Cake and sipping Jamaican coffee from white diner-style mugs Audrey had bought at a yard sale.

Brett's Tommy and Bella playing in the tree house, Hugo working his deltoids at Fitness East.

"We were so goddamn sophisticated, Bodie and me."

Julia's eyes welled. "God, I hate sophistication." She pulled her green bathrobe close. A crow hopped toward them over the brick and paused on one leg, brown eye in its glossy black head weighing danger versus the lure of a sugared crumb.

"Something Asher once told me," Audrey said. "Twenty years into a happy marriage the sex is for shit anyway. Incestuous. Like shaking hands with yourself."

"The thing is Bodie needs you emotionally, but physically he digs men," Brett said.

"My husband also on occasion digs *me*. I'm kind of a warm up for the main course, an *amuse bouche*."

"As Woody Allen said, being bisexual doubles your chances for a date on Saturday night."

Audrey made a moue at Brett. "I don't get it, it's almost 1980, we're not in Kansas City any more. Bodie's always danced to his own tune, since we were kids, staging plays when the other boys were in Little League. Why hasn't he just come out?"

"Because he was born when he was," Brett said. "He's been imprinted to lead a double life. Allen Ginsberg told me that for years he thought homosexuality was a disease he could conquer. I mean, there's still some goddamn thing called 'gay conversion therapy.'"

Julia said, "Bodie's a law unto himself. He says *Yes!* to everything: marriage, sex with men, gay, bi—Yes! We're allowed to do it all! Ain't it grand?" A dry sob escaped. "Just think, ten years from now there won't be any more women married to gay men and wondering why they drink in the afternoon and what's wrong with them that they're so undesired. We'll be obsolete, like the milk man from my childhood. God, remember milk men?"

"I'm afraid so. How about Charles Atlas and the 97-pound weakling?"

"*The Good Wife's Guide.*"

"*The Amboy Dukes.*"

"What would I do without you guys?" Julia said. "Thank God for you both." She held out a clump of crumbs to the Dachshunds. Wily Min scarfed most of it. "Bottom line, we're not a true couple, Bodie and me."

"The hell of it is you *are*," Brett said.

*   *   *

"Oh Jule, what a cliché to run home to Mummy."

"This is not about style, Bodie. Don't make me hang up on you. Okay, I'm going to hang up now."

A call from Tip DeGroff proposing an evening of solace came as no surprise. Digger Osborn, her former somewhat fiancé, now divorced, surfaced to invite her to lunch. Julia screamed at Mother, whom she suspected had alerted him. Bodie, they said, was drinking, and worse. He totaled the yellow BMW on the highway service road to Islesford. An attention-getting device, Julia decided from her perch at Mother's in Mt. Kisco. She took his call finally, he was in the hospital, after all.

"I can't get enough oxygen without you—"

"Ask the nurse for some."

"You'll have my life on your hands."

"You sound like a bad play. Let me go, and go my own way."

"I'll cheerfully murder any man who so much as looks at you —"

"Don't make me hang up on you. Okay, I'm hanging up now."

New York's fall cultural and social season kicked into gear. The ginko trees shed all their leaves overnight, as they do; by next morning their gold fan shapes lay plastered on the ground. Julia saw the ginko's sudden defoliation as symbolic, of what she wasn't sure. One evening a black Lincoln Town Car pulled up in the curved driveway at Mt. Kisco. A blameless indigo evening, unnaturally still, as if the birds were alert to some event unavailable to humans. The driver of the Town Car got out and handed Julia an envelope. He said he'd been instructed to wait while she dressed. Julia startled: in the back seat, unmoving, *a passenger*. She moved cautiously toward the car. Goddamn, if it wasn't a mannequin of a man in black tie. Like out of a department store window. Or like the dummy cops the Islesford police propped up in squad cars at strategic crossings to discourage speeders. Julia looked closer. The mannequin was even fitted out with a neck brace! She squelched a smile, as she tore open the envelope: two tickets to the premiere of "Evita." The chutzpah! His own ticket, too, the bastard had been so confident. Something constricting her chest burst free and laughter barged out of her. The chauffeur stood stiffly inclined from the waist, looking past her at the bare ginkos and thinking there were worse ways to make a living.

He was so overjoyed at having her back she had to be a little happy for him. Weekends they drove to Islesford and walked the winter roads around Millstone Drive. Often they ended up at Swan's Bridge where they hung over the stone balustrade and watched the tidal waters race out to sea with a rattle and suck, exposing rocks mantled in emerald seaweed. Once, over her protests, he clambered up on the balustrade to pose, arms outstretched like Jesus in Rio, against the sunset. Evenings they read, each on a separate brown velvet sofa, in the cavern-like living room on Millstone. Julia cooked the sweet local bay scallops, pinching out the tiny muscle, or sometimes just heated up a can of Dinty Moore's Beef Stew, a salute to her old sailing days, and Bodie would chide her about polishing off solo a bottle of Chablis. They ate on bar stools at the kitchen's island. Their years together had accrued interest in the form of comfort.

Bodie made promises, they made love, planned a work-free trip to Antigua, but even before they'd left he'd slipped back. She went willfully blind, all the while certain he knew that she knew. In a twisted way the shared knowledge was a bond. Occasionally she even got aroused picturing Bodie and Simon Gorgeous entwined like two gladiators. He kept it back-alley, Bodie; he knew, their unspoken agreement, he must never humiliate her in public. One evening, high on whatever he was snorting, he confessed that years back he'd logged time with a shrink who specialized in converting his patients to "a traditional lifestyle."

Julia regarded them as a broke-backed simulacrum of

a couple. Simon disappeared but a new Simon was bound to come along, maybe this one a keeper. Together she and Bodie fashioned separate lives. They slept in separate bedrooms. She didn't want to smell him after—she couldn't finish the thought.

"There's nothing I like better than going home with you," Bodie said one February evening after the Art Fair at the Park Avenue Armory. He sighed with ease as they shimmied their bottoms into a cab. "And there's no one I'd rather come home to." He burrowed his nose into her hair and neck. "You *are* home. I can only truly be myself around you." Julia stared through the rain-pocked window at the ruby and blue smear of lights along Park. With his great con man's heart, Bodie had worked it so he could have it every which way.

Their social friends, all smiles in her presence, must call her fag hag behind her back. She caught herself sounding like Tallulah Bankhead. Next she'd join the conga line of "Hello Dolly" at the Botel at Fire Island Pines.

Following a concert at Tanglewood one night, she and Bodie found themselves at a party for Felicia and Leonard Bernstein, a husband notorious for outside interests. Toward midnight, everyone smashed, Lenny stood framed in the doorway and dramatically surveyed the roomful of guests. "I've had you all!" he announced.

"Such a pity," murmured a woman on the sofa next to Julia. "Felicia once said, 'I've spent my life waiting for Lenny.'"

Well, that will not be me, Julia thought. That will not be me. With its usual mystery time had ferried them to 1980, a new decade, and surely—she could almost smell it—something new awaited in the wings.

THE CHORD

Memorial Day 1980

Julia scanned Audrey's Memorial Day party. As the first of the eighties, Audrey had give it a patriotic spin: blue cocktails, servers decked out in stars 'n stripes, the works. Ever more guests arrived, pushing onto the terrace in that feral Islesford way, as if they had to get there first, for what they didn't know. Nothing super exciting here, Julia thought. The men around her—she aborted a yawn—seemed like a third gender. This lord of Leveraged Buy Outs wanting to tell her at length about the Maccabiah Games, an Israeli Olympics. A guy introducing himself as "Michael Milken's cousin." A parking garage baron talked up his latest Bouguereau. The baron's art consultant must have told him he could snag Bouguereau's on the cheap, neglecting to mention they were considered kitsch or softcore porn.

Julia bet these men now slept in separate bedrooms from the blooming girls they'd married. Even the marriage re-ups seemed oblivious to their age-proof second wives, with biceps sculpted from working the trapeze at "Nick" Kounovsky's on 56th Street, training for some circus act never to launch. The only passion here was money. And to live forever since what was the point in having money if you couldn't keep on making even more?

Julia spotted Audrey. She'd gone mysteriously AWOL at her own party. She'd just re-emerged and was chatting with an old classmate of Bodie's from Yale—Julia couldn't remember his name. Now *there* was someone with a little juice. Outdoorsy red-blond, lived-in-looking. Of course he'd be tiresomely married. Julia wondered about the color of his pubic hair.

A ways off her godson leaned, one hip out-thrust, against a free-standing staircase spiraling to nowhere. Smoking what looked like a joint, pinched between thumb and index finger. The cream jacket and Ray-Bans from *Miami Vice*; designer-mussed hair and *pajama* bottoms—the whole package was calculated to drive his elders berserk.

"Auntie Julia!" Miles approached with a mocking smile and his gait of a wary animal. His left cheek wore an indentation like a high dimple—in fact, a scar from a bite he'd acquired from trying to ride his childhood Gordon Setter. His eyes dark blue, the bowed upper lip like an old roue's, incongruous in his boy's face. He landed a *m-wah* kiss near her cheek.

"I've hardly seen you all summer," Julia said. "Why don't you come for dinner next Saturday. And bring your friend." The current girlfriend favored transparent dotted swiss tops that challenged you to keep your eyes on her face.

"You mean Samantha?" He scratched his head. "I think we broke up."

Julia frowned. "You can't remember?"

"Been seeing Tiffany. I need to check with her. Can I let you know?"

"Actually, next Saturday it's really just old friends. Come alone."

"Tiffany's gonna freak out." *Women*, he shrugged. "I hope you haven't invited my old man. He's helping bankroll Reagan and his cronies. And he'll rag me about 'dropping out,' when I could be working in 'wealth management.'"

"Well, I hardly think your father would bring up anything unpleasant over dinner." Least not till the third drink. "And Bodie would love to see you."

Tip and Lyndy had reason to be concerned. The two

younger brothers were model sons, one a college track star and Phi Beta Kappa, the other an investment manager at Prudential. While Miles had spent his leave mooching around the New York theater world and acquiring a greenish pallor; then moved out to that cottage near Islesford Harbor to build ocean kayaks and sculpt. A decorative fixture at Islesford parties, he could be spotted evenings cycling on his Motobecane 10-speed hybrid through the "estate" area toward gated enclaves—untroubled by their owners' fondness for Ronald Reagan. Princeton was poised to cut Miles loose. Tip was little help. He made no effort to conceal his distaste for his eldest son, and anyway was too absorbed in long distance ocean racing—where you can "sort out what life's all about"—to sort out Miles. Lyndy, when not absorbed in adjusting her meds, at least took an interest.

"What's going to become of him?" Lyndy said one evening in her unstrung way. "I mean, what was he thinking, with that acting career? Ten years from now he'll be selling driftwood 'sculptures' at a farm stand out here. Julia, dear, you always had a special rapport with Miles, maybe you could talk to him."

"I've barely seen him in the past ten years."

"I know, but, well, maybe you could help point him in a good direction."

"I'll give it a shot. I'm just not sure what I can do."

Lyndy turned her blue eyes on Julia. "Dearie, you'll think of *something*."

And then she did.

An opening at Art Barn on Route 27. Art lovers jammed the warren of rooms to check out who was still in Islesford, who was still married, who was still alive. The event, perversely called for Friday rush hour, as if Islesford were still mainly a colony of artists and not a fiefdom of Wall Street, had turned all east-bound traffic into a conga line of cars.

Julia pushed through the galleries in search of Miles. She chatted briefly with Bodie's buddy, the Polish builder, who appended every sentence with, "I own that." Her eye alighted on the red-blond guy from Audrey's party, freckles a melt of bronze; his head swiveled to shoot *her* a look—like dogs "marking" their territory, Julia thought, holding his gaze. She had no qualms about married men; after all, she was married herself.

She found Miles in the gallery's grassy inner courtyard. He'd acquired a nasty little mustache and a pimple on his chin.

"Sweetheart," she said, collapsing time, "I have an idea for you."

"Fire away."

She frowned at the arrogance. "Okay, here's what I'm thinking. Bodie needs a kind of office manager for the Houses on Lilac Close. Right now, it's sheer chaos and he's going batty trying to run it all. He needs someone to handle the public relations, write releases, deal with the press, both local and New York. Work with brokers to generate interest. I was thinking"—warming to her idea—"why couldn't you help him get his shop in order? Just temporarily, of course, during your leave of absence. Princeton will be impressed. It would dress up your resume. And working for Bodie you'd make all kinds of connections. *And* get Tip off your back."

"An office job? I don't see myself sitting at a desk in an office."

"God, you know nothing about business or the world. As a PR person you'd be taking people to lunch—"

"Bodie comes on like Cecil B. DeMille crossed with P.T. Barnum. He'd be hell on wheels to work for. I don't see myself as his go-fer—"

"Well, maybe you *should* see yourself doing something that can lead somewhere. Develop a new skill set."

"Is that like a swing set?" A pout. "Oh, Jule, now you're singing *their* song."

Bodie's name for her. "Don't call me that," she snapped. A moment. "You know? You *are* a pain in the ass."

She'd stood up too fast from dead-heading her Grandiflora petunias, and went light-headed. If she'd fallen, would either have noticed? Over by the table beneath the roof's overhang they were still futzing with the photos Miles had assembled for a new prospectus for the Houses at Lilac Close.

"Love *this* one, the way it shows the dynamic roof line." Bodie's hand mimicked the shape. "And in this one you see how the windows along the roof flood the interior with light. Next we'll shoot the McManus House." He re-lit his cigar. Bodie had recently returned from a project in Miami where he'd discovered the joy of stinky Cohibas. Five minutes in a room with his cigar, and she smelled it in her hair.

"The McManus, by the way, just won an AIA Housing Award. Where's that piece?"

Miles seized a magazine off the table and paged to the article: "'The house functions, physically and psychically, on multiple levels,'" he read. "'As much an intimate retreat for two as an accommodating host to an extended family—thus promoting multiple, overlapping narratives.'"

"Maybe you two could promote the narrative of lunch by clearing the table." It had come out fag hag. Not that they paid her any mind. She repeated it nicer.

From the shade they both peered at her beside her pot of pink Grandifloras as if sighting the lost tribe of Dan. She wore an ankle-length navy-and-white striped tee and brought to mind a zaftig barber pole.

"Do I have a gorgeous wife or what?" Bodie said. Miles murmured something from behind the photo he held up to his face.

Julia went into the house to help Blanca assemble lunch: shrimp salad and slices of avocado, *salade de tomates* with fresh basil from her kitchen garden, a baguette and two bottles of dry Rose. Her matchmaking, Julia reflected sourly, had proved an unhoped-for success. Since starting in Bodie's shop in July Miles had taken to public relations as if to the business born, schmoozing at A-list parties with the design and architecture mafia to plant a story. Miles now virtually lived in Bodie's office, phone to ear, working contacts at shelter magazines; placating prima donna starchitects; "partnering" with the Maxfield Museum's upcoming show on modernist architecture. He'd just placed a piece on The Houses at Lilac Close in the Style section of the *New York Times*. The little ruffian now wore his hatchling's hair in the trendy "wet" look, dressed in blue-checked shirts and a navy blazer; tooled around in a second-hand red Datsun. Julia found Miles's sudden self-importance unattractive. Maybe because of his lack of gratitude to her. The truth was she'd long ago lost what she termed a "working husband," and now, in a sense, she'd lost this surrogate son—and she was the architect of her own isolation! He'd put his cool silky cheek to hers and his little arms around her neck, and stood on the sofa snuffling with a cold and messing around with her hair, and proudly printed on red construction paper, *To Nana from Miles DeGroff, You are the best godmother i ever had!* Dammit, she wanted the best for Miles, of course she did! Children left and moved on, it was the nature of things.

The following week, a final working session on Millstone Drive, and the prospectus was ready for the printer's. Bodie rose, bent to kiss her, and announced he was needed at the office. Julia suspected he was needed west of Islesford in Quogue, where the current Simon was assistant tennis pro at Bath and Tennis. Miles lingered on at the table in the lazy heat, sipping ice tea with fresh mint from her kitchen garden and grousing about the vanity of starchitects. Trying to rekindle their old easy intimacy, Julia sensed, the days of shared smiles over the world's folly. She'd once taken him to see the ballet *Petrouchka*, and Miles had cried when the Moor killed poor Petrouchka and got the girl, and Julia had thought, oh God, he's going to be an artist, let's hope Tip is gracious enough to foot the bill.

Miles kept glancing around, foot bobbing, wired. He'd doubtless lined up some afternoon mischief but feared it would be rude just to split. Clouds snuffed the sun; the cool felt heaven-sent.

"How 'bout we hit some balls?" Miles said abruptly, nodding toward the court set behind the pool house. Leaning forward, he angled his arm to scratch the small of his back with his thumb like an ape.

"Oh, I'm pretty rusty, haven't played much this

summer." She'd acquired her good tennis virtually as a birth-right and still hit a wicked backhand. But these belly-rolls she'd acquired . . .

Miles leaped to his feet and pranced in place. "Didn't bring my whites but we won't tell anyone. I'll go grab one of Bodie's rackets."

Julia sighed. Typically nervy just to assume she'd agreed.

She emerged from the house in shorts and an over-size tee. Miles stood there bare-chested over faded trunks, a battered tennis hat of Bodie's clapped on his head. He was finely made, skinny like an adolescent. Julia flashed on him as a five-year-old, his amusingly muscled biceps and legs of a miniature athlete to delight Phidias.

After some abortive rallies—Miles kept dropping junk shots just over the net—they found a groove, sending the ball back and forth in what seemed a silken skein as if they were bound together on separate sides of the court. He took the first set 6-2, pausing for a smoke between games. He took the second, 6-3. The sun burst through like a blast of trombones. Sweat mingling with Sea & Ski ran into her eyes.

"I'm wiped out."

Miles pushed back his hat. "Huh. Already?" He'd bare-ly broken a sweat. "We'll have to schedule a re-match."

They sat under an umbrella on two court side chairs and knocked back bottles of Evian. Miles crossed his leg, ankle to knee. She recognized from when he was an infant the dark freckle on his ankle. She tipped water out of a bottle for her dogs, pushy Min getting most of it. She'd forgotten a towel, her skin was basted in a slimy impasto of Sea & Ski and sweat; her cheeks, she suspected, were a roseaceous pink. She won-dered if she weren't what the doc had called peri-menopausal.

Miles chose that moment to say, "Can I kiss you?"

Julia wasn't sure she'd heard right. She plugged the awkwardness with a laugh, tucking damp tendrils into the elastic holding her hair. "Bit sweaty, dear, but of course." She leaned sideways and gingerly presented her cheek. The cheek went un-kissed.

"No, I mean a real kiss."

What? A trill of laughter, and she shot him one of their

private "do-you-believe-it?" smiles. His dark blue eyes stayed steady, unamused.

"Kiss me," he said.

She took in his bowed upper lip, his air of a young animal newly hatched. His smell of sweat and mown hay turned her head. "Miles, that's not funny."

He looked wounded.

"I mean, *honestly.*" She heard her own laughter. She'd taught him how to blow his nose. . . . She pursed her lips. "Sweetie, I think we both got too much sun."

He pulled on his tee shirt and stood. She stood, too. She boxed him lightly on his upper arm. "Seriously, Miles."

He was sullen and silent on the way back to the house, which suddenly seemed a long trip, and after he'd showered in a guest room he coldly said see you around.

Two weeks later.

In honor of the evening's benefit, Julia shimmied into a white jumpsuit. It struck her, bizarrely, as a grownup version of the "onesies" she'd once wrestled onto her squirmy godson. Her lips longed for the iced rim of a wine glass and the first sip of chilled Pinot Gris ballooning warmth through her chest.

She found Bodie at his on-site office hunkered down with his office manager. In record time Miles had made himself essential to the Houses. His impersonal greeting grated. She hadn't seen him since that ridiculous business after tennis. He wore a dark shirt and off-white blazer and was so slim-hipped, a wonder his pants stayed up. Somehow the least detail of his person was grounds for annoyance.

"Jule, have you met Mireille, our new intern?" Bodie said. "Mireille's studying landscape design in Paris and working in our office for the summer." Julia absently greeted an eel-thin girl with tiny hillocks pushing at her tanktop. She was trying to decode Miles's chilliness. Surely he couldn't still be pissed about the tennis nonsense.

"So we'll see you at the play I hope?" Bodie called over his shoulder at Miles.

"Yup, soon's we wrap it up here." He and Mireille headed toward a drafting table spread with blueprints, Miles briefly touching his hand to her waist with a formal courtesy not usually in his repertoire.

The gesture flickered in Julia's mind like a dying light bulb. Where was Tiffany, from earlier in the summer? Bodie turned the Beemer onto the highway, then down Beldover Road toward the bay. Julia had no appetite for a tiresome play by some Czech genius that marched viewers through different rooms for each scene. But the event benefited Conscience Point, a summer workspace for musicians, painters, performance artists. Through the trees its main house loomed into view, a neo-Gothic stone apparition with crenelated turrets that some robber baron had literally shipped from the Hudson Valley and plunked down on the bluffs overlooking Devon Bay. The pianist Madeleine Shaye had inherited the estate from a pair of crazy siblings in a story as Byzantine as the castle itself, and now part of Islesford folklore.

Bodie pulled up before a vast copper beech, where a valet took over. They strolled down the curving drive toward the castle Bodie called "dementia writ in stone."

Armed with a flute of champagne Julia retreated to Maddy's "autumn garden" hugging the castle's south side, a riot of zinnias and dahlias. Irritation at Miles buzzed her like the no-seeums emerging from the dusk. She'd long since dismissed his absurd "come-on" as a variation on the contrariness he'd shown as a boy. Like the time he trawled a crayon across the living room wall to protest Lyndy's talking on the phone.

She stooped to snap the head of a frazzled zinnia. Had she actually been *flattered*? She hardly lacked proof that she could still count on male attention. Really, there was no reason on earth why she and her godchild shouldn't be on the coziest of terms. She would not let his nuttiness wreck a bond of twenty-one years, she would not permit it! She frowned up at a wedge of geese passing in formation like a stealth bomber. Then she spotted Miles strolling head down toward an allee leading to a grove of gardenias.

"Miles!" She hurried over. She tucked her fist in an armpit. "Miles, dear, I sense you're annoyed with me in some way, and I'd like to clear the air. If I've offended you in some way I'm sorry."

His dark blue eyes were neutral, lips bowed in a faint smile. "Annoyed? Not at all. Why would I be?"

Damn him, for some reason he wanted to make her squirm. "Oh, I don't know, maybe you thought the other day, whenever, I was, you know, mocking you. I didn't mean to be unpleasant." *Why wouldn't he understand?* "You know, after"—she could be cue-ing a moron—"the other day," she said, voice up-ticking.

He looked puzzled. To piss her off? She didn't like being toyed with. Unless in his harebrained way he'd *forgotten*. Everything about him abraded.

Miles scratched his head and then a feral glint invaded his eyes like someone getting the call to hit the john. "Let's not make a big deal of it," he said with a shrug. "I acted like a jerk."

Julia pivoted and fed into the crush of guests heading toward the porte cochere over the main entrance. Why had she bothered?

"Julia Curtiz, just the person I wanted to see!" Tip De-Groff's lidless eyes and lack of lip gave him the look of a dapper shark. This man who spread rumors about her husband was just the person she *didn't* want to see. Lately he'd taken to house-guesting in Ilesford, maybe to escape Lyndy in Marion. "Come sit with me," Tip said, taking her arm. "I gather for this play we're meant to move from room to room and I'll need you to tell me what the hell's going on. You look fetching in that white get-up." They rounded an alabaster statue of Cupid and Pysche and found a place in the rows of chairs set in a solarium.

"I've been wanting to thank you for looking after my impossible son," Tip said. "This job at Bodie's shop—it's certainly set him on a good path."

"I'm pleased it worked out so well."

At that moment, Miles and Mireille headed down the aisle between the chairs. They sat a few rows down to the left. Julia saw him in profile, the curve of his upper lip, an ear lobe beneath his spiky hair.

"Worked out in all sorts of ways," Tip said. "Mireille's from a good family, very 'Deep France,' brother at Lazard Freres."

"Is that right."

Miles whispered in Mireille's ear, she gave a voluptuous little shudder.

"Before I forget, I know it's a ways off, but I hope you and Bodie can tear yourselves away from Islesford and come to Marion over Labor Day. Your mother would be thrilled, of course, and we're christening the new Herreschoff Newport 30. Be like old times."

There would be croquet and talk of "stiff breezes" and a sail aboard the Herreschoff to Cuttyhunk, and she would drink too many bullshots and G&T's. Dusk browned the solarium like a sepia photo. Julia squirmed, invaded by a sense of waste. It had gone by so fast, and *before us lie / Deserts of vast eternity*—her beloved Marvell. She pictured tangled limbs in a room with white muslin curtains billowing.

She craned her neck around. Bodie was likely sequestered in an oak-paneled parlor deep in the castle, hatching a new deal or hitting on the hot new architect he'd just hired for The Houses. Bloody hell, she wanted to split. Tip looked up in surprise, rose and cupped her elbow. "Are you alright? Why don't I come with you?" She pushed past him, crushing toes, and hurried out under the porte cochere into the evening, sandals crackling the gravel. Bodie's latest Simon could drive him home. She turned the key in the ignition. She must have misjudged the turn around the copper beech, she heard a metallic screech from the right side of the car as the Beemer took leave of its fender. Flashes strobe-lit the trees. Two valets ran toward her, shouting.

Julia stepped out of her jumpsuit, leaving it puddled on the floor, fixed herself a Dewars, headed for the terrace.

Could I be in love? She bent double and her knees went wobbly, she needed to get on the ground. She lay palms up, legs splayed. Above her pulsed the tiny torches of fireflies. The boyfriends, Obrecht, Bodie—nothing came close to this. She'd married Bodie out of vanity. In this new country none of the old coordinates held. *When the fox asks the Little Prince to tame him, he'd peer up at her face to see if she would cry*— No, this couldn't be. It was monstrous, she couldn't conceive a world that would permit it. Daylight would dissolve the madness like a vampire. She saw him standing hip to hip with Mireille in all their youthful perfection, poised to seize their portion of heaven—heard her own groan above the chorus of katydids and tree crickets. Phèdre got to die on account of lust, but in life you just slogged on with your awfulness. She'd been a functioning, normally fucked up person, and this boy had carelessly disabled her. On a whim. He couldn't remember! *Why would I be offended?* She would wall her self off in some basement like the Elephant Man and toss the key.

She'd racked up a bill for a couple of grand to repair Bodie's Beemer.

The thing about Brett, you could tell her anything. She was shock proof and never went judgmental.

"I mean, 'A girl's gotta celebrate everything passing by,'" Brett said slowly, "but, uh, *twenty-four* years younger?"

Apparently Brett had standards after all. She hadn't even told Brett the ghastliest part. She and Miles were distant cousins through Lyndy DeGroff.

"Look, I tried to keep it on the up and up and make amends. But the little creep basically blew me off." Julia poked at a morsel of grey soy with serrated edges, one of many items masquerading as edible at Food on Prince and Wooster in Soho. She eyeballed Brett. "What really kills me, if the sexes were reversed we wouldn't be having this conversation."

Brett struggled to jimmy up some support for what Julia so did not want to be talked out of. "Guess amends is not what Miles wants to make. Maybe he was hurt by your brush-off."

"Rejection must be a first for Miles." The notion of thighs falling open at his approach made Julia madder;

indignant for the Tiffany's *she'll freak out* and Samantha's and all the others he wouldn't remember.

"If you, uh, pursue this, just understand you could be humiliated," Brett said, staying on message.

"There's also the small detail of Mireille, his girlfriend."

"Oh, forget that, there will always be a Mireille, she's a cosmic constant. There's surely a constellation in the heavens named Mireille. Have you thought Miles might be using her to get back at you?" Brett speared something turnip-like. "Hey, I just thought of a precedent: didn't Georgia O'Keefe have a boy lover? Considering the deprivation on the home front, it will keep you healthy."

Brett believed, a holdover from Jason days, that a regimen of Reichian orgasms prevented cancer. "Why not just conspicuously ignore Miles? One of the great classic maneuvers. Though, I have to say, you could ignore him better if you had an occupation of some sort. I mean, being married to Bodie and all you must feel . . . underemployed."

Starving at the banquet. She would one day leave Bodie of course; she'd known she would leave since last summer, the Summer of Simon, though she played to perfection the role of willfully blind spouse. In fact, she took pride in the craft of her performance; when everything's shot to hell, you can still muster up a bit of style. She just hadn't organized her exit yet. If you're going to jump, better land on *terra firma*. She knew that for all the braggadocio, Bodie was plagued by a cash shortfall. Trophy architects with big egos had emptied the coffers, he needed more investors. The sordid truth was, they couldn't afford a divorce right now. Or rather, she couldn't. She was waiting, with reptilian patience.

The August gala at Conscience Point always marked a high point in Islesford's social calendar, which grew more frenzied as summer peaked. This year the gala would feature an evening by the artists-in-residence of cutting-edge "installations" and performance art on the grounds of the estate. Those who ponied up the hefty sum for tickets cared deeply about cutting edge art, of course, but perhaps even more about a chance to mingle with a Who's Who of other Islesford money.

Maddy Shaye kept a tight rein on the Point's budget. When the photographer she'd hired to cover the gala jacked up his fees ten days before the event, she fired him.

On impulse Julia said, "Why don't you let me shoot it? I'll be more reasonable."

I'd like to help you out, but this is no amateur hour, she could hear beneath Maddy's polite smile. That was before Maddy flipped through Julia's rejiggered portfolio. Julia bought a new Nikon. Working Bodie's contacts she signed on to shoot the gala for the *Islesford Star.*

Her photos captured performers popping out of the scrub oak in white snow-monkey costumes; dancers in nude body stockings hanging from branches in net pods like opossums; a man buried in sand to his neck. She slyly caught the guests looking as clownish as the artists. There was a shot of a woman in her Lily Pulitzer kneeling, like Mother Teresa, to offer the guy buried in sand her Mimosa. Another of a cigar-chomping magnate leering at a dancer's gilded boobs, an image from George Grosz (which the mogul blew up and proudly hung in his media room).

The reddish outdoorsman Julia had ogled across crowded rooms approached her at a party. He was the publisher, as it happened, of *National Geographic.* "I was very impressed by your pictures of that gala, their wit. Maybe you could do some work for us." And maybe fuck, Julia translated, flashing her loveliest smile.

She put the invitation on hold. Since the gala, she'd become a regular presence around Conscience Point, shadowing the artists and documenting their visions as they evolved. She persuaded Vera Tang to include her photos in a show in her gallery on multimedia works. That Vera Tang was Simon's wife scarcely registered on Julia, so far had she journeyed from that watershed evening at Millstone Drive a summer ago. Thanks to Bodie's magic fingers, Roy Lichtenstein allowed her to photograph him painting in his studio just west of Islesford. She'd begun gathering material for a larger project, a coffee table book called *Artists at Work.*

Julia would occasionally spot Miles at benefits around Islesford, and duck behind a hedgerow. Her disease was merely in remission, but her youthful ambitions, idly luffing all these years, caught the wind and sailed her robustly through the days.

"What the hell's going on?"

A voice from her sweaty, love-wracked nights. *Excuse me?*

He hung over her, face semi-visible, as guests arrived on the beach for George Plimpton's Labor Day fireworks. The event was a benefit for—well, no one quite knew.

"Seriously, would you tell me please?"

"Tell you *what?*"

"You've been, like, avoiding me. Why?"

"I haven't in the least," Julia said pleasantly, tucking her long skirt around her legs. "I've been working." Savoring the novelty of the phrase.

"Yah, those photos of Conscience Point really nailed that crowd. Whenever I see you"—dropping his voice—"you act like I'm carrying the plague."

"Miles, that's not fair, we're all busy—"

"Well, whatever game you're playing, it's way out of line."

Me . . . games?

"Hey, Miles old buddy." Hugo lowered himself to the blanket beside Julia. "Bodie coming?"

"Eventually. He's been detained in Quogue."

Miles hovered, phantomed by the darkened sky. "I'd like to show you something."

"Stick around, you don' wanna miss fireworks by the Grucci bros," Hugo said.

"Something over by the house," Miles said.

"By the house," Julia said.

"Something you need to see."

"Need to see." She rose as if hypnotized. Miles guided her over a tidal hem of seaweed and shells, and up a grassy path toward a garden. Above, as in a stage set, rose an Arts and Craft-style house, lights firing its windows. From the beach a series of staccato cackles, then the crowd's *ahhh!* A blue geodesic dome rocketed skyward to expand in the velvety black, trailing tentacles of sapphire slowly dying.

Julia's hand encountered a low stone wall. Moving forward, she followed the wall, left hand tracing the way along rough stone. She stopped where the wall formed a corner and turned to face him. Another volley of reports—then a diadem of gold stars exploded above, pierced by green rockets. She kept an after-image of his drawn face. From across the bay, a smell of sulfur.

"I miss you." An adolescent break in his voice. "Why have you disappeared, why don't we hang out like we used to?"

"Oh, you know, we're both just . . . getting on with it."

"Hey, we've seen plenty of fireworks. Why don't we bug out of here?"

"But the Grucci Brothers . . . "

"Yah, it's always the same."

"And go where?"

"Dinner? Let's have dinner."

"Not sure that's a good idea."

"What, do I disgust you?"

She shrank back. "Don't be absurd."

A fusillade of reports, the Gruccis laying one over another . . . Sprays of fuschia hosed the darkness . . . A dome of emerald balls expanded, then again and again . . . Giant silver palm trees limp-wristed fronds of gold down the night.

The blessed dark.

"What's wrong Julia," came his low voice.

Everything.

"What's going on? Could you tell me please?"

"I don't know, I don't think I can."

"I think I can," he said.

The bands constricting her chest relaxed.

"It's just about killing me," Miles said.

She braced herself against stone, the lichen cool and rough under her palms.

"I've known for a while," he added almost impersonally.

Known what, she didn't dare ask. "No, don't touch me." High strains of laughter sparked off the beach. Why was it always women's laughter you heard? "You knew before me. What an idiot I've been," she murmured, scarcely knowing what she meant. "It's all wrong . . . so so wrong—"

"What does that even mean? And who the hell cares? All I see is right."

"Your latest conquest—?"

"What?"

"Always the gentleman" she started, but his mouth came down on hers, lightly, a dream within a dream. He was tentative, trembling as if fearful she'd push him off. His curved lips, his smell made her weak, his arm came around her waist and held her. For a second it hung in the balance, the ghosts of themselves crowded between, but Julia shut her eyes and he pulled her in. His hands on her felt sacramental. He was skinny beneath his jacket and she swollen with desire, powerful, they were equals in strength which aroused her the more. He kneeled down and pushed up her skirt. She came instantly, arched and spasming over him like a portrait of grief. From another earth came a pop-popping and voices *the sky's early light.* The rocket's red glare caught the cleft on his cheek. She sank and took him in her mouth, and he groaned and abruptly drew out and she felt the beat of him between her fingers, the warm spurt against her throat.

The tall white-shingled house was built on an outcropping of rock so it all but cantilevered over the Sound. Julia was well acquainted with derelict houses overlooking water—but Miles's Aunt Lila's place made Edie Beale's Grey Gardens look House Beautiful. The vast living room was furnished in decrepit pieces ready for a bonfire; everywhere lay stacks of cartons, magazines and newspapers piled high like giant cairns or stepped to the floor in frozen cascades.

"At least there are no corpses of Collyer brothers here," Miles said, merry and at home.

She needed a drink. They broke out a bottle of Pouilly Fuisse from the half case they'd bought in town. Julia scoured a pan filmed in grease and broiled fluke in lemon sauce and fixed a salad with the season's fine tomatoes. They opened a second bottle and ate in the wood-paneled "boat room" among stuffed loons staring at eternity, photos of the Montauk bluffs in every light—and of the hatchet-faced DeGroffs who seemed their human extension.

The second story bedroom rose plumb with the cliff like a giant prow; from the windows you saw only water. *The white curtains* . . . The house wasn't winterized. Julia found her teeth literally clattering. They dove into bed and undressed under the covers and grasped each other for warmth under layers of thin, ratty blankets, their feet icy.

She woke, achy and stiff, to a golden band of sunlight seeping under the threshold. Miles, dun-colored hair over his eyes like a sheepdog, emitted a little whiffle-snore. Propped on an elbow, she looked around the near-bare room. Wherever she'd landed was neither to the good nor the bad, just fact.

They leaped into their clothes and jigged around, laughing, to warm up. Julia made a pot of coffee, while Miles drove into town and brought back milk, eggs, apples, croissants. Julia gave the downstairs bath off the kitchen a pass— moss and other vegetation grew in the shower—and claimed a third floor one with ancient fixtures. Later they hiked the rocky ledges surrounding the Montauk lighthouse, the angry surf wanting at them, and then the Walking Dunes, its doomed trees drowning in sand.

Dusk robbed the house of daytime's warmth. They countered with stiff shots of Maker's Mark. "*L'amour est simple,*" Julia said. "Arletty to . . . Jean-Louis Barrault," Miles said on cue, then changed the subject. She'd taken him a *very* long time ago to *Les Enfants du Paradis*. Where escape the cold but in bed? Upstairs he pulled her to him, one hand grabbing her ass. *Wait,* Julia pleaded. She crouched in the claw-footed bathtub, thankful for the hot water. Everything hurt, his elbows, teeth, knees, they locked on like lethal gladiators. Miles came instantly. Julia lay eyes fixed on the ceiling and throat twisted to the side like a crime victim. They burned off the madness enough to make love. She woke in the night. *This is the best it will be.*

The difference in age that she found mortifying, the dip of her breasts and forward cant of her belly, seemed only to delight Miles. He adored her laughter, the smell of her hair, everywhere, loved her mouth and teeth, her mouth on him, lolled in her groin, then plunged at her, deep, deeper, till she lost who ended where. The filial tinge, when Miles sucked at her and burrowed into her shoulder, added to the frenzy. Bodie undertook love as a chore, like flossing, though cheerfully embraced.

By some divine dispensation, Bodie spent long stretches out of town, consulting with planners for a mixed use shopping center strategically placed near a ring road outside Miami. He was also scouting for a residential parcel on Long Island's North Fork. During his absence Julia and Miles stayed at Lilac Close. Audrey rarely used it off season. After her initial dismay at Julia's liaison, she'd handed over an extra key. Ever since Foxleigh their merry band had pitched their tents in outlandish locales. So why balk now? Her father Imre currently planned to wed a sitar player younger than his daughter. Julia-and-Miles righted some sort of cosmic balance.

They hid from the world. They parked behind the barn at Lilac Close, her silver Honda Accord, his red Datsun invisible from the road. They felt rich beyond measure. Miles sometimes stood bearing his weight on the left leg, hip hitched, other leg bent at the knee, like Greek sculptures of languid boys. He could also be rough and commanding, pursuing pleasure with male ruthlessness. She lived in a state of continual arousal.

She'd insisted on the downstairs bedroom/study just off the living room. Audrey had closed off the second floor master, where a girl had once stood on the windowseat and wrung a bloody towel. Even Julia's three Dachshunds suspiciously sniffed under the door. The downstairs bedroom was musty with mildew but Miles scrubbed down the walls and they lay the mattress out to air in the sun on the bricked terrace behind the house. Julia cooked ratatouille with zucchini, eggplant, and tomatoes from the farm stand on South Main, swordfish they bought from a fisherman on a cul-de-sac off Lilac Close. Sometimes for fun they gleaned potatoes in the falling light of dusk from neighboring fields.

A bit of a culture shock when Miles blasted his faves from the record player—"punk and post punk" he informed Julia; Blondie, the Talking Heads; reggae and "ska influenced stuff" like Madness and the Specials. Julia's idea of pop extended to "My Sweet Lord," which Miles, she shuddered to think, would have heard at ten.

Julia's ear wanted Richard Strauss. The prelude to *Der Rosenkavalier*, a musical depiction of the Marschallin and seventeen-year-old Octavian going at it, which was clearly depicted in the music down to anatomical details, those orgasmically whooping horns. She learned to tolerate Miles's musical tastes—partly to sidestep the world of high culture they'd once shared. Better to prance around together to the reggae beat of Madness's "Night Boat to Cairo" and "the oarsman grinning a toothless smile." The volume so high it sent little Min scuttling under the highboy.

Miles seemed puzzled by the notion of household chores. He simply stepped out of clothes and left them on the floor, or draped over the sofa with yellow cabbage roses; he ran through untold numbers of towels. Julia called in Blanca, her Ecuadorian housekeeper from Millstone Drive, who'd seen plenty around Islesford and knew to turn a blind eye. Julia suspected Blanca might also be keeping house for Bodie and the latest Simon in Quogue. In any event, Blanca had her own games going. Over the summer she'd split for Ecuador to visit an ailing father and returned to Islesford sporting a creditable eye job.

They were both expert skiers, and spent a week in Alta, Utah. His ass in ski pants, she thought she might not be up to tackling the slopes. When he pushed off from High Rustler it called up a lovely springy move in bed. Mostly it was bitter and blizzardy, their goggles always fogged, but one day the sun appeared, spangling acres of white, and they took Grizzly Gulch in a delirious swooping descent. A photo of them in the den at Alta Lodge smiling at each other in profile. "February 10, 1981. Such happiness," she would pencil on the back of the print. In another shot Miles stares straight into the camera, his bowed upper lip.

They lived in "the now." She hated psychobabble, but Julia had embraced the term after discovering an old paperback in Audrey's bookcase by human potential guru Fritz Perls. "If you are in the now you have security. As soon as you jump out of the now, for instance into the future, the gap is experienced as anxiety." Loving Miles felt entirely right to Julia, so long as she stuck in the now. Miles greedily met her there. Marriage to Bodie had convinced her that she'd grown disgusting. Lush, Miles called her body, which he roamed and entered like a blind man seeking his way, yet domineering, stern. It went beyond sensation: coming into her he brought them both to the edge of oblivion. Then like a horny kid he wanted to start again. She would feebly bat him away. He lingered wonderingly in her groin, his lips and tongue. Sometimes he was all pointy elbows and jabby . . . She walked around tasting them, the smell of semen in her hair. She expected to wake one morning staring into the muzzle of a shotgun.

She signed a contract with Abrams for her book of photos *Painters at Work*, which now included Esteban Vicente and other Ab Ex painters based on the East End. Nights, at the wood farm table in the living room bay, Miles pored over her contact sheets with a loupe, weighing in on the best shots.

"I got back working as revenge on you."

"For what?"

"For not loving me."

"Wasn't it the other way around?" Miles said.

"Never mind all that."

He ambled around the living room. Took a pull of his Heineken. "Julla, why didn't you leave Bodie long ago?"

Love—loving her, she liked to think—had brought Miles a personal elegance that had never been his hallmark. Without saying much he'd let on that he knew about Bodie's style of being married. The Hoover's Dam of backed up libido he'd unleashed told him the rest.

"Bodie and I care for each other in some way that's off the spectrum. We're each other's history. Even the bad stuff is a bond. And I didn't yet know my life is with you."

"I didn't *have* much of a life till you. I mean, my *family?* Tip comes on like I'm the product of a rogue gene. I always had this biblical hate thing going with the bros. Lyndy's in gaga-land."

"But Princeton, surely—"

"Tip kept ragging me to join his old eating club, Tiger Inn, the frattiest of them all—home to America's future leaders! They've kept this medieval ritual, 'bicker,' to get into the clubs and hang with the cool crowd. Pledges choke down live goldfish and eat dog food. The clubs are also big on barfing contests and guys standing on tables and strumming their 'penis guitars.' Someone once set off a 'butt bomb'—on himself. Guess I was born old, or without a sense of humor." He kneeled beside her chair. "Julia, I was in freefall and you caught me. The job's great, especially if I get a piece of the action so we'd have some money. But it's just a job, there'll be others. What matters is being with you." He roughly pulled her to him, squeezed hard so her ribs cracked, she almost cried out.

Spring came grudgingly to Islesford; with the wind chill the temps never hit fifty. Undaunted, willows hosted a fuzz of yellow-green, brambles flushed a come-hither red. The magnolias unclenched a mingy few blossoms, like reluctant Madonnas in Flemish Annunciations.

A Sunday brunch thrown by a major donor to the Maxfield Museum. "I hear you've been photographing Esteban Vicente," the curator said, eyeing Julia from behind purple harlequin glasses. "I'd like to see what you've got. We're planning a show right after Labor Day on the Ab Ex artists like Vicente who've lived and worked in the area. Here's my thought . . ."

Julia stepped out into the garden, elated. To think her photos might hang in the Maxfield! The curator had spoken of grouping them around Vicente's paintings to "illumine the artist's process." Though hardly a done deal—the curator had yet to see her work—Julia couldn't wait to tell Miles. They'd break out the prosecco; they always toasted each other's success. With Elliott her role had been to prostrate herself before his genius. Bodie had bought a single photo of hers twenty years ago, then her "hobbies" had fallen off his radar. Miles had a terrific eye and spent hours weighing in on her photos. "We live creatively together," she told Audrey and Brett.

Over by the azaleas she spotted a stunning girl with caramel skin and an afro interviewing a collector. Julia recognized Rachel Dempsey, the adopted daughter of George Dempsey. The Dempsey's had a place, she dimly remembered, somewhere below the Cape near Marion. Julia couldn't pull her eyes away. Rachel, who wrote the Social Diary for the *Islesford Star*, seemed a different species from the languid, lovesick girls of her youth. She strode around Islesford in riding boots and did vodka shots at The Black Buoy off Main Street. Julia had heard from the gossip mill that Rachel had recently broken her engagement to a lawyer just named Undersecretary of State—*why stagnate in a faux Tudor in Chevy Chase and preside at official events when your career was in New York?* Women might chart their own course these days, people nattered, but Rachel's choice defied understanding. Imagine dinking about as a freelance writer when you could be Mrs. Undersecretary of State!

With a pang, Julia recognized in Rachel something of what they'd reached for, she and the friends. Except for Audrey, they'd fallen pitifully short. But they'd given it their best shot, and that had to count for something.

Rachel caught Julia's eyes on her; responded with a rude stare—you lookin' at *me*, lady? Julia's amusement lasted only a moment. Rachel a perfect match for Miles. Youth, sass, those bedroom lips. They'd make bi-racial babies. Julia sank onto a Luytens bench of bleached wood.

Hold on—did Miles even know Rachel? Her family might spend the summer near the DeGroffs, but Julia suspected that Rachel had been quick to vamoose from that world. "I'm not interested in girls my age," Miles liked to say. "Why would I be when I have you?"

Julia took herself in hand. Really, it was not possible to live this way. In fact, she ought to help Miles. If she truly loved him, she would engineer a meeting with Rachel.

The idea did not survive the turn off to Millstone Drive.

*   *   *

Julia became absorbed with plans to come out of hiding, to make a life with Miles. People would raise holy hell of course . . . *the horror, the horror!* Mother would feel vindicated, as if her daughter's depravity were now officially confirmed—and in her cups might pump her for prurient details. Lyndy DeGroff would take up permanent residence at McLean's. Tip DeGroff could pull something seriously ugly. And there was the small matter of dealing with Bodie after he learned that his chief steward was boinking his wife. When Julia paused to consider all this, which she didn't much, she worried about the fallout on Miles's fledgling work ethic. She worried about how to protect Bodie. Through some bizarre algorithm, Bodie's marriage to her made his life possible.

She decided Bodie had such joy in him he wouldn't remain unhappy for long. Brett liked to say, no need to worry about men; tossed from a high ledge, they always right themselves like cats—usually with the help of a divorcee bearing a casserole. As for the town bigmouths, after a time, the shock and novelty of her and Miles would cease to titillate and they'd become part of local folklore; around Islesford you could count on some fresher *scandale.* And 1981 wasn't the world she'd been born into, people no longer sacrificed love for the sake of appearances or the kids. It was me-me-me, now and forever. Follow your bliss, everyone else be damned. They'd landed right in the zeitgeist, she and Miles.

They would live modestly and obscurely on the unfashionable bay side of Islesford favored by locals. Buying a house and other such practicalities were daunting of course. Julia had only the dimmest grasp of things financial. There would likely be a payout from Bodie (the word alimony was too sordid), which Julia thought of as "guilt money."

"After all," she'd said to Brett, "I married him in good faith. And he was maybe *shtupping* Leland."

"Maybe when Bodie married you he didn't know he was gay. Or bi, or poly-whatever."

"Or thought I might be the cure. We tell ourselves fables in order to be happy."

"Y'know, I don't see the term *schtupp* for gays," Brett said.

"Maybe you're right. I once sneaked into this gay German flick at the Quad, *Taxi Zum Klo*. It was wildly educational, helped me know more about my husband."

She guessed that Bodie, after an operatic tantrum, would be generous. Con man though he was, he had a good heart, he would wish her well. That Miles was embedded in Bodie's projects complicated matters of course—heavens, they were all as intertwined and ingrown as high end Kallikaks. But knowing Bodie—well, he had a worldly, quirky sense of things and might actually be *intrigued* by her and Miles. Congratulate her on her taste! Who better than he to understand?

It freaked Julia that the new generation of gay men, who'd never hide beneath the skirts of a white marriage— would be roughly the age of her lover.

Spring had popped. Pear trees shook their frou-frou of white, lawns lay petaled with magnolia blossoms hemmed in brown. Audrey flew to the coast to oversee the screen adaptation of *All You Could Want*. Come Memorial Day she would join the massive summer migration to Islesford, and Julia and Miles would be ousted from their nest. A second problem: Bodie's projects were taking ever larger bites of Miles's time. Bodie had set up camp on the North Shore to launch a version of The Houses near Greenport—leaving Miles in charge of the office in Islesford.

Rather a privileged problem, Julia decided, delighted that Miles now ran the shop. But it fell to her to go house-hunting. She scouted out properties in the townie side by the bay that the LBO crowd ignored. The green frame house way out on Gerard Point was simple but comfortable—two bedrooms and sleeping loft, livingroom facing the water. The single bathroom a drawback—Miles made worse messes than a teenager —but there was an outdoor shower. Best, they'd have a dock where they could keep a boat. Julia had already found one in a catalog: a Catalina 16.5 sloop with main and genoa, the pivoting mast and forestay housed in the headsail, that could be sailed singled-handed or carry up to six people.

Every time she asked Miles to drive by Gerard to look at the house he was "trouble-shooting" some new office crisis. He went back and forth on where they should live. He loathed Princeton and hoped to finish his degree at NYU, so wouldn't it make more sense for them to get a place in the city? And then the house on Gerard was gone.

Julia was careless about keeping track—but at some point it became clear she'd missed her period.

"I'm either pregnant or it's early menopause," she told Brett.

The jocular tone was a cover-up. In truth, Miles had reignited her longing for a child. *Miles's child.* It seemed a natural extension of their love, his seed swelling her. She felt like an African fertility figure, heavy through her belly, nipples tingling. And weren't women having babies in their forties? She'd failed to get pregnant in the past, they'd eventually discovered, because of Bodie's "low sperm cell motility" (and maybe because it didn't like mucking about in women). Miles's sperm, and she loved his taste, felt like it meant business.

After finishing up one evening at the dark room she'd rented in Islesford, Julia drove to the General Store on Wainwright Drive. She bought milk, eggs, oj, and a quart of the first local strawberries. Carrie, the owner's teen daughter who worked the register, had a sly manner and lingering gaze. Julia disliked the way Carrie and her younger sister would gawk at Miles whenever they shopped there together, then confer in a dark corner by the cooler.

Julia went next door to the stamp-sized post office affixed to the General Store. She was eager to see an article on The Houses Miles had placed in the June issue of *Architectural Digest*, likely to be in today's mail.

A new postal clerk was at the counter. When Julia asked for the mail, the woman eyed her for a moment, slowly processing bits of information like a balky machine. A wen with a couple of hairs sprouting from it sat on her cheek.

"The mail for Vosburgh and DeGroff has already been

collected," the woman said. "The young man, uh, your son picked it up this morning."

Behind her Julia heard a giggle. Her head swiveled. Carrie and her sister were loitering by the door. Carrie smothered another snicker with the back of her hand, and stumbled out with her sister, the screen door slapping to.

Bitches. Then, like in an eye exam where you peer at the colored pinwheel, the future came clicking into focus. My God, who was she kidding? In twenty years, when Miles was her current age—and in his prime—she'd be in her sixth decade. She had no imagination for existing in the world undesirous of Miles—but why would he want *her*?

She sat in the Honda outside the General Store, bag of groceries on her lap. *You got what you wanted and now you're stuck with me,* she would tease.

I want to be stuck with you. I'm stuck on you . . .

The age thing —

—just an accident of timing, someone else's story. We belong together. I'm the luckiest man alive.

And when they roll me away in a wheel chair?

I'll be pushing it . . . or you'll be sitting on my lap . . .

She pictured herself a crone lover. The landscape was littered with versions of the amorous old goat: hair piece, earlobes to here, shiny shanks . . . But what about amorous old women? She could come up only with Georgia O'Keefe, in her 80's and half blind, with a young potter . . .

Her passion for Miles sometimes wore him out, Julia thought, taking heart.

And if by some miracle they made a child? *Miles as an undergraduate dad?* She swerved to avoid a truck bearing a load of saplings.

Julia pulled onto the shoulder of 127 and put the Honda in neutral.

She couldn't very well parade her big belly around Princeton's Tiger Inn. Or even around way hipper NYU. She'd be like that mom from hell in the novel by Bruce Jay Friedman, who follows her son to college and haunts his dorm.

She would not in any event survive this. She had no Plan B. You did not find such happiness and walk regretfully but sensibly away. She parked the Honda behind the barn at Lilac Close with visions of old-guard Islesford forming a posse with pitchforks.

She was not, as it turned out, pregnant. What she had was a bladder infection. The doctor stopped scribbling in his chart and eyed her over his half-glasses. "No baths for two weeks and no intercourse for six."

Julia didn't make it to six and didn't care. She was ruled by a new recklessness. She could sense her time with Miles silting away. She searched for some impulse in herself to be graceful. To let go graciously, if with melancholy and regret. Like the Marschallin in *Der Rosenkavalier*. Julia thought at length about this middle aged Marschallin—well, probably thirtyish, but dentistry in the Belle Epoque left much to be desired. She thought about how this elegant, charming woman gives up her boy-lover Octavian. The Marschallin seemed to be telling her that in life one must take lightly and with light heart and light hands—and then let go. Richard Strauss's time-addled music, pulsing with beating clocks, sounded the same message. It all felt vaguely Christian and resigned to Julia and she herself was in league with the devil.

Strauss's opera gave Julia the idea of letting the grand daddy clock in the hall wind down, and stowing the other clocks in cupboards.

"Is there no working time piece in this place?" Miles groused. "We supposed to use sundials?"

He'd become absorbed in a fresh crisis threatening the Houses. Local environmental groups were setting up a squawk about a "toxic plume" of water that ran deep underground all the way from Noyack through Bodie's site for The Houses in Islesford, fallout from dry cleaning chemicals dumped by Rowe Industries. The chemicals, it now appeared, had contaminated the aquifer in the environs. Bodie, from his perch in Greenport, appointed Miles chief troubleshooter. The supposed toxic plume stopped way short of his land, Bodie insisted, and the scare was nothing more than grandstanding by local pols to exploit a false issue that would garner votes. Still, any rumor linking the Houses to toxic land presented a PR nightmare that needed to be adroitly defused.

Miles worked later and later at the office; Julia was often asleep when he arrived home. Sometimes he spent the night at a B & B near Houses #2 in Greenport. She, too, was busy, meeting in New York with a writer for *Artists at Work* whom Abrams had hired to provide an introduction and text. The book was slated to appear in the winter catalog, positioned, in part, as a Christmas coffee-table book.

With Bodie in Greenport, she and Miles sometimes stayed at the house on Millstone. But he couldn't really move his stuff in, and the arrangement felt to Julia like back-pedaling, transient and tacky. Millstone crackled with Bodie's presence, his voice and laughter ghosting through the under-furnished rooms, along with a whiff of Cohiba cigar. Miles seemed oblivious to problems. He was high on work. He was now effectively running two offices—the one in Islesford and the spinoff Houses North in Greenport. Lately he arrived at Millstone Drive with the smell of Bodie's wretched Cohibas in his hair.

"Great news, Julie," he said one evening. A raw sea mist had blown off and they'd taken their tumblers of Islay double malt to the terrace to enjoy the sunset over the potato fields.

"I'm getting a big raise. *And* Bodie's about to hire two new assistants."

"Darling, that's wonderful!" She kissed his stubble cheek. "And *I* have something to show *you*." She placed a booklet on his lap. "The Abrams catalog. 'Artists at Work,' check out page 12."

He inspected it with a practiced eye. "Fan-fuckin'-tastic." He reached a hand around her waist as she hung over him.

"We bring each other good things."

"C'mere." He pulled her closer and grabbed her ass. "I can think of more good things to bring."

"Wait, we've got to get a little practical here. Maybe we

can afford a nicer house now. One on Gerard Drive's gone, but Islesford's gotten really overbuilt, we'll find something else."

"You do the legwork, could you Jooj? Check out the year-round rentals. I trust your taste. And I don't really care where we live." He yawned, suddenly sleepy, like a child.

Bluebell. Charming historic cottage, Islesford Village street, two bedrooms, French doors off living room opening on terrace. The ad in the Classifieds had not mislead, the terrace was even flanked with purple-blue bellflowers, reminding Julia of the terrace at Gentian Court where she'd married, knowing nothing of love, a lifetime ago. The landlord was offering a two-year lease, it was perfect.

When Miles finally checked it out, he pronounced it too "cutesie."

Next up a shingled ranch house set among the scrub oak, hard by a split level with an above-ground pool. The neighbors were playing the radio. *Baby I think tonight / we can take what's wrong and make it right . . .*

"Is that *siding*?" Miles said, frowning at the ranch house.

He wore a black linen shirt with Mandarin collar, sort of Eurotrash, his hair slicked and combed straight back. She might as well be asking him to live in Levittown.

"The thing is, any place I find you shoot down. *You* look for a change."

"I don't have time, Jooj."

His distracted eyes told her he needed to get back to the office. Different eyes, she suddenly thought, from the night of the Grucci fireworks.

"Well, I'm short of time, too." She heard the sharpness in her voice. "I've got the Vicente show coming up at the Maxfield, you know. We can't live like gypsies or graduate students. But if you don't care, why put me through this charade of looking?"

"Of course I care, but can't you understand I'm overwhelmed at the shop? Those toxic plume nuts . . . Now this hydro-geologist guy is on the case." He ran his hand through his hair. "It's getting nastier. Some locals want to picket the turnpike near the Houses with signs: 'Contaminated Groundwater Area' . . . 'Cancer Causing Chemicals.' *Ay caramba.*"

A moment. "Do they have a case? *Is* the land contaminated?"

"The toxic plume of ground water—about seventy feet deep—well, it extends farther than was thought. Much farther. Locals are claiming a higher cancer rate in the area. They want to hold Rowe responsible."

"Look, you've got a thorny situation—but that doesn't mean we can't find a place to live."

"I wish you wouldn't take that tone."

"You're always 'in a meeting.'"

"Julla, after things calm down we'll take a little vacation. We'll go to Paris, that hotel you like near the Luxembourg."

The St.-Gregoire. A yellow box of white cyclamens nesting before the fireplace . . . A gigantic tub to play in. . . . "For *now*, though, we can't stay on at Millstone Drive. Bodie could sell the place out from under me, I'm surprised he hasn't already."

"I don't think you understand, we could be in deep shit."

We. Who was "we?"

Fall 1981

The Maxfield was mounting a gala opening for its big group show of second generation Abstract Expressionists based on the East End. Esteban Vicente claimed an entire wall. Framing the paintings were photos of Viccnte in his studio by Julia Vosburgh Curtiz.

A few artists groused under their breath about the swift ascent from nowhere of Julia Curtiz. Had a husband on the board helped her edge out photographers who'd put in their dues for years? Elsewhere in the room Julia inspired spicier gossip. For all its glitz, Islesford was essentially a small town that hummed with rumors, and sightings by nosey parkers had led to random remarks that had lead to further remarks that had sparked speculation on a deliciously appalling liaison in their midst.

Julia broke free from a group to give her face a break from its smile. For the opening she'd bought a vintage Pauline Trigere number—red, tightly seamed, shoulder pads, zipper cuffs. Her eyes scanned the crowd packing the galleries, yammering, weaving, planting *m-wah* kisses. Occasionally someone glanced at the walls.

"It's your evening, enjoy it," Audrey had said. Julia was more interested in yesterday's item in the real estate classifieds: *Artist's summer bungalow, option personal chef*—an amenity they could skip. She longed to be liberated from her scarlet carapace, which permitted only shallow breathing. Till recently, she'd kept some small control over the big story of her life. Now other players, other forces were running with it.

Where the hell had Miles got to? Well, they couldn't exactly move around as a couple, could they? Once it was finally in the open and they had their own place, they could get on with their lives . . . *Mint post and beam home, fireplace and Japanese garden . . .*

She glimpsed Miles through a gap in the crowd. He wore a pinstripe vest under a dark jacket and loosely knotted yellow tie, and looked so cool it stung her that he was there for all the world to admire. She tried to catch his eye. He kept chatting with Bodie and a couple of louche types. They could have have been regulars at the Swamp, the gay disco west of Islesford the good burghers were up in arms about. Damn Bodie! Just last week she'd found him and Miles doing lines in the bathroom off his study on Greene Street. The two of them like hogs bent over the marble counter snuffling up blow through a rolled dollar bill. Miles pinching and messing with his nostrils, altogether too expert. Then he and Bodie went roistering off like frat boys to Regine's, or that other club where Barbra Streisand got her start. Lately Miles was sniffly and pink around the nostrils, up half the night, little appetite—symptoms she knew well.

She'd accosted Bodie one evening. "You're corrupting that boy, you've gotten him hooked."

He looked at her coolly. "Jule, don't be naïve. He was doing blow in prep school. *And* dealing, which is not in the Princeton curriculum so far as I know."

Carriage house in Belle Estate. Beautifully furnished, all amenities.

"Julia, your photos are mah-velous, they add a whole new dimension!" Lyndy DeGroff. They sketched a kiss. Lyndy's Breck Girl pageboy was so dated it had circled back to chic. Her medicated gaze looked as if the real Lyndy were held hostage behind it. Between the coke heads and the medicated, standard issue alcoholics seemed positively wholesome.

Julia's attention was hijacked by a private image of Miles, lids fluttering, his sharp upthrust jaw forming almost a right angle.

Tip DeGroff sauntered over, ice cubes clunking. He gestured with his head toward a girl with an electric cloud of hair. "That Rachel Dempsey's some piece of work." He shook his head, confounded by the existence of such a girl.

Rachel wore a plaid mini, fishnet pantyhose, and Frye clodhoppers. She was in heated conversation with an official of Islesford Hospital. Julia caught the phrase *new disease.* She edged closer. "Karposi" something, she heard . . . Why were afflictions named after people from Frankenstein land? "Pneumocystis" . . . "Limited to homosexuals."

"The point is," Rachel put in loudly, "the government is stigmatizing the gay community as carriers of this disease. And using that as a way of dismissing the situation."

Heads turned at Rachel's belligerent tone. "*But*"—Rachel waved her finger—"cases have started to be seen among drug addicts and straight people who received blood transfusions—"

"Heavens, how unattractive to talk about diseases at an opening," Lyndy murmured.

"Rachel's a piece of work," Tip affirmed.

"Julia Curtiz!" Rachel closed in on her, ignoring the others. "I've been wanting to catch up with you. I'm doing a feature on women in the visual arts out here and I'd like to include you and your photographs of painters in their studios. Could we talk some time this week?"

Julia wanted to question Rachel further about the mysterious disease but this wasn't the moment. "I'm awfully flattered, but—well, there must be many more prominent women. Is your story for the *Islesford Star*?"

"Actually, it's for the *New York Times*, the Long Island section." Rachel let that percolate. "Hey, you're on the radar"—she gestured toward the photos of Vicente—"don't undersell yourself. In fact, you're exactly what I need for my piece: a homemaker who's reinvented her life." Rachel cocked her head at Julia as if sizing up a prize Orpington hen.

Well, Rachel wasn't subtle, but such virtues were likely oldschool. Julia said she'd be happy to set up a time.

"Work work work," Lyndy said, "that's all anyone does. . . ." The chatter in the galleries crescendoed and she seemed to lose the thread. "I hardly recognize Miles," she picked up.

Julia spotted him in a corner, now chatting up the editor of a "shelter" magazine.

"I mean, the boy's positively slaving for your husband, don't you think, Julia? Not that I'm grateful for all you've done. What did I just say? I mean I *am* grateful, so very grateful." Lyndy looked at her with her peculiar muzzled gaze and Julia thought, *crazy like a fox.*

"Before this job with Bodie all Miles did was play," Lyndy went on. "Now it's the *other* extreme. But I *finally* persuaded that boy to take some time off. He's promised to spend Labor Day in Marion with the family. Rachel dear, you'll be coming, too, I hope? Your father said you might all be up for the weekend. . . . "

Miles had said nothing about his Labor Day plans.

Julia heard Rachel say, "I'll have to see, may have to work that weekend."

"Over *Labor Day?*"

"Oh, you know, the press. Deadlines don't know from national holidays."

Lyndy's gaze settled on Julia. She waved her hand in front of Julia's eyes. "Yoo hoo, earth to Julia! That's what my boys used to say."

She felt like that cartoon critter that rides off a cliff on a bike and keeps pedaling furiously over the void. When the broker called Monday morning about the Belle Estate property—*3 bedroom carriage house on 2 acres, bike to ocean and bay beaches*—she let him take her round. For a moment Julia was tempted to question the fey broker about that disease Rachel had mentioned. What was she thinking? The man was a total stranger. Such thoughts vanished as they pulled up before an English-y cottage nestled in a grove of bamboo. The moment they walked in Julia saw *home*: beamed cathedral ceiling, stone fireplace, wide floor boards. Wood paneling in the bedrooms; a skylight in the bath; a red Japanese maple beyond the kitchen window.

When she finally reached Miles in Greenport later that day, a mega crisis. Some prima donna architect threatening to pull out . . . Accusing Bodie of not abiding by the specs and cutting corners to save money . . . Talk of a lawsuit . . .

Julia found she was trembling. "Will you be tied up over Labor Day, too?" She heard his silence on the other end.

"Julia, of course I was going to tell you, but with all this shit going on—"

"Why am I the last to know your plans?"

"I thought you'd be pissed, frankly."

"You've gotten sly like Bodie. His worst traits have rubbed off on you."

"Look, I thought I should go to goddamn Marion for one weekend on account of Lyndy. To please Lyndy. You know my mother's a fucking mess."

"Will Rachel"—hating herself—"be there to please Lyndy too?"

"*Who?* You mean George Dempsey's daughter? They're old family friends. What the—what do you want me to say? Really, I have no time for this."

The following evening he didn't call, nor the next, nor the evening after that.

Julia hit the back roads around Millstone, where she did her heavy mental lifting. A shaving of moon, her shadow long on the road, the scent of woodsmoke. Her Nikes all but floated off the ground, as if rage had winged her feet. Miles's timing, in his lingo, "sucked." Drifting away just as he gets his shit together? Too ignoble. If not for her he might still be surviving on chicken satay from parties, a house pet like the dwarf in a Spanish court only prettier. That he was childish and self-absorbed was a given. But opportunistic and calculating?

Some piece of the jigsaw lay tantalizingly out of range.

Back at the house a message from Miles. Not the coded message they'd agreed on in case Bodie played the answering machine. No, there it was—she replayed it—Miles's voice scratchy from a cold, she could see the high dimple, saying he was sorry he'd been so abrupt the other day, all hell had broken loose at the shop, but they'd managed to salvage the project, he'd be back in Islesford Friday and could they have lunch at Bobby Van's at one— "Now the crisis is over I was thinking we could take a little trip. . . ."

She replayed the message several times, partly to hear his voice. A voice, she allowed herself to remember, she'd heard through all its stages. She sat on the stool in the kitchen island staring at the fridge's stainless steel door. A toddler's soprano *Hi Aunt Joowa* on her answering machine; Auntie's gone out, comes Lyndy's voice in the background; *Where she went?* The cracked voice of adolescence. Overnight, it seems, a man's tenor; when she first hears it from another room she startles, fearing a break-in.

Through it all, in truth, he'd remained a boy. And she, their silken cocoon, would keep him there.

Julia stared in the bedroom mirror at her face above the black turtleneck, grey circles under her eyes, silver hair encroaching on the auburn.

Perhaps she'd been unfair to Miles. She wanted now not to think the worst of him. During her walks on the back roads she'd seen the future. She'd refused the future like a wild horse getting broken in. Then, lying down in the ring, she accepted it, pacified and furious; accepted the unimaginable. Now, suddenly, it had become all she *could* imagine. She must cut him loose. Pull some grace from the inevitable, scrounge up a bit of elegance. In how we endure life's cruelties, there lies all the difference. A noble quote from somebody noble, which she could pretend to be. Their dream of a shared future—she'd nurtured it, force fed it. As if playing games with the clocks at Lilac Close could change anything! She must try to forgive herself. It had driven her mad, this love arrived from nowhere and for the first time, midway through her life. She would sooner have murdered than miss it. You imagine there's a fair share of love to go round for everyone. Not so, some don't get their share. She'd been blessed. She thought of the *Marschallin*: take lightly with light heart and light hands, hold and take, hold and let go. The moment had come lightly to let go. She must embrace the next step grandly.

The prospect robbed her body of heat. She went to her bedroom and crawled under the blankets with her shoes on.

She'd made a list of things she would not say, tones she would not take, boundaries she would not cross. She owed herself; she owed *them*.

"I especially wanted you to see the house in Belle Estate," she heard herself say, already brimming with poison—and only five minutes in!—"because now we—you—are in a position to afford a nice place." She paused before lobbing her grenade. "I mean, now that Bodie's giving you a piece of the action in the Greenport Houses."

His eyes skidded away. He upended his glass of Campari. "Julia, I wanted us to have lunch so I could tell you in person for Chrissake. Not over the goddamn phone."

"Of course. Still, it was damn creepy hearing the news from your father. I ran into Tip in town the other day."

They'd both been sneaking ice cream cones at The Scoop, she trying to decide between chocolate or rum raisin, with chocolate or mixed sprinkles on top. "I won't tell if you won't tell," Tip joked about their guilty errand. "Let's sit by the windmill and enjoy our little secret." There he'd relayed the news about his son's "*coup*."

"Just between us," Tip said, "I'm surprised Bodie's cutting him in, Bodie's a clever businessman. And I'd say Miles is rather a lightweight, even if he is my son. . . ."

Julia said, "Maybe you've helped *keep* him a lightweight"—in the same instant she absorbed Miles's latest deception. . . .

Miles's eyes glittered. He'd acquired some kind of designer fuzz around his chin. "Julie, did you actually think I wouldn't tell you? Do you think so little of me? I mean, I *owe* you—"

"And I owe *you*, I've never been so happy," Julia said, skirting dangerous shoals. The waiter set their crab cakes on the table. They eyed their lunch as if he'd plated toxic fugu-fish.

"Listen," Miles said, brightening, "I'll come look at the place in Belle Estate this week, I promise. And now that I'm gonna have a bit of money we should plan to get away. Thanksgiving in Paris, I thought, perfect time to escape the family. We could stay in that place you like, the Saint Gregoire."

A lurch of hope. *The Saint Grégoire.* The boxes of white cyclamens in the lobby . . . A quiet room on the courtyard . . . A morning stroll in the Luxembourg, metro St. Placide. In France they would appear less ridiculous. . . . She looked around at the lunchers: Wall Street guys with Dumbo ears, their youngish wives with ironed hair auditioning to be widows.

"If only we could," Julia said. If only they could. She trotted out her spiel, the hateful language of sense. Getting no traction from the words as if steering a car over water.

"I thought we'd settled all that," he said hotly.

He had so much ahead of him, she pushed on, keeping her eyes from his mouth, the too-high dimple, his beauty that others would have. "Miles, I'm so proud of you and what you've accomplished. It was *you*—you don't owe me. All I did was what any friend would do. You're on your way. You'll find a woman of suitable age—"

"Don't be grotesque."

"—and marry and I'll love your babies. We both need to move on."

He was looking at her as if she were peddling croc oil.

"*I* need to move on." Where, she couldn't exactly say. There remained the labor of surviving the death of love, a kind of TVA project of open-ended duration. There remained the not negligible detail of work: a curator from L.A. had seen her photos of Vicente in the Maxfield show and asked her to shoot Richard Diebenkorn in his studio in Santa Monica.

He lifted his fork and set it back down. "Julia, I didn't want anything but to be with you."

So. It was done.

"And I with you, but it's not to be."

"I hate that religioso talk."

She ignored this. "You saw it first, stupid me—I think these last several weeks you've been giving us practice in how to be apart, the hassles at work be damned." He shook his head no yet in the same moment something knocked them into a new alignment: their bodies together felt no longer possible. His eyes told her he recognized this. "You saw it first the way you saw us together first," Julia said. "In a way you've always been ahead of me, darling. We're not about to change the world."

She'd imagined—hoped—he'd at least fight for it a little. Instead . . . he grew busy lining up his cutlery beside the plate with its untouched crab cakes. She must memorize him. She inhaled him through her eyes. Keep the momentum. Focus. Take lightly and lightly let go. It was a lot to bear.

"Go," Julia said, "I'd like to sit for a bit." How one bears it makes all the difference.

A waiter was signaled, a check got paid. His face grave like at a memorial service. He rose. "No, don't touch me, please," she said. She kept her eyes down as he threaded through the lunch time crowd. When she looked up she saw he'd reached the wide-open French doors in front of the restaurant. He threw back his head and, adjusting his shoulders and stretching his neck, walked smartly up the street with the gait she knew.

On a night of storms some weeks later Julia picked up the bleating phone in the kitchen, hoping she hardly knew what.

"Julia, is that you? This is Rachel Dempsey. I thought you should hear this before it hits the *Islesford Star* on Monday."

Julia decided that the best place to "hear this" was seated on the Spanish tiles.

"The cops raided the Swamp last night in some kind of drug sting—though of course it's also an attack on gays. Basically, Islesford wants to shutter a club that—quote—'brings the atmosphere of the baths and New York's downtown meat racks,' blah blah, to a family community. The piece of this you should know—here, I'll read the damn thing. 'Implicated in the drug bust and accused of lewd conduct in a public place are real estate developer and theater producer Bodie Curtiz and Miles DeGroff, his partner in The Houses at Lilac Close.' I'm so sorry, there's a photo of them both."

PART IV

INVINCIBLE SUMMER

"What happened . . . to our light-hearted youthtime?
— Allen Ginsberg (Tangier, Morocco)
to Peter Orlovsky, December 22, 1993

*"In the midst of winter, I found there was, within me,
an invincible summer."*
— Albert Camus, "The Stranger"

Paris 1998, seventeen years later

Bells from the Eglise Saint-Merri. On the stroke of twelve a good smell of charring meat genies up from the street. Brett abandons her galleys on Julia's little Empire desk and pushes the tall windows wide. Below, workmen renovating the Atelier Brancusi are cooking lunch, maybe lamb sausage, over a charcoal fire improvised on the site. Hunger comes knocking, but her pages await.

She's holed up correcting the galleys of her novel in Julia's apartment in Paris, three light-struck rooms on the fourth floor catty-cornered to the Pompidou museum. Julia's in Africa—not its beauty spots, as in the old days, but a hellish refugee camp in Liberia to photograph the children. Brett is looking after Lark, the surviving Dachshund of Julia's last brace of three, now semi-blind and incontinent. Miraculously, for several hours now Lark has failed to dribble on the parquet floor. Brett laughs out loud to think how the Dachshund and her sprinklings accompany Julia to Paris's finest restaurants; how Julia greets protests by exclaiming in Brahmin French, "*Ce sont des gens sont mal élevés!*"

Lark is whimpering and Brett decides not to push her luck. She'll take the poor beast for a walk on the Left Bank, now hostage to Yves St. Laurent and Prada. Paris is fast becoming a Disney franchise, a theme park of itself, far from the days of madness with Allen Ginsberg and Gregory Corso. She's in search of details for "her" Julia's memory of Hotel Saint Gregoire that she can wiggle into the galleys. She'll also dip by the former Beat Hotel on Rue Git-le-Coeur, today a four-star, barely recognizable—perhaps during a full moon the ghost of Gregory Corso barfs down the stairwell. She may want to tweak her portrait of that place, now a shrine to a group of grubby writers who changed the world. She scribbles in her little notebook, *Weave into earlier chapters mention of Julia's silver fox hat.* Yes, it's expensive to make changes to galleys. But the truth is, she's lived in her stories a long time and can't let go.

Brett locates the Saint Gregoire between Saint Germain and Montparnasse. Sure enough, it's much as her Julia character imagines: a box of white cyclamens at *Reception*, another set before the fireplace. Brett asks to see a room. She studies a painting of a sylvan frolic, vintage flea market—that Julia might notice—but suddenly the receptionist cries, *Ah, ca alors, c'est vraiment trop!* Poor Lark has christened the Oriental.

Brett walks down the Rue du Cherche-Midi, following no particular route back to the Pompidou, lost among her stories. Abruptly, she remembers that in her final draft Julia never got to the Saint Gregoire, least not with Miles.

Which is sadder, the lovely places you never got to, or got to with the wrong person?

The previous fall, before she left for Paris, the friends had gathered again at Lilac Close. Allen Ginsberg had died that spring, April 5, 1997, after kickstarting a world he would scarcely have recognized when he set out, hungry-eyed and geeky and desperate to be loved. A world she and her friends now inhabit like immigrants lacking language and skills, but gamely winging it.

They sit out back on Audrey's terrace, layered in polartec against the autumn chill, Julia in her ratty silver fox hat. Time has taken them down a notch or three, but not so they couldn't be players still, especially among connoisseurs of hot flashes. The radio has warned of an approaching hurricane, 100-knot winds. For now only a breeze pirating the sweet-sour mash of fallen apples and acrid scent of marigolds. Glossy black crows wing by, chatty and important with business. It feels like once-forbidden topics are up for discussion. Bodie's "fall" from Swan's Bridge into the creek at low tide— is it already five years ago? The death of a classmate thirty years back, a subject they've avoided like a malarial swamp.

Audrey sets a bottle of Vouvray and red cut glass goblets on the wooden table. For herself, Lillet. It's early, but hell, they're on Islesford time.

"Thank God for you people, you know?" Brett says. "I love us. To us." She raises her goblet, joined by the others.

As if on cue, a snowy Great Egret lifts off from the tawny marsh, its thin black legs stretched taut behind it like a ballerina. They follow its slow, pumping flight.

"Before we get maudlin," Audrey says, "I s'ppose you've heard that Tip DeGroff wants a divorce? He's no longer 'in love with Lyndy.' He's seeing a younger version of Lyndy who will surely want kids of her own."

DeGroff. Nerveless scar tissue there, though it's healed ugly. Julia regularly thanks a God invoked for such moments that by some divine dispensation she escaped the Plague. How she knows that Miles escaped, too, she couldn't have said. "Tip must believe the planet exists to house his offspring. Has the man never heard of Zero Population Growth?"

In college Julia barely knew Ike was president, but a trip in the 80's to Angkor Wat spun her around like St. Paul en route to Damascus. It was not the temples that leapt out at Julia—it was all the folks in the town of Siem Reap missing limbs from landmines. It was the women crouching on the filthy street holding their babies. It was the swarms of child beggars (pimped by their parents squatting out of sight) that the government hoped to expunge from the area like vermin, lest tourists such as her be grossed out. It was the woman who hobbled toward their group as they piled onto their Mercedes minibus and thrust a baby girl at Julia, crying "Take this child!"

"It's ironic when you think that Lyndy's the one who

did everything 'right,'" Brett says. "I once saw her by the subway on 79th and Broadway looking like the bag lady we were afraid of becoming." Hem dragging, eyes innocent and wild. "Allen Ginsberg saw the best minds of his generation destroyed by madness. Guess that didn't include women. He literally didn't 'see' women, much less consider they had minds to destroy."

"Well, never write off the old crowd," Audrey says. "Lyndy's on new meds. She's getting 'mentored' by a Jewish chaplain from her penal reform board. *And*, wait'll you hear this—she's about to enroll at Hebrew Union College to become a rabbi."

Julia hoots. "You couldn't make this stuff up."

In the downstairs loo Julia touches base with the mirror. The shadows have deepened under her eyes and the uniform of sweaters and tights on her "Junoesque" form is beyond fashion, yet she's kept—Leland's words—a sort of "ruined allure." After the *scandale* at the Swamp Julia moved to a shabby-genteel building in Gramercy Park. She sat unmoving at the kitchen table like a black bear shut down for winter, eyes fixed on the twigs encased in ice outside the chicken-wired window. Replays of that night flickered by on an endless loop. *You put your filthy mark on him, the one person I ever loved . . . seduced him with money and the job . . .*

"For fuck sake, Tip, it's past midnight and pouring," Bodie says. "Why are you in my house?"

"You know purr-feckly well. My son makes his home with you perverts—"

"Listen, you're shitfaced, I don't need to hear this. If you won't leave, I will."

The door fails to catch, a rogue gust swings it wide. Bodie backs up the car, swings left, crunches gravel into the murk ahead. "Where's he think he's going?" Tip mutters.

Headlights bloom through lashings of rain and she sees the red Datsun pull up beside Tip's jeep. She edges toward the door, stretching her hand out. The Datsun douses its lights. She hears the door go *thunk*. She hears Miles standing, invisible, among the Montauk daisies on the rise behind the parking.

Tip stumbles past her out the door. He climbs into his jeep, slams the door, the ignition coughs on.

"*Your lights!*" she screams as the car bucks *forward* and leaps the rise till something solid halts it.

Lyndy decoupled from reality and set up full time at McClean's. Tip checked into the Betty Ford Center to ponder, among other things, why he'd tried to run over his eldest son. The twigs outside Julia's kitchen window made white flowers. News filtered through that Miles was doing well in rehab, that lawyers had been retained to smooth over any difficulties the "accident" might cause his father. Lyndy rejoined the turning world and threw herself into penal reform.

"*Rachel Dempsey and Miles DeGroff were married Saturday November 14 1983 at the Carlyle Hotel in New York. A friend of the bride's family who became a Universal Life minister for the occasion, officiated. The bride, 29, is keeping her name. She is a reporter in the Style Section of the New York Times. The bridegroom, 24, is Assistant Vice President in charge of Client Relationships at Fiduciary Trust.*

Julia was sighted one night sitting in the snow outside a singles mixer at Tavern on the Green, silver fox hat askew. Till then, she'd been "doing better."

The Houses North in Greenport caught on big and Bodie got rich again. Julia had underestimated his largesse. Or the scope of his guilt. Or his "undying love," which inspired deep thinking about what people mean by the word love. Bodie's adieu bought her the apartment in Paris overlooking the Pompidou, the one-bedroom in Gramercy (now a co-op), and the privilege of working for no pay. Sara and

Gerald Murphy, Julia concluded, were a tad off. Living well was a fine revenge, but money was even better. "Fuck you money," in the phrase of one of Audrey's characters.

"Of course the assignments are harder to come by without Bodie's access," she emailed Brett from Paris on her new IBM PC. "And I'm competing with cocky young embeds in flak jackets ready to journey to hell and back. The niche for my art books has shrunk, too, and there's not a heck of a lot I can do about it. Art often feels like a bourgeois indulgence. I want to photograph the bad, the hideous and the invisible— like my old boyfriend Elliott (luckily there's enough misery to go around). Just finished a series on girls in Bangkok's bordellos who are literally slaves. Next up, the folks who survive by salvaging trash in the world's dumpsites. I'm leaving soon for a place called Bantar Gebang in Jakarta. It's literally a garbage mountain that has spawned a town of its own, population 2,000, complete with cafes and movie theaters."

"As for men, well, you do need someone to pick you up after the endoscopy. And I don't expect what we used to call 'the sleeping giant' to stay asleep. Thankfully, the age-blind French are on hand when the giant stirs awake. I look forward to becoming a dirty old woman. After all, love was our profession, don't you agree? There's a wonderful quote by Stendhal—something like, 'Love has always been the most important business in my life, I should say the only one.'"

A kicky breeze drives them off the terrace into the house. From the hall the grand-daddy clock, ancient guardian of Lilac Close, gears up for a strike, and Julia remembers how crazy love had driven her to halt it at twelve. Audrey opens a third Vouvray—it's early, but it's the country, right? They have a good laugh running through the vast lexicon of their youth for "drunk"—smashed, shitfaced, plastered, sloshed, schnookered, stewed, zonked, tanked, bombed, blitzed . . .

"Remember Leland used to say, 'time for my transfusion'?"

Audrey sets Greek olives, smoked bluefish pâté, and poppyseed crackers on the coffee table. She mostly lives in

Islesford; country life agrees with her. She's still the hue of Paper Whites, and flashes with the old salty cheer, and is never without a long V-neck cardigan—which she owns in several colors—like a French provincial woman.

She takes the phone in the kitchen. Brett and Julia share a smile at the sound of her voice, intimacy's warm, easy shorthand.

Audrey garnishes a crock of hummus with parsley from her garden. She'd brought the old friends together five years back—after Bodie's memorial—with a vague hope of laying ghosts to rest. Instead, waylaid by pettiness, she came down on Brett for wanting to cop their stories. Which have surely found their way into the new novel Brett's about to publish. That they continue to mine similar turf in their books, she and Brett, can still get dicey. Especially as they like to weave bright threads of each other into their characters. A major difference is that Audrey Marsh has become a "brand" and her books walk off shelves. Brett claims that writing has made her poorer and the sex scenes embarrass her children. Whatever one might think of "the latest Audrey Marsh," she's made her own money. How many of her classmates could say that?

"I really admire how you've made it on your own terms," a fiftyish woman said at a book signing at The Tattered Cover in Denver.

Well, dear, did I have a choice? Especially after Imre left all but a few dimes to wife #4 and Bodie.

She's kind of made her peace with being a writer of "women's books" or chick lit—or whatever genre they say she invented. We can't all be Herman fucking Melville. As for the critics who dismiss—or, worse, routinely ignore her—the checks for film rights salve the old vanity.

Audrey sips from her goblet of Lillet and rinses a few of the season's last good tomatoes. A publishing friend has alerted her about an "Audrey-Douglas" story in Brett's new novel. Audrey's intrigued to see how Brett handled that weekend in Lonelyville, August '57, may it live in infamy. Maybe some day she'll set Brett straight about what actually happened.

For now she'll just raise a glass to Brett; what's success for if not to make you generous? Especially since that first novel of Brett's sank like a stone. She pictures their yearbook photos at Foxleigh, their clear eyes and freshness like the flesh of a cut apple. Brett's eagerness to take it on all but busting out of the photo's frame, a girl plainly heading for trouble. The boys would be lawyers, dentists, admen; the girls, where was the harm, would be artistic.

A sudden gust manhandles the windows; she worries the ailing Dutch Elm close by the house could do major damage to the roof. She rinses the last of the red lettuce from the garden they'd planted four years ago.

She'd been housebound with pericarditis, legacy of the Lyme disease she'd chosen to ignore. One morning she woke with a face to scare the horses: an eyelid curtseying, lips yanked into a hideous grimace and leaking drool. She hid, she and her Bell's Palsy, in the darkened house, curtains, blinds drawn. Hugo, his Cookalong launched, had simply dropped away like Cee Vosburgh's gangrenous toe.

A plumbing disaster forced her to phone Alex. At his knock she wanted to slap on the Phantom of the Opera's mask. Maybe the thought that it was "just" Alex prompted her to open the door. Half-expecting him to turn to stone at the sight of her. She kept her face down, wiping away a bit of drool with the back of her hand. With his usual calm manner of getting on with it, Alex disappeared into the basement.

He made a return visit with new parts—and a Pyrex bowl of chicken and rice.

"From your wife?" Audrey asked, cradling the bowl. Remembered too late that the missus had taken up with a bond trader who sidelined as a junkie.

"My daughter."

Audrey's latest novel included a character based on a Foxleigh debutante who'd married a bandleader from the Dominican Republic. One day when Alex finished up around Lilac Close, she invited him in for a beer and asked him to translate some Spanish phrases. The following week Alex asked for help with language in an application for a bank loan.

The earth warmed. Alex proposed a garden that harmonized with the great swathe of marshland out back, limiting the color spectrum to shades of lavender. Audrey had never given landscaping much thought and took more pleasure than she'd imagined watching Alex and his workmen transform the property. Her face remained torqued in its cruel grimace. Alex had the grace to pretend not to notice.

The anti-inflammatory medication for the pericarditis stopped working. The doc said, you should be in the hospital, you need—some mumbo jumbo about sticking a needle in her heart. Were they kidding? "Why are you smart about everything but your own health?" Julia groaned. Audrey leaned over the cold porcelain of the bathroom sink and wrote her obit: "Audrey Curtiz Marsh, an inspiration to other women, pioneered chick lit. She was married to Asher Lind."

Her world contracted to the living room sofa under the red and blue mohair blanket. She could see through the bay window to the field where Alex and his men were spading up earth for the vegetable garden. Sunlight glossed Alex's black hair, he looked fiercely alive. She wanted not to die in some medieval ward without a view of the Matterhorn. She wanted to lie in the orchard and be rained on by apple blossoms. If Alex came into the house she could ask him to carry her outside.

Her lurching steps across the terrace . . . Alex laying down his spade . . . Then a spike through her chest, she can't reach the next breath, chases after but can't—

Next thing they're settling her on the sofa.

Mrs. Marsh, I'm going to call 911.

You'll do no such thing.

Your doctor then. Where's the number please?

I don't want a doctor.

Oh, Mrs. Marsh. Eyebrows arched in dismay, like you'd admonish a child.

He sometimes stopped by Islesford General after work. Other visitors were well-meaning but tiresome—Brett and Julia battling doctors, threatening malpractice suits, herating nurses. Berating *her* for ignoring symptoms and "letting it come to this." She preferred Alex. He seemed content to sit quietly in a corner chair, understood her lack of desire for pretty much anything. Maybe in his immigrant culture the cycle of self-neglect and suffering were in the normal course of things. Stroked out on her pillow she took in the wide set of his eyes in his frank face, the glossy brows. His gold skin felt ancient, soothing. He brought dishes cooked by his daughter, Daria—*caldo de pollo, arroz con lima, flan.* "You can't get well if you eat the food they serve here."

One day that she felt markedly better they walked together in the hall. "Tell me, Alex, what are your hopes for your business?" As always he was neatly dressed in long khaki shorts and work boots, his arms a deeper tan than the pale honey of his face and calves.

Alejandro was his name. That he'd been harboring a meticulously thought-out plan took her by surprise. The weekenders in Islesford regarded the service people with their pickup trucks as so much lawn furniture; she'd been no better. He was adapting the garden designs of the Brazilian landscape designer Roberto Burle Marx—a name not familiar to Audrey—to the Islesford terrain. He'd already created such a garden for a client using Marx's signature grasses and flowers in the same color spectrum. Now the client's friends on Schuyler Lane wanted a similar one. After the initial loan from a local bank, he needed another infusion of capital. Immigration issues made it tricky. . . .

"I just realized, I've seen your garden! The Hayworth place over by the bay. It's gorgeous!"

The next day: "Now you tell me," he said. "Why do you make all the men so bad?"

A lopsided smile. "So you've been reading me! I write what I know." With one exception.

Smiling, he shook his head, as if not quite believing her.

Home from Islesford General, there awaited a fresh setback: the absence of Alex. It took her off guard, the disappointment that bit into her. At the hospital he'd doubtless just been making pro forma visits to an employer. Perhaps he'd suddenly recognized she looked hideous.

She was too old for this and far from well and to entertain

any further intimacy with her, well, glorified handyman, was preposterous. Even if between them she'd sensed this . . . affinity. Did she think she could play Lady Chatterley out here with a Latino Mellors? Hell, she wouldn't use such a story in one of her own plots. Islesford was rife with construction guys with six-pack abs and tool belts who took up with the area's lonely, real estate-rich widows and divorcees. Sex would probably kill her. Though it might, as Brett and Julia liked to say, cackling, "be just the thing."

Leaving the IGA one afternoon she hooked a detour onto Schuyler Lane. No reason to take the long, scenic route to her house, she scolded the face in the rear view mirror, none whatsoever. Aliens must have seized the wheel.

Slowing, she noted Alex's trademark hues of white jonquils and cream tulips mingling with silver-green grasses. A boyish form bent to a wheelbarrow. His white tube socks stuck up above his boots. Wolverine DuraShocks, water proof (her snooping had revealed). She killed the ignition and got out into a drizzle of light sieved through mist. From behind the hedges a merengue, its drums and tinny horns festive and sexy. Someone dialed down the volume and Alex came round to greet her.

A horrid flush suffused her face, she felt her heart *whompety, whomp*. He held her gaze.

"I want to thank you for helping me through a rough time"—*oh God the drool*. "It meant a great deal to me, your kindness and—help." *You are lovely to me*, her eyes finished.

He inhaled deeply. He had immigration problems, he would need to return to Mexico for five years.

So that's what it was. "Five years," she said dully.

"My wife is expecting a child."

So that's what it was.

He was shaking his head. "Eche a mi esposa. El bebe no es mio. Ella se fue. Ella se fue con otro muchacho."

Eche . . . She rummaged in her meager vocabulary. *Echar . . . To exit? Ella se fue*—she left? With the bond trader? Anything in that category would do. It would do just fine.

Something fell open between them bringing new awkwardness.

"Please. Let me show you what we're doing here."

He guided her around to the land sloping behind the house and into a succulent garden of greens: reeds, ornamental grasses, "walls" of boxwood and bamboo. It was planted architecture. They arrived at a lily pond backed by a stone wall. The place formed a dreamy, mysterious retreat out of time. Audrey exclaimed over the beauty, mind going like a spinning jenny. It was pretty radical, but a solution to his immigration woes had suddenly offered itself. Beyond a stand of bamboo the workmen had dialed up the meringue. The singers, drums, horns put a sway in her hips. She hadn't danced since Asher. It might be fun to dance.

Turns out a major nor'easter—a "non-tropical super storm"—is indeed barreling toward Long Island. Winds up to 150 knots, coastal damage, when it will make landfall still uncertain.

"Well, since it looks like we're here for the duration . . ." Audrey begins. Digs her fists into the pockets of her long cardigan and pivots to face them. "There's something I've been wanting to talk about, and also not wanting to talk about."

"Nina," Brett says.

"It's always been on my conscience, too, or some back room of it." Julia, from the yellow chintz sofa, still wearing the silver fox hat.

"Well, don't put it on mine." Brett's never tamed her snappiness. "Look, I realize we're supposed to feel guilty about Nina's suicide." *Like in one of those by-the-numbers scenes from Audrey's novels.* "But what did we know? It was *cool* to be crazy back then, no one called it paranoid schizophrenia. There was a glamour to checking out young."

Julia tucks a fist into her armpit. "Maybe some are guiltier than others."

"Meaning what?"

They startle at the scrape and bumpety-bump of an empty flowerpot scuttling across the terrace.

"Back in college," Audrey says slowly, "can we honestly say Nina wasn't somehow . . . egged on?"

Brett hears her twenty-year-old self in Obrecht's class, attacking Antigone—or Nina?—for refusing compromise and "humdrum happiness." *"I am disgusted with your life that must go on come what may."* Later, in the common room in Dudley they all piled onto Nina, a girl mob, combusting with private angers . . . Julia especially rabid. *"You make a mockery of real tragedy. My brother was so radiantly alive."*

"May was the worst," Brett says abruptly. "May wouldn't let up, she was terribly envious of Nina's talent, and then Nina stole Bodie away."

Julia's eyes, after the third glass, like a Charolais cow's. "Y'know, years after I married Bodie, May somehow convinced him my 'posse' had pushed Nina over the edge. That became Bodie's default position in our fights: that I was to blame for the loss of his precious Nina—who he *never fucked* of course. He never forgave me," she went on, bellicose and teary. "In Bodie's twisted logic, it gave him permission to seduce Miles."

The Eglise Saint-Merri tolls twice. Brett can still smell the char of lamb in the air; true to French protocol the workmen have enjoyed a two hour lunch. She herself has grabbed a *sandwich jambon* and Badoit at the old Beat hangout, the St-Michel. Communing with the ghosts of her young self and Allen Ginsberg . . . From the square below, opposite the Pompidou, the whine and put-put of a motor scooter. The sound brings back her misspent youth and the nights of careening around the Place de la Concorde, arms wrapping a lean waist, cheek pressed to a leather jacket—quite a feat back then to misspend your youth, since most people back then had never been young. She remembers a night in the Pantheon coaxing forth the ghost of Victor Hugo with Gregory Corso, while Pablo Sobotka twists in his chair and anxiously checks his watch. *When is it* our *turn?*

He'd called some time before she sold her new novel— after an interval of maybe fifteen years. She flung herself out of her Brooklyn one-bedroom, where she'd moved after Bella left for college. Headed toward Prospect Park along Flatbush, a stretch immune to yuppie aspiration, past the liquor store where the Korean owner presided behind bullet-proof plexi-glass punched with tiny air holes. The start of Memorial Day weekend and anyone who could had skipped town. She joined the harried moms and loosely-employed dads piloting strollers, a guy shouldering his cache of bottles in a dark green garbage bag, a woman in a redingote from the Napoleonic wars mouthing a monologue. Odors rose off people uninvited.

What did Pablo want from her? Why was he exiled in New Paltz, a college slash hippie town in upstate New York, where he lived, he claimed, in a *bus*—he who liked to hang with VIP's at galas? Licking his wounds? She'd read in *Business Week*—in the waiting room of her periodontist—that Pablo Sobotka, mega media entrepreneur, had gone bust. Something about "over-leveraging" and other such arcana from the world of commerce.

Now his phone call. Did he still hanker after the road not taken? Maybe it was part of human DNA to loiter around the fork where you might have chosen *the other* way, the path that would surely have lead to El Dorado! Of course, the girl ensorcelled by Amory Blaine no longer existed. The current edition worked three underpaid gigs as Adjunct Professor, and was definitely behind schedule in becoming, as Rufus Porter once put it, the person she was meant to be. As for the golden boys of yesteryear, Rufus had indeed published his novel at twenty-five. Then he jumped from a window in Piazza Barberini, and later surfaced near Boston and wrote manuals on the Holy Ghost. "Dismayingly glamorous," Leland once called call him. *Rufus Porter*, read the obit in Alumnae News, *was one of the shining lights of Yale's class of '57.*

Her romantic career had been scarcely more distinguished. She'd managed to bollix herself out of the marriage market, a la Lily Bart, even though feminism had made marriage so, well, *yesterday*, and she was supposed not to mind. Aborted romances piled up like riders on a blocked escalator. The Wall Street Wolf who arranged a meet-'n-greet with his fiancee—*the better to test the limits of possessiveness, my dear.* The architect with bad teeth who gave her a multiple orgasm so she screamed with joy / Who saw no reason to cohabit with another man's brats / Who today had failed implants and a date for a quadruple bypass. The yeast researcher she should have loved.

Now, fifteen years out, Pablo, again. She wondered what his business reversals had done for his character. That he was now poor again chloroxed any taint from her own motives. To reconnect so many years later, after bad timing, missed connections, "almosts," and so forth—hell, it would make a story for the Weddings section in the *Times*.

She'd last seen him mid-eighties. "It seemed like a fresh start with May," he'd said over Stolis in the Russian Tearoom. "But when I saw you in the Plaza that day I had this sinking feeling that you get when you make the wrong turn. The thing had been set in motion, though, sometimes life slides out from under you and all you can do is traipse after. A sign from you, and I'm not sure what would have happened. May was pregnant then, did you know? She threatened to kill herself if I left. When is it our turn?"

In the 80's it was always someone's "turn."

Damned, if he didn't actually own a bus. Yellow with black trim like a friggin' bumble bee.

The bus lived on the grounds of Rose Cottage, a grey three-story Victorian nattily crowned with a diadem of black, wrought iron lattice work. The air smelled resinous and green and an orange sun roosted on the horizon through June's freshly minted leaves.

He zoomed in, a manic gleam to his eye, as she herself went for the double Euro, but he smashed her against him, one hand on her ass. *Whoaa.* She wasn't quite ready for Omar Sharif. Omar with sheepdog bangs, jeans and moccasins, scraggly half-moon beard.

"C'mon, I'll give you the tour."

She eyed the bus suspiciously.

He'd had the thing gutted and fitted out with a tiny kitchen, dinette, bathroom perched on a rise above the wheel, couch that must double as a bed though he'd be too tall to fit. *Why?* To emulate the preppies who'd thought it cool to tool around in a stripped down hearse?

In the kitchen alcove he fixed her a vodka tonic in a plastic glass; for him plain tonic.

"You don't drink?" Wary at lack of parity.

"Not with this I don't," he said gaily. He knocked back a blue pill. Prozac? Or that new guy pill?

They sat on flaking white Adirondack chairs behind the house. Birds that do their heavy flying in evening cut nervous angles against the pale violet sky.

"Pablo—tell me what's happened with you. Why are you here?"

"What's not to like?" He unpacked the story of his business woes: the new FM stations failed to perform as planned, throwing off insufficient cash flow blah blah . . . competition took market share from his company's stations . . . outside investments in trouble . . . She got the part about the city's economic crises, which had iced hiring at CUNY and her shot at earning a living wage. After a "fire sale" of his company, he'd fallen off in his alimony payments to May, and her lawyers wanted to take possession of this house.

So he hadn't been kidding about the school bus!

"The good news is for the first time in thirty years May won't be getting my money."

She didn't buy it, quite. Audrey, a student of Islesford uber-consumption, had observed that when the rich crash and burn they manage to salt away a few clams in Mauritius and the Caymans. "I'm sorry you've taken such a shellacking. And the deals with Bodie? I always thought Bodie had the Midas touch."

"Well, The Houses at Lilac Close got a bit complicated, lemme tell 'ya," Pablo said. And didn't. He looked half-way troubled yet pharmaceutically cushioned against it.

"But you, Brett"—he leaned in—"here *you* are, here *we* are, after so many years. I've been wanting this since—since that time beneath the bluffs at Lilac Close."

He reached over, slid off her sandal, and massaged the instep of her foot. His hand brought joy to her instep, the opening chords. He looked up at her, face darked. "Let's go inside and lie down," he said thickly.

She glanced at the bus. "You mean—in *there*?"

"We'll christen the place."

"Wait, I just got here. You've taken me by surprise." And what about her own story?

"Surprise? Really?"

Okay, she'd hit the Walgreens on Flatbush Avenue and Lincoln, slipping the packet onto the counter under four items she didn't need but included as camouflage, and she'd bought a navy silk teddy from the Lingerie Addict. Not *so* surprised.

His hand had found a zone behind her knee. "You know," he said, "the profiles in Forbes, the galas and private jets and rest of the bullshit—when all's said and done, the things a man and woman do together naked in bed are what it's all about."

Yes and yes. But she didn't like that it was still light. She wasn't quite so beautiful any more. The middle-aged should cavort only under cover of dark like vampires or horseshoe crabs.

The interior of Rose Cottage, home to funereal Victoriana, was mercifully low on wattage.

He was no longer twenty-two, but she liked the way he looked and told him so.

"I keep myself nice," he said.

They fell together on the bed, still semi-dressed, and he moved over her.

"Wait. I brought something." Her hand scrabbled around for her bag beside the bed.

"No."

"*No?* We have to. I mean, lotsa crazy stuff out there now. God knows, we've neither of us been monks." That they could draw on knowledge banked over half a life bumped up her desire.

"Uh uh. Can't." He'd shimmied up to sit against the headboard.

This was doing little for ambiance.

He raised his second finger and bent it downward. "That's what happens."

"Look, it's not ideal, but, well, we're friends in this."

"I can't feel anything that way. Look, I'm healthy.

Perfectly safe. I'm sure you are, too. I've only been with nice women like you. Your age."

"And you're sure I'm safe?" Jesus, what was she saying.

"I trust you."

"But suppose—" *oy gavolt*—"the 'nice' people have been with not nice people." *A walking collection of STD's!* "Pablo, it's not like the old days when all we worried about was someone getting knocked up." She thought of the terrors Julia had endured—a long-married woman with an adoring husband. Was Pablo even in the loop about Bodie?

"I mean, if you're gonna worry . . ."

The mood here had taken a bad hit—even if she could pivot on a dime.

Some confusion, and it was somehow agreed they would do everything but. No matter how she gave it her all, he never quite rose to the occasion. Down at her south end she could sense his ebbing interest—and his dismay that up north he'd stalled out at half-mast. And was now MIA. She felt all dressed up with nowhere to go. Poor men. He switched on a lamp and looked glumly into space—*I told you*. He stood beside the bed naked, his furry chest, slight belly-roll, his nice Jewish cock. Which her demands had offended.

"Guess we're fated just to make out," Pablo said. He had the mother of all headaches, he added, and was still traumatized by his business woes and the battles with May. Brett suddenly wondered if those pills he'd scarfed were meant to keep it up or anxiety down. Perhaps he'd been popping both and the messages got crossed.

He sat on the edge of the bed shaking his head no. "Maybe it can't work with us cuz you saw me when I was nobody. It's not your fault. It's too late, we've missed too much of our lives together. I been married most of my adult life and now I just want to see different women. But you've always been at the top of my list."

Brett looked up at an elaborate ceiling fan with double blades like something for slicing luncheon meat. She rolled out of bed, braving his eyes on her body. She collected her clothes—she was still wearing the teddy from Lingerie Addict—plucking dignity from the air.

"In a way it's just as well," he said. "I wouldn't have wanted to fuck if you were going to *worry*. God, I would have hated getting phone calls from you saying, I've got a discharge or an itch. I don't want anyone calling saying they've got a discharge. May once had a discharge, something that was maybe herpes, but it was never diagnosed. Whatever it was, she never stopped blaming me." He pulled on his shirt. "Maybe this monster headache is on account of I'm hungry. How about we have dinner? There's this place in New Paltz, the Gilded Otter."

In college they'd loved to quote Samuel Beckett: "Nothing is funnier than unhappiness . . . it's the most comical thing in the world." Back then, they couldn't have imagined *how* funny.

"An 'ischemic event,' they called it at SUNY New Paltz hospital," Brett says. "Pablo was basically okay, though bad show to mix Viagra with other meds." She eyes a red wine stain on the skirt of Audrey's yellow chintz sofa, a memento from a house party thirty years ago. *We miss our lives regretting what we've missed.* Some great writer had said that; maybe all the world's wisdom was spoken for. Well, since Audrey once accused her of stealing her friends' lives, might as well annex that line too.

"In the hospital waiting room that night," Brett said, "Pablo gave me some idea of what may have happened to Bodie. He said a bunch of things came at Bodie all at once. But mainly it was about the Houses at Lilac Close. Which has kind of stalled out, as you know. Apparently, they didn't go through the banks for money. . . ."

"We assembled a group of wealthy investors, friends of Jason Schley, who basically didn't want to waste time doing due diligence and an environmental site assessment. Then we hear people from the Turnpike, twenty miles west of the Houses, are talking to a lawyer, claiming they're getting sick. High rates of cancer, miscarriages, deaths. And next thing, the do-gooder lawyer's threatening to sue Rowe. Which dumped thousands of gallons of solvents containing toxic chemicals into the soil. So all this dreck's been released into the ground and now it's poisoning wells and making people sick. Or so the lawyer claimed."

"Then it turns out the sandy earth out there's very porous and the toxic plume ran farther east than anyone thought. I mean, Bodie was not exactly cautious going in— the scrub land was awfully cheap, which made it attractive— but this took even him by surprise."

"You're saying the plume ran all the way to the Houses at Lilac Close?"

Pablo had turned his head as if tuned to a different frequency. "Meanwhile Bodie—well, suddenly he snaps or something, wants to go public with it and blow the whistle on the whole Houses project. On him*self*, for Chrissake. And us, his investors."

Brett felt elated. What inner muscle it must have taken to kill his dream project!

"We decided to quick cut our losses—before word got out—and sell to a group called EastEnd Realty—Chinese, Russians, Israelis—sleazeballs who operate beneath the radar with their own money stream coming from outside the country. They were willing to take the risk on account of the Houses had cachet. But Bodie wasn't on board. He was itching to 'go public with the mess,' he called it—and screw us out of the sale. For all I know some goon from EastEnd Realty sneaked up behind him on that bridge."

The wind whistles like a banshee through loose sashes. Audrey switches on a couple of lamps. "I don't buy it, that my brother was offed by thugs. Bodie was wildly overextended, and that night on Swan Bridge he was probably zonked on coke, booze, meds—he was hooked on Ativan. . . . The moonlight on the water under the bridge can be hypnotic. . . . He could have lost his balance."

"There was another wild rumor around Islesford that Bodie *was* murdered," Julia says. "A man who lived near the Turnpike had a daughter who got leukemia and he blamed the toxic chemicals. He actually *boasted* about shoving him off the bridge."

"Yes, but then the cops found the guy had been no-where near the bridge that night and was likely insane," Audrey says.

"So many stories." Julia sighs, looking wise and cat-like around the eyes. The other two watch her. "We create stories to make sense of things," Julia says. She tucks a fist under her armpit. In a past life, they would have all lit up. Audrey works a cork free with a pop.

"Some stories, though, are truer than others," Julia says. The other two wait. "Not so long before Bodie went off Swan Bridge he and I met with lawyers about some property we still co-owned. I looked at him across the table at the lawyer's and—something about him seemed 'off.' After we left the office on Madison Avenue and 41st, Bodie asked if I'd have lunch with him. We'd barely spoken in years. We went to the Oyster Bar a couple of blocks uptown. Sat at the counter on those little stools. That's when he told me . . . T-cell count below 200 . . . A seizure. So that's what I'd been looking at." She brings her fist to her mouth. "I've never felt such terror." A moment. "After I tested negative for the third time I phoned Bodie and told him I was with him and he could count on me. And then, shortly after—I don't know what happened on Swan Bridge. But I believe Bodie broke ranks with his partners because he was on the way out and wanted to do what was right."

"He stage-managed his own myth," Brett says. She pictures Bodie extravagant with dreams before the luck ran out. The night he walked into Gilbert with Rufus Porter, the two of them straight and clear-eyed like young gods. The Gatsby of Lilac Close, his stretch smile and creaky laugh. *We'll create a new theater, fly to Paris, smoke Beckett out in his lair . . . Gotta press on, m'man . . .*

The crab apples bend every which way, one moment bowed, the next furiously flinging branches at the sky. Loose shingles scuttle across the terrace.

"Whoaa, it's the big blow," Julia says. "Why don't we drive to the beach to see the surf from the bluffs."

A thud against the side of the house. Audrey runs to the bay windows. "Damn, the ginko. Never thought that one would go, it's the big Dutch Elm I'm worried about. *Beach* did you say? We could get carried out to sea, along with the houses on the dunes."

"Last I looked, the bluffs are pretty high."

"Wait," Brett says, "I just remembered, there was that party with Nina." The friends turn toward her. "It was pretty soon after the *Antigone* class. A party in a pad on 115th Street near Columbia. Belonged to J.P. someone, a Harvard drop out . . . "

They'd been smoking bad stuff, green. Some wise ass cooked up hash brownies. She panicked, Brett remembered, at being trapped in the high, heart in overdrive, beset upon by ants only the ants were *inside* her. A small figure in black climbed onto the windowsill of the kitchen overlooking 115th Street. A scraggly little potted cactus on the sill. The window was opened wide because the apartment was insanely overheated.

Alright, knock it off, come on down, Nina.

Another voice: *Oh, Why* don't *you. I dare you. You talk a good game, but you'd never—Hell, why* don't *you go and* do *it already?"*

"I'm sure that was May. But May," Brett goes on, "was only ever channeling the desires of whoever she most wanted to impress." Her eyes flick toward Julia.

"That party was thirty years ago and we were wasted," Julia says, sweating belligerence. "Y'know, Bodie respected you more than anyone and you could have convinced him to get Nina help. I'm willing to bet you backed off because you always sucked up to him and needed him to love you."

"And you've always been pissed you married a closet gay and fucked up your life."

"Oh. Very classy. I wouldn't talk about marriage, Brett. Tommy once told me all you cared about was work, you were an 'absentee wife' who never loved him and did 'marriage lite,' always one foot out. No wonder he dumped you with two kids and disappeared to New Guinea."

Brett's suddenly distracted by Audrey. She's been watching them, fingers steepled at her chin. "Audrey, you're not thinking—? This is not material, this is off bounds."

"Hell's bells," Julia barrels on, "I wasn't going to tell you—"

"Julia, wait—unless you want to see it in print!"

"—your charming Pablo was conning you in New Paltz. He cornered me at a benefit once. He says, 'do you think it's okay to compromise to avoid being alone?' Julia nailing the burred voice. "Apparently he's been seeing someone for ages—but for whatever reason, wanted to test the waters with you, maybe keep his options open. He was always a dentist's waiting room reproduction of Bodie."

Brett launches herself into the room, dangerously quick. "Y'know, you hear about incest among drunks and half-wits. Or upperclass Brit psychos who molest their own offspring. But with Miles you took it to a whole new level—"

"Oh, I'd call it incest lite," Audrey says.

Julia's eyes well. "Bodie tried to make the physical part work, and the *trying* was the worst. Miles—he was a miracle, the great happiness of my life. Miles was everything and everyone to me, lover, child, family, all in one person. Something so rich and joyous and strange could only be good. Couldn't it?"

Julia's silver fox hat sits slightly askew on her head, and Brett's heart aches suddenly, something about the cockeyed hat, she aches with love for Julia, the rest is just noise.

"Yes," Brett says, "it could only be good. The very best."

Audrey's lips curl in a Cheshire smirk.

Julia drains her glass. "Y'know, Audrey, you're so condescending and superior. Because with you and Asher of course—everything was perfecto!" Brett shoots her a look: *don't*. "Asher was a pathetic wannabe player, tied to his wife like mommy. I bet the whole time he was 'married' to you—"

"Leave it alone, Julia," Brett says.

"—he was screwing around with that ski bunny—Ingrid . . . Inger . . . I gather they had an annual fuck date. There was probably an Inger in every resort."

Audrey walks to the bay window and peers out. She turns to face them, hands dug in the pockets of her sweater. She looks radiant. "I wouldn't have cared," she says.

A thunderous blow on the roof. They stare upwards toward the east bedroom.

"Oh not the Dutch elm, I *knew* it. Bet it's put a hole in the roof. I been nagging Alex to take it down but he says, can't cut down a mature tree . . . *Damn!* Must be blowing a hundred knots out there."

Brett smiles. "There's something strangely freeing about saying the worst. Though I wouldn't recommend it on a daily basis.

She moves to the Queen Anne chair, sits facing them, hands on knees. "I saw Bodie once, a few years ago, after I'd dropped out of his league. I brought up Nina. He went on about her talent and 'the psychic risk in being an artist' and all the rest. And then he said—quoting someone or other—Nina 'had the suicide inside her.' Nina didn't want to live. That's the story, basically."

A blast gives the windows the what-for.

Brett raises her arms to the ceiling in a monster stretch and throws back her head. "D'you realize how lucky we are? We get to find out what happens next."

"That line of Antigone's," Audrey says. "How did it go? 'I'm disgusted with ordinary humdrum happiness—'"

"—'and life that must go on come what may.'"

"That's the horror and wonder of it," Julia says. "Life that must go on."

"I'll take humdrum happiness," Brett says. "And the compromises, and petty self-seeking, and all that life that must go on. Audrey, what a luxury, d'you realize? To have to worry about fixing the roof. Isn't it marvelous?"

"Not if you have to goddamn pay for it. I'm going upstairs to see if there's a hole. And then—linguine with arugula pesto from the garden."

"Sounds *divine*," Julia says in the honk. "But first—before it's totally dark—let's drive to the beach and look at the sea from the bluffs."

She sits over the galleys at Julia's Empire desk in the swarming dusk. Doesn't pay to work after five, she turns sentimental. On the streets below workers from offices and visitors to the Pompidou stream toward cafes. October, with the tourist herd thinned, Parisians get their city back. Brett decides on her usual, Cafe Beaubourg, down the square from Julia's *appart'* and a magnet for chic Parisians, slender men with narrow Italian shoes, women with to-the-nipple decolletage. She orders a glass of Chateau Margaux—an homage to Hemingway—and a half dozen Belon oysters. She scribbles a note for the galleys. Why is it easier to find words after walking away from them? She orders a second glass. As Julia likes to say, otherwise *it's just all too grim.*

She'd contracted with her original editor at Scribner's to write a memoir. But the editor got axed because the boss hated his face, and along its tortuous route True Confessions from the Dark Ages found a new editor. And slyly morphed into a novelized memoir (or memoirish novel). Thank God for fiction! Unvarnished truth can be dispiriting God knows, and reality could use a little varnish.

So some of the book she ended up calling *Wild Girls* belongs, you might say, in the realm of alternative reality. Not to be lightly dismissed. She's lately become entranced with books for science illiterates (and at Foxleigh, where drawings of orgasms passed for scientific inquiry, didn't they all share that dubious honor?) Respected thinkers now posit the existence of multiverses, where alternative versions of our lives could conceivably be playing out (see reference in Acknowledgements).

Here in our humble dimension—which at moments feels like a shadow version, a holograph of some truer, realer life—the union of Audrey and Alex was never actually cemented. A canny lawyer made Alex's visa woes go away. Illness and too-many-lives syndrome had scribbled over Audrey's porcelain beauty of a girl in an old cameo, while the Verrazano Bridge couldn't span the culture gap between a best-selling author and her Latino handyman. When the junkie/bond trader dumped Alex's wife, five months pregnant, Alex sucked it up and took her in. The gardens at Lilac Close were featured in *South Shore,* Islesford's glossiest shelter magazine. Alejandro Landscaping Associates now has more work that it can handle.

After a long fallow stretch Audrey is bringing forth a

new novel that's been touted as her return to form—and never mind the cattier sorts who detect the deft hand of her ghost. Articles are planned in book sections of the country's newspapers about the re-emergence of Audrey Marsh after a long "block." Her new book, it's said, features two competing novelists who work similar turf, women from a generation for whom scribbling or some artistic endeavor was the ticket out, an alternative to stewardess or secretary or suburban house-wife. One of Audrey's characters is marked early in life by a traumatic event.

For all her born-again ambition, Julia's career merely shambles along. She's been overtaken by the new digital photography and "age-ist attitudes" (every week, she laughs, brings new opportunities to become obsolete). "Retirement art" the cattier sorts call Julia's work; it keeps her active, like sitting on the board of Visiting Nurses or playing doubles and bridge. But never write off the old crowd, Audrey likes to say. Julia recently snagged an assignment from *National Geographic* for a photo-essay on pollution in the Persian Gulf. Only a churl would suggest it came about because the magazine's newly-widowed publisher had always found the ex-wife of Bodie Curtiz a woman of breath-stopping beauty.

In an earlier draft, Brett hoped to give Pablo and the girl named "Brett" he once adored a happy landing. It would have been so satisfying to close the circle. And how cruel that "Brett," the all-for-love one among the friends, should be left flapping in the breeze; she's too old school, too broke, and too man-crazy—still; always—to find happiness as a single woman. But Brett-and-Pablo had no legs. Try as she might in scene after to scene to bring them together, they just sat woodenly staring off in opposite directions.

So Brett's taken to dreaming about a candidate outside her pages. She keeps circling back to Jordan Frankel, the editor who urged her, the summer she turned twenty, to write her generation's story. She keeps a vivid memory of their last encounter—'81, it would be—in the lobby of the Four Seasons before her lunch with Kristi; his sexy hangdog look and how the air went wavy around them when he eyed her under his tented brows. Nothing volcanic like Julia's Tristan chord; more a lovely little phrase asking for completion. She's heard that Frankel, a charter member of the flameout club, is now an antiquarian book dealer in Cornwall, Connecticut, and separated. One day he must have opened a yellowing copy of her first novel to the jacket photo of her toothily smiling self. Next thing, he's on the phone to Audrey inquiring about Brett Eigerman's marital status, and then shows up at Audrey's book party, in the hopes of maybe reconnecting with a former author. But the fates weren't game. As Brett remembers it, the evening of Audrey's party she was on a train returning from the Bedford Hills Correctional Center after an interview with Jean Harris. It's entirely likely that during that same evening, as she and Frankel respectively journeyed homewards, the two Metro North trains crossed.

Brett orders a final glass of Margaux before leaving Cafe Beaubourg for dinner in a little Moroccan place in the *quartier*. In Paris, it's easier than in New York to dine alone. These days she sails through dinner with good grace, phones Tommy and Bella, rises early. With the galleys of her book due by the first of November, she keeps a military routine.

Lately, taking inspiration from her book—just as "her" Audrey did from *her* characters—she finds herself conjuring up ways to engineer an encounter with the actual Jordan Frankel. Waiting on circumstances is a luxury for the young. Perhaps on her return from Paris she'll do a little sleuthing. How many antiquarian book dealers can there be in Cornwall, Connecticut? And how delicious it would feel to sit across from Jordan Frankel over a glass in Ye Olde Tavern, and present him with a copy of the book he set in motion some thirty years ago! The air smells of scooter exhaust and *frites* and a citrus-y perfume called *Eau d'Hadrian*. Brett asks the waiter for *l'addition* and sits a bit longer dreaming into the gathering dusk.

The wind wallops their car before it's out of the driveway of Lilac Close, and wags them down the road to the beach. The parking lot is bereft of the usual lone pickup truck—only crazies would go out in this. A battle merely to wrestle the car doors open, then shoulder them closed. They file singly up a trail to the top of the bluffs. An army of waves froth and fume at the far horizon, a closer layer shooting spume skyward, while crossed walls of water schuss toward them, hissing, wanting at the bluffs. And the wind! It's a billowing wall, a medium all its own. The friends move close together. They're whammed by an outsize blast, they reach for each other, as three, they form a bulwark. They hold on tight as the wind whips and pounds them from behind, their scarves streaming before them like standards. They lean against the wind.

The End